STREETS OF HUNGER

Streets of Hunger

MISTY THOMAS

Contents

Dedication

To those of us entering our villain era, burn it down.

Author's Note

As with Tower of Blood, the second installment comes with a content warning. This story includes either the mention of or depiction of the following:

Physical assault (depicted)
Sexual abuse (referenced, not depicted)
Cursing
Torture/Removal of limbs and organs (depicted)
References to parental death
Death

Please keep your mental health in mind as you continue.

Chapter 1

Elora

She wasn't aware these sounds could erupt from her or any other living being. They were the screams that accompanied her reality disintegrating around her, leaving her in a void with only the cries that were currently being ripped from the core of her being. The only thing she could see beyond the tears and windshield was Lukas's pale gray eyes brimming with acceptance and what she knew now was love.

"Please, you have to go back. You can't leave him!" Her voice was loud, shrill as she watched the garage disappear through the back window. Elora's hands struck out at anything she could reach—the back of the seat, Damien's shoulder, anything. Each breath was erratic as she attempted to take in as much air as she could while pleading. They had left him behind as a single gunshot rang out through the underground garage. The image of Lukas bleeding out on the concrete with a bullet hole in his temple, his laughing eyes blank and dead, as Viktor stared down at him in disgust wouldn't leave. Damien didn't respond, but kept his focus on the road, weaving in and out of traffic.

"Please! He's your friend!" she screamed at him as her hands latched onto his sleeve, the fabric gathering in her fist before she pulled it towards her.

Again, silence was the only response, and she choked back a sob. There was nothing to do. Nothing for her to do. Lukas was dead. Dr. Montgomery was dead. And Viktor —

She hoped and prayed with every dark part of her he was dead as well. The damage Lukas had done could do the trick. There had been a long gash along his face and wounds along his neck while blood poured down the front of his shirt. A sharp pain radiated through her chest as she tried to take a breath, but it felt like her lungs had collapsed, like her ribs had shrunk down to hold her in a vise.

It was defeat that resulted in her throwing herself against the seat and closing her eyes, trying desperately to calm herself. But she couldn't shake the image of the one friend she had made. The shocked expression on Dr. Montgomery's face as her dead body stared up at them. And for what? For her to escape? Elora had already accepted her fate, had already been prepared to do whatever was needed to make sure Killian would never hurt her again.

Was her life really worth theirs? And what would happen now? Her mind raced with question after question as she struggled to come to terms with her new reality. Would she live the rest of her life with only Damien, the vampire who kidnapped, drugged, and pushed her until she lashed out? She wanted nothing to do with him, nothing to do with his inability to decide if he hated her or not.

She just wanted — Elora wasn't sure what she wanted. All she knew was that whatever the future held, it didn't involve Damien and wherever he was taking her. Maybe she could leave the city, move to a place where she could live the life she and Elizabeth had always discussed. They had dreamed of a small, picturesque town near the mountains or a lake. They would open a shop, perhaps a bakery that sold coffee and books. Elora could sell her sketches if she wanted. They would get to know everyone in town, have conversations with everyone who came in. Even as they laid in bed each night, shoulder to shoulder, negotiating the décor for the apartment they would share above their shop, they had known it was a dream and nothing else.

People like Elora didn't have lives like that.

"The safe house isn't too much farther. Once we get there, just follow me inside. I'll need to make sure everything is secure." Damien's voice was curt and strained, and she curled up, pulling her legs into the seat with her.

"How do you know they aren't already there?" She didn't say Viktor's name, refused to let it pass her lips again.

"Only Lukas was involved in securing it. Only him and I knew its location." Elora winced as he said Lukas's name, noting that he did the same, though it was subtler than her own, a tightening of his lips and a muscle feathering along his jaw.

She didn't respond. There was nothing to say. Instead, they sat in silence until he turned down a street that led to the industrial district. On either side of the road were warehouses mixed with short apartment complexes. Most of them were only a few stories high, but at least a dozen apartments long. Others were taller, but maybe a few apartments per floor. They all looked the same, though, with their red brick façade, windows covered by steel bars, and single entrances. He finally pulled into a side street and stopped the car before taking a deep breath, as if preparing for the next stage. His hands gripped the wheel so tightly that his knuckles were white, and his head hung in what seemed to be defeat.

"I need you to follow me and do what I say. Can you do that?" She had never heard this tone from him. It was utter exhaustion and devoid of any emotion. It was what she imagined he was like when he dealt with Killian's problems. Elora nodded, and he got out, making his way to the back of the car as she followed him. Her hand went to her nose as she tried to block out the overwhelming stench of trash and urine that assaulted her senses. The concrete beneath her feet was somehow sticky, and she felt her shoes hesitating with each step like the sidewalk was trying to hold her in place. Silently, he pulled two large duffle bags from the trunk and gestured for her to follow him.

This building looked exactly like the others, and she noticed a sign above the front door that read Garden View Apartments. Her eyes darted around, searching for any hint of a garden or even a single flower before she snorted. This particular part of the city wasn't exactly known for its view or anything even resembling nature. A joke and not a great one.

Damien gave her a quizzical look before he used his key to enter the building, holding the door open as she entered behind him. The lobby area was empty, filled with a staircase and an elevator to the left that had caution tape across the front. Sickly green wallpaper was filled with some sort of floral pattern and the wood beneath their feet felt warped somehow. She trailed behind him as they made their way up the stairs to the second floor. With each step, his eyes darted around, searching for any sign that their location was betrayed somehow.

It was only now that Elora remembered she was still covered in blood. Silently, she prayed that no one would come out to take out their trash or leave the building. Whoever it was would be met with a woman whose skin and clothing were drenched in drying blood and whose hair was a tangled mess around her face. Damien, at least, didn't look quite as shocking. There was some evidence on his jeans from where he kneeled beside Killian's body and on his shirt from where he had carried her out of the building, but nothing else.

Finally, Damien stopped and unlocked the door before he stepped inside and gestured for her to wait in the entryway. She held her breath as he made his way through the apartment, checking each room and partially concealed spot—closets, behind the couch, behind doors. From her spot where he left her, she could only see the kitchen to her right and the living area, complete with a television and couch directly in front of her. The kitchen was dated from what she could see. Cabinets were painted some strange off-yellow color that matched the stove and refrigerator. There was no division between the kitchen and the living area beyond a counter that provided a type of divider between the two. There were a few stools lining it, as if it was meant to function as a dining table.

In the corner of the counter near the sink was a coffee machine. No, it was more than that. It was expensive looking, similar to the ones she saw at the coffee shops she had frequented with Elizabeth. Tears flowed down her cheeks once more at the gift Lukas had left behind for her, and she had to bite her lip to keep from collapsing on the floor in a sobbing mess.

Elora scratched at her arms where the dried blood had begun to crack and itch, flaking off underneath her fingernails as she dragged them across her skin. She didn't bother looking down at her clothing, but she could feel how stiff the dress had become from Killian's blood. Her hand spasmed slightly as she recalled the feeling of the knife in her grip, how it had felt as she drove it into his chest. It had been a pale imitation of every fantasy she had ever had, but it had been pure satisfaction. She only wished she had gotten to see the light drain from his eyes, hear him plead for mercy.

Damien emerged from the hallway to her left and set the keys on the counter before finally meeting her gaze. Shadows hung beneath his dark eyes, and his lips were turned down at the corners as he scanned her from head to foot before hesitating at the blood on her hands.

"Let me give you the tour and you can take a shower if you want. But then we need to talk." She nodded, unsure that she could speak. Even his voice sounded exhausted, as if each word was forced from his mouth.

He gestured to the space beside her. "The kitchen." He opened the refrigerator to reveal four collection bottles, a small jug of milk, and an assortment of coffee creamers. His face contorted slightly as he took in the contents and he shut it, leaving the reminders of Lukas inside.

"The living area." He waved his hand in the general direction of it before he headed down the hall. He threw open the first door and stepped to the side as she peered in, not sure what she would find.

"Bedroom one. Yours if you want it." He moved to the second door and did the same. "Bedroom two. And that door there is the bathroom. There's only a shower."

Elora peeked into the second room before moving towards the bathroom. Both bedrooms were identical, containing a single bed big enough for two and a nightstand with a lamp. There was a closet with missing doors and a small three-drawer dresser. Thick curtains that looked as old as the building itself covered the windows along the far wall. She winced at the carpet that seemed to move slightly, as if something lived in it. The bathroom was equally simple. A sink, toilet, and shower. A pile of towels sat on the counter, along with bottles of soap and shampoo.

"I'll take this one," she muttered softly before pointing to the one he called bedroom two. He nodded and tossed a duffle bag on the bed, causing dust to float into the air.

"There are clothes in there. I'm not sure what exactly. Denise was in charge of that." Her eyebrows narrowed at the name.

"Dr. Montgomery. Her first name was Denise." She nodded once more, ignoring the pain in her chest. She had so many questions for her, so much resentment and anger that would never be expressed. Elora had imagined herself raging against her psychiatrist, screaming and yelling, demanding answers for so many years of gaslighting and false diagnoses.

"Go ahead and take a shower. We can talk after." She listened as he shut the door, and his footsteps disappeared down the hallway. A part of her wanted to break down, to curl into the bed and wrap herself in the quilt that looked worn but loved. But she also wanted answers and proof that Lukas's sacrifice was worth it.

Chapter 2

Elora

The shower was as old as the building itself and the water temperature couldn't decide what it wanted to settle on, oscillating between burning hot and freezing cold. It didn't matter as long as the blood was washed from her skin. She wanted all traces of Killian gone. She may not be able to remove the scars that lined her flesh, but she could at least wash away everything else.

The apartment was silent as she made her way to her room and shut the door. With the towel wrapped around her, she dumped the duffle bag and searched for something comfortable to wear against her sore body. It was strange to search through another set of clothes that Dr. Montgomery—Denise—had picked out for her. It was too close to when she had bought her things to wear at her job and at the transition house. She had taken such care when she picked them, opting for jeans and high collared shirts, because despite everything Denise had known her better than anyone else.

Based on what Elora now saw tossed out all over the bed, Denise had done the same as before. It was a collection of pants, long-sleeved shirts, and a couple of long dresses and cardigans. Simple clothes that were worn mostly for comfort. She grabbed one of the dresses—a dark blue cotton one that went down to her feet and wrists with a high neckline that stopped just below her collarbones. The fabric was soft against her skin, hanging off of her loosely as if it was a size or two too big.

She pulled the towel from her red hair, squeezing out the water before running a brush through it. During her time with Killian, it had grown longer than she had ever had it before and it now lay flat, ending around the middle of her back. The hospital had always kept it around shoulder length, claiming it was easier to take care of if something happened, but it always felt like a control tactic more than anything else. Slowly, she sank down onto the mattress as exhaustion finally caught up now that her heart rate had calmed, and the adrenaline had worn off. She just wanted to lie back and sleep, pretend that Lukas was alive, and that Viktor didn't betray her, that she could still believe he cared for her. Even now, she felt his hands on her jaw, softly turning her head as he changed the bandages in the hospital, could feel his lips on her forehead after she stabbed him on Killian's orders.

Lies. It had all been lies.

She scoffed at her own stupidity, her own ridiculous desire to be loved without them wanting something from her in return. With Viktor, she had thought she had found that and had ignored every sign that she was wrong. When he discarded her after she was released, claiming his job was done or when he revealed that he had known everything about her from the beginning. Elora had savored his words when he said she was worth more than being in Killian's control. She had foolishly thought he meant something other than being controlled by someone else.

A harsh breath was forced from her lips while she played with the end of her hair and prepared to engage in whatever the conversation with Damien would include. She stood and shook out her shoulders before smoothing out the dress. As she turned from the bed, something white sticking out of the duffle bag caught her eye. An envelope tucked into a side pocket.

Elora

Her name was written in a looping cursive, the strokes smooth but deliberate. Her hand reached out, shaking slightly as she picked it up. Slowly, she pulled the thick paper out and gently unfolded it before sinking back onto the bed to read.

Elora,

If you're reading this, then my part in your escape went wrong and I won't be able to tell you any of this in person. I'm sorry about that as I know you have questions and are probably incredibly angry. You have every right to be, but I do hope you'll read until the end and give me an opportunity to explain.

Her skin bristled as she took in Dr. Montgomery's words. She had wanted an explanation, needed her words more than she had thought. Yet, she hadn't expected to feel this level of desperation for something as simple as knowing and understanding the motivations for each medication increase, each visit to the green room, each disappointed sigh at Elora's words.

I lied to you. Repeatedly and for years, as you know. I'm sure you think I should apologize for that, but I'm not sure I can. All I can say is that I was trying to keep you safe. I knew who you were, who Killian was, and everything that you confessed to me that first night in the emergency room. At the time, I was working with the Resistance, and we had been searching for you, hoping to use you as leverage against Killian. We had gotten a tip about a girl around the right age who had attacked her family and was screaming about vampires. I was sent to follow up and take you if you were who we thought. I was expecting not just a vampire, but Killian's daughter, born and raised in his image.

But all I saw that night was a broken girl, someone who needed to be protected and not used like a pawn. I convinced the Resistance that we should keep you in Blackwell Hospital under my care, where I could research your blood. Our intel told us that there was something unique about you, but we had yet to get anything concrete from our sources inside Killian's labs.

So, I kept you in the dark, doing and saying whatever I had to in order to keep you there. Viktor helped me with this. He knew who you were and what you represented to not just humans, but vampires. Do not let him tell you otherwise or believe him when he says it was all on my orders. He was brought in to not only keep an eye on you, but also on me. I stopped reporting back to those in power, and Viktor was meant to fill the gap.

Elora, they want to use you and are willing to kill you in the process. Your blood and abilities surpass anything anyone thought possible. Whatever Killian did, he hasn't been able to replicate despite his best efforts. They will come for you and use you until there is not a single part of you left.

DO NOT LET THEM! It will be war, and you will pay the price.

I can't tell you what to do. I won't beg you to forgive me. I had a plan to get you out of the city, to get you far away from here and from everyone who wanted to use you. You don't have to believe me, but it was to be my last act as your psychiatrist, as your caretaker. All I can say is that in my time with you, I came to love you as my own.

Denise

The wetness on her cheeks came as a surprise as she finished reading the letter for the third time, cradling each word to her. She could hear Dr. Montgomery's voice, could imagine her sitting behind that massive desk that took up so much of her office while her face softened with each line of script. Their relationship had been tumultuous at best and hostile at worst, as Elora fought before submitting to her care. A part of Elora wanted to scream at her, shake her by the shoulders as she demanded to know how lying to her had kept her safe. In the end, her efforts failed. Elora had ended up right back where she started.

Her hand brushed away the tears before Elora jumped up and shoved the letter under the pillow as a soft knock came from the door.

"If you're ready, can you come out here?" She yanked on a pair of socks, not wanting to feel the carpet or whatever may be inside it on her bare feet.

Damien was standing right outside the door in a fresh shirt and jeans when she opened it. His wet hair was hanging over his forehead, the sides no longer shaved close to his scalp. His throat bobbed as he swallowed and turned from her to head back down the hallway, his steps hesitant and slow. Unease curled in her stomach as she watched him retreat. She had never seen him look defeated, never seen him without either a cocky grin on his lips or an irritated scowl.

A part of her would do anything to see them again.

After a minute, she followed him and even with the thick socks, she could feel every bit of dirt in the long carpet. The walls were lined with discolored squares and spaces where the family photos or paintings once hung in wooden frames, smiling families staring out at everyone who passed by. A seemingly happy moment in time in an otherwise harsh world. They probably argued as they got the children to sit still while they fixed the hair of the youngest and made them plaster on a smile.

She had no photos of her family. None of her foster family, her mother, or even Killian. There were no family pictures to present the illusion of them all living happily together, arms wrapped around one another with fake smiles on otherwise empty faces.

Elora stopped as the hallway opened into the living area. More discolored spots lined the wall behind the ancient couch that was covered by a hideous geometric design. In front of it was a long coffee table and two matching end tables sat on either side. Damien was seated on the far end of the couch, his arms resting on his knees as he leaned forward and stared at something on the chipped table.

She stayed there for a second, not sure where to sit before he patted the space next to him, a silent answer to her unspoken question. He didn't look up as she sat on the opposite end and pulled her legs under her. The silence was unbearable and yet felt necessary as they both gathered their thoughts, searched for the right words even though they were unsure what to say.

"I'm sorry. About Lukas." Her voice was low and unsteady. She could feel the stinging of tears again and for once, she didn't feel the need to hide them. Damien had seen her at her worst, had seen her covered in blood, seen her prepared to end her own life. Tears were nothing compared to that. And Lukas had been her friend, despite everything. In Killian's office, she had finally understood why he had acted as he did when he had joked coldly about her stabbing Damien. She had mistaken the empty gaze in his eyes for not caring, for annoyance, or even plain dislike.

"Me, too." Damien cleared his throat and sat up, still not looking in her direction. "We need to talk about what happens next." She said nothing and allowed the silence to settle again. He sighed heavily and ran a hand through his now damp hair, pushing it away from his face.

"The Resistance wants you. I don't know why or what they need you for, but Viktor was obviously working with them." His dark eyes turned to her, distrust and something else on display, something she couldn't read before his focus shifted away once more.

"We need to keep you from them, find somewhere to keep you safe. I have a couple leads I was looking into with—with Lukas, but I'll need some time." Again, she said nothing, not sure what there even was for her to say. She could apologize again, explain that she hadn't been worth his death no matter what the two of them had believed. Any words she would offer now would be hollow and pointless. No amount of them would bring him back.

"This means I need you to listen to me, do what I say. Can you do that for once?" Elora sat up straighter as irritation raced through her system, forcing away the grief.

"When have I not listened to you? When you were my kidnapper? When you were being an asshole?" She knew this wasn't the time for an argument, for her anger to come out to play with his own. But she couldn't help it, and the words were out before she could stop them. How dare he ignore his own role, which was the very reason she had fought him at every turn?

He let out a harsh breath that may have been a laugh before he tilted his head back to stare at the ceiling for a moment.

"How about when I told you to behave, to not run off, to just do what you needed to do? How do you think Jonas found you at the party? Because you ran off. Because you didn't listen to me!" His voice rose with each word, and she leaped to her feet, refusing to cry yet again because of him. She had been willing to weep with him over Lukas, to share in his grief and mourn together in the space their friend had found for them. Lukas had probably imagined them staying there, watching horrible shows and making lattes together. They would play cards and share stories as they kept the darkness out. Lukas hadn't simply talked to her for the sake of making his time with her more palatable. He had listened. Remembered. The thought made her hands constrict, as if she could reach out and bring him back.

But she wouldn't cry when Damien was faulting her for her actions when he was her jailor.

"Jonas would have found me either way and you know it. Don't throw that at my feet. I wouldn't have been there if it wasn't for you! I would have been out of the city, long gone, where Killian couldn't reach me." She crossed her arms over her chest to keep herself from hitting him, to keep herself in control.

"How do you know that? Some grand scheme you and your precious Viktor came up with while he was pretending to care about you?" She jerked back as if he had hit her, the words landing like a physical slap across the face. The sneer on his face told her he had known exactly where to aim and had hit his mark.

She shook her head, trying to erase his words from echoing in her ears. "It was Denise's plan to get me out. It had been her plan all along. You messed that up and took me back to that monster like the loyal pet you are. You drugged me and left me in that room. Don't pretend you're better than Viktor. He isn't the only one who pretended to care if it suited his purpose." She silently cursed herself that she now sounded hurt, not angry. But she refused to break eye contact even as his own narrowed and the sneer fell from his lips. He ran his hand over his face.

"I wasn't pretending. And I think I've shown that by now." His words were desperate, pleading. It was her turn to smirk at him, at the pain now on his face.

"No, you haven't. You've simply shown the lengths you will go to in order to appease your own guilt."

She turned on her heel and marched towards her bedroom. The questions she had entered that room with didn't matter anymore. It no longer mattered if he was able to answer them either. Once more, she was at the mercy of someone else while hiding from those who wanted to use her.

"We aren't done!" He yelled down the hallway, and she froze.

"Yes, we are. Find whoever you're giving me to next." The door slammed shut, and she leaned against it before sinking to the floor. All the bravado of her words disappeared instantly. She didn't want to cry yet again. It was all she had done since they left Killian's rooms, since they had left Lukas behind, since they had arrived in this apartment that felt smaller and smaller by the minute.

And yet tears came in cascades until she succumbed to them, becoming a hysterical weeping mess on the floor. The potential bugs in the carpet were no longer a concern, neither was the fact it smelled like vomit and mold. For once, she simply let herself cry, let herself rage against everything that had happened. Not just at the Tower, not just under Killian's control, but since the abuse started and her mother disappeared.

Sobs tore through her body, leaving her shaking as her throat constricted with each cry that was ripped from her. She mourned them with every nerve in her body, with every part of her soul, no matter how dark and shattered it was. Lukas. Denise. Even Viktor, or who she had thought he was.

For a moment, she swore she heard footsteps stop right beyond her door. She could have sworn she could feel Damien standing just beyond the cheap wood, listening to her fall apart once more.

Chapter 3

Elora

Denise's letter haunted her every thought as she tried to sleep. Each time she closed her eyes, the psychiatrist's unseeing face stared at her from the other side of her desk. But the office wasn't hers. It was Killian's. Elora's own sketches lined the walls but were twisted and splattered with blood. Dr. Montgomery's lips moved in exaggerated shapes and blood dripped from the corners of her mouth. Guttural groans that may have been words erupted from her mouth before becoming a scream that destroyed everything around her, breaking it into shattered pieces that collapsed, and Elora's cries merged with that of her psychiatrist's.

The room was dark when she woke, panting slightly as she tried to center herself and shake off the remnants of the nightmare. She could still smell the blood that had coated every surface in the dream office. Her stomach growled slightly at the reminder, contracting in a way that was almost painful. Elora hadn't realized how much Denise's death had unsettled her, had broken the hope inside her that questions would finally be answered. She had wanted to demand an apology even though Elora knew she would never forgive her for the medication and lying, for keeping her locked up with the label of dangerous stamped across her forehead.

Denise had claimed that vampires weren't real even though she knew that they were, had been fighting against them, had known exactly how dangerous they were. Elora wished she had been correct, and that this was all a fever dream brought on by her trauma and delusions. One that an increase in medication would make go away.

If the lies Denise told had been true, then Elora wouldn't have killed her father. She wouldn't have stabbed Killian repeatedly, felt his blood splatter across her face and pool beneath her feet as she lost herself to her vengeance. The smile that had spread across her lips as Killian bled out had been feral, been born of satisfaction and relief so dark she almost didn't recognize herself. Some part of her knew she would always regret not having more time. Killian had deserved so much worse, had deserved hours upon hours in which she flayed each inch of flesh from his body, had ripped the fangs from his mouth, made him beg for mercy before she clicked her tongue in disappointment like he had done each time she had pleaded for him to stop.

She shifted on the bed, cringing at the feel of the rough blankets against her skin. It took a moment before the weight across her torso, along with the hand that rested against her stomach, pulled her from her thoughts. She inhaled deeply, filling her lungs with as much air as she possibly could, and held it. The walls of the bedroom began to close in, the blanket becoming silkier, her wrists feeling the coolness of metal as her hold on reality began to weaken.

It can't be him. You killed him. Just breathe.

Once, then twice, she repeated the mantra before craning her neck to see who was beside her. Despite having a fair idea of who it would be, Elora's heart still stuttered as she stared at Damien. His breathing was even as he slept and his dark hair laid against his face, shielding the eyes that always seemed to look at her with such disdain. Or at least, they used to. Now, she wasn't sure what she saw. His soft lips were parted slightly, and she studied the tattoo of the moth along his neck. It was a black and grey work of art. Clean and consistent lines, with no blow-outs or hiccups. Right beneath one of the wings, she could still make out the puncture marks from where Killian had turned him.

Damien was beautiful in a strangely classical way. But there was an edge to his features, a harshness that revealed a darker history that had been etched into each part of him. A part of her wanted to ask, wanted to know what was under the smirks and irritation and coldness. But Lukas had been the one to share his own past, had seen her as worthy of his secrets. She didn't think Damien felt the same.

She laid back on the pillow and gave herself a minute to just enjoy the warmth of his body, the feeling of being held without any expectations or demands. There was a comfort in his embrace that she didn't fully understand. But for a moment, she could pretend that she wasn't a commodity that would be pawned off at the earliest convenience. That he wouldn't hand her off at the first opportunity.

Until he ruined it and moved slightly, forcing her from the illusion she had built. With a grunt, she tossed the blanket from her body and slid out from under his arm to stand up. Now that the comfort of his presence had worn off, she didn't remember him coming in, hadn't felt him crawl into bed beside her.

"Get up." She called out as she marched over to the dresser that held her meager amount of clothing. "Come on. I want to change."

"Don't let me stop you." His voice was low and gravelly from sleep as he threw his arm over his eyes and rolled over onto his back. With a huff, Elora yanked a jacket from the closet and tossed it at him. Damien cursed as it landed on his face and a grin stretched across her face as she dug through the drawers.

"That was rude, love." She rolled her eyes and stole a glance at him. Her breath hitched slightly as he tossed the blankets off, revealing a toned chest covered in tattoos that she couldn't tear her focus away from.

"Just get out. What are you doing here, anyway? I don't remember inviting you in." Not that she was necessarily complaining. But his ego didn't need another boost.

"You had a nightmare. I came in to help but fell asleep." He smirked at her as he stood up and headed towards the door. The image of Denise's bleeding mouth and her screams flashed before her, rendering her unable to utter a single word. She swallowed tightly and pulled out a black cotton sweater dress that reached her knees.

"Thank you, I guess." He quirked a brow at her words, and she wondered if she could force them back into her mouth.

"Don't bother. I can't sleep very well if I have to hear you in here crying and whimpering." He gave her a vicious smirk, and she nodded in recognition that they were back to this. The hot and cold, the cruelty and kindness that left her reeling and searching for something to hold on to. It wouldn't be him. That much was clear.

He hesitated for a second before turning away from her, his hand resting on the doorframe as if there was something else he wanted to say but couldn't. Or wouldn't. Instead, he left and a moment later, she heard the shower turn on.

She quickly finished getting dressed, pulling her unruly hair into a messy braid to keep it contained. With a sharp cry, Elora doubled over as her stomach clenched once more, contorting and hollowing out. It felt like something was trying to claw its way out from inside her. Her mind went back to the collection bottles in the refrigerator along with the coffee machine and her lip twitched into an almost smile. With slightly uneasy steps, she made her way into the kitchen and pulled out two chipped mugs from the cabinet. Moving quickly to prevent another wave of pain, Elora poured a cup of blood, leaving half for Damien once he came in.

A soft moan escaped her lips, and she threw her head back as it flowed down her throat. Her skin broke out in goosebumps, and she tingled throughout every limb. It was euphoric, and she wanted more and more until there was nothing left, almost like she would never fully be satiated.

How long had it been since she had fed? Yesterday, before the meeting with Killian. Roughly twenty-four hours or so, considering it was fairly late in the day. Are vampires supposed to get hungry so quickly? Or was it because she expended so much energy attacking both Damien and Killian? She could ask him, she supposed, but Elora had a feeling he would only mock her and argue she already knew and was only playing at being uneducated. It was what he had done the last time she asked questions.

Thump. Thump.

The mug in her hand almost fell into the sink as she jumped at the sound of knocking. Her eyes shot to the door, mind racing through every possible scenario that could lie beyond it. Someone one from the apartment building — a maintenance person or neighbor. Or Viktor. Her mind conjured the image of a smiling Lukas, dirty and bloody, but otherwise unharmed waiting just beyond the door. The tightness in her chest increased until it felt like something was strangling her.

Thump. Thump.

Elora set the mug down and looked through the dirty peephole into the hallway. There stood an older woman with what looked like a small plastic container. Her gnarled hands gripped it tightly to her chest as she seemed to rock back and forth on her heels. After a quick glance to make sure the collection bottle was out of sight, Elora unlocked the door and inched it open.

The woman's face, lined with wrinkles, lit up as Elora finally opened it enough to see her properly, keeping her hand on the frame in case she needed to slam it shut. A large smile broke out across her face, revealing no fangs, just aged and crooked teeth. Human, then. Elora's shoulders relaxed since she highly doubted the Resistance was in the habit of recruiting elderly women and sending them on missions to find the only thing they seemed to want.

A large mass of grey hair sat atop her head in a messy bun and her blue eyes were bright with excitement as she looked Elora over from top to bottom. But the scrutiny didn't make Elora squirm, didn't make her want to shut the door and hide. Instead, it felt like the assessment that someone gives a friend after not seeing them for months or years. Checking each inch of flesh for cuts or bruises or any sign that something had occurred. The woman's T-shirt and jeans were partially covered by a black apron littered with flour and pieces of dough. Elora glanced down to find a pair of slippers with little cats printed on them donning her feet.

Her shoulders relaxed even more, and Elora returned her smile as the old woman held out the plastic container with trembling hands.

"Good afternoon, lovely. Welcome to the apartment! I'm Constance, but call me Connie." Her smile was brilliant, encouraged everyone who spied it to fall under her spell. For a moment, all Elora could think about was Sarah, the seamstress who had made her gown for the so-called birthday party.

"Thank you. I'm—" She hesitated, not sure if she was meant to use her real name or not. With everything else they had talked about, this wasn't one of them. But how would this woman even know who she was?

"Elora. What's in the container?" In response, Connie lifted the lid to reveal roughly half a dozen muffins with tiny dark spots — blueberries or chocolates.

"Just something I made this morning. I bake like it's breathing, and it's only me and my nephew, so looks like you'll be getting some treats." Elora laughed softly at the explanation, even as her stomach curdled at the thought of eating what she had brought.

"These look amazing! Thank you so much." Connie's smile grew impossibly wider, and she shrugged slightly, as if a gift of baked goods wasn't a big deal.

"Anything for a neighbor. This apartment has been empty for a long while. Maybe I'm just excited to have someone here again."

"Trust me, it's clear it's been empty." Connie let out a deep laugh that reminded Elora of thunder cracking across a silent field and she joined her, unable to resist as the feeling of the weight of everything, of her actions and who had been lost faded away.

"You'll need to meet my nephew. He takes care of me now in my old age. He's quite the handsome man." She raised a brow and Elora almost snorted at the cliché plot unfolding before her, where she would be a key player if Connie got her way. Elora had only seen this happen in romantic comedy films she had watched with Elizabeth. Even then, Elora had found them silly, but Elizabeth had eaten it up, hugging a pillow to her chest as she sighed over the male lead and his selfless actions to get the woman of his dreams.

"Nephew, huh? Well, we should definitely meet him." Damien's voice broke through the bubble of happiness as he opened the door the rest of the way, revealing his shirtless torso to Connie. To her credit, she didn't betray anything on her face as it cooled slightly, and her eyes dimmed. Instead, her assessing eyes met his for a moment before returning to Elora, a clear dismissal of the interloper.

"I'll be sure to send him over the next time he's here. Let me know how you like those treats." She gave Damien one more withering look and turned, entering her own apartment across the hall.

Elora stifled a laugh as she returned to the counter, set the container down, and grabbed her cup, still halfway full. It had warmed slightly, and she grimaced as she finished what was left. One by one, she pulled the muffins from the container, trying to figure out a solution to this newest issue. It was a small one, manageable to handle when everything else seemed so monumental, but it felt wrong to simply throw them away.

"You do remember you're in hiding, right?" He pulled the collection bottle from the refrigerator and grabbed a cup, sitting down on a stool while he poured the second half out.

She gave him a deadpan look. "I'll be sure to avoid the obviously dangerous old woman."

He glared at her and took a deep drink from his cup. "She may not be a threat to you or me, but her nephew could be."

Elora grinned slightly at the warning. "I think I should meet the nephew. I can assess if he poses any danger. Then we can be prepared, especially since you seem worried a human is a problem for you. Think of it as reconnaissance."

Damien's eyes darkened, and he set the cup down. The sound of the porcelain hitting the countertop echoed in the empty apartment. He stood, slow and deliberate, as he stalked towards her, cornering her where the two counters met. His hand gripped her chin, forcing her to meet his eyes. She stared at him completely defiant, refusing to break or submit.

He had no say or power over what she could or couldn't do, who she could or couldn't see. Her hands trembled, the only sign that she felt the closeness of his bare chest against her.

"If he steps foot in this apartment, I'll kill him."

Elora scoffed and attempted to jerk her face free, but his hold tightened and brought her to face him.

"I mean it. Don't let him in here. This is a safe house, meaning no one comes in but me and you." He dropped her chin and moved again, disappearing down the hallway as she struggled to catch her breath. Her heart raced in her chest, and she wasn't sure it was from fear, but from something that felt like a betrayal from her own body. After a minute, he returned fully clothed and grabbed the keys off the counter.

"I have to leave for a while. I should be back before dark." Damien threw his jacket on before he picked up a folded knife and shoved it into the pocket. She had never seen him with a weapon, but she supposed he probably didn't need one while living in Ashcroft Tower under Killian's protection. And neither of them had that anymore. She made a mental note to search the apartment to find anything she could use.

"Are you going to tell me where you're going? Or am I supposed to stay behind and be quiet like a good girl?" Irritation lined each word as she rested against the counter, watching as he tightened the laces on his boots. The last five years of her life had been spent indoors, except for the daily hour of sunlight they were given at the psychiatric hospital.

His head jerked up at her question, a devious grin on his lips.

"Do you want to be a good girl?" She rolled her eyes and crossed her arms over her chest, forcing herself not to blush at his question. He was simply toying with her once more and a part of her knew that. It was the same tactic he had used in the Tower—kind and caring one moment, and cruel and inappropriate the next. But that didn't calm the rush of blood through her veins, the way her heart seemed to miss a beat.

Damien stood and headed towards the door before stopping, his hand on the handle. There was only the rise and fall of his body as he breathed, and his head hung slightly. He turned towards her slowly, glancing back at her one more time before opening the door and leaving. The door clicked shut, and she listened to his footsteps disappear down the hallway as she chuckled slightly.

He said no one could come in. He said nothing about her leaving.

Chapter 4

Damien

The coffee shop was busier than he would have liked with the line to order three people deep. All the tables were taken by either chatting housewives or students with their books and laptops, leaving only a few booths open.

He sighed and shoved his hands into his pockets, waiting for his turn to order. His contact was supposed to be there soon, and he wanted to be set up at a booth before that happened. There were questions that needed to be answered before he could decide what to do with Elora. Staying in that apartment was not a long-term option, not even a short-term option. He had ended up in her bed and that couldn't happen again.

Despite what he had told her, Damien hadn't slept last night. His mind had simply replayed the scene in Killian's office over and over. He rewatched the way Killian's blood had splattered across her face when she pulled the knife from him. It wasn't that her actions had surprised him, but the pure rage behind each time the knife plunged into him had. For days, she had barely moved or spoken or showed any hint of emotion. She had fallen into herself, sunk into a chasm so deep she couldn't seem to climb out. But to see every emotion concentrated in that moment, the pure power and force behind each strike was indescribable. He had been relieved that she had acted, but it was nothing compared to the pride that had rushed through him as she took her vengeance.

And when he had heard her crying out and sobbing uncontrollably, there hadn't been a single hint of hesitation. He had jumped from his bed and laid beside her, running his hand along her spine until she quieted. It wasn't a lie that he had fallen asleep there, both of them comforted by each other's presence. And now—he didn't know what happened now. He would get her somewhere safe and then move on, join another vampire family or leave the city all together. But the thought of leaving her behind made something inside him twist uncomfortably, made him want to rush back and never leave her side.

It was ridiculous. She needed someone who could take care of her like she deserved, and he couldn't do that.

He placed his order for a latte and stood off to the side, eyeing the various patrons. Vampires were rare on this side of town, at least those from the Ashcroft family. The industrial district was known as somewhat neutral ground among the various groups. There weren't necessarily defined territories, but the families had claimed so-called ownership over the areas surrounding their headquarters.

The Radcliff family controlled the city center, and Ravenwell controlled the area along the east side of the city, mostly on the outskirts. The Ashcrofts had always held the largest portion under their control, including the business district and a bit more outside of that. Killian had worked tirelessly to extend his reach, to control more and more of the city. The Corvin vampires didn't claim any control, not officially. That would require giving up their location, something that had been a closely guarded secret. That would be the next issue to figure out if he wanted to try to meet with Silas Corvin — the head of the family, and Elora's uncle.

Finally, his order was called out using the fake name he gave the cashier, and he collected it before he slid into a booth in the back of the shop. He positioned himself so he could watch the entrance, not just for his contact, but for anyone else. No one had followed them when they fled, and he knew Lukas had covered his tracks when securing the safe house. Still, the paranoia built into him by working for Killian and living on the streets was difficult to put aside.

A sharp pain shot through his chest at the thought of his friend, as he remembered him standing there with a sad smile on his face while Viktor held the gun to his head. He had only nodded at Damien before saying goodbye to Elora. And it had broken her, the final strike against a woman who had been too strong for too long. Her sobs had reverberated off the concrete walls, shattering everything left in Damien as he grabbed her arm and forced them both away, leaving Lukas to his sacrifice.

Lukas had done what Damien would have in his place. He just wished neither of them had needed to do so. Denise's and Lukas's death were both at that bastard Viktor's feet, and his hand tightened into a fist at the reminder. Elora may have ended Killian, but he would be the one to destroy Viktor, dismantling him piece by piece. She hadn't really said anything about the human since the confrontation in the garage, where he revealed exactly how little he had cared for her, about his plans to use her. Damien had seen her face fall and tears flow from her eyes, but beneath it all had been rage. Fury akin to what he had only witnessed in snippets up until that night.

And he had used that fact against her, thrown it at her like a blade that hit with perfect accuracy. He knew he was a prick, pulling her in before holding her at arm's length. She deserved better than that, better than him after everything he had done to her. He couldn't give her the type of love or consistency or devotion she had earned with every scar and scream. It didn't matter that he couldn't get her out of his head, that she plagued every waking moment and dream.

The chime above the door sounded, ringing across the cafe, and he looked from his latte to find his contact scanning the crowd. He raised his cup to signal to her, but instead of making her way to him, she nodded and stood in line to order her own drink. Black coffee, no cream or sugar. An easy order that he remembered from a different life. Within minutes, she was sitting across from him, looking no different from the day they met after he had been turned.

"Damien." Her voice was breathy in a way that was calculated, relying on the stupidity of the men around her to fall for her act. He had learned the hard way to not be taken in by it.

"Korina." His own voice was flat, empty as he studied her features for any sign that the events at the Tower yesterday were causing damage.

Nothing. Not even dark circles under her hazel eyes, more brown than green. Her whiskey brown hair was pulled back into a braid that looked too complicated to be worth the effort, and her full lips were painted a purple color that matched her complexion perfectly. She was beautiful, had always been beautiful. But she was also ambitious, ruthless, and had turned on him when Killian gave him the mission to find his runaway daughter. Korina had assumed the job would be hers, that she had earned it.

She sighed and leaned back in the booth. "I'm assuming you want an update on what's going on since you disappeared so suddenly." He nodded and waited, watching for the slightest hint that she was lying or worse.

"It's a bit of a mess. No one knows what happened, and Killian's body was removed before anyone got into his rooms after the whole thing in the garage." She took a drink before smirking. "Do you want to tell me what happened?"

"No, I don't. What do you mean about Killian's body?" She pulled her braid over her shoulder and played with the ends.

"Exactly what I said. The current story is that Darian has it and is planning to dispose of it. He seems to be making a bid to become the Ashcroft head. But that means he had to of killed Killian, wouldn't it?"

Her eyes landed on his, scanning for any reaction. Damien leaned back and rubbed his hand over his jaw. If Darian was trying to take over, he would need to prove he had taken out Killian. And he couldn't do that. If they accepted him as head, then he would need to gain their approval without proof. Technically, the new head should be Elora, but that seemed like running directly into the enemies' hands, gift wrapped and ready for them. Plus, she would also have to prove her actions beyond just her word. There had been five of them in that room and two of them were now dead.

"Most in the Tower are calling on you to come claim the title since you were his second in command. Their loyalty is to you. If you want it."

He didn't. Not even the tiniest shred. But there were things in the Tower that he did want.

"Of course," she drawled, stretching out her arms along the side of the booth, "there are many who want his daughter to take over. If she really is his daughter, of course."

His eyes hardened and jaw clenched as Korina leisurely looked over the shop, eyes lingering on one or two humans with a hungry gleam. The last thing he needed was Korina interested in Elora, seeing her as a threat or obstacle to something she believed she was owed.

"Could you get me a few things if I told you what to look for?"

Korina nodded, her eyebrow arching in interest at being called for a mission. Maybe she had aspirations of Damien taking the title and pulling her up through the ranks. Throughout their short-lived dalliance, Killian had never seen her as any-thing more than a pretty face, someone to sleep with when he got bored. Korina had thought she would become Killian's new wife or consort, replacing Iris at his side. Damien guessed that he would make a consolation prize now that Killian was no longer an option.

"There are some journals in Killian's office. Last time I saw them they were in a drawer in his desk. They look like medical textbooks, but there's a little symbol along the spine. Then I need you to gather the clothing left behind in my room, along with anything in the closet."

"Anything else?" Her eyes were bright and hungry, and he forced himself to meet them even as he wanted to retract each request he made.

"Cash. I have some stashed in my own rooms, but any that you can get from Killian's safe would be useful."

"Can I ask what all this is for?"

"No, you can't." His tone was hard, edged in hopes that she would recognize that this line of inquiry was over. She had her orders and not another word needed to be spoken.

"And what about Killian's blood whore? Or daughter? Any word on her? Apparently, she disappeared last night as well."

"Don't fucking call her that." His voice was more fury than anything else and he watched her eyes narrow, the hunger re-placed by anger and jealousy. He had stepped right into her trap, but Elora always brought out something in him that couldn't be fully restrained. A protective urge that was almost overwhelm-ing at times.

"Testy, Damien. That temper did cause problems once upon a time." She giggled, like this was the funniest joke in the world. "Don't worry. I'll get everything you need and contact you once I do."

She gave him one more grin, her lips curling sharply in the corners, and sauntered to the door. Just as his shoulders lowered and his jaw relaxed, a vibration erupted in his pocket, and he cursed as he pulled it out. No one had his number. Only Killian and Lukas. And now Korina, but that was a necessary evil. Across the screen was an address along with a date and time, and he had a fairly good idea who it belonged to.

Chapter 5

Viktor

"So, you failed." The voice came from the woman sitting at the head of the kitchen table. Two people sat on either side of her. Together, they made up the council that assisted in making the major decisions of the Resistance. For now, the main headquarters of the movement was housed in an old, rundown apartment complex along the edge of the city. It had belonged to one of the members who donated it to the cause in return for a seat at the table, a say in the moves that were made. But Viktor supposed such a trade was worth it since they were able to house people there and use it as the main base despite having others, especially since those kept getting shut down, raided by vampires in order to stop their cause.

The kitchen had been updated to wooden cabinets and steel appliances since it was built. The wood floor was partially covered with a large rug where the long, banquet style table stood. Apparently, the person had been remodeling the home before going broke. They only managed to renovate a few rooms before losing their money. The movement had done the rest with the donations that came in from people seeking help or safety.

Viktor held the gaze of the woman who spoke—older, roughly mid-forties, with dark auburn hair and deep green eyes that were almost black. Her navy-blue shirt and jeans complimented her deeply tanned skin that was littered with scars from battles long since passed. Her eyebrows furrowed, and her eyes hardened as Viktor interlaced his fingers behind his back and squared his shoulders.

"The target was taken by an enemy vampire during the extraction." He repeated the line he had practiced in preparation for this moment. He wouldn't admit that he failed. Plans had simply shifted due to unforeseen changes. They would need to adapt and luckily, he had an idea of how to do that.

"Again, you failed." He didn't respond, just met her eyes until she smirked, an agonizingly familiar look he had been struggling to place for years.

"But you brought a consolation prize, from what I understand."

"Yes. I brought her foster sister, Elizabeth."

"And she's useful how? She's a threat to every human here." Viktor turned to who spoke, a small man who was older than anyone else at the table. He was always careful, from what Viktor had seen. It made him the rational voice when the rest of them had wanted to rush into a raid or an attack on a group of vampires. But he was also the voice that had spoken against taking Elora from the hospital itself. If he had kept his mouth shut and opinions to himself, they wouldn't even be in this situation.

"The target cares about her, for one. She could be used as leverage. Another aspect to consider is that Elizabeth is the only vampire turned by the target. Even Denise said she wasn't sure what the consequences would be of her being turned by someone like the target." He didn't use Elora's name, couldn't bring himself to do it. Every time it passed his lips, it brought with it a twinge of guilt. He had seen her tears and heard her screams, the sound of her voice cracking as she forced out the words in between sobs.

"You think we should study her, test her blood, and see what happens?" The question came once more from the woman at the head of the table, fingers interlaced under her chin.

"Yes, I do. She can do both at once. We can use her and study her. We just need to keep her contained and fed if necessary." There was a collected groan of disgust at the idea of feeding her, but blood banks would work well enough. Elizabeth was uncharted territory, just as Elora was.

"I agree." The woman nodded her head at Viktor before she gestured a dismissal at those sitting at the table, leaving just them two. Viktor didn't move as each one shuffled out, muttering their discontentment at the way the meeting had gone. He had known that bringing Elizabeth wouldn't be a popular choice, but he also knew that he was right about her being useful. Luckily, the only person whose opinion mattered agreed with him.

"Coffee, Viktor? Tea?" Viktor shook his head and took the seat next to her as she stood. "Mind if I make myself some?"

Once more, he shook his head and studied his hands as she busied herself with the kettle, placing it on the stove and turning it on. After she chose a tea bag and placed it in the mug, she twisted around and leaned against the counter, hands gripping the edges.

"What else did you learn while you were there? Anything about the target?" He noted the small wince as she said the word target, as if she found rendering Elora nameless as distasteful as he did.

"What do you want to know, Thorne? The abuse continued after she was brought back. I didn't see anything, and she didn't tell me details. She's also feeding once more now that the medication is out of her system, so Denise's theory was correct." Thorne hummed a small noise and then poured the boiling water into the cup, returned to her seat.

"Denise was right about most things. Did you find her journals? Patient notes?" She dunked the tea bag a few times, watching it intently as the water's color turned darker each time.

"I checked her office and her condo. Either they are hidden really well, or someone beat us to it."

"Hmm. I thought that might happen."

"My guess is Killian. He would have had them taken right away." Viktor didn't regret seeing his death, had enjoyed watching Elora drive the knife into him over and over until she was forced to stop. He knew that if given the chance, she would have kept going until there was nothing left.

"I'm inclined to agree." She took a sip and smiled softly to herself as if they weren't having a conversation about the future of not only the Resistance, but human life in general.

"Do you want me to try to retrieve them?" She considered it for a heartbeat as she stood and looked for something in the cabinets.

"Maybe." Thorne seemed to pause briefly before continuing. "When did the target begin feeding again?"

Her eyes went everywhere but to Viktor as he attempted to trace the timeline. So much of it was hazy with periods of blackouts after he was fed from. It had left him wondering if it had been like this for Jaime when he worked as a source. Their tuition had been increased during college and Jaime had struggled to pay it. Instead of confiding in Viktor, asking for help, Jaime had taken the job.

"A couple of weeks ago. Her birthday was the first time. It was the party Killian held for her." He thought for a second. "So, since—"

"I see." Thorne's interruption was followed by her silence as Viktor considered how she seemed to know Elora's birthday.

"The files we have on her contain all the basic information," she explained curtly, as if she had heard his thoughts. Her eyes never left the teacup in front of her. Of course, they would know all the mundane facts of her life. He had gained it all from her files at the hospital, so it wasn't as if it was hidden. It had probably been why Denise had kept her journals separate from the online files. It seemed like most parts of Elora were known, set up in tiny display cases for them to study and memorize. It felt wrong somehow. No matter who or what she was. For a moment, he wished he knew all that information because he had asked. Because she had found him worthy of telling.

"About Elizabeth." Thorne shifted the conversation, and Viktor straightened in the chair, pushing away the confusing and dangerous thoughts from his mind.

"I don't know anything, really. Everything I said earlier is a hunch. Denise thought her blood would prove useful, but she never said how." Thorne waved her hand, dismissing what he had said.

"We have people for that. They're already getting started. She should have been fed and had blood gathered by now. Someone will be going in to ask her questions later to see what, if anything, is different about her compared to other vampires." He nodded, and they fell into silence. The only sound was her sipping her tea.

"And the target? Do you think she'll come to us willingly?"

Viktor took a breath, deciding how to word his response.

"I'm honestly not sure. My time with her was limited at the Tower and she never really talked about her opinions on vampires. I know she hated Killian, but I'm not sure about the rest of them."

"Hmm. I think we'll need to take her by force." She took another sip of her tea, eyebrows knitting together. "You'll need to. Find her, Viktor. It's obvious they're hiding somewhere, so find out where and bring her here." Thorne placed her cup in the sink and left the kitchen, leaving him to plan how he was going to not only find her, but drag her back.

"Wait!" Viktor jumped to his feet and followed her out, hoping that she hadn't gone far. Thorne froze on the stairs, her hand resting on the peeling banister.

"I have an idea about finding her."

Chapter 6

Elora

Damien returned late while she sat on the couch, drinking blood from another mug and watching some reality show where women planned their dream wedding. It was asinine, and she loved every second of it. Every snarky comment by the bride's best friend and insult from the future mother-in-law. She didn't even bother to look up as he shut the door and shrugged off his jacket, leaving it on a stool in the kitchen. Her eyes remained on the television as he disappeared down the hallways for a few minutes before returning.

She could feel his focus on her as he collapsed onto the couch, leaning against the back cushion with his head resting against it. For a moment, he simply took in a series of deep breaths, as if he was releasing every ounce of tension and exhaustion from his body. He pulled his head up and watched the show with her while a woman began weeping from joy before turning towards her.

"Can we please shut this off?" His voice was strained, like he was in physical pain as a woman on the show squealed after being shown a potential wedding cake—a massive five-layer monstrosity covered in buttercream flowers and thick ribbons.

"No."

"We need to talk." She made a show of sighing dramatically and turned it off before she twisted her body to face him. Elora pulled her feet under her body and adjusted the dress to cover as much as possible before gesturing for him to continue. If he wanted her undivided attention, he would get it.

"We need to be careful with blood intake, for one. Try to feed once every other day to make our reserves last as long as possible. I'll have to call in some favors to get us more." She nodded, suddenly guilty for consuming a full bottle that day.

"How often do vampires typically need to feed?" She didn't want to ask him, didn't want to see his smug smile as he got to explained something so basic to her. But the sneer never came, only the barest flicker of concern.

"A vampire can usually go two days before hunger starts to set in. Anything after that, and it becomes dangerous." She bit the inside of her cheek and quickly stifled her panic. It felt like she would need to feed more than that. The hunger had come on so fiercely earlier in the day that she thought she would pass out, hence the blood in the mug she now held. Was it because she was so new? She may not be newly turned, but the medication had only been out of her system for a couple of weeks.

"I can do that." Her voice sounded more confident than she actually felt.

"Can you?" He gave the mug a pointed look, and she took a deep breath.

"Now that I'm aware that we are rationing, I can do what's needed. It's amazing what can happen when someone has some basic information." She watched him swallow back a retort.

"Good." He twisted his neck one way and then another as he seemed to consider what he wanted to say next. "I met with a contact today when I left. She's bringing us supplies that I left behind. She's also bringing some journals that could be useful."

Elora wanted to ask about the journals, but her mind got stuck on one simple word— she. To prevent herself from saying anything that would embarrass her, she pulled at the sleeves of her sweater and let him continue. He didn't need to know what part of his explanation she had focused on.

"She's a vampire I've known and worked with since I was turned. She's loyal, or at least enough to not turn us in."

"I see." Her words were curt, and she could practically feel him smirking at her, his stupid smile making his face light up with a devilish gleam. "What are the journals about?"

"You. Denise kept all her patient notes for you separate, wrote it all in journals. I got them a while back." She raised her brow at him.

"For Killian?"

He swallowed thickly, as if he knew exactly where this would go and was preparing for it. "Yes, it was on his orders."

She let out a bitter laugh that she hoped would hurt him. "So, the journals are all my patient notes from her. Every session?"

"Yes."

"I want to read them."

He nodded. "Of course. I wouldn't keep them from you."

"When will we get them?"

"I'm not sure. Hopefully in the next couple of days."

The urge to scream that a couple of days wasn't soon enough rested on her tongue. That morning wouldn't have been soon enough. The letter Denise had left her felt like a tease, a hint at answers to questions she hadn't realized she had. And the journals were a lifeline, a raft in a raging sea that was trying to pull her under. She brought her finger to her lips, chewing on the loose skin around her nail as she thought through their sessions and what she may have written down.

"And after we have the journals? What happens then?" Her voice was quiet as she stared at the weird stain on the couch, not actually seeing anything.

"I don't know, honestly. Like I said this morning, I'm following up on some leads. I have another meeting tomorrow."

"With who?" She couldn't help the distrust in her tone, the paranoia that seeped into her skin and forced her to tense up.

"Don't worry about that."

"Why wouldn't I? You're meeting with someone to discuss what to do with me. Why the fuck wouldn't I worry about that?" Damien rubbed the back of his neck, closing his eyes as he struggled to get his temper under control.

"I understand why you feel that way. But you need to trust me. I don't want to get your hopes up." His words were perfectly measured, as if he were talking to a rabid animal that could attack at any moment. She cackled and relished the way his eyes widened before narrowing. Damien shifted away from her as she leaned towards him, as if he was uncomfortable with how close she was, and she savored the effect she had on him.

"I don't trust you. I'll never trust you. All I'll ever trust is your own self-interest to get rid of a problem."

He scowled at her promise. "Self-interest? That would have been leaving you to Killian. That would have been letting Viktor take you in that garage."

"Maybe you should have." Her voice was barely a whisper, but he froze, going unnaturally still as he studied her. If he had let Viktor take her, Lukas would probably still be alive. To her, it was worth it, worth being taken to the Resistance.

"You truly have no sense of self-preservation, do you?"

"Of course I do."

"Really? When? Was it when you offered up your neck to me in that room? Was it when you stabbed me with a fucking fork? When you ran off at the party knowing there were vampires there who would hurt you?"

She laughed loudly, the sound mingling with the harshness of his breathing. There was a wildness, a desperation in his features as he crossed his arms over his chest, mouth pressed into a thin line.

"Or was it when you shut down for days and decided death was the best option for you?" She flinched at the question, unable to form words to defend herself. It was cruel to throw that back in her face, especially when all he had done was leave her to drown in the dark place she had no control over. She studied her hands, then let her fingers rest on her wrists, toying with the scars there.

Lukas had been the one to attempt to drag her back to the surface, to help her see the light again. Because despite everything, Lukas had been the sun and warmth. Now he was dead.

"Exactly. You have no thought for your life, and it drives me insane." He stood and started heading towards the hallway, shoulders slumped like there was a weight there. She didn't know how to explain to him it was difficult to have any thoughts for your own life when the reminder of your worth was etched into your skin.

"The only thing worthwhile is my blood and we both know that. It's the reason I was created. The only reason anyone has bothered to pretend to care about me, including you. So forgive me for not caring." He stopped mid-step before marching back to her, his gait heavy and quick to the point she could feel it reverberate through the floor and into the couch. In an instant, his arms sank into the cushion on either side of her, trapping her between them.

Damien leaned down until his face was so close she could feel his breath as the corners of his lips curled down. "Don't play that game, love. You're worth more than that. You're worth more than what they have used you for. And I'm going to make sure you come to believe that." He stood back and watched her for a reaction he didn't get.

"Funny. That's exactly what Viktor said."

"The difference is that I mean it." She shifted slightly and turned the television back on. The show she was watching was over, but it was a baking one now. Honestly, that was a much better option.

"I'm sure you think you do." He watched her for a moment longer before he shook his head and disappeared down the hallway. The last thing she heard, other than the show, was the sound of his door slamming shut.

Chapter 7

Damien

Got it. Coffee Shop. 1 hour.

The message from the unknown number came early the next morning and he tensed, each muscle growing taunt and twisted. Meeting Korina always left him feeling uneasy, like she knew a secret that he needed to know but refused to disclose. And maybe she did. When they had first met, she had been sweet and eager to help Damien acclimate. And he had been so new, so inexperienced in what it meant to be a vampire, especially one in the Ashcroft family. He had taken her help without question. She was one of the few who had been turned by Killian. Most were turned by others, usually with permission from the head vampire. But mistakes happened. Their growing numbers was proof of that.

They had fallen into an easy friendship before it had grown into something resembling a relationship. It was physical — nothing more. But as Killian gave him more and more jobs, Korina had grown angry and distant, blaming him for her lack of status. That was when she had moved on, sleeping with Killian instead. He had thought it would hurt when she broke it off, but it had felt more like a relief, leaving him wondering when being with her had started to feel more like a chore rather than easy companionship.

The door to Elora's bedroom was still closed as he pulled on his jacket. For a moment, he debated knocking to let her know he was leaving in an effort to be transparent. And there was how last night had ended, what words were said and couldn't be taken back now. They were volatile together, and he understood why, even if it left him questioning every word he said, every move he made. She had no reason to trust him, nothing beyond his promise to keep her safe.

Then there was her declaration about her worth, about her blood being all that mattered. His pulse had raced as the words lingered in the air between them. It was what they had taught her throughout her entire life, and it made him want nothing more than to bring Killian back so he could be the one to kill him this time. Every word he had said in response had been true, even if she didn't believe it. She saw herself as unlovable and unworthy. Until she was safe, either with or without him, Damien would fight tooth and nail to replace every belief she held about herself.

His hand hovered in the air as he hesitated and considered finding Jonas since Killian wasn't an option. He could destroy him the way they tried to do to her. Because they had failed. Hidden beneath her beliefs that she was worth nothing but the blood in her veins, that she was broken and disfigured, was a fierceness that could end worlds.

Damien's fist fell to his side as he moved away from the door. Korina wouldn't wait and would take him being late as an insult. Besides, there was a more important place he needed to visit. Gently, he grabbed his keys and left, closing the door so softly not a single sound was made despite the rusted hinges that somehow held the door up.

The drive to the coffee shop was relatively quick. It was close enough that he could get there easily, but far enough from their location that it was not an easy connection to make should someone spot him. As he approached, his focus moved over the surrounding area and the few people sitting at tables outside, taking in the last of the warmth. Coffee mugs were held in their hands and thick coats hung on the chair behind them. Easy smiles and soft laughter filled the air, despite the way their breath frosted slightly in front of them.

Damien's eyes scanned the crowd as he entered. There were fewer people here this time, and he easily spotted Korina sitting in the same booth, only this time she had taken the seat facing the door. He nodded in her direction before ordering his drink and sitting across from her.

"Good morning, handsome. I was thinking you weren't going to show." He stiffened at her greeting before returning a forced smile.

"Just a slight delay. Nothing to concern yourself with." He glanced around the shop, lingering on each face.

"Do you think I brought back-up? That I plan on betraying you?"

He gave her a deadpanned expression. "I think you serve your own self-interest and if that includes betraying me, then you would."

She tossed her head back and laughed loudly. It was a sound that was at odds with who she was underneath the façade she put on. A few years back, she had killed a human because Killian fed from them more than once, claiming she was doing him a favor since he was obviously getting attached. What would she have done to Elora if she knew the truth about everything? After Elora was brought back, Korina was sent away from the Tower. Killian never talked about it, and her name was never mentioned. At one point, Killian had enjoyed Korina's bloodlust, her willingness to become violent. But once it became obsessive, it was over. Damien was sure Killian hadn't been willing to risk Elora, and so Korina was removed from the equation.

"I suppose that's fair. Here. I found everything. I even threw in some bottles of blood I found in Killian's private rooms." His hand hesitated as he reached across the table to grab the bag that she was handing him. If the bottles were in Killian's room, then the blood belonged to only one person. That also meant that the blood was useless. Elora couldn't drink it, and he had vowed never to do so.

"Thank you. Anything new?"

She shrugged and the loose curls moved along her shoulders.

"Nothing new. The division is getting worse, and I think there may end up being a problem. Vampires killing vampires. Not enough of them support Darian. It's either you or Killian's—" Her eyes met his, mischief shining as she uttered the next word, "daughter. Killian's daughter."

He leaned back, refusing to make the same mistake as last time. "And who do you back?"

"Whoever gives me the best offer." She smiled sweetly, then stood, carrying the coffee cup he hadn't noticed with her.

"I'll let you know if anything changes." She called over her shoulder just as she threw a smile at the young man running the counter, a smile that had spelled death for many humans over the years.

* * *

This was the one place Damien had never expected to be willingly invited to, and yet here he was in Silas Corvin's foyer, waiting to be escorted into his office. No one had even known where the Corvin family resided, let alone were invited to visit. Any human who was turned by a Corvin vampire was sworn to secrecy with an old-school and ineffective blood oath to never talk about the manor or anyone who lived there. They thrived off secrecy, and it had driven Killian insane to know he couldn't even find the address. He wasn't even able to secure a meeting despite being married to Silas's sister.

Damien studied the entryway and its tasteful décor: paintings of nature scenes and portraits of Silas and a woman who bore a striking resemblance to Elora. The woman could only be Iris, the secret that was kept close to Killian's chest. Elora shared her mother's hair, though Iris's was a darker red in the painting. While Elora's was nearly the color of blood, Iris's was more of a dark auburn. They also shared the same green eyes, high cheekbones and thin lips that curled slightly at the end as if she was always smirking.

Silas's painting revealed little resemblance to his sister or niece. Maybe the same face shape and bone structure, but his lips were a bit fuller, and his eyes were narrow, almost hiding the icy blue irises. His long hair was a dark brown that fell in waves over narrow shoulders.

"Those are old paintings. We've moved on to more modern technology. Large portraits are framed in other areas of the manor. Though that is the only one we have of Iris." Damien took one final look at the painting where Iris and Silas stood side-by-side before turning towards the voice—a deep timber that sounded like it would vibrate in his chest each time he spoke.

Silas stood in front of a door just down the hall. His hair was shorter now than in the painting, falling in a haphazard way around his ears that made him appear younger. Damien tossed him a grin before strolling forward until they were face to face.

"Why keep these up at all if they're so outdated?" His tone was joking, hoping to ease any tension that may exist between the two of them. Damien had never been sent specifically after Silas, but he knew Killian had used him as a threat. More than once, he had been tasked with coercing information from Silas's vampires.

And then there was the role he had played in his niece's kidnapping.

"Call me sentimental. Shall we?" He gestured to the office and stepped to the side so Damien could enter first. For a moment, Damien studied his face, searching for any hint at how this meeting would go. There had been no context given in the text message. Only the address and time. But there was nothing. Not a single hint. Not a curl of his lip, a flare of his nostril, or a twitch in his brow.

Blank. Unreadable. Infuriating.

Damien stepped into the large office that was reminiscent of the others he had seen over the years. A large desk sat in the center of the room with two chairs and a side table in front of it.

"Have a seat." Silas pointed at one of the chairs before shutting the door and taking his own. Damien studied the room, noted the books on the shelves and the paintings that looked similar to those Killian had lined the halls of the Tower and his office with. He had a feeling if he checked the corner of them, he would see the same initials.

After he settled in, Silas interlaced his long fingers and rested his chin on them. "We don't need to worry about pleasantries. I won't try to kill you while you're here if you promise me the same."

"Of course. Glad we're on the same page." Damien laid his ankle on his knee and reclined against the back of the chair.

"Why don't you tell me what happened with my niece and Killian?"

Damien scoffed. "Why don't you tell me what you know, and I'll fill in the gaps."

A small chuckle sounded from Silas as his eyes narrowed until there was no hint of blue.

"If this is going to work, you need to trust me." His words were gentle, like he was placating a child, and Damien forced himself to not tense in response.

"The short version is I was sent to find your niece, and I found her a psychiatric hospital. Killian ordered me to bring her back, which I did. He publicly claimed her as his daughter and then she killed him. I have her in a safe house somewhere in the city."

His nostrils flared. "You're the one who took her back from Denise?"

Now it was Damien's turn to be surprised, to try to understand why Silas would know Denise that well.

"Yes," he responded, hoping that his tone was as cool as he was attempting to make it.

"Did you know what would happen to her if she was brought back?" Damien flinched at the question because even though he hadn't, it was no excuse for what he did. If he had thought it through instead of acting like a loyal soldier, he could have put two and two together. She ran away and was covered in puncture wounds. It wouldn't have taken much thought. But he had been blinded by his own history, his disdain for who he thought she was.

"No, I didn't. Once I found out what was happening, I worked to get her out."

"Oh, I know. Denise kept me informed of what was happening."

"And why would she do that?" Damien couldn't help it. He knew Denise had defected from the Resistance, but he hadn't known she was working with Silas. He had never asked if she was being aided, and she had never offered the information.

"Not your concern. She made sure Elora would know everything." That was also new information, and he was getting tired of having secrets alluded to but not revealed.

"The question, Damien, is what happens to my niece now." Silas leaned back in his chair and waited.

"Isn't that the point of this meeting?"

"Are you that anxious to get rid of her? From what I was told fairly recently, my niece is quite wonderful."

A jolt shot through him at the thought that someone was in the Tower and reporting to Silas. Killian had obviously grown too complacent, too secure in his position. Not only had Resistance members infiltrated them but so had the Corvin family. How many others were there now, reporting back secrets to their masters?

"I'm done being her babysitter." His tone was cold, and the corner of Silas's lips twitched, like Damien said something amusing.

"And if I hired you to do the same job? You are in need of a new family, aren't you? From what I understand, Darian is poised to take Killian's role, and he's no fan of yours. Something about interfering where you weren't wanted?" He raised a brow as he waited for Damien to think about his offer.

"Technically, Elora should take over. She was the one who stabbed Killian and ended him. Isn't that the rules?" Damien's response purposefully ignored Silas's question concerning Darian and instead asked his own. He could only assume that he was referring to Jonas and his interference there. It was interesting that Darian cared enough about it to make him an enemy.

"Is there proof she did that?"

"We both know there isn't." The assertion was met with a nod from Silas, as if he had known exactly what it would be.

"Do we now?" Silas's question lingered for a minute before continuing. "Either way, we return to my original question. What to do with her?"

"What are you offering?" Damien wanted details from the vampire. It didn't matter to him that Silas was her uncle and seemed to have an interest in her safety. Killian had been her father and had appeared obsessed with keeping her protected. This time Damien would ask questions, demand each and every potential detail.

"Is there something you want in exchange for her?"

"No! That isn't what I meant." Damien ignored the amused and knowing smile on his face. "I simply want to know what you're offering her. A place in your manor? Protection from the Resistance? Protection from Darian and everyone else?"

Another nod from Silas. "Yes. All of that and more. I want to help her come to understand what she is, what Killian did to her when he tried to play at a god. She's unique, completely new. And that can be a blessing and a curse, as she can attest to. I also want to get her help. I can only imagine the pain she's in."

Damien assessed the expression on Silas's face, the tone of his voice. He sounded earnest, sincere. But so had Killian when he had given Damien the job, when he had tasted her blood and asked him to bring her home. He pushed himself up from the chair and shoved his hands into the pockets of his jacket.

"I'll take your offer to her. Let her decide." Silas's lips turned downward into a frown that was harsh on his features.

"How generous of you. And what if she turns it down?" Damien stared and lifted his shoulder in a shrug. He didn't have an answer to that. He wasn't even sure which choice he wanted her to make. Without any rationale, it almost felt like asking her to decide between Silas and himself, even if Silas had offered him a place here. In this mind, he imagined each of them taking on their role within these walls — hers as the niece and him as another vampire who happened to be under Silas's protection. The chasm between them would widen, turn into a gaping void that could never be bridged, no matter how desperately he wanted it to be. They would see each other in passing, maybe chat about mundane things if they saw each other or found themselves in the same room or social function. Their relationship, volatile as it was, would be rendered sterile and devoid of any emotion.

And yet, it was an enticing offer that would bring safety, comfort, and purpose to both of them. It was these things that had kept him tethered to Killian in the first place. But if Silas kept his word, Elora would be protected, and that was what was important. He would sacrifice whatever he needed to in order to make sure she was safe.

"I'm surprised you don't have more questions. About Iris? About Denise?"

Damien grinned as he stared down at him. "Oh, I do, but she has those questions, too. And I think she should be the one to ask them."

Silas chuckled and shook his head. "It makes sense now why you risked so much to get her out, even betraying your own vampire head."

Damien tensed, all the projected ease evaporating from his limbs. "Even I can't stand a woman in pain. Being treated like that."

"No, Damien. I don't think that's the reason at all." He gestured towards the door, a clear dismissal. "I'll expect an answer within three days. In the meantime, be careful. There are plenty of people who will do anything to get their hands on her."

Chapter 8

Elora

Damien was gone when she woke, which wasn't necessarily a surprise. She had expected it, but his absence was still a blade in her ribs, hindering each breath she tried to take. Last night, she had said too much, had let him goad her into revealing thoughts she had kept only to herself. And then there had been the emotional whiplash that left her unsure of anything. In one moment, it was all hateful comments aimed at her darkest insecurities and the next it was the sweetest reassurances that she had worth.

She took a quick glance at the collection bottles in the refrigerator and slammed the door shut, struggling to ignore the gnawing hunger in her stomach. It was agony with the way it contracted and cramped until she was on the verge of tears. Elora clenched her hands, attempting to ease the trembling as she tightened her jaw. It was fine. She could do this, could conquer the hunger and stick to the rations Damien had implemented.

It would be fine.

Elora glanced around the room before taking a deep breath, centering herself in the way Denise had taught her to do when thoughts and emotions became too much. In the early days of her stay at the hospital, she had been easily panicked. Her heart and thoughts would race at the slightest provocation. She knew now that she had simply been terrified of being found, of Killian dragging her back. At the time, she had merely known she couldn't stand being near anyone, that the nurses who checked her vitals at night had left her screaming.

Until Viktor. She shook her head, scolding herself for falling back into those memories, into the lies he had told for years.

And then Damien had taken her back, put her back in Killian's reach and under his control. He hadn't known what would happen to her and a part of her understood that. But she couldn't bring herself not to blame him to a certain point. He had been the catalyst for it all, following orders until she appeared broken on the floor of his bedroom.

Yet, she blamed herself more. It was a weight that never left. A grime that coated her skin, leaving her feeling dirty and ashamed even before she remembered why it was there. Denise had tried to help her work through these feelings, had explained their irrationality, and Elora recognized the truth of that when she wasn't trapped in those thoughts. But the rational part of her, the part of her that knew, had always been quieter. It had always been drowned out by the screaming refrains in her head, the repeated names and labels that left her unable to meet her gaze in the mirror.

"You should have fought," she whispered into the empty room. "You should have tried to run away. Or killed him." Elora wrapped her arms around her as if it would protect her from the accusations that she threw at herself. It was always the same. A spiral of unwarranted self-hatred that she could never fully convince herself to emerge from.

"You should have fought." The walls started to move, slightly shifting at first, before inching closer and closer. With a sharp exhale, she retreated step by step until her back hit the counter.

"Breathe." She reminded herself, but the words meant nothing when the room threatened to swallow her whole. Her breaths came too quickly as she struggled to control the speed at which the air came rushing in, becoming more of a shallow pant than anything else. The walls were so close as she threw the door open and raced out into the cool air of the hallway that smelled vaguely like cookies and cinnamon. Behind her, the door to the apartment slammed shut as she stood on shaky legs and paced, hands alternating between clutching her hair and scratching at her palms.

The floor! Focus on the floor.

Denise's advice somehow made it through the haze of panic, the strategy of finding things to ground herself in reality. She stared down at the intricate pattern of tan, red, and black tiles until they grew blurry and indistinguishable. There were chips in them and places of discoloration from years of abuse without repairs.

Count the squares. Inventory each imperfection.

The words screamed in her mind as she fought against every desire to curl up on the floor and become another decoration. She collapsed to her knees, not even feeling the stinging pain that radiated through her body at the impact.

Breathe, damn it!

"I'm sorry?" Elora froze, and so did her breathing. The air itself stuck in her throat and lungs as she glanced up through her lashes. She must have said that out loud. Her eyes locked onto the tile, which was now much clearer, before she turned away from the voice.

Count the squares. One red. Two tans. One black. One —

"Are you okay?" She raised a hand, waving it slightly to try to make them leave her alone, leave her to her panic. As soon as her breathing decided to cooperate again, she would be fine.

There! A gouge in the tile, revealing the pale floor underneath. She begged her body yet again to breathe, but it ignored every plea she made. Once more, Elora pulled a breath in, but her body wouldn't hold it. Her lungs refused to expand, to allow for the very thing that would stop the lightheaded sensation that was quickly taking over.

Hands. Her hand was suddenly in someone else's as they held it with her palm up, using their thumb to rub circles in the center of it.

"Focus on this. On this feeling. You're not in danger. Focus." She did as the voice asked and allowed the strange sensation caused by their fingers on the sensitive part of her palm to become the only thought in her mind. Slowly, so slowly, her breathing eased.

"Okay. Good. Now, try to take a deeper breath. Not a deep one, just more air than before." Again, she followed their instructions. The hallway was coming back into focus along with the discolored walls that desperately needed either a new coat of paint or wallpaper. Anything to cover up the stains.

She finally sucked in a deep breath and smiled even as she lifted her face to the ceiling. Each breath was deeper than the one before and she finally glanced down at the hands holding her own, cupping them like they were precious. The hands were a deep tan, rough and calloused, like they worked somewhere that required manual labor. In the city, that could mean anything—mechanic, factory workers, or something more underground.

"Is everything alright?" Elora knew that voice as it rang out in the hallway. Her eyes darted up and locked with Connie's, whose furrowed brows scanned Elora's crumpled form on the dirty floor.

"All fine, Aunt Connie."

"Bring her in, Wyatt." The hand, which she now knew belonged to Connie's famous nephew, closed around hers while his other went underneath her upper arm as he lifted and led her to his aunt's apartment. She didn't fight him, simply centered herself as Denise taught her now that she could conjure up a rationale thought. His hands were warm, the heat reaching her skin through the thick sleeves of her sweater. Her shaky fingers reached up, feeling the collar around her neck, and sighed in relief at how high it went up. Very little was showing, was on display for these humans she knew practically nothing about other than Connie lived across the hall. Again, the smell of cookies and cinnamon reached her, a sign that Connie had baked something already.

Slowly, as if she was a scared child, Wyatt led her to the couch. Elora tried to take in the apartment to distract herself from the embarrassment that was rushing through her, but there was simply too much to look at. Framed pictures crowded the walls, smiling faces gazed out from blank backgrounds or various locations. There was one at a lake while another looked to be outside the art museum downtown. Some of them were black and white, older photos of who looked to be Connie and who Elora could only assume was her husband—a handsome man with hair parted on the side and a sly grin that screamed mischief. Connie was a younger version of herself — beautiful, with long hair that fell in curls around her shoulders. They looked so happy and in some of them they were simply gazing at one another, smiles on their lips.

Elora noted that the couch was much newer than the one in her own apartment as Connie shuffled to the kitchen. There was a large coffee table with mugs and a teapot sitting beside a plate of what looked like scones and cookies. She glanced over everything as she sat down, and the hands disappeared. With a slight groan, Elora leaned against the back of the couch and took another deep breath, closing her eyes for just a minute. She could hear whispering in the kitchen but didn't bother to make out the words. It was obviously a conversation about what had happened in the hall.

And what had happened? She had panicked, had another anxiety attack brought on by thoughts of Killian. Even now, he controlled her in a way she had never expected. He was a plague, a curse, and a disease that would never leave her system, forever infecting her every thought and emotion.

Now she was here in Connie's living room, intruding on her time with her nephew.

All because you can't keep your shit together. Elora shifted slightly as the thought came, the truth of it eating her alive.

"Feeling better?" A masculine voice she vaguely recognized sat in a chair that must have been pulled up from some-where—the dining room, perhaps. This apartment looked bigger than her own. The kitchen was actually separate from the living room, along with a dining room with a small table and three chairs sitting near a window.

She gave him a small smile that was more of a grimace and nodded.

"Yes, thank you. I'm sorry to bother you both with that." She finally studied him, took in his features. He was around her age, maybe a year or two older. Chestnut hair hung around his face and his amber eyes were framed by dark lashes. A clean-shaven face revealed a sharp jaw and a slightly crooked nose, like he had been in fights but never got it properly set. The smile that stretched across his face was genuine and inviting, like they were old friends catching up over tea.

"No need to apologize. I'm just glad I was able to help." Connie strolled in from the kitchen, another plate and coffee mug in her hands. She gave Elora a bright smile before she nodded towards the man in front of them.

"You got to meet my nephew. He was bringing me my groceries. It's hard to get out at my age." She placed the cup down and poured whatever was in the teapot into the three cups, handing Elora one before sitting next to her on the couch. Elora struggled to meet her eyes, sipping her tea instead.

"He's quite the gentleman and very helpful." She glanced up at the old woman, taking in the concern in her eyes as Connie watched her. With a small smile that she hoped looked more real than it was, Elora took another sip and fought back a wince. It was bitter compared to how she usually drank it.

A look of comical despair forged itself on Wyatt's face as he jumped to his feet.

"I left them in the hall!" Elora giggled at the display, the sound strange to her ears considering the tingling sensation throughout her body and the gnawing hunger in her stomach. He rushed from the apartment, his stride wide and heavy on the floor. Elora almost cringed for the people living underneath as she imagined how it must sound for them.

"Handsome, isn't he?" She didn't wait for a response. "I told you." Connie took a drink of her tea and grimaced slightly, reaching for the sugar cubes waiting in a small bowl on the table. Elora chuckled and nodded as she reached for her own.

"Yes, he is. And here I thought aunts tend to exaggerate these things." The old woman laughed so loudly Elora was surprised the numerous knickknacks didn't reverberate from the force of it.

"What's so funny?" His voice, warm and deep like honey, broke through as he returned with his arms crowded with canvas bags. A grunt sounded from the kitchen as he lifted them onto the counter and began taking items out and putting them away. Sugar in the upper cabinet by the sink. Coffee creamer in the re-frigerator.

"Come sit, Wyatt. I can still take care of that." There was a playful bite to her words, as if they had had this conversation before, and Elora smiled into her tea. Wyatt pressed a kiss on his aunt's cheek before retaking his seat and resting his ankle on his knee.

"My aunt says you moved in across the way." Not a question, but a conversation starter. It was an opportunity for this to start on her terms, and she found herself strangely appreciative of the small gesture.

"Yes, very recently. A few days ago, I think." She huffed a laugh, forcing her thoughts away from Killian. "She said that the apartment had been empty for a while and seemed surprised to see someone living there." Wyatt grunted in confirmation and held his cup, not taking a drink as he watched her. Elora shifted slightly under his gaze, not sure why it was making her so uncomfortable. All she could think about was how her hair must look after her panic attack in the hall.

"The last occupants were a cute family, but they disappeared once the kids were out of school a few years ago. No one moved in after. The apartment was in rough shape but was fixed up about a month ago." He shrugged and Elora nodded, not sure what to do or say next. In the kitchen, Connie hummed as she put her groceries away, no doubt eavesdropping on the hesitant conversation happening.

"What brought you to the neighborhood?" She held the cup halfway to her lips, considering how to answer the question in a way that wasn't a lie. But she couldn't see any way around it unless she wanted to explain she had killed her father and ran away. His brow quirked as he waited patiently, sipping his tea.

"It was the best option we had at the time. We had to leave our last place fairly quickly, and this seemed like a good fit." Not a lie. Just not the whole truth.

"We? Oh, my aunt did mention someone else lives there. A roommate?" There was a smirk on his lips as he watched her, and she nodded.

"Damien. My roommate." He grinned as she repeated the word that felt wrong on her tongue. That felt like an understatement for whatever their dynamic was.

Chapter 9

Elora

"Have you explored the neighborhood at all? It's not the greatest area, but there are some good restaurants and coffee places. If you like coffee, that is." Wyatt's pointed question barely passed his lips when Connie settled in next to Elora again and took her probably lukewarm tea in hand.

"You forgot the vanilla for the cupcakes." She took a sip, her keen eyes passing between the two of them.

"Maybe you should take her to the corner store? You can fix your mistake and show her that one coffee shop at the same time." Elora started to shake her head in response as the fact that she was in hiding began screaming at her. She had to admit that Connie was a master at this game, and she wondered exactly how many times she had played it, had attempted this very thing. From the eye roll and wink Wyatt gave her, she was assuming many, many times. Why hadn't any of them stuck? Was there a glaring issue with him she hadn't seen yet that drove the women off? Considering her previous luck, she wouldn't be surprised if Wyatt ended up being a serial killer or something along those lines. Though Elora supposed as long as he didn't pretend to care about her or kill her only friend, he was better than most so far.

"No, Elora. You'll let him take you. Don't argue with an old woman who needs her vanilla extract." She stood and grabbed the tray from the table, returning it to the kitchen. The conversation was apparently over.

"Go on, Wyatt. You know I like to have a treat for the maintenance worker when he comes to fix things." He glanced at her, eyes practically begging Elora to agree. Damien never said she couldn't leave, and why was she even considering listening to him to begin with? Yes, technically, she was in hiding and wandering around the city probably wasn't the smartest idea for someone in her position. But wasn't he meant to be in hiding as well? He was on the run just as much as she was, but he was out there and meeting with whoever he wanted while she waited in the apartment with nothing but reality television to keep her company.

Mind instantly made up, Elora stood and grinned. "Let me get my boots." She glanced down at her sock-covered feet pointedly, a little embarrassed about the fact she was barefoot in Connie's apartment.

"And a coat. It's a little chilly." Connie's voice filtered in from the kitchen and Elora scrunched up her nose, wondering exactly how she would know that if she never wandered out. Wyatt must have seen the question on her face because he gave her a faux serious expression that sharpened his features.

"She knows the weather. It's a superpower that was annoying as a kid, but very useful now." Elora laughed, the first genuine laugh in days, if not longer. Without another word, she darted across the hallway and pulled on the boots Denise had left for her, lacing them up quickly before grabbing her coat. It was only once she reached the doorway that she hesitated. There were no keys for her to take, no way for her to lock the door. She would have thought Damien would give her one, would have left her one on the counter. But no, he hadn't left her anything at all. He probably never expected her to leave.

"Asshole." She muttered before slamming the door shut, no longer worried she couldn't lock it. It wasn't her problem. If he had left her a key, she would have done so.

Wyatt was waiting for her, resting slightly against the peeling paint in a dark canvas jacket she hadn't noticed earlier. With a dramatic flair, he offered her his arm, amusement gleaming in his golden eyes. Elora chuckled softly before placing her hand into the crook of his elbow and he gave it a cursory glance before giving her a mischievous smile.

"Shall we?"

"Of course. We can't have your aunt mad at you." He let out a soft laugh, a light sound that reminded her of Connie's. Nothing hidden underneath, no sharp edge. It was refreshing, and she wanted to wrap the sound around herself like a shield. He led her down the stairs, keeping pace with her while pointing out the paintings along the walls. Apparently, they were done by various residents over the years, as the owner of the building enjoyed having the personal touch of those who lived there.

"This one is my aunt's." He pointed to a large painting, roughly 24 by 36. It was a cottage—small, with a blue door and shuttered windows. In the background was a lake, the same one from the photos in her apartment. Wyatt cocked his head, as if trying to view it from a different angle.

"My aunt's cabin. I only went there a few times growing up. It was her special spot, especially once my uncle died about ten years ago. I kind of took over taking care of her a little while back once I got a bit more stable." She nodded even as she took in the details—the brushstrokes, the tiny flowers around the lake's edge and around the cabin. It felt peaceful, and she wondered what it would be like to leap inside of it, lock herself in the building and never come back out. It would be simpler there. She could hide, pretend that she was normal twenty-six-year-old woman. Not even a vampire, but a human without anything unique or special about them.

She felt him turn to head down the rest of the stairs and she followed suit, hesitating briefly as they stepped out into the sunlight. Her eyes squeezed shut and her spare hand reached up to try to block the light even as she heard him chuckle slightly.

"Don't get out much?" She knew that he was teasing, using the moment to try to draw another laugh from her. But she bristled slightly, cursing the rush of irritation that flooded her veins. A deep breath went in as subtly as she could manage before she exhaled, ignoring the feeling of his gaze on her. But she didn't look up at him, simply studied the street before her as her hand returned to her side, fingers clenched. The area was different in the light, busier but less terrifying despite the dozens of people marching up and down the sidewalk.

"I don't. And it isn't like those windows let in much sunlight." Elora tried to follow it up with a laugh, but it was hollow, and he pulled her hand back into the crook of his arm. She hadn't realized it had fallen back to her side.

"Very true. Filthy things." She glanced up at him to see concern, and something else marring his features.

"So, where's this store? I don't know this area." Elora almost added that she didn't know it at all, but that felt like it would invite too many questions she would either not be able to answer or would force her to lie.

Wyatt jerked his head to the left and started heading that way, weaving them through the people marching towards their own destinations. Her hand spasmed slightly at the overwhelming nature of everything around her. The scents and sounds surrounded them even as people bumped into her as they passed by one another. She hadn't been around this many people since before the hospital, and Elora felt her heart jump into her throat and her pulse race. Her grip on Wyatt's arm tightened, and she felt him rest his other hand on top of it, his thumb softly stroking her finger in an effort to calm her, comfort her. The kindness of the gesture was not lost on her, and she wanted to hold it close so it could be there whenever Damien decided to be an asshole.

But the smells—dark and coppery. Each person who hit her, who touched her, who simply came too close, radiated an intoxicating scent. It was vast, and she took a breath. She had been able to ignore the lure of Connie and Wyatt, their individual scents easy to block out as she chatted and drank her tea. But now there were too many, all intermingling and calling to every instinct that needed her to feed.

The gnawing increased, almost forcing her to clutch her stomach and fold over in pain.

Finally, a street later, Wyatt led her into a small store tucked into the corner of a building. Next door was a tiny restaurant, only available for takeout since there was no seating other than two tables and a couple of chairs. Sandwiches, maybe. The store itself had a few aisles with the most random assortment of items, everything from snacks to medication to sunglasses and hats. And vanilla extract—three or four variations in tiny bottles. She grinned as Wyatt placed one of the options, along with a chocolate bar, on the counter and paid.

"My aunt loves it, but never buys it for herself," he explained as he took the small bag and receipt from the cashier—a tiny man who was balding but seemed to be fighting it, considering the way his hair was combed over the top. The gesture and reason reminded her so much of Elizabeth, of the time she had saved up to buy even a single bar. There had always been an expression of pure bliss on her face when she took the first bite, eyes closing as she savored the taste.

Wyatt gave her a sheepish smile and led her further down the street, where a sign advertising coffee stood in the middle of the sidewalk. People swerved around it without really noticing, eyes either dead set ahead of them or on the ground, watching each step they took.

"Do you like coffee?" He positioned them in the line where four people were lined up ahead of them. The room was somewhat empty, mostly people casually drinking while reading or talking with whoever they were with. Coffee beans were painted in random spots along the cream walls, like they were thrown at them and had merged into the paint and plaster. It was inviting, made for people to come and spend time with one another.

A wave of pain hit her, and she exhaled a harsh breath. She and Elizabeth had spent so much of their time in shops like this one, giggling over lattes and hot chocolate. For a while, Elizabeth had a crush on one of the workers, giving him sly grins and watching him as he worked. Homework didn't get done whenever they went there. Her eyes had been glued to the guy wiping down counters and making drinks. It had been as adorable as it was annoying. And when he gave her a free coffee with a wink, Elora had thought her sister was going to faint, turn into a puddle right there in front of the counter.

"Are you okay?" Wyatt's voice yanked her from her memories.

"Just thinking about the last time that I was in a coffee shop." He nodded, as if understanding her meaning, and leaned in close. She could smell the blood rushing through his veins, could feel the way his pulse quickened a bit. Coppery with a hint of spice, like winter. She wondered briefly if he would taste that way as well, and her mouth watered slightly while the gnawing roared once more.

"I always get a caramel latte with an extra shot," Wyatt explained, and she thought back to what she normally had ordered—a simple hot chocolate with extra whipped cream at first. Then, it had been vanilla lattes, but she didn't want to think about the last time she had gotten one.

"I normally get lattes, but I've never gotten caramel." She admitted with a shrug before looking up at him, her mouth twisted into a conspiratorial grin. "I'll just get what you get." He only matched her smile as his eyes twinkled slightly.

"Excellent choice. I'm sure it won't disappoint." Once they reached the counter, he ordered their drinks — two caramel lattes, one with an extra shot and one without. She shoved her slightly shaky hands into her pockets to pull out the few dollars she had found in the duffle bag, along with the jacket. Whether Denise had left it there on purpose or if it was forgotten by the last person who used the coat didn't really matter.

He narrowed his brows and shook his head as he handed the woman across the counter a twenty. As she returned his change, she shot him a small smile meant to entice and brushed her hair back behind her shoulders before leaning forward just a bit. Elora almost rolled her eyes at the display. With a slight incline of his head, he grabbed Elora's hand and moved off to the side as the cashier huffed slightly.

They settled into a booth near the pickup counter to wait for Wyatt's name to be called out. He had given his for both drinks, sparing her from having hers announced to every person in the shop. Wyatt rested his forearms on the table and leaned forward slightly. She could feel him watching her as her gaze ran over the space, lingering on the crowd that seemed to have grown. Or she had grown more paranoid, seeing threats on each face and hearing them in each voice that carried and lingered.

"Tell me about yourself. My aunt seems to think we should be friends, so I should at least get to know you." Elora played with her sleeve, twisting and pulling the ends of the sweater until it looked too loose, the elastic breaking down.

"What do you want to know?" Her voice was low despite the cacophony of sounds that surrounded them, but he seemed to have no problem hearing her.

"Hobbies. What do you like to do?" She brightened, finally meeting his eyes and taking in the wide smile on his face. Elora studied him for a moment as she chewed on her cheek, pretending to think, pretending that there were options to choose from. He had a scar above his eye, dashing through the thin end of his arched eyebrow that she hadn't noticed before.

"It's boring but reading. I used to draw—sketching and simple things like that. Nothing fancy." His grin widened.

"I doubt that." Wyatt's eyes rested on her, forcing her to meet his gaze. Then he leaned back, hands still on the table in front of him. "What do—"

His name was called out, and he stood, winking as he moved to grab the two coffees in to-go cups. The waitress who desperately wanted his attention was there, fingers brushing his as she handed him one of the drinks. Elora coughed to cover up the laugh that wanted to barrel out of her. Wyatt turned, now with both coffees, and rolled his eyes as he sat back down, as if this happened every day. And it probably did. He was handsome enough and the ease and welcoming nature of his features could draw anyone in.

Hell, they had drawn her in, and she didn't exactly have the best history with men—human or otherwise. Viktor had lied and betrayed her. Killian, Jonas, and Darian had used her. And Damien. Well, Damien was complicated. Only Lukas had been straightforward and kind, had been a beacon when she was lost.

Another pain, sharp and persistent, settled into her chest and she rubbed at her sternum before standing to take the coffee from him.

"Let's get that vanilla back to my aunt." Elora nodded and muttered thanks before following him out.

The walk back was comfortable as easy conversation flowed between them and he asked about what books she liked to read. He had scoffed slightly when she said that she would read anything, claiming that she had to have a favorite or preference, at the very least.

"Fine! I enjoy fantasy. Far away worlds where good triumphs over evil. It's appealing."

"I figured you would say romance." She made a face at him, scrunching up her nose as they approached the apartment building.

"I don't mind romance. Most fantasy has some type of romantic sub-plot or storyline. But I have a hard time with pure romance type books." He opened the door, holding it so she could enter first.

"Why's that?"

"They are never realistic. Random miscommunication and love winning at the end of the day, no matter what. It just always seemed farfetched."

"More than fantasy?" He raised a brow, questioning her reasoning.

"Sometimes the idea of dragons and wizards and fairies is more believable than someone declaring their love no matter the cost, claiming that they love you unconditionally. Love like that is selfish, more about the person who loves and their desire to hold on to those feelings. And self-sacrificing is always more about being able to use it, to be able to say they gave up something. It's always self-serving at the end of the day." Elora shrugged as if her explanation was meaningless, as if it didn't reveal some broken fragment of her psyche. Wyatt stopped at the foot of the stairs, and she managed to climb two of them before she noticed he hadn't followed. She waited, glancing down at him as he watched her with something akin to devastation on his face.

"That's heart breaking, Elora. And I'm sorry you've been led to believe that love is conditional. That it's transactional."

She opened her mouth then shut it, gripping the banister as she struggled to find words, any words to say in response. But she had nothing. There was no way to refute it, no way to explain that he was wrong.

Instead, she resumed her climb and felt him follow, quickly falling in line beside her. They were both silent as they reached the top, both obviously stuck in their own thoughts. Had she been led to believe that? Killian's love as a father had been based on what she gave him, whether that was power, influence, or her blood. And Viktor's love had been a lie that he used to gain access to her.

No, hatred was more realistic than love. At least then there was truth in it. No hidden motives or vying for whatever they could get from the object of their affections. Damien's disdain for her was clear and obvious. The rationale for it made sense, at least in his head. But it meant that he didn't want anything from her, didn't demand anything in exchange for his hatred. It just existed as an inky thread that stretched between them.

Hatred was more palatable, more plausible.

They paused between the two doorways, both holding their coffees that had long since gone cold. She glanced behind him, wondering if Connie was watching through her peephole. Elora wouldn't have doubted it. She had worked to set this up, moving the pieces into place, and the old woman would want to see the finale.

"You know, she didn't actually put vanilla on the original list she gave me." Her attention darted to Wyatt, who had a small grin on his face. He looked pointedly at the bag hanging from his thick forearm and she laughed. Of course it hadn't been.

"Your aunt is crafty. Apparently, she thinks you need help in the romance department. Too bad she didn't see the cashier at the coffee shop." He gave her a shy smile as he ducked his head slightly, sneaking a look at the door behind him as if she was standing there. He sighed dramatically and ran a hand through his hair.

"She means well, of course. You're not the first neighbor she has tried to send with me to get something, suggesting a coffee shop or lunch to go with it." Elora placed her hand to her heart and gasped loudly, faking shock that she wasn't the only one.

He turned slightly, reaching for the handle.

"But you are the first one I have actually taken." She stared at him for a moment, once again rendered speechless. He just grinned, shyness creeping into his face, rendering him almost boyish. "Next time, we can get sandwiches or something."

Before she could respond, he entered the apartment, and she heard Connie's voice ringing out to ask how it all went. Not a single mention of the vanilla she so desperately needed. Elora smirked as she played through the afternoon, reminding herself of the feel of his arm under her hand, his thumb stroking her fingers when he sensed her unease at being outside.

She shook her head. Stupid. It wasn't even an option. She wasn't sure how long she would be here or if she could even handle being around him the longer she had to go without feeding. His scent was already intoxicating, lingering on her skin where he touched her. But it was nice to imagine a future where something could come from it.

Finally, she opened the still unlocked door and stepped through to find a very tense, very angry Damien waiting for her.

Chapter 10

Viktor

Thorne played the role of the grieving and distraught aunt better than he had thought possible. When he had put this plan forward, he hadn't expected it to work quite this well, hadn't expected her to embrace the role so completely. Her sobs and tears had the police officer shifting uncomfortably and reaching out to touch her arm repeatedly. He was incredibly young, which was probably why he was here on desk duty, recording various complaints or reports from the people who came in.

And throughout the entire performance, Viktor sat beside her as the son she brought with her for emotional support during this difficult time. Despite the conversations occurring all around them, he kept his focus on her. He knew there were people filtering in and out of the station, could hear the screams and cries of those who had been arrested. In his mind, they were being tossed in a holding cell or being led to an interrogation room that would be similar to the ones at the hospital for interviews. He couldn't see anyone smoking, but the scent hung heavy around them as it mingled with cologne and sweat.

This was the first time Viktor had ever been to a police station. After Jaime's death, he had wanted to turn himself in. He had even argued with the Resistance members that it was the right thing to do, that Jaime's family deserved some type of closure about what had happened to him. They had only shaken their heads and dragged him to Thorne, bloody and injured. In return, she had given him a purpose and a way to atone for his crimes.

Thorne grabbed a tissue from the desk and patted both eyes as she sniffled pathetically. He rubbed her shoulder, brows furrowed together as he watched her. If he didn't know better, Viktor would think she was truly worried about a missing niece.

"Please, sir, you must understand. I'm all she has left. Her parents passed in a car accident years ago and she lives with me." Her voice broke periodically as she explained. It was truly the perfect addition to her speech, even if Viktor wanted to roll his eyes at the entire display.

"I understand, ma'am. Explain what happened." He picked up a pen and pulled a notepad close, flipping through to find a blank page. Thorne wiped her eyes again before swallowing.

"She left to visit a friend from school. They were going to see a movie and then spend the night at her house. But she never came home the next morning. I called her friend who said she left after breakfast but didn't know where she was." A sob and another tear rolled down her cheek. The officer nodded once more, frantically writing down snippets of what she had said.

"The friend's name?"

"Bethany, I believe. Bethany Wood." Viktor nodded beside her, touching her arm in what he hoped looked like a comforting gesture. He wasn't sure how to play this role convincingly, despite how similar it was to how he behaved with Elora. The difference was that this was a true performance. With Elora, it had stopped being fake fairly quickly. Luckily, the officer didn't seem to notice that he even existed. Thorne rattled off an address from the housing area the Resistance controlled since the majority of the homes belonged to various members. It was also the location of where all incoming calls would go, any tips where Elora may be hiding.

"What happens now?" she asked in a broken voice that left Viktor with a swirl of guilt and unease in his stomach. This poor officer had bought the act completely and the expression on his face said as much.

"Well, we start by putting out emergency announcements on all the local channels, sending out alerts to anyone with a phone. It will include her picture and where she was last seen, along with the number you gave us for contacting you."

Thorne nodded her head and brought the tissue to her eyes despite the fact they had been dry for a while.

"I want to warn you, ma'am, that in cases like this there are a lot of fake leads reported. People do it for some sick sense of amusement. We just want you to know in advance." The officer rested his hand on hers and offered her another tissue, a strained smile plastered across his face.

"I understand. Thank you." Her voice was low, soft as she looked up at the officer.

"Is there anything else you need, ma'am?" Thorne stood, and Viktor followed suit while she gripped his arm as if she needed his support in this fragile moment. A genius move based on the sympathy in the kid's eyes.

"No. Thank you for everything." Thorne leaned against Viktor as they exited the station and made their way to the waiting car. She slid into the back seat with him beside her. Only once the door had closed did Viktor let out the breath he had been holding during the whole performance.

"Genius acting, Thorne. I think you might have missed your calling." She shot him a sarcastic grin before her face hardened.

"Take me to the suburb house. I want to be there when the announcement goes out." The driver nodded and started to pull away.

"Can you drop me off at the house? I want to see Elizabeth, see if there is anything new." Thorne sighed and nodded to the driver, who turned on his signal to make a right down a side street. Now that the announcement and missing person report was happening, Viktor needed to make sure Elizabeth was ready to play her part in this.

* * *

They had her in the basement, which had been renovated slightly to include a makeshift lab and a few cells. Nothing as nice as Killian had, but they had limited funds and weren't trying to keep their food comfortable. Elizabeth was resting on the small cot in the corner of the tiny cell that was maybe the size of a walk-in closet. There was a toilet behind a privacy screen and a small sink, but that was all. Even with her small frame, she was hanging off the edge of the bed, feet almost touching the floor.

She glanced up as Viktor approached before closing her eyes once more, not saying a word. He studied her as he tried to decide how to begin the conversation that needed to happen.

"Just ask me about her. It'll be less painful for both of us." Her voice was low, but girlish. Viktor recalled Elora describing her during the few times that she discussed her sister, explaining that her voice was like spring—innocent and fresh, like new flowers. Now, it was wholly at odds with what she was.

"To be honest, I'm not sure what to ask." Elizabeth sat up at his admission and turned so she could recline against the wall.

"Interesting. Can I ask why I'm locked up here if I'm supposed to be helping? Partners don't usually lock each other up."

Viktor huffed a laugh and crossed his arms over his chest. "They do if one of them has a habit of feeding from the other. We can't risk a house full of humans." She grinned, revealing her sharp canines, all predator beneath her girlish veneer.

"They keep taking my blood. Why?"

"How much do you know about Elora? About what kind of vampire she is?" She shook her head at his questions, and he felt his hope die just a little.

"No one was very forthcoming concerning her. And most of my information about vampires comes from movies."

"She wasn't turned, despite the scars." Viktor watched as Elizabeth's brow rose in response. It was unheard of to have a vampire who wasn't turned by another. The Resistance had researched it, going back over a century in the documents they had managed to collect.

"She was born a vampire, impossible as that sounds. Her father had her genetics altered, using artificial insemination to impregnate his wife."

Elizabeth tried to hide the surprise on her face, and he inclined his head as further confirmation.

"So, she's special. What a surprise." Her sarcastic tone was something he hadn't expected, and he took a step forward.

"Such hatred for your sister. I thought you were grateful for being turned?" She giggled as if he had told a fantastic joke.

"Not hatred. Not at all. But I knew she was something different when she showed up on our doorstep, dropped off by someone who somehow convinced my parents to take her in. As far as I know, we had never even seen her before, never seen the person who was with her either. At least I hadn't."

Viktor stayed quiet, taking in her explanation as he wondered if perhaps whoever had taken her used compulsion on Elizabeth's family, convincing them to take her in without question. Elora had never talked about the night she ended up there, only said she didn't remember, and Viktor had been inclined to believe her. He had seen the frustration and utter devastation when she couldn't answer such a simple question.

Killian had done so much damage, breaking her over and over until there was nothing left but tiny pieces that needed to be picked up and glued back together. He wasn't sure it was fully possible. But at least she had gotten to end him. It had been disturbing and for the first time in their time together, he had feared her at that moment. During all the years in the hospital and knowing the whole time what she was, he had never been scared of her. Not even after the medication was gone from her system. But the rage and grief, the power beneath each fall of the knife, had been enough to render him speechless, make him step back and put space between them despite needing to gain control of her.

Killian had deserved it. Every stab, every rip of his flesh. And now Viktor knew that a similar fate could be waiting for him if Elora ever managed to get her hands on him.

"And if you don't know anything about her, you don't know anything about me. What type of vampire I am if I was turned by such a special specimen?" Elizabeth chewed on the ends of her hair, considering her own question. Viktor nodded and let her continue her musing about what was essentially the nature of her own existence.

"Did you know I didn't even have to drink from her to turn? Her bite did all the work. I always thought it was more complicated than that. That's how the movies and books always made it seem." Elizabeth was right, from what he understood. Usually, it was a process of draining the human before they drank from the vampire, an exchange in a way. That was how Jaime had described it the night when Viktor's reality started to shift. Jaime explained the extra shifts, the bruises and the gauze that was always wrapped around his wrists. He had truly believed Viktor would listen to the explanation about how humans turned and agree to the process. Instead, they had fought viciously with screams and curses and tears before Viktor left in a flurry of slammed doors and shouts.

But if Elora's bite didn't require that, then Thorne needed to be told. It could be a problem. Would the same be true for a bite from Elizabeth? And if they couldn't control their hunger, would the city see an influx of new vampires, children of whatever this altered version was?

"I can see your wheels turning. Considering how quickly my sister and I could overrun the city? Maybe you should do away with us now. Remove that potential problem from the equation before it can become one." Viktor grunted, not sure how to respond.

"Do you want to know what else I've noticed?" She glanced at him, a small smile on her lips. He raised his brow, encouraging her to continue. "I need to feed more often. I heard that vampires feed every couple of days. Some feed every day, but they don't need to. Except for me. Except for Elora, I bet."

Elizabeth lay back down on her bed with eyes locked on the ceiling. He couldn't read her expression as she whispered softly. "You have no idea what Killian created. Or what Elora created that night."

She waved her hand in dismissal and rolled over to face the wall, leaving Viktor to retreat. Because the truth was that Elizabeth was right. Killian had no idea what he was doing when he played with Elora's genetics, altering them in ways they still didn't understand. Denise had tried, had studied her for years and came no closer to a real answer. All she had managed to do was care for her, which she then nurtured with every act of resistance, every refusal to allow her release.

After Elora had been there for about a year, the Resistance had demanded her release into their hands. Their plan, ironically enough, was very similar to the plan Damien had successfully executed—release her to a halfway house or something along those lines and then take her from there. Denise had fought ve-hemently against it, arguing for days that she needed more time with Elora, that she wasn't ready to be told the truth and take up her role in their schemes.

"She will break. And any hope we have of using her and bringing her to our cause will disappear."

The council, headed by Thorne, had relented, but not with-out conditions. His presence in the hospital being one of them. As much as he was there to watch Elora, gauge her progress and mental stability, Viktor was also there to watch Denise and re-port on her and the relationship between the two of them. And he had in the beginning. He had diligently paid attention to every interaction, the aftermath of every therapy session, and went to Thorne. But once Elora had started to confide in him, started to view him as more than another nurse, his reports be-came less detailed.

Thorne had noticed but said nothing. Just kept an eye on him, a smirk on her face each time he showed up and shared nothing of real value.

A buzz in his pocket, followed by a siren-like sound, brought him from his memories. With a grunt, he pulled the phone from the back pocket of his jeans and unlocked it, already know-ing what he was going to see. The alert. There on his phone was her picture. Her face was blank yet beautiful as she stared at someone with her hair loose around her shoulders and lips pressed into a line. Viktor recognized the area behind her from the Tower. Whoever took this either got the picture inside the elevator or as she was about to step out. And underneath was the headline:

Missing: If seen, call the number below.

Chapter 11

Damien

The apartment had been empty when he returned from his meeting with Silas. He had entered, already done with everything and everyone after Silas's offer, and had stopped dead in his tracks. It had been quiet. No sounds of ridiculous television shows, no obnoxious humming that he wasn't even sure she knew she did when she thought too much. He had checked each room, each closet. Checked the shower despite the lack of running water.

Nothing. She was gone.

A rage like nothing he had ever known struck him and he went into the same mindset he had when he originally found her, when he had been hunting for her on Killian's orders. He considered the situation as he leaned over the counter, arms resting on the cool faux marble. Strategize. Think it through before acting. She couldn't go far. She didn't know the city, didn't even know the area. Maybe she had left to find something, a household supply he and Lukas had missed or overlooked when they had set up the apartment. Damien had bought everything he thought she may need—brushes and combs since he didn't know her preference, toothbrushes, and everything else that came with it. Shampoo and conditioner, even buying the more expensive type he had seen in her bathroom at the Tower. Denise had taken care of everything else. Lukas had brought in extra items, like the coffee machine. Yet another thing Damien hadn't known about her.

And then he heard the old woman's voice in the hallway, talking to who he imagined was another neighbor.

"I sent them off to buy vanilla. I have some in my cabinet, but it seemed as good an excuse as any." The other person laughed—a woman by the sound of it. "This was after he brought her into my apartment, of course. I'm not sure what happened, but she looked so pale. And she was shaking! It was probably that brute living in there with her." Damien curled his hands into fists as he listened to each word. The famous nephew had made an appearance.

And Damien was the brute, obviously.

But what had happened? What had caused her to end up in this woman's apartment? And where the hell was she now?

"Wyatt took her with him to buy the vanilla," another chuckle from both women, "and then to get coffee. He seems very taken with her. Attentive. You know how long I've been using this plan, and it's never worked!"

"Well, it has now!" Both women descended into a cackle that grated on his ears, made him want to scream and force his hands over them like he had as a child when his father came looking for money or when his mother wept after being left empty handed. Damien wished he could say that he was reacting like this because Elora was meant to be hiding, because people were looking for her, that she was a target.

But it wasn't. It was the picture in his head of some human walking with her down the street, making her laugh, buying her coffee, and earning a smile from her that wasn't coated in sarcasm and vitriol. Like his were. Not that he didn't earn it, didn't continue to earn it.

He perched himself on one of the stools and waited, listened as the women continued talking about bread and a new muffin recipe she wanted to try. He figured that Elora would be given a batch of those as well, even if she couldn't eat them. But Elora would take them either way, smile and thank the woman before putting them somewhere out of sight. She would never deny the woman or reject her gift. Despite everything, that streak of kindness was just as fierce as her fire. Finally, the women said goodbye to one another and silence ensued, punctuated by horns sounding outside and faint steps in the hallway that never got closer.

Until they did.

And he could hear her outside as she talked with him.

Damien listened to her laughter, free and unhindered by anything that had happened. He had only heard her laugh like that a few times, and never by anything he did or said. There would be a smug smile on the nephew's face, or what Damien imagined was his face, as he told her about the vanilla extract not being on the list. How this was the first time he had taken his aunt's bait. Whether it was true or not, his blood boiled. The calm that had eased over him in the time since he discovered she was gone started to break as his pulse began to race.

And then he had invited her out again, and she hadn't said no. She hadn't said anything at all. Damien wanted to vomit, felt the bile in his throat even as the door opened, and she took in the sight of him waiting for her. Her eyes widened a bit before a cool mask of indifference settled across her features. Her shield was now firmly in place as she entered, closing the door and locking it before sitting on a chair to remove her boots. Carefully, slowly, she unlaced them, fingers working on the knots before she loosened the laces and pulled them off.

Silence. Complete silence.

"What part of in hiding do you not understand?" Damien's voice was low, and she flinched slightly, barely enough to notice unless one had spent a lot of time watching her, studying her.

And he had. For weeks he had noted each facial expression, each unconscious tick or reaction. He had filed away how she always tucked her legs underneath her as if it would help her hide. Had noticed how she pulled obsessively at her collar and sleeves, ensuring that everything was hidden. How little lines appeared between her brows when violence was brewing and how fiercely radiant she became when she was about to hurt someone. It had started as reconnaissance for Killian and then intel for his own protection, since he was usually the target of her rage. Then, it became an obsession. He had wanted to identify each piece of her to gain some insight into who she was.

"You go out. Aren't you hiding as well? Or is it just me who was there when I murdered Killian?" Fair points, but there was no way in hell he was going to give her that.

"And what about not seeing anyone? Not seeing the nephew? We discussed this. We agreed." Finally, anger, raw and unfiltered, flashed across her face as she stood. That fierce look she had before she stabbed him with a fork was there, and a part of him wanted to make sure nothing was in her hands.

Then she smiled. Cruel and cold as she took a step towards him. His body unintentionally tensed as he watched each move. Every step she took was calculated as her eyes absorbed every tiny flinch or twitch. It was like being prey that a much bigger predator was sizing up. And that scent intermingling with hers. He knew hers like he knew himself, the perfect blend of lavender and jasmine. But now there was something like spice—cloves or cinnamon. It had to be the nephew.

"You said he couldn't come into the apartment. And he didn't. I went with him."

Damien's lips hardened into a straight line, and he felt his jaw clench slightly. For his scent to be on her like this, he had to have touched her. And not just once, but multiple times. Did he embrace her? Hold her hand? Had she let him pull her close to him?

She pushed her hair away from her face while the rest hung loose down her back and smirked, believing she made her point. And she had, only not in the way she thought.

"Find your fun where you can, I guess. I'm just saying you have a horrible track record." Elora stepped back, the pain clearly displayed on her face, and he instantly wished to take back his words. He knew they had been vicious and that they would hurt. Yet he had said them anyway, wanting her to feel the same betrayal that he did. She nodded, slowly and steadily, as she ran her tongue over her lips.

"That makes two of us. But at least I was never someone's lapdog, blindly licking his boots."

"No, you took whatever scraps Viktor gave you, no matter what he wanted in return or that he was using you." She stepped back again, arms crossed over her chest, fingers playing with her sleeves in a motion that he knew so well. He knew that there had to be something rotten inside him with the way he felt the need to push her away. Some part of him wanted to make sure she hated him even as another part wanted desperately to apologize and beg for the forgiveness he didn't deserve.

"I didn't know!" Elora's words were shrill, even as she threw her shoulders back and lifted her face in defiance. He widened his stance, waiting for the hits to come as her face contorted into a mixture of pain and fury, of betrayal and hurt. And it was his doing. He had hit a spot he knew would do damage, and he wanted to take it back. But they were both too far gone, too encased in rage to stop the argument that was coming.

"Of course you didn't," he sneered at her. "You were so starved for affection you would have overlooked any glaring red flag that popped up. Overlooked anything as long as he gave you that stupid smile and touched your hand." She stepped forward, a snarl on her lips and Damien knew that what was coming was going to decimate them both, that she was willing to destroy herself just to hurt him. He had seen it that night in Killian's office when she never intended to survive because to her it didn't matter as long as he didn't live past that moment.

"And you, Damien, were so desperate for any praise from your master, so desperate to be told 'good boy' that you were willing to overlook the physical proof of what was done, willing to take me back to him for him to use and give out as a gift. Don't talk to me about ignoring the obvious. At least no one but me was hurt by my ignoring Viktor's red flags."

Damien opened his mouth to respond, but nothing came out. Because she was right, every word out of her mouth was a simple statement of truth. He had been willing to overlook the obvious, willing to latch onto the belief that she was a spoiled runaway who had gotten stuck in a hospital.

"You're right, except for one thing, Elora. It cost us both someone who sacrificed himself for you, who died because you trusted Viktor."

He watched her shoulders slump as the fight left her, how she retracted into herself like he had seen her do so many times under Killian's watchful eyes. Damien's hand itched by his side to grab her, force her to stand up straight, to insult him, hit him, something. Could he possibly explain that he couldn't seem to control himself when it came to her, that he was drowning in grief and the loss of not only Lukas, but the first home he had known? He wanted to explain that he needed to keep her at arm's length, that she needed time to heal just as much as he did. But that didn't excuse his words, or how easily they hit.

Instead, he took a deep breath and moved on, trying to ignore how the light that had been so radiant when she opened the door had disappeared, leaving only emptiness behind.

"It doesn't matter. Your uncle has requested your presence, has asked for you to come live with him so he can take care of you." She raised a brow before she settled on the couch and folded her legs underneath her. An attempt to make herself smaller, to contain whatever she didn't want to come out. And this time he had been the one to cause her desire to disappear, and that was fucking agony.

"Good. When do I leave?" He stared at her. Damien had expected questions or even demands. Not simple acceptance.

"I told your uncle I would talk to you, lay out his offer, and give you a chance to decide on your own."

"Kind of you." She murmured, staring at her fingers. "And what was his offer?"

"Protection, for the most part. From the Resistance and Darian and others like him. He also wants to take you in and treat you as his niece. He wants to get you help to deal with everything that happened."

"And does he know what happened?" Her voice was sharp, and he flinched. She wasn't going to like the answer, and he steadied himself, prepared for what would come.

"From what I gathered, yes. He knew what was happening, what Killian was doing, and what he did to create you." Her eyes darkened as they narrowed, focused on him where he stood in the middle of the room.

"Why didn't he do anything? Take me out of there?" Damien sighed and shoved his hand through his dark hair.

"I don't know. He offered to answer any questions you have. For what it's worth, I think he's mostly sincere. Probably motivated by guilt and loyalty."

"Two things you know a lot about." Damien let the barb slide, refused to rise to her bait. He had already said enough that he regretted.

"I would—" she hesitated, chewing on her finger. "I have requests." He cocked a brow, a grin playing on his lips. Of course she did.

"I expect nothing less. Am I to take your demands to him or do you want to speak to him yourself?" She considered his question, that low humming noise making an appearance. A lullaby, probably.

"I—" Damien's phone went off, the siren-like sound that indicated an alert. He rolled his eyes as he ignored it while Elora watched him, eyes pointedly staring at his pocket.

"Well?" He huffed a breath and pulled it out, unlocking it to see what the alert was about. More than likely, it was a missing child or something like that. A common enough occurrence that he usually ignored them. But Elora apparently wouldn't continue the conversation without checking it.

The phone lit up, and he stared at the alert, his blood instantly freezing in his veins. Damien took a sharp breath and started pacing across the living room, staring at the phone screen as if it would change if he just watched it long enough.

"Fuck!" His voice reverberated off the walls, sounding louder than he thought it had been. Damien could have sworn he whispered, but from the look on her face when he glanced up, he knew he had yelled.

"We have a problem."

Chapter 12

Elora

It was her face staring up from Damien's phone. She thought it was from one of the days she was taken to see Viktor. That was the only time she was in the elevator. Or maybe one of her visits to Killian. Dark circles hung under her eyes in the photo, and she noted the haunted expression—broken and empty. Elora hadn't realized exactly how defeated she had appeared while there.

She also hadn't noticed anyone taking a picture.

"What does this mean?" The question was born more out of panic than confusion. She knew what it meant. There had been alerts like this before she went into the hospital—notifications to find people who went missing. And technically, she was missing and had been since she never showed up at the transition house. And there was only one person who would have used that to find her.

"It means someone really wants to find you. It's just a question of who." She glanced at him, finally looking up from the screen and the phone number listed at the bottom.

"What now?" Damien sighed at the question and rubbed his jaw, shoving the phone back in his pocket.

"I'm not sure. I'll have someone track the number, see if we can find out who put out the missing person's report. Then we would at least know who to look out for." She nodded as she sat back down. Damien had made her come to him to see the alert and the photo that accompanied it. Now, she felt too exhausted to stand. It was never ending — running and hiding before running again.

Elora knew that it was the Resistance, and her money was on this being Viktor's idea. She could imagine him presenting the idea, using the knowledge he gained as her friend and nurse to sell it to whoever was in charge. Other than those involved in her kidnapping, no one had really known that she was meant to be at the transition home.

A fierce wave rushed through her and her stomach tightened, partially from her realization concerning her previous friend and partly from hunger. Elora's focus shifted to Damien, who didn't seem to be struggling like she was. There was no sign of hunger or desperation, no sign of discomfort or waves of agony. Was he feeding somewhere else? Or was she truly that weak? She grimaced, trying to ignore the gnawing hunger as she moved her focus to her hands, picking at the skin around her nails. The cuticles on most of her fingers were destroyed and tiny beads of blood appeared. Being angry and arguing with Damien had been a distraction, but now the steady emptiness and hunger was back with a vengeance.

"Don't bother," she muttered before glancing up at him. "It was Viktor. He's the only one who would think to report me missing." Damien nodded with each word, even as his own focus narrowed in on her hands. Instantly, she wrapped her sleeve around the bleeding fingers, praying that the scent hadn't reached him.

"I think it's best to go to Silas's as soon as possible. We don't have time to negotiate. Enough people saw you today while you were out that we can't risk staying here." She stiffened, then relaxed slightly, reaching for the remote and turning on one of the shows she knew he hated. Elora listened to him sigh before he stood in front of her, blocking the screen.

"Did you hear me?"

"Of course I did."

"And?" She gave him the briefest of looks as she adjusted her expression to one of confusion.

"And what?"

"What do you think?" She huffed a laugh at his question, and his jaw ticked slightly.

"I think I don't have much of a choice. At least you get what you want."

"Which is?" She met his eyes, her lips curling slightly. He knew what her response would be, but he asked anyway. He wanted her to say it so he could either deny it or make a cruel comment about having been waiting for this opportunity. It would annoy him more to not say a word, to not give him any-thing. With a disappointed shake of her head, she turned off the show and stood. She gave him a slight smirk as she brushed past him and made her way down the hallway, pausing only for a mo-ment to tell him one last thing.

"Do what you need to do. Agree to what you need to agree to." She listened to him call her name, demand she stop and talk to him about it. But she walked into the bathroom, locked the door, and took the hottest shower she could manage.

* * *

Sleep didn't come easily that night. She had tossed and turned until finally falling into something akin to sleep. Every time she fell asleep, Elora was plagued with dreams of Damien dragging her back to Killian, of Wyatt rubbing circles into her wrist with his thumb, whispering that it would be okay. Damien never came, even though she knew she cried out a few times, and it bothered her more than it should.

Maybe Damien was right. Maybe she did latch onto anyone who gave her the tiniest shred of kindness. Maybe that was what she was doing with Wyatt, what she did each time Damien was kind to her for a single moment. But was there something wrong with wanting to be loved? For someone to look at her like she was something precious? For the world to melt away as she found solace in their arms? After a minute, she scoffed. Pathetic. Absolutely pathetic.

She pulled a long-sleeved shirt over her head with a pair of sweats. After a quick run of the comb through her hair, she left the room and entered the kitchen. Damien leaned against the counter, a cup in his hands. Blood. They would get to feed, and her muscles constricted as she took in the scent that filled the room. Instantly, her mouth watered, and she swallowed before a moan almost escaped her lips. Her steps were easy and even as she approached the counter despite every instinct commanding her to run and snatch every drop from Damien's hand. She didn't need him to know exactly how much she was struggling. He nodded to her before taking a sip, leaving a tinge of red along his lips.

Without a word, she poured her ration into the cup and savored it, holding the blood on her tongue for a long moment before swallowing. A part of her mind screamed at her to consume, to take and take until she was satiated. Her hands trembled as she brought the cup to her mouth and took another small drink, forcing herself to drink it slowly. Damien simply watched, eyes dark and face blank.

His head jerked towards the end of the counter where a stack of medical texts sat waiting. She stared at them, confused about why Damien would have them, let alone bring them to her attention.

"Denise's journals. Your patient notes. Everything from every session you had based on what I saw."

"You read them?" He winced. The movement was so subtle she almost missed it.

"Some. Only a few entries while I was gathering them for him." Elora quietly thanked him for not saying Killian's name, for leaving it unspoken between them. The name still elicited a reaction from her, a tightening of her breathing, her nails digging into her skin. A reminder. His name was a reminder.

"And how were they? Fascinating? Engaging? Was I a good story?" He glanced away and stepped towards the door.

"I'm going to see your uncle this morning to relay your message. I'm sure he won't be surprised by your response, given the newest development." She nodded as she eyed the stack of journals. Three of them, each one equally thick. How should she approach reading them? Would she go cover to cover or would she look for entries that were the most telling, the ones from sessions she recalled most vividly? What had Denise written after the session where Elora attacked her? What had she written about Elora's attempt on her own life?

"Please don't leave today. The missing person alert will have gone out to everyone with a cellphone. And if it was sent out like that, it was probably on the news as well." He ran a hand along the back of his neck. She barely heard him, so lost in her own thoughts that she only nodded and agreed to his request.

His phone made a noise—another alert. He simply glanced at this one and shoved the phone back into his pocket. Not about her, then. At least she didn't think so.

"I'll be gone a while." She quirked a brow, considering making a comment that his absence sounded perfect to her, that he could stay out as long as he liked. But she drowned the words with the rest of her meager ration before setting the cup in the sink and grabbing a journal. There was a number one on the inside cover followed by a time stamp—the years that this journal covered. It seemed to cover the sessions from her first year or so.

She wandered over to the couch and nestled into the corner, using the armrest to prop her arm and the book up more comfortably.

"Did you hear me?" His voice broke through, and she gave him a fleeting look. He sighed and looked towards the ceiling, as if begging for strength. "Look, just please stay here. Promise me?"

She bent her head in acknowledgement, refusing to let the words leave her lips. After all, she didn't owe him her voice or words. If it wasn't for him and Killian, Elora would be working and making friends. She would still be taking her medication that kept the hunger suppressed. In this alternate reality, Elora would be, or at least could be, happy. Instead, she was there with a few new scars on her body, hiding away from everyone who wanted to use her for her blood. Maybe they could drain it, and Damien could sell it to the highest bidder before living out his life of luxury.

The idea had merit.

She was tired, so very tired, and the thought of it all being over, of the guilt and shame disappearing, was more tempting than it should have been. Denise would have been concerned, horrified even. She would have ordered her medication increased and called for her to spend time in the green room until they were sure she wasn't a threat to herself. But Elora didn't have that now. There was no padded room to protect her from her darkest thoughts, from the urge to remove herself as a player in whatever this game was.

The door opened and shut with an audible click as she opened the first journal, flipping through the pages. Denise's cursive handwriting was loopy, yet elegant even in the areas that were smeared and difficult to read. It was strange to read about herself as if the journal was describing someone else, a patient she had never met. But one thread became clear, something she now knew—Denise had known she was telling the truth, had used Elora's trauma against her, encouraged her to think that vampires were a product of her guilt.

It should have made her angry to find this, to read each time Denise claimed it was all for her own good so Elora wouldn't be taken back to her Maker, to Killian. The designation of Maker felt so much more appropriate that Elora latched onto it, branded it across every memory she had of him. The title of 'Father' implied protection, love, and support. Killian had given her none of that, had denied her it at every moment. 'Maker' denoted a detachment, a coldness that spoke to the hierarchical relationship between them. He had been in control, had owned her.

She read through the entries surrounding the first denial of her release and absorbed Denise's version of what happened and why.

Elora attacked me during our session with a paperweight. I knew she was still angry about her release being denied, but I hadn't expected it. It wasn't like with the resident. She did not try to feed—only to harm, to inflict pain. Her rage is immense and hidden. It comes out and is aimed at either those around her or herself. I'm concerned but not upset about the attempt. I should have seen it coming. She was removed before any damage was done to my person, but it took multiple nurses and staff to escort her to the green room. Her strength is growing. I'm not sure Killian accounted for the changes that could come with his alteration. He was focused on creating a new vampire, one who could become a feeding source outside of humans. A capitalistic approach to gaining power.

She will need to be more closely monitored. Someone is being sent in to watch her. I know he will be reporting on her behavior and more than likely mine, but if it keeps her safe, then I will tolerate it and play their game.

Elora took a deep breath and rested her head against the back of the couch. Denise had known that Viktor had been sent to spy on her for the Resistance. But that only begged the question that if the group knew where she was, why hadn't they taken her earlier? Why leave her to be found and kidnapped by Killian, ripped out from underneath their noses? Quickly, Elora skimmed through the entries, searching for any other references to Denise's role in the denial of her release. But there was nothing. Not even the subtlest hint.

With a grunt of frustration, she tossed the journal aside before grabbing another one, which contained mostly basic entries. Thoughts on her breakdown and how it had been handled badly. Information about Viktor reporting back, her growing unease with working with the Resistance, that she no longer agreed with their goals. No longer agreed with what they wanted from Elora. She let out a huff as she flipped through more pages. Not once did she mention what they wanted from her, what their goal or plan was. Another gap. Another secret.

Finally, another entry towards the end of the journal:

Their goal is no longer my goal, and it has caused friction between myself and the Resistance leader. To use Elora would be to kill her, to harvest everything her body contains and leave nothing but a corpse behind. I cannot condone or support that. Not now.

Elora turned another page and then one more, even as her heart raced at Denise's admission. To use her meant she would have to die, a literal sacrifice for the survival of humans. She shook her head as she continued. That told her nothing beyond what her fate would end up being. A part of her wanted to know if Viktor was aware of this fact, if he had been growing close to her to make handing her over easier.

She rubbed her palms over her face and grabbed the last journal, searching for anything interesting, anything that could tell her something important. As Elora started rifling through the pages, she jumped at the knock on the front door, soft and hesitant. She stood slowly, leaving the journal on the arm of the couch, and made her way to the door. Another knock, this time a little louder. A curse fell from her mouth as Elora's heart raced a bit faster, beating against her ribs as she approached. Through the peephole, she could see Connie as her head turned from side to side, looking down both sides of the hallway. Anxiety filled her entire being as she creaked the door open, just enough to stand in the frame.

Connie let out a soft laugh as she ran her eyes over Elora, searching for something.

"I'm so glad to see you're okay." Elora furrowed her brows, trying to figure out what she was talking about.

"Of course, I am." Connie shook her head before she grabbed Elora's hand and pulled her towards her own apartment. For only a moment, her feet refused to budge, locking her in place as she debated leaving. But this didn't feel like breaking her deal with Damien. She wasn't going outside, merely across the hall. There was no one between the two apartments who could spot her, could report her location to the number listed on the missing person alert.

The missing person alert!

Elora wanted to laugh at herself for not understanding Connie's anxiety instantly, for not recognizing her words for what they were. She must have seen the message and thought the absolute worst. With a sigh, Elora let go of the door frame and shut it behind her, allowing Connie to drag her into her apartment to push her down onto the couch. Already the teapot was there, prepared for whatever this conversation was going to be.

"I had fun with Wyatt yesterday." Connie grinned at her words even as she flitted around the apartment, a bundle of nervous energy, while she gathered a small bowl of sugar cubes and a plate of cookies.

"I told you he was handsome. And such a charmer." Elora laughed softly as Connie poured the tea into the two cups, immediately adding sugar to her own. "It's always too bitter for me."

Elora took a small sip, grimacing at the taste and added her own before trying again. They sat in silence, both drinking their tea. The tension between them as they waited for the conversation to start was a third person, snuggled between them on the couch.

"Dear, you know if something is wrong, you can tell me. I can take care of you. Wyatt could help you." Connie sat her teacup down before gathering Elora's free hand in hers. Her face contorted and her wrinkles became more pronounced as anxiety and fear stretched across her features. Elora gave her a lopsided smile and set her own cup down, resting her hand on top to nestle Connie's in the middle.

"I'm perfectly fine, Connie. Please, I promise." She scoffed before jumping to her feet and grabbing a phone off her dining room table, muttering about the stupidity of technology and how Wyatt had forced her to get it as she wandered back over. Even as she sat back down, Connie thrust the phone at Elora to reveal the missing person alert. Her haunted face stared back at her, along with the phone number at the bottom.

"Then explain this. Please, I can help you. All we need to do is call—"

"No!" Elora's words were harsh, and she forced herself to breathe, to soften her tone before she continued. "Connie, please. The people who put out this aren't looking for me to help or protect me."

Connie shook her head and brought her hand to Elora's cheek. It was warm and rough against her skin, and she leaned into it, closing her eyes and pretending that everything was normal, that everything was okay.

"Connie, listen to me." Her wrinkled eyes met Elora's as she held her gaze. Desperation fueled every movement and word. She needed the woman to believe her, needed her to understand that Damien was not the danger she thought he was. At least not to Elora.

"Do not call that number. I'm not missing and the people looking for me want to hurt me. Just delete the message. Please, Connie." She sensed the change before she realized what had happened. Saw the way Connie's eyes glazed over and went slack and the way her face relaxed as a smile curled over her lips. There was a moment of pure silence as she waited for Elora to say more before she shivered slightly and laughed.

"Goodness, it's a little cold in here. Let me grab a sweater. Would you like more tea?" Elora stared at her, not sure exactly what had happened. But all that mattered was Connie was no longer talking about calling the number, was no longer discussing the alert in general.

Elora smiled and shook her head. "No thank you, Connie. I need to go back." She only gave Elora a sad look, promising to let Wyatt know she had fun with him before she closed the door.

Chapter 13

Damien

The number of missing person fliers with Elora's face on them forced his muscles to tense each time he saw one. Corner shops, markets, and streetlight poles were all covered with her face. He watched as people stopped to look them over before moving along. Damien could only be grateful that no one seemed to pull out their phones to dial the number. He wasn't sure how many people had seen her when she was out with that human or if they had gotten a good enough look at her to even recognize her. Most people were so wrapped in their own reality that they never saw the people around them. Damien hoped that would be the case this time.

The gates to the Corvin manor opened instantly as he pulled up, closing behind him as he followed the driveway up to the front door. The grounds, from what he could see, were massive, with acres upon acres of trees and well-manicured gardens. It was annoyingly beautiful and picturesque. And the exact type of place Elora deserved. He could picture her here, wandering the grounds with that small smile she wore when she was content, humming that song he had come to know. The manor itself was huge, and he wasn't sure how many rooms there were. It was all red brick and iron, with ivy creeping along the walls and flower beds along the windows. Damien parked off to the side after spotting Silas waiting on the patio, hands in his pocket as his eyes blazed from rage.

As he turned off the car, Damien took a breath and got out, locking it before shoving the keys in his pocket.

"What is this? Who put this out?" He stared at Silas, watched the way his mouth formed each word, the feverish nature of his eyes. The vampire was terrified. At first, Damien had thought maybe Silas had put the alert out to force Elora's hand, to ensure that she would end up here. But now, he wasn't so sure.

"A missing person alert. Elora thinks it was someone in the Resistance that she knew did it." The rigidity of Silas's stance softened, and a sense of calm fell over his face as he rubbed along his jawline.

"I apologize. It just took me by surprise." He stared off behind Damien for a moment before returning his attention to the conversation at hand.

"Understandable. At first, I considered that you put the alert out." Damien gauged Silas's reaction to his words, but the vampire simply laughed.

"Not exactly my style. I want my niece to come here, but not enough to alert everyone else to her presence," he replied with a light laugh before the concern on his face reappeared and they both realized the repercussions to this could be disastrous. Everyone, including Darian and Jonas, would try to use this to their advantage. If Damien was still in charge or working for Killian, he would start by finding out who the number belonged to and then hacking each phone call. Instead, he could only hope that they didn't have someone like him working for them.

"Fair enough," he replied as Silas opened the door and entered, leaving Damien to follow along behind him as they went to his office. As they entered, Damien took the same seat and Silas took his, both watching the other.

"Your niece says she accepts and is willing to come on the condition you answer any and all questions she has." Silas leaned forward, resting his arms on the desk as he took in the update.

"The response is quicker than I expected, but I assume the alert has something to do with that." Damien grinned at Silas's assumption, and let his arms lie along the sides of the chair.

"Which is why I thought you might be involved," Damien responded, and Silas blew out a small laugh.

"The logic makes sense, even if I don't want to admit it. I'll just say that I'm glad it's working in my favor, even if there is quite the potential for unforeseen consequences."

"Such as?" Silas leaned back, eyes looking towards the ceiling as if he was considering what to say and how much to reveal.

"Obviously, it shows us someone is looking for her and they are willing to involve the human authorities in finding her. That is desperate, since it gives everyone else an idea of how valuable my niece is. Other vampire heads, specifically Darian, have been discussing her, arguing that she either needs to be brought under control or needs to be removed from the board. I know which of those options Darian would prefer, and I refuse to give her to him." Damien let out a breath at the vow Silas offered, at his refusal to hand her to Darian or Jonas. The image of her lying on his bedroom floor, covered in blood and bites and cuts, was never far from his mind. Once more he saw it as if she was there in the room, eyes glazed over as she pushed the pain deeper and deeper inside her, as she left reality behind to escape if only for a moment and he winced.

Silas clocked the movement and raised an eyebrow.

"And what will you do, Damien? Once she's within these walls?" Damien was quiet for a while because while he wanted to say that he would leave, drive out of the city and never look back, it wasn't the truth. And it wasn't what came out of his mouth when he finally did respond.

"I would like to take you up on your offer to join the Corvin family." Silas nodded, as if he knew what the response would be.

"And my offer to look after my niece?" Damien stiffened.

"I think that should be left up to her."

"And what if I want to know your thoughts? What if I want to know if you'll look after her? If you would want to?" Damien stood and strolled over to the bookshelf, pretending to look over the titles he thought he recognized. Almost absentmindedly, he took one down from the shelf, studying the title. A fantasy novel, which seemed strange to have in the office of someone who was in charge of an entire vampire family. Damien knew his answer, knew that he would protect her for the rest of his life, if only to atone for what he had done, for the role he had played.

"I would do whatever the head of my family requested, including watch over Elora."

"And if she didn't want you to? Even if I ordered you to do so without her knowledge or permission?"

"That, Silas, would be where I draw the line. I won't do anything she doesn't consent to. I think she deserves that much after everything." The words tasted bitter as he spoke, like lies because they were. There was no reality where he wouldn't protect her, no matter what noble bullshit came out of his mouth. It would tear him apart to do so.

Silas stood and walked over to him, handing Damien a set of keys and a long plastic card. "Here are the keys to the manor, and this will open the gate. I'll let you know when she can come. I need a few days to get everything ready for her, since the timeline has been pushed up. Is there anything she needs? Anything you need?"

"She needs clothes, and she prefers long sleeves and high necks." Silas nodded with a grim look that told Damien he knew why.

"Understood." Damien turned away from him and started towards the door.

"Silas, you need to be ready for a lot of questions. She's pissed and hurt that you knew about the abuse. She wants answers."

"And she'll get them. Thank you." Damien said nothing but waved the book in his hand at Silas, who only inclined his head in silent permission. The feeling in Damien's chest forced all words from his mouth, forced all thoughts from his mind as a horrifying realization came crashing down around him. This could be the end of his time with her. Once they were at the manor, she could send him away and he would never see her again.

His feet seemed to sink into the gravel as he made his way to the car and started it, thinking through the logistics of getting her there. It wasn't a long drive, an hour or so. They could simply leave early in the morning and come straight there once they got the word from Silas. It would be easy enough as long as she didn't change her mind before then. Silas's question echoed in his head as he drove towards the apartment. If Elora didn't want him to continue protecting her, would he respect that? He wanted to say yes, wanted to swear that he would follow her wishes. But he knew he would still find himself looking into every conceivable threat, still find himself hunting down her enemies and removing them one by one.

No, even without her permission, he would still protect her. That was the only thought in his head as he parked and headed inside, purposefully ignoring the old woman who was probably watching him through the peephole. He couldn't see her, but he could sense her there, declaring him a brute once more and calling her nephew to come rescue Elora. He chuckled darkly and unlocked the door, pushing it open. This time, it was his turn to be faced by a very irritated Elora, their previous roles reversed.

"What did he say? We need to leave, Damien. Now or soon. But now would be better." Her words were frantic, rolling off her tongue so quickly he had to take a second to figure out what she was saying, what she was asking. For a heartbeat, he watched her, tracking her movements as he took off his boots and jacket, tossing the former into the corner and the latter onto the kitchen counter. Elora was pacing back and forth between the couch and the hallway, hands wringing together as she stared at something he couldn't see. Even as he called her name, she didn't glance up or answer.

"Elora!" She stopped for a moment and let her hands fall to her sides, biting her bottom lip.

"We need to leave. Soon." Damien nodded slowly, noting the panic in her eyes, the way her mouth was tightened into a line.

"What happened?" She jumped a little at the question, fingers picking at her sleeves before pacing once more.

"I don't know. Or I think I do?" For a minute, she went still, as if figuring out what to say. Damien leaned forward on the counter, resting on his forearms as she worked her way through whatever this was and tried to quell his own rising panic.

"She came over, knocked on the door and offered to help me. I was reading the journals, which are fairly pointless by the way. They say nothing important. Or at least nothing that I didn't already know. Connie said that she would protect me and keep me safe. She really doesn't like you, by the way. Thinks you kidnapped me, which is funny in a way since you did. But I didn't tell her that, obviously. Anyway, I let her take me over to her apartment and we drank tea and she showed me the picture on her phone. Wyatt had bought it for her so he could contact her, and she would be able to call him if she needed help. They also text sometimes if she forgets something."

"Elora," he said softly, and she pulled on the ends of her hair, studying each strand. She was rambling, but that wasn't what had caught his attention. It was the use of the human's name, the ease with which it had rolled off her tongue. Damien started to piece everything together as Elora collected herself. Constance, or Connie, must have gotten the alert as well and offered to help her. He almost wanted to laugh at the entire situation since he didn't kidnap her this time.

"Then she started talking about calling the number on the alert and I started panicking, begging her not to. I tried to explain that the people who put out the alert are the ones I'm hiding from. And—" Damien listened as Elora fell silent and finally met his eyes, finally gave him a glimpse of the torment and confusion there.

"I compelled her. I think? She was staring at me as I told her that I was fine, not to call the number, and that I was safe. Then she—I don't know. She relaxed and got quiet. And after that she never mentioned it again, just deleted the alert on her phone when I left. I was worried she would figure out what I did." It was only then that he saw the tears in her eyes and understood.

Damien straightened and calmly approached her. She seemed so fragile that he was terrified even the slightest semi-harsh movement would scare her. He stood in front of her before placing his hand on her arm while the other cupped her chin, turning her face to his. She needed to hear what he had to say, needed to listen and believe every word.

"You only compelled her not to call a phone number. You didn't force her to hurt herself or let you feed from her. You didn't make her do anything harmful to herself or anyone else. Okay?"

"But I forced her to believe me, forced her to listen to me when she was just trying to protect me." Elora's eyes brightened for a minute, fierce and determined as she jerked from his grip.

"Maybe so, love. You compelled her to believe you because the alternative was her calling whoever put that alert out and telling them you're right across the hall." Damien approached her once more, and she stared at him with such desperation that his breath caught in his throat.

"Don't you think it's possible she would have believed you? That she would have trusted your word even if you didn't accidentally compel her?" He watched as her face softened, as her lips returned to their natural state, as her shoulders lowered. Elora took a step forward, and he reached for her, heart racing as he forced himself not to question this, to not say something stupid. To just let them both enjoy this moment.

Damien extended his arms slowly, allowing her time to move away or deny him, even if it would have destroyed him. When she didn't move, he wrapped his arms around her and pulled her close. For a second, she was stiff, and he worried that she would jerk away from him, would remember what an asshole he always was. Finally, she melted, falling against his chest, her head nestled along his collarbone. The scent of lavender reached him even as she shuddered, and her breathing became gentle. With trembling hands, she grasped the front of his shirt, and her grip tightened as if to make sure he couldn't leave.

"Are you okay?" A stupid question and he felt her let out a breath before she attempted to shake her head.

"I'm not, Damien. I don't know what I am or what's normal. I just—" She stopped, and he tightened his hold on her, lowering his lips to her head. It was distracting to be so acutely aware of her in his arms, of every place they touched. His heart raced even as he screamed at himself to not mess this up, to not say something wrong. To not push her away like he always seemed to do, even if it was best for both of them.

"Thank you. I don't think I ever thanked you for getting me out of there and for not leaving me, despite what you think of me. I never said that, and I wanted to before I go to live with Silas." He swallowed, mouth suddenly dry, like every drop of moisture was removed from his body.

"You don't need to thank me, love. I owe you for my part in everything. I'm trying to even the score." Something flashed in her eyes before they settled into a cold expression. Her hands let go of his shirt as she pushed away. He felt the loss of her instantly, the absence of warmth and of her keeping him grounded.

"And how long until we are even? Until I'm with Silas?" Her hands trembled as she moved towards the couch, settling into it. For a moment, he debated following her, debated sitting on the couch beside her and pulling her back into his arms.

"A few days. He needs to get everything ready for you." Elora nodded and stared at the stained and ripped fabric beneath her, her attention suddenly far away from their tiny apartment. With his entire being telling him it was a mistake, he left her and went to take a shower.

Chapter 14

Viktor

The calls that came in were a strange collection of ransom demands and psychics mixed with a couple of potential leads. After roughly seventy calls throughout the first day that either asked about a cash reward or claimed they knew where she was but would only tell them if they got something in return, Thorne had grown frustrated. Viktor stood in the doorway, watching the five Resistance members taking turns answering phones with a stack of paper between them. Most of the time, they repeated the line that had grown too common — "No, we are not offering a cash reward at this time." That line was closely followed in frequency by, "No, we are not looking to hire anyone's services. Please only call with actual information."

Nothing was written down during those calls. But at the end of the second day, they had a small list of potential locations, but nothing concrete.

"I think I saw someone who looks like her at the library on Main."

"I saw her at the store on 4th street, the place called Natural Market."

The person in charge of the phones kept glancing towards Viktor and Thorne, who was busy reading a report from the Resistance scientists. He snuck a glance, just a quick peek, and saw Elizabeth's name across the top with a chart with varying numbers with notes beneath it. His lips quirked as he fought the urge to ask Thorne about it, and his hands itched to take it from her grasp. Instead, he turned his attention back to the living room that had been transformed into a call center.

It was a cute house, one that was bought with donations from members. Technically, the walls were painted a pale pink but were covered with maps and notes that had been pinned to various places. The map, which took up most of the space, had been highlighted to show the areas that the more credible tips had mentioned. The couch was pushed into a corner to make room for the long collapsible table where the various workers sat, answering calls and taking notes.

Until one of them, an older man with graying hair and a bald spot at the top of his head, gestured frantically to Viktor. Despite the enthusiasm on the man's face, Viktor kept his expectations low as he rushed over. A voice filtered through the speaker as the worker kept talking and his eyes narrowed at whatever was being said.

"I understand, sir." The man started scribbling on the sheet of paper, an address and the name of a store. "Yes, thank you so much for your help." He hung up and handed the sheet of paper to Viktor.

"What do you think?" The question was met with the worker stretching his back slightly and twisting his neck, resulting in an audible cracking noise.

"I think I've been taking calls for over 24 hours and that is the best one I've heard yet. The man works at a little store in the Industrial district. He said she came in with another man, bought a few things and left. But he remembers that she had scars on her neck, that it seemed odd, which is why he remembered her and recognized her photo."

Viktor's heart leaped into his throat at the mention of the scars. They had kept those out of the alert, had chosen a picture where they were mostly covered up. He hadn't expected something so credible to occur so quickly. Until now, he had been working off the assumption that Damien would keep her locked up to keep her safe until he had somewhere to take her. Viktor hadn't seen him taking her to the store when they were both meant to be hiding. Unless that hadn't been Damien, which could present another potential problem.

"Thank you." The man nodded and returned to the phone that was once more ringing, sighing heavily before answering. Viktor left the man to his job and marched to Thorne, still completely engrossed in the report, and cleared his throat.

"What?" She didn't glance up, just kept reading and playing with the pen in her hand.

"A lead. A credible one, I think." Finally, she tore her focus away from the report, eyes wide as she snatched the paper from his hand. Her brows narrowed as she read the few words again and again. It was almost like Viktor could see the wheels turning, the commands falling to place before they left her mouth.

"I want you to look into this. Go down there first thing in the morning. Find out when the place opens, talk to whoever was working that day, and check out any houses or apartments in the area. Take a printout of her photo and start canvasing. Ask people if they've seen her." The words erupted from her mouth in rapid succession, each word breathless and laced with anticipation or excitement. Viktor wasn't entirely sure which one it was even as she handed the paper back to him.

"Of course." He paused as he turned to leave, hesitating as Thorne returned to the file on her lap.

"Can I help you with something?" She drawled, sighing as she spoke.

"I was wondering if there was any information about Elizabeth. From the tests that they've been running."

"It's only been a few days, Viktor. We haven't learned too much."

"I thought you would want an update from my visit with her yesterday."

"That depends. Did she have anything useful to say, or was it all crazy nonsense again?" Viktor wondered briefly if Thorne had been down to talk to her, or if her impression was based on what others saw. He wasn't entirely sure Elizabeth was insane, just unhinged in her obsession, in her dual drive to both love and kill her sister. It was an all-encompassing desire that didn't seem to have any boundaries or rules.

"She doesn't know very much, as we guessed. But she did mention something that was interesting. It was about how she was turned."

Thorne sighed and closed her eyes for a moment, as if reminding herself that patience was a virtue. "I am aware of how turning works, Viktor. Some would say I am intimately aware." Viktor recalled the rumors he had heard, the legend of Thorne who took the Resistance from small-time vampire hunting to a full organization complete with leaders and funding.

The story was that Thorne had a wife and child, had been married and they both worked in the blood banks, collecting and storing donations. During a shift, Thorne's wife was attacked, and the entire supply had been stolen. When the vampire heads learned of what happened, Thorne's wife and child paid the price. She only lived because she was gone that night, had taken on an extra shift at a second job.

"That's the thing, Thorne. From what Elizabeth said, it was different. El—the target only bit her. There was no exchanging of blood, no draining, nothing like that." Viktor relished the satisfaction he felt as Thorne's eyes flashed with surprise, her grip on the file in her lap tightening until the pages were bent and crumpled.

"That's impossible." Her words were almost a whisper, as if speaking too loudly would make it all real. Viktor shrugged in response, shoving his hands in the pockets of his jeans.

"That's what Elizabeth said, and I know that the target never spoke of a blood exchange, only an initial attack."

"Fuck. If this is true, then it's bad. You understand that? This cannot go beyond the council members. Am I understood?" Viktor inclined his head slightly, shoulders back and spine straight, ever ready to take on her commands. Thorne placed the file on the table beside her and stood, hands in her hair as her eyes moved wildly over the floor.

"If this is true, and I do mean if, then it means the target and potentially anyone she turns could then turn more and more humans into vampires. The process would be so simple, so instantaneous that there would be no stopping it." Viktor stilled with his hands clasped behind his back. Thorne wasn't truly speaking to him, but to herself, talking through the consequences of this new hit.

"Then what do we do?" His words were low, unsure if Thorne would tolerate being interrupted, but needing an answer to this question. She stopped, arms limp at her sides, and she shook her head. Instantly, the panic subsided, and her face became a mask of indifference, of harsh realities and the willpower to alter them.

"Nothing changes. We still need her. We still need her blood. If anything, it only makes it clearer that we need her to make a weapon."

"And Elizabeth?" Thorne glared at him, her gaze assessing, and Viktor shifted uncomfortably.

"Again, nothing changes. Once she has fulfilled her role of bringing the target here, then we get rid of her. She's a liability, a potential plague upon every human in this city. Don't forget what she is. We'll remove you like we did with Denise." Again, a curt nod. He didn't bother to defend himself or declare his innocence at whatever Thorne believed was happening.

But why did I even ask?

The thought rushed forward, and he shook his head, not wanting to investigate that right now, not when there were missions to prepare for. He believed it came from the obsession with proving himself after the failure with Elora. If Elizabeth was useful to them, perhaps the stain on his reputation would disappear. Or at least ease. Thorne sat but handed him the file from the table and he took it, flipping through the pages, not understanding a single word.

"I don't know what any of this means." He admitted after a minute. Thorne chuckled and took the file back.

"Honestly, it doesn't say anything that we didn't already know from Denise's research. The blood is more potent, and we now know that the same is true for Elizabeth as it is for her. We know that it works as a replacement for human blood, which was Killian's goal. And we know it has unique properties. However, so far it doesn't look like Elizabeth's blood holds all the same ones, but we are going to go ahead with trying to make a vaccine of sorts from it and see what happens." His stomach twisted as he considered what that would probably require, the trials and how they would even test it.

"Does it say anything about time between feeding? If the potency of the blood has something to do with it?" Thorne's eyes snapped to his, narrowed with suspicion.

"No. Why would you ask that?" Viktor cleared his throat and met her gaze.

"Elizabeth said something about needing to feed more often, but explained she wasn't entirely sure is that was the case. From what she knows about vampires, they need to feed every few days and she was growing hungry after less than twenty-four hours." Thorne studied the file once more, flipping through the pages as if the answer was there. Finally, she sighed and ran her hand over her face.

"She's right about the time period between feedings, but only if we are talking about the need and not the desire to feed."

"There's a difference?" She looked at him like one would look at a child who asked an incredibly stupid question.

"Yes. Humans are similar in a way. A person may eat something because they want it but aren't necessarily hungry. You can call it a craving, a desire, a lack of willpower. Whatever you want, but it's the same for vampires. They get hungry and feed, like we do. But then there are those who simply want to feed and do so without needing to."

"She claimed it was hunger, something that she felt. But I can't say for sure whether she's telling the truth."

"Which is why the girl would be very helpful right now." He winced, visibly and violently, to the point that Thorne gave him a confused look. That was Damien's term for Elora, his way of rendering her nameless and unimportant while he claimed to hate her. And even with that, she had gone with him. Maybe he had approached the garage all wrong, too aggressive. The council members were right that he had messed up the mission. He could have waited, taken her from the safe house once they got there.

The reminder of his failure was not lost on him. Thorne had meant for it to hit home, and it had. But now he had a chance to fix it, and he was determined not to mess it up again.

Chapter 15

Elora

"I need to meet with someone today. They have information and supplies." The peaceful bubble Elora had built while watching a new baking show was ruptured by Damien's announcement. Irritation rose slightly at the sound of his voice. She had never seen this one and didn't exactly appreciate the distraction. Her thoughts oscillated between the show and the way she had compelled Connie, the way she had forced her to do something against her will. For Elora, it didn't matter that it had been for protection, or that she hadn't forced the woman to do anything other than not dial a phone number. It was about the lack of will, the lack of consent. At the thought, the phantom teeth and fingers reappeared on her scarred skin after days of them being held at bay. Yet, they now roamed over her limbs as she struggled to watch someone make a three-tier cake.

"What?" She gave him a side glance. He was already dressed in his jeans and fitted t-shirt. With a grunt, he pulled on his boots and gave her a searching look before using his fingers to brush his hair away from his face. The effort was wasted as it fell back onto his forehead in a way that was annoyingly distracting. It made it all the most difficult to return her attention to the television when she wanted to drink him in.

"I said I need to leave to meet with someone who has information and supplies for us." Elora nodded before turning back to the show.

"Okay. I promise not to leave." She heard him sigh and stand.

"Really? That's it? No sarcastic comment or question about where I'm going?"

"Would you tell me if I asked?" He studied her before taking a few steps towards the couch, hands clenching at his side.

"I'll tell you anything you want to know." His words sounded like a promise, like a vow. She almost believed him.

"How long until we can feed again?" Damien raised his brow, either because he was surprised by the question or by the fact she didn't ask about the impending meeting.

"Depends on if I get these supplies. If I do, then as soon as I'm back. If not, we'll need to have a conversation." She grunted in acknowledgment and felt him settle onto the couch beside her.

"Are you feeling like you need to?" She stared down at her fingers, fighting the urge to bend over in hopes the gnawing in her gut would stop. It had been like that all morning after the sharp pang in her stomach and chest had woken her, leaving her with a salivating mouth. The scent of every person in the building filtered in and out of the air ducts like they were teasing her, tiny threads that wrapped around her limbs to drag her forward to each one. It was intoxicating. Knowing that only a wall or flimsy piece of wood stood between her and the humans occupying the building was torture. It was disturbing to know how desperately she wanted to feed from them, to work her way into their homes and drain them dry.

You're your father's daughter. She shook her head and gave Damien a small smile that she hoped would encourage him to simply turn around and leave.

"Just a bit, I suppose." He scooted forward and took her hand, the warmth of his skin forcing her mind from the agony in her stomach.

"The truth, love. Tell me the truth." She smiled once more as a notification sounded on his phone. He cursed softly and used his free hand to study the screen, face contorting with agitation as he read the message.

"You can go. I'm fine. I'll just wait for you to get back." He shook his head, tossing the phone onto the cushion behind him.

"Tell me." She bit the inside of her cheek, not sure what to say or where to start.

"I get—" Elora hesitated for a second. "Hungry, I guess. I get hungry more often than I think I'm supposed to, if I'm like you or the others. It feels like need to feed every day, or I can sense every human here. I can smell their blood. Hear their hearts beating." She watched Damien nod as she spoke, his focus never leaving her face, even as his eyes filled with anxiety. Was he worried about her? Or the others in the building? Was he afraid of what she was?

He sighed deeply before speaking. "I'll try my best to get you some so you can feed more often. Every day, if possible. Once we get you to Silas, it shouldn't be a problem anymore."

Damien dropped her hand before he stood and grabbed the phone from the couch cushion. He didn't say anything as he left and locked the door behind him. Elora sat there, attempting to make sense of the kindness and the newest nickname, waiting for the cruelty that would inevitably follow. It always did without fail. Yet, she craved the moments when his face and eyes softened, when he looked at her like there was nothing else in the world besides them. She could only wonder how much of that was in her head, a desire to find affection anywhere she could, just like he accused her of.

A knock on the door made her jump up from the couch, her heart racing in her chest from the shock. If it was Damien, he would simply unlock the door and come in. With easy steps, making sure she was as quiet as she could be, Elora made her way to the door, peering through the peephole. She huffed a small laugh as she unlocked it and pulled it open, a bright smile on her lips as she took in Wyatt standing there with two coffees and a plastic bag hanging from his wrist.

"Good morning. I thought I'd bring the coffee to you." She beamed at him and moved out of the way, waving a hand in a gesture to enter. For a brief, very brief moment, she considered what Damien would say if he saw she had let him in, if he caught Wyatt here.

Her eyes followed him as Wyatt studied the space, standing awkwardly in the middle of the room as she shut the door. The floor creaked as she returned to her spot and sank back onto the couch. Only after she turned off the show did she pat the seat next to her. He flashed a devastatingly handsome grin at her invitation and sat, setting both coffee cups on the table.

"I wanted to bring you a gift." His smile was sheepish as he handed her the bag and a soft giggle erupted from her. She couldn't remember the last time someone had given her a present.

"What is it?" she asked as she started to open it, hand trembling slightly. He said nothing, simply stayed quiet and watched with hesitant delight as Elora pulled the items out of the bag, gasping slightly at what she now held in her hands. A leather-bound book roughly the size of a piece of paper. She felt her brows knit together as she opened it before her lips stretched into a grin that she was sure made her look like a fool.

"A sketchbook?" He shrugged.

"You said you like to draw. I didn't think you had anything." She reached into the bag again and brought out a small package of sketch pencils, complete with a sharpener and eraser. Tears formed in her eyes as her body flushed with intense heat. The gesture felt wrong, like she didn't deserve it. Not after everything. She forced the thoughts away, locking them behind a wall so she could enjoy this. It was a simple gesture of someone who seemed too kind for the world, of someone who saw only the good in others even if it was buried underneath secrets and guilt. Elora let the sketchbook rest on her lap as she reached for his hand, grasping it between both of hers.

"Thank you. I can't remember the last time—" Elora stopped mid-sentence, unsure she could finish it. He nodded, understanding clear on his face, and they sat for a moment in silence until he cleared his throat.

"Now, I think you should draw me something."

She laughed, the sound ringing out in the quiet. "Like what?"

"Anything. I don't care what. If you do, I'll give you your coffee." She placed her hand over her heart as if she was insulted.

"Bribery? Really?" He chuckled softly as she turned to a blank page, pulling up her sleeves as she opened the package of pre-sharpened pencils. Her eyes narrowed slightly while she ran her fingers over the paper, marveling at the rough texture of the page as she considered her options. She hadn't drawn anything in years. At the hospital, it had been triggering, leaving her curled up in her room for hours. For a while, she had begged for supplies. The answer had always been no, that she hadn't earned that privilege yet. When they finally relented and gave her paper and pencils that could be checked out at the desk, she cried. Screamed. Hid in the tiniest of corners she could fit in. Eventually, it was the green room and no more sketchbooks outside of art therapy where even there she was heavily monitored. Even after numerous sessions with Denise, Elora had never understood the reaction to something she thought she loved.

She cracked her neck and started putting down line after line, no matter how foreign the pencil felt in her hand, how hesitant her marks were. She let out a huff as once again she erased something, only to redo it or alter its shape slightly.

Elora chuckled as she started to finalize lines, trying to decide exactly how embarrassed she would be by this. Luckily, she never said she was any good, just that she enjoyed it. She turned it around, revealing a sketch of his face. It wasn't very detailed, but she had captured the strong jawline, his lips, his warm eyes that crinkled slightly when he smiled.

"Don't laugh." Wyatt smiled even as she started laughing. "Do I get my coffee now?"

"Of course. As soon as you sign it and give it to me." She did as he said and signed her name at the bottom before tearing it out.

"What happened there?" Her brow drew together in confusion, thinking he was talking about a rogue line in the drawing or one of the burn holes in the couch. She glanced around them, trying to identify what he meant when his hand gently gripped her wrist, turning her arm over to reveal her forearm, now exposed from where she had pushed up her sleeve.

Elora's body stiffened as her blood froze and her breathing hitched as she pulled her arm back, tugging the sleeves down.

"It's complicated."

"Was it the roommate?" There was a hardness to his voice, an anger that radiated off each word, off him as he studied her face, eyes shifting between her and her arms as if he could see through the fabric. But for once, she didn't want to hide. She didn't want to curl into herself, make herself small, so she was beyond anyone's notice.

"No! No, it wasn't Damien. It was the people he helped me escape from." She sighed and rested her hands on her legs, watching his face for any sign of revulsion. "I was—"

"You don't have to explain. I shouldn't have asked. You don't have to tell me about it if you don't want to." Wyatt grabbed her hand, pulling it close, gripping it tight between his own. She closed her eyes, savoring the touch of someone who didn't know who she was or what her blood meant. Enjoyed being what she imagined normal was for just a single moment.

"I know. I was abused by people who were meant to protect me. The scars are from that." It felt strange hearing even that tiny morsel come from her mouth, that revelation and confession all wrapped into one. A piece of her soul lay bare as he handed her the cup of cold coffee and they heard familiar voices outside the door.

Chapter 16

Viktor

It took whoever was inside a few minutes to reach the door. Viktor could hear their feet shuffling towards it as he shifted, gripping the picture in his hands. This was the sixth apartment or so in this building. Honestly, he had lost track at that point and was done with the whole mission. Once he finished up the last few apartments, he would be able to move on. The shop where the lead had come from served numerous blocks and who knew if the shopkeeper even saw Elora. Maybe it was someone who looked like her. Maybe the shopkeeper had been able to see the scars in the photo.

Finally, the door opened to reveal an older woman in a blue house dress and what looked like cat slippers. Flour covered her hands, and she wiped it on the apron that covered her dress before glancing up at him, scowling. Underneath the bundle of gray hair on top of her head, her eyes narrowed as she studied him.

"Can I help you?" Her tone was biting as she eyed him, gaze moving from his face to his feet and then back up again, lingering on the photo in his hand.

"Yes, I'm sorry to bother you. I'm looking for this young woman and I was wondering if you had seen her." Viktor repeated the words he had said so many times at this point and held out the picture, letting her take it to get a better view. There was still flour and what looked like bread dough lingering on her fingers and palms. He could only hope it didn't transfer over as she handled it, holding it further away and then closer, eyes squinting as if she needed glasses.

"Lovely girl," she murmured, eyes hesitating on Elora's face, before darting to the hallway.

"Yes, she is," Viktor agreed. "Have you seen her at all? We had a lead that someone in the neighborhood had seen her nearby." She took another look at the photo before meeting his eyes, face the very image of disappointment.

"I'm sorry, but I haven't. But I don't leave my home very often. Stairs are tricky for me." She shook her head and touched her hip, as if to explain her comment.

"Are you sure? If you could—" the woman cut him off, her thin lips pulled into an even thinner line.

"Young man, I told you that I have never seen this girl before in my life. I do hope you find her and find her safe." The old woman's voice was stern and impatient as she handed back the photo.

"And that apartment there?" Viktor jerked his head towards the door behind him and the old woman shook hers in response.

"No one lives there. Not for years since that poor family moved out. Headed out of the city from what I understand. Once their kids graduated, they had no reason to stay. Sad story, really. They were lovely neighbors. The children loved my cupcakes." Viktor held up his hand, hoping she would take the hint to stop. Her eyes darted to the door once more before moving back to him. Her shoulders were tense as he shifted on his feet again, letting the uncomfortable silence stretch between them.

"Is that all? I have something in the oven I need to check on." Viktor nodded.

"Thank you. I appreciate your help. Please call if you see her." Viktor handed her a small card with the tip line number on it.

Begrudgingly, she took it before waving her hand at him as she shut the door. At the click of the lock, Viktor spun on his heel and took a moment to look over at the other apartment, searching for any sign someone was in there.

He didn't believe for a second that the apartment itself was empty or that the old woman was telling the truth. With each step away from the allegedly empty apartment, with each step down the stairs, with each person on the first floor he spoke to, Viktor kept glancing back, as if something kept drawing him, something in his core that told him to go back and break in. It screamed, the sound echoing inside his head, that he would find her there, huddled in hiding from the Resistance, from him. All he needed to do was bust down the door and his failure would be fixed.

But he didn't. Instead, Viktor knocked on three more doors, asked three more residents if they had seen Elora. He studied them as they took the photo from his hand, stared at her face before shaking their heads, voices revealing a kind of strained disappointment. They weren't sorry they hadn't seen her, weren't sorry that they had no information to give him. If Viktor was in their position, he would feel the same way about a random man searching for a young woman. They were probably grateful they couldn't send him in the right direction.

But there was that apartment one floor up.

"Does anyone live in that apartment above you?" The man in front of him, a middle-aged human with dark hair and leathery skin from working outside his whole life, shook his head.

"I haven't heard anyone, and these floors are thin. But I also don't spend much time at home. I work construction and that keeps me out of the apartment most of the day." He shrugged before turning slightly. "Marie!"

Viktor stamped down the disappointment as a young woman came lazily towards the door, brown hair pulled back into a ponytail and a television remote in her hand.

"Yea?" She stared at them both, curiosity and annoyance making her features sharper. She looked to be an older teenager, maybe seventeen or so.

"This guy wants to know if you have heard anyone upstairs."

"I guess. Footsteps, maybe. I think I heard arguing the other day, but I'm not sure. It's not like our neighbors are exactly quiet most days, so I ignore them. And people break into the empty apartments all the time." The man nodded and gestured for her to leave, obviously not wanting to allow room to ask follow-up questions. Viktor inclined his head slightly as the girl turned away, returning to whatever she had been doing before being interrupted.

"There you go." The man declared and started to shut the door.

"Wait. If you do see her or hear anything else from that apartment, can you call this number?" The man grumbled something as he shut the door in Viktor's face, the sound echoing in the empty hallway. With a harsh breath, he ran his hand through his hair and left, quickly making his way to the door of the lobby and out onto the sidewalk. The late day crowds had emerged from their various businesses, mostly warehouses or factories, to find food or run errands.

The Resistance had intel that this area had a high concentration of blood banks that offered people money in exchange for giving donations. The official statement was that it was for the hospitals and would be used in surgeries or emergencies. It was a half-truth. While it was true that some of it did go to the hospitals, a lot of it went to feeding the vampire population, bought by the various vampire families to distribute.

But it was a dying practice and a floundering business. The amount of human feeding had increased over the years, with people either being lured off the streets or simply taken. Viktor had seen them in the cells in Ashcroft Tower, humans who were used for live feeding. The ones he was able to speak to explained that they were paid, that this was their choice. Others explained it was better than living on the streets. At least in the cells, they were fed and had a place to sleep.

Exploitation. A loophole in the Accords. That's all it was. Preying on the most vulnerable of the population. Vampires like Killian saw themselves as heroes, as saviors who offered opportunities for employment, a mutually beneficial arrangement. At least until the humans were bled dry, or the vampires lost interest in them. Viktor had seen humans taken from their cell and not brought back. Instead, workers came and cleaned it out, disinfecting every surface before someone else was brought in—haggard and usually too thin from their time on the streets.

He shuddered despite the warm weather as he recalled the feeling of teeth in his neck, his wrist, his thigh during the first part of his time there. He had been communal food, two or three vampires feasting while he was tied to a bed. As they drank, he almost allowed himself to fall into a pit of rage. Almost allowed himself to weaken his resolve to take Elora and hand her over to be utilized by the Resistance.

Almost.

Viktor's hand clenched at his side as he risked one last look at what he thought was the correct window. A grimy layer of dirt made it difficult to see much of anything. His breath hitched slightly as the curtains shifted and he saw her face staring down at him. Even through the filth, he recognized the mixture of pure devastation and fury on her face. To keep himself from doing something stupid, he forced his hands into his pockets and turned away, unable to look at her. He didn't want to consider the squirming sensation in his chest, the way her expression brought something to the surface that he didn't understand.

This was why she was always nameless when he spoke to Thorne or the other members. She had to be 'the target' and never Elora. At least not out loud. Viktor never thought that he and Damien would have something in common.

The drive back to the suburban house was long and by the time he got there, he had already outlined what he would say, the script ready on his tongue. He pulled the car up across the street from the blocked driveway and tossed Elora's photo in the glove compartment. The house itself looked like every other one on the street. Single level in an L-shape where the garage stuck out. The lawn was well manicured, and there were flowers along the walkway to the front door, which was flanked by two large windows. If it wasn't for the small collection of cars surrounding it, Viktor wouldn't have recognized it amongst the almost identical houses surrounding it. There was no flag outside, no insignia painted on the front door.

He didn't bother knocking before he went in and was hit with the smell of food, reminding him that he hadn't bothered to eat while canvasing the neighborhood. Viktor had wanted to talk to as many people and cross off as many apartments as possible. That area was primarily large complexes, either fenced in with multiple buildings all together like a community or tall buildings with numerous apartments on each floor. It had taken hours to get through the ones that he did. And he stopped after the Garden View apartments. Elora was there. He just needed to prove it, get backup or someone else to assist in getting her.

Thorne was reclining in a chair in the dining room, an empty plate in front of her. Her eyes were closed, and her hair was pulled back. For a moment, she looked years younger than she was, the weight of running an entire organization aimed at protecting humans removed from her shoulders. Viktor cleared his throat as he stood in the doorway, hands clasped behind his back.

"Anything?" Thorne didn't open her eyes or sit up, but he caught the way her fingers twitched on the table, the way her shoulders tensed.

"The lead was good. I talked with the shopkeeper first and showed him the photo. He confirmed he saw her and gave me more information and a starting place." She waved her hand, eyes still closed.

"He said that the target was in the shop with a man, and they bought a few things before leaving. The description seemed to indicate that the man she was with is human. I canvased the area surrounding the shop. No one else recognized her."

"I thought you said the lead was good." She bit out, eyes finally opened as she sat up and glared at him.

"It was. I spoke to an older woman in the Garden View apartments. She said that she'd never seen her, but I'm sure she was lying. She claimed the apartment across the hall from her is empty, but the people who live below it say they've heard people up there." The heat from her eyes eased away, and he saw her considering the report.

"You think the target is in the so-called empty apartment." Not a question. A statement and he nodded.

"Yes. I would like permission to return and get in." Thorne bent her head in an almost nod before gesturing towards the kitchen.

"Get some food and we can talk it over. I'm willing to bet you didn't eat while you were out." Viktor laughed at her correct assumption and wandered to the kitchen, grabbing a plate before filling it with the chicken and vegetables in the roast pan. It smelled like rosemary and garlic, and he felt his stomach clench as he finally took a fork from the drawer and returned to the table. Thorne raised a brow at him as he started eating.

"A lesser person wouldn't use a fork after being stabbed with one." He glanced up at her and swallowed.

"It wasn't too bad. I think she held back when she did it." He shrugged. "It was either her or Damien, and I preferred her to do the stabbing." Thorne nodded.

Viktor had told them everything, or almost everything. For hours, he had sat in a chair with Thorne and the other council members across from him, telling them what happened and answering questions. He had only left out little things, like kissing Elora's forehead after she stabbed him, and telling her it was okay when she fed for the first time. He didn't need to be labeled as soft or have his motives questioned. Viktor didn't need to be equated to Denise, someone who fell under the vampire's spell.

"I had been told you two were close." Again, he shrugged as he chewed slower, hoping to buy himself time to consider her statement.

"I suppose so. It was part of the job. To get close to her and then use the information I got from her." Thorne said nothing, just studied his face before letting out a breath and leaning back from the table. Viktor forced a disinterested expression onto his features, hoping that the regret that raced through him every time she was mentioned, every time he heard or said her name, didn't show. Over and over the betrayal, the absolute anguish on her face when he demanded Damien hand her over, when he said she was a weapon played inside his head, a personal form of torture he had no control over.

"I agree that the target is probably in the empty apartment. I also agree that you should go back and search for her. Break in if you have to." Viktor continued eating, taking a quick drink of water as he waited for her to continue.

"I want you to take Elizabeth. All necessary precautions will be taken, but I think she can be helpful in this."

"How?"

Thorne laced her fingers together, letting them rest on the table. "We managed to get a hold of the patient notes from when Elizabeth was in maximum security. She made a lot of very interesting statements, similar to the ones she made to you concerning feeding. But she also talked incessantly about being able to feel her sister, like there was a tie between the two of them. She said she could feel her, could sense her. The doctors, of course, brushed it off as crazy nonsense, but I'm not so sure." Understanding rushed over him. If Elizabeth was telling the truth, then she would know that Elora was in that apartment. Elizabeth would be able to sense her, and the so-called tie would be useful in finding the object of her obsession.

"And we control her how exactly? She isn't stable, mentally or otherwise." Thorne nodded and pulled out a syringe.

"This is how. It's a milder form of the medication the target was given during her time in the hospital. It'll dull her strength and desire to feed, but hopefully not enough to dull the tie between them."

"You think the connection is real, then?" Thorne nodded carefully and chewed her lip as he took another bite.

"I do. It's a strange concept that there would be this tie between them. But the target is uncharted territory. We don't know exactly what her bite did to Elizabeth."

"I understand." Thorne stood and stalked towards him, face unreadable as he took a drink of water.

"Give her the medication before taking her from the cell. There will be another one for you, more powerful, in case the first starts to wear off or she behaves in a concerning manner. Don't double guess it or overthink. If she starts becoming unstable, then drug her and bring her back. I won't risk the target because Elizabeth is obsessed."

"And how do I get the target here?" Thorne gave him a cold smile.

"You were close, as you say. I'm sure you have ideas." With that Thorne left the room, not giving him an opportunity to tell her that he and Elora weren't close, that she despised him, that she may kill him as soon as she set eyes on him. And part of Viktor knew that he deserved it.

Chapter 17

Damien

His phone had been continuously going off since he sat down with Elora on that couch, begging her to confide in him, to tell him the truth. But she had only given him that sad smile that told him that she didn't trust him, that he had possibly messed up so fantastically that there was no chance of repair.

It would be a lie if he said he wasn't concerned about her or the fact she was feeling hunger so quickly. He hadn't been surprised that she could use compulsion, or that she had felt so guilty about doing it, even if it had been by accident. But the fact she felt hunger less than twenty-four hours after feeding was different from using an ability all vampires seemed to have. Damien could go two days without feeding and had gone longer when doing various jobs for Killian.

Korina was waiting exactly where she said she would be. They had decided to forgo the coffee shop out of an abundance of paranoia on her part. He had just rolled his eyes as he responded that they could meet outside the blood storage building instead. Damien honked as he pulled up beside her where she sat on the bench, an insulated bag sitting next to her. She threw him a grin and tossed her hair over her shoulder before grabbing the bag and sliding into the passenger seat.

"Good morning, lover."

"Not anymore, Korina. Let's not start like this." Her smile didn't falter for a second as she patted the bag on her lap.

"I got what you asked for. Plus an extra just for you." She winked and turned slightly to set the bag in the back seat.

"Any news?"

"Not even a 'thank you' or anything? Whatever you're up to has you very cranky, Damien." She gave him a faux sad expression, complete with pouting lips. He kept his eyes on the road as he pulled back out into traffic.

She let out a dramatic sigh. "Fine. Darian wants a meeting." He huffed out a bitter laugh before glancing over at her. "No, seriously. He wants to meet with you."

"Why?" Damien could probably guess the reason, and from the amused edge in Korina's voice, he knew it was bad.

"Do you want the official reason or my theory?"

"Both."

"The official reason he gave us when he told us to find you is that he wants you to resume your position as second-in-command. He's familiar with your work and wants you to continue it, as he said." She shifted in her seat, turning so she faced him. "The rumor, however, is that he needs you to inspire loyalty. Most of the vampires who already belong to the Ashcroft family don't support him, and there have been outright rebellions and whispers of an assassination plan. In his mind, having you working for him will help make him seem more legitimate."

Damien made a noise, something between a chuckle and a snort of disbelief. Darian had been a fool to think that the vampires would simply accept him. The succession requirements were ingrained in their very bones and flowed in their veins. Walking in and claiming the seat without any proof he earned it was never going to work. The position he was desperately trying to hold on to belonged to one person, one vampire.

"I have a feeling that there's more to this than me simply offering my loyalty." She laughed at his comment.

"You would need to prove your loyalty, of course. Many vampires in that Tower think you were the one to do away with Killian and that you should be in charge now. You would need to offer up a very special gift to prove you view Darian as the new head." His hands tightened on the steering wheel, the sides of his vision going dark as he took in the offer. Darian wanted Elora, either because of the past or because of what she represented. Maybe both. Use her for who she was in public and then for what her blood offered in private.

"Why her? What's the reason he's giving?" Damien snuck a look at Korina, who was studying him, eyes lingering on where his hands gripped the wheel, knuckles bloodless and white.

"Not sure. But of course, there are rumors. None that you would want to hear and none that I want to tell you. I would like to remain intact."

"Tell me, Korina." She flinched at the command before recovering and sitting straighter in the seat, eyes darting around the car as if to check where all the exits were.

"Darian wanting her as a bride is the most popular and tasteful rumor. It would help to legitimize his claim to the Ashcrofts. If Killian was telling the truth, then she's the heir to the Corvin family. Darian forcing her to marry him could combine three vampire families into one that he happens to control. Then it would only be a matter of bringing the other one into submission." She sighed before continuing.

"There are discussions of him and Jonas, who has resurfaced, sharing her in the past. Gossip about her blood and what Killian did when he played with her genetics. Darian doesn't dispel the rumors and makes comments about how she's practically his bride already."

"I want Jonas's location. Where's he staying? The Tower?"

"No. From what I understand, he's staying in a condo a few blocks away. I think he doesn't want to risk being in the Tower in case the vampires turn on Darian. He was always one for protecting himself first and showing loyalty second." Korina paused for a moment as he pulled up alongside the sidewalk near the blood bank that he had picked her up at.

"I suppose you want something more concrete, something like an address and condo number." Damien grinned at her correct assumption as he put the car in park. "I'll get that for you. And any other information I can."

"Thank you." She stared at him for a long moment, eyes tracing the features of his face as if trying to figure out what was different.

"Why is Killian's daughter so important? What has everyone searching for her, fighting over her? Why are you so loyal to her? You always said you hated her, that she was everything wrong with people who had money, that she was selfish and stupid for costing so many vampires their lives."

He leaned his head back on the seat, hands still on the wheel as he tried to figure out how to explain it and if he even should. Her loyalty was fickle at best, always latching onto whoever gave her the highest bid.

"You were there for the party and dinner he gave in her honor, right?" She nodded. Damien knew she had been there, had seen her walking arm in arm with various high-ranking vampires. Since Killian brushed her off before Elora's return, Korina had taken to getting cozy with others who had some power. She was nothing if not ambitious.

"You heard what he said about her and how he made changes to her genetics. She's the only vampire who was born, Korina. Not made, but born." He let his words sink in and felt her shift in the seat.

"And her blood is unique, in terms of what it does and its properties. Everyone wants control of it for what it can do. Killian wanted it to replace humans — a new and better blood source. Humans want it to attempt to create some type of cure or vaccine, maybe even a weapon."

He didn't say that Elora was the key to either the continuation or eradication of two species that had been fighting for centuries and were at war before the Accords were developed. Damien didn't explain that he fought to get her away from Killian, not because of any moral code, but because it was her. He didn't tell Korina that his foul mood came from the fact he let himself fall in love with her even though he knew it wouldn't work, that she would go to Silas's manor with him as her shadow.

"And you? What's your stake in this? You have her hidden away somewhere. We all know that." There was a line of desperation in her words, a lingering hint of what they once shared before he understood who she was.

"Jealousy doesn't suit you. It never has." She scoffed before checking her make-up in the rear-view mirror.

"Jealousy implies she has something I want." Damien grinned, cold and cruel, as she ran her finger under her bottom lip. He knew her tells, knew when she was lying or deflecting.

"Doesn't she though?" He laughed, the sound filling the otherwise silent car, watching as she flinched, and her gaze hardened.

"I expect something in return for my help, Damien. A favor of my choosing."

"I knew we would get to this part. What favor?"

"I'll let you know."

"Any favor, as long as it doesn't involve or hurt her, Korina. Understand?" She rolled her eyes and opened the door, hesitating just long enough for the car behind them to honk at her.

"Fine. But she'll be the death of you." Damien stared straight ahead as the door slammed shut. Little did Korina know Elora already was. The death of every belief he had held about Killian, every belief about her. She was the death of almost every selfish urge he had, every desire for anything and everything beyond her.

He checked his phone before pulling out into traffic, leaving Korina to report back to Darian. Damien hadn't given an answer to his offer, but Korina knew him well enough. She would tell Darian that he refused, and the vampire would rage, swear to find him and Elora, promise to drag her away from his dying body. The vampire always had a flair for the dramatics when his temper was tested. He would send someone after them, if he hadn't already, adding to the growing list of people who wanted her.

It wouldn't matter soon. She would be safe behind the walls of Corvin Manor. He forced out a breath at the thought, at the fact Silas had thought he wouldn't take accept the invitation to join him, as if there were other choices. Even if he hadn't offered him the job of protecting her, Damien would have done it anyway. He would have watched as she found her place with Silas, watched as she learned who she was and what Killian did, even watched as she fell in love with someone other than him.

Chapter 18

Elora

They listened while the footsteps grew quieter as they descended the stairs and disappeared. Elora could hear Viktor's voice traveling through the floor as he spoke with the people below them. Neither of them said a word, each listening as the feminine voice told Viktor she had heard arguing, proving Connie to be a liar. She winced as Viktor's muffled thanks reached her and she rushed to the window, parting the filthy curtains to watch as he exited the building. But she hadn't expected him to look up, to look back.

She wasn't sure if he could see her through the dirt and grime on the window, but it didn't matter at this point. He knew Connie was lying and would come back. If anyone would recognize a liar, it would be him.

A wave of pain forced every muscle in her body to contract and she hissed slightly, almost doubling over. She knew that one part of it was from seeing Lukas's murderer, from the flashes of memories that came with him glancing up with such an empty expression, none of the warmth she had known. Instead, she only saw him holding the gun to Lukas's head, felt his lips on her forehead, heard his voice as he talked her out of a breakdown in the hospital. Lies. It was all lies. She wanted nothing more than to run out the door and chase him, scream at him, demand that he explain, and then — Elora took a deep breath, closing her eyes as she exhaled. Then she wanted to hurt him, destroy him like he destroyed Lukas, destroyed her.

Wyatt's hand touched her shoulder, and she spun around, suddenly achingly aware of his presence, of the scent of his blood filling the room until she couldn't escape it. It was in the air, the couch, the carpet. She gasped softly at the contact, at the tiny sharp points she could feel touching the inside of her lips. Slowly, Elora ran her tongue across them, wincing as they drew blood.

"Are you okay?" His words were a whisper, barely audible, but still she nodded, unable to explain who Viktor was, explain what she was. For Wyatt, she was a human of no real consequence, someone with a troubled past. She wanted to live that existence as long as she could. Until she left both the apartment and him behind.

"He's one of the people looking for me." Wyat pushed back a strand of her hair.

"Can I ask why he's looking for you?" She shrugged at his question.

"I left a very dangerous situation, and he's one of the people who wants to take me back." Not a lie. Viktor didn't want to take her back to the Tower, but he did want to hand her over to those who would use her.

"Well, my aunt and I will do what we can to help you and keep him away from you. You don't need to worry about that." She smiled at him even as her eyes wandered to his neck, to the pulse she could sense beneath the surface. Her stomach clenched once more, and she felt herself raise a hand towards his face, caressing his cheek. Wyatt's amber eyes widened in surprise even as he leaned into the touch, closing his eyes, and she took a step forward. Under her touch his pulse quickened, the blood rushing as she moved closer, letting her hand wander down to his jawline and then his neck. He shuddered at the touch and her grin grew until her fangs were on display for him to see if his eyes were open.

The scent of his blood was intoxicating, overwhelming every screaming and silencing voice in her head that wanted her to stop, to remove her hand and send him away, make him promise to never come back. But instinct, or what she assumed was instinct, shut those voices inside a box, tossing them off the edge of a cliff and into oblivion until all she could hear was his pulse and the rush of blood just below the surface.

She leaned forward, letting her lips trace his jaw, tiny nips and kisses as he moaned and melted into her touch, into her arms. He was putty in her hands as she savored the feeling of control above everything else. Wyatt shuddered slightly as Elora's lips found his neck, kissing along his pulse until his breath hitched. Under her shirt, his rough hands caressed her skin, roaming along her ribs in a way that made her body break out in goosebumps.

"What the fuck is going on?" Somewhere in her blood addled consciousness, Elora knew a voice was raging through the space as a door slammed, the windows behind her rattling in their frames. She heard it all as if she was underwater, muffled and incoherent even as she gave Wyatt's pulse one more kiss, running her tongue over the vein she could sense. He was delicious and the promise of what was to come was almost too much.

"Back up." Elora cried out as Wyatt was ripped from her grasp, her fangs aching at the loss of him, of what he had to offer. With her balance unsteady, she staggered back, blinking frantically as the room slowly came into focus. The first face she saw was Wyatt's, dazed with his eyes like glass, distant and unfocused as he stared at her. Then Damien's, the very image of murder and wrath, as he grabbed Wyatt's shoulders and shook him. Wyatt's head thrashed around on his neck, body limp in Damien's grasp.

Understanding struck her like a fist to the face, pummeling her to the ground as she took one step back and then another until her back hit the window. Her hand rose to her mouth, feeling the sharpness of her canines, something that had never happened before.

"Hey, it's time for you to go." Wyatt's eyes finally focused and shifted to Damien, who released his shoulders.

"Who are you?" Wyatt's voice sounded distant and strangled as he forced the question out. Damien turned on his heel and opened the front door, gesturing for him to leave.

"I'll only leave if she tells me to." Elora's gaze moved between the two of them, between Damien's expectant expression and Wyatt's confusion. Her heart had stopped racing, and the gnawing had settled into a dull pain. Somehow, the denial of what she had almost tasted was worse than the hunger.

"I'm okay, Wyatt. Go ahead. My roommate and I need to have a conversation." She gave him a wry smile, and he nodded.

"I'll see you tomorrow." She jerked her head into a nod at his statement even though she knew he wouldn't, that Damien would make sure of it. They needed to leave before Viktor came back. Wyatt hesitated a minute before stomping towards her and pulling her into an embrace, locking his arms around her waist as she wrapped hers around his neck, pushing her face into his shirt. Elora inhaled softly, taking in the scent of cinnamon and blood, feeling the heat from his body. And then nothing. He reluctantly removed his arms, and she followed suit, watching him leave with tears in her eyes, feeling the loss of him and normalcy so intensely it hurt.

The door slammed shut and Damien locked it, listening as the sound of Wyatt's footsteps grew quieter and then disappeared completely. Elora wrapped her arms around herself, preparing for whatever Damien had to say, preparing for both cruelty and kindness, since she never knew which one she would get.

"What the fuck were you doing?" His voice was rough and forced through his clenched jaw and gritted teeth.

"Nothing." She declared as she leaned back against the window, feeling the coolness through her shirt.

"Really? Because it looked to me like you were about to either fuck him or feed from him, probably both." She didn't say anything. There was nothing to say since she couldn't deny it. Damien knew the truth, had seen it with his own eyes. There was no hiding from that. She considered making a comment about jealousy but bit her tongue since that topic always brought out his vicious side.

"Exactly." He spat out before turning to the bag on the counter she hadn't noticed. Slowly, he started pulling out collection bottles, four in total, before putting three of them in the refrigerator. The door to it slammed shut with so much force, she heard the bottles clink together.

Elora swallowed and hugged her arms closer as she edged towards the counter. Damien raised a brow as he opened the bottle he had left out and gestured to the stool along the edge. She dropped onto it while Damien moved through the kitchen with a tense efficiency, selecting a glass from the cabinet and filling it to the brim. With a glare, he slid the glass over to her.

"Here. Drink before we have any more problems." Elora didn't even bother with a response, just grabbed the glass with both hands and drank, each swallow easing the tension in her body, her muscles finally relaxing and leaving her sore from how tightly they had contracted. Within seconds, the glass was empty, and her eyes were closed in satiated ecstasy. She let out a little moan as she opened her eyes and found Damien watching her, a dark expression on his face she wasn't sure she wanted to read.

"Better?"

"Yes. Thank you." He grunted as he finished his own glass and put both in the sink before clutching the edge of it. His shoulders rose and fell as he took a deep breath and shook his head. Finally, Damien turned back to her and reclined against the counter, hands shoved deep in his pockets as if it would help keep him under control.

"What the fuck happened?" Elora glanced at the front door before moving away from the kitchen, sinking onto the couch. The fabric was rough against her skin, and she felt it even through her pants and shirt as her eyes landed on the gift Wyatt had brought with him. The sketch book was still there, along with the two coffee cups and the forgotten sketch. Carefully, she moved them onto the coffee table and leaned back, trying to figure out how to explain.

"Viktor showed up." Whatever Damien thought she was going to say, it probably wasn't that. He pushed off the counter and rushed towards her before hesitating at the edge of the couch.

"What does that mean, Elora?"

"Exactly what I said. Wyatt and I were talking, and I heard voices in the hallways. It was Connie and someone else. It was Viktor. I recognized his voice." Damien cursed loudly before he started to pace, hand running over his hair and down his neck.

"What did she say?"

"She told him that she had never seen me before in her life and that this apartment was empty. But then he talked to the people below us." He cursed again without her needing to tell him how that went. "I saw him. When he left, I looked out the window, just a little bit." She pulled her knees to her chest.

"So, we have multiple problems today." He was talking more to himself now, eyes frantically roaming over the room, but never settling on anything. Elora doubted he was even taking in anything until his focus landed on the sketchbook and pencils.

"Wyatt get you that?" She nodded and refrained from grabbing it, suddenly protective of the gift. He met her gaze, eyes devastated in a way she didn't understand.

"I didn't know you liked to sketch." Elora laughed, loud and obnoxious, and he stepped back.

"That would require speaking to me, Damien. It would require asking me questions about myself. You were always too busy avoiding me or being hateful." For a minute, he was perfectly still in a way that was unnatural. Not even the rise and fall of his chest as he breathed was visible. Before she could blink, he was sitting on the couch beside her, face in his hands, shoulders hunched over.

"I—" he stopped and took a breath. "I was a prick, Elora. I can admit that."

"Why?" It was a question she had asked him back in her room in the Tower, back when she had given up on surviving, on living, on escaping. In that moment, she had told him it didn't matter what his response was and yet the question rushed past her lips, her desperate need for an answer surpassing any dignity she had left.

"At first and for a long while, I despised you." Elora let out a harsh laugh, and he did the same. "I know it's a shock to you, but I did. In my mind, you represented everything I hated. You were the daughter of one of the most powerful vampire heads. I had been told he had given you everything. I thought that you had been given everything I was denied—a home, food, protection, security, everything." She shifted slightly, leaning closer as he kept staring at the sketch book on the table, at the sketch of Wyatt's face.

"Before Killian turned me, things were rough. Lived on the streets for the most part. Or abandoned buildings or houses. Food was scarce. My mom—" He paused. "My mom did what she could. Worked as a source for money. But it was underground then, and she didn't usually get paid much. My dad was a piece of shit. He stole from Killian and offered me up as payment when he got caught. I was turned instead after I killed him. A part of the bargain. His life as payment instead of mine."

Elora listened to each word as he seemed to struggle to speak. The pain he felt seemed to radiate from his body to fill the space between them. It was a physical thing that wrapped itself around him like a barrier that would protect him as he told her his story. It shattered something in her and yet she could recognize the way they were both broken and simply trying to pick up the pieces to fuse them back together. Perhaps that was why they always seemed drawn to one another even as they fought it. The darkest parts of their souls sang a song to each other that only they knew. Maybe that was why she always felt safe with him, felt at peace.

"I despised you for throwing that away because of a stupid act of rebellion. I had heard of the vampires who were there the night you disappeared, had seen what happened to the ones who failed to find you. Killian's wrath was legendary. Their deaths took hours. And when I saw you in the hospital, when I found you, all I saw was a person willing to throw away what others would kill for, a person who caused the deaths of dozens of vampires. And I hated you for it, even as I started to question everything. Even as I stopped hating you."

He finally looked at her as she took his hand, pulling it away from his face and holding it in hers. His eyes were bright, glistening slightly as if tears were just on the horizon. His free hand cupped her cheek as his mouth opened and then closed.

"I was wrong, and I'm sorry. I would never ask you for your forgiveness, not when I took you back to him. But I'll do everything I can to keep you safe now, to make up for what I did, for what I allowed to happen to you."

"You didn't know, Damien. I didn't even know until I saw his face again, until I heard his voice that first day after I woke up. You don't need to make up for anything." He gave her a small smile, and she leaned into his hand as his thumb brushed along her cheekbone.

"I do. And I am. I'll stay by your side until you make me leave, until you force me away." She moved closer, her hand never leaving his, as she closed the space between them and kissed his cheek. He stiffened, his hands spasming slightly at the touch. Elora met his eyes, deciphering the myriads of emotions warring for supremacy—shock and resignation fading away to leave behind something soft and tender. He never had looked at her this way, never looked at her as if she was something to be loved and not used, something to be protected and held, not handed out as a prize.

Her heart skipped a beat as the overwhelming desire for him to kiss her, for him to pick her, took over every thought. She wanted to choose him when nothing else in her life had been her choice. She wanted him to touch her with her permission, not someone else's.

She realized then that what she wanted more than anything, more than her freedom, more than anonymity or normalcy, was for him to consume her.

Damien leaned back, hand falling from her cheek as he pulled the other from her grip and stood. He cleared his throat and stared pointedly down the hall.

"I'm going to take a shower and then we should talk. Between Viktor showing up and what I learned today, we may need to leave here sooner than I thought."

"Okay." Her voice sounded pathetic, and she scolded herself as he walked away with muscles tightened and steps stiff. All she heard was his bedroom door open and shut as she reminded herself that he was simply settling the score he saw between them. Once they were even, this would all disappear.

Chapter 19

Damien

"**F**uck." It was the only word that would come to mind as he closed the bedroom door and pulled out his phone to send a message to Silas.

Need to come now. They're too close to finding her.

Damien didn't expect an answer from him right away and he pulled off his shirt before collapsing onto the bed. The blanket was rough on his bare back, the coarse threads digging into his skin. But he welcomed the sensation, welcomed anything that forced away the feeling of her lips on his cheek, her face in his palm, the sight of her in Wyatt's arms.

That had been too close, too dangerous. Elora never would have forgiven herself for it, would have seen it as proof she was Killian's daughter through and through. The accident with the compulsion had been difficult enough for her, but feeding from Wyatt would have shattered her just as she was recovering. Damien could see it in the way she held her head higher, how she met his gaze, how she responded with snarky comments. He wanted her to fight with him, wanted her to push against what he said because it was proof she was beginning to heal, that she wasn't the shell of a woman he had seen on that bed the night she killed her father.

Damien cursed once more and got in the shower, trying to filter through everything Korina had said, everything that he needed to tell Elora. Darian and the offer he extended that required her to be handed over. That wasn't even an option, considering what Darian wanted with her. Revealing that would have to be handled with care. She remembered Darian, remembered what he had done. He knew where her mind would go, what would be dragged to the forefront.

He sighed and turned off the water, drying off quickly. He wasn't sure what mentioning the vampire would do to her, what reaction it would cause, but he knew it wouldn't be pleasant. But keeping it from her would be worse since Silas probably knew, would tell her once she arrived and got settled. No, the information needed to come from him. She had to know he wasn't going to accept the offer and give her away.

Elora was exactly where he left her, the sketchbook on her lap as she shaded something with her pinky, brows furrowed together. He smiled softly, watching her even if the fact Wyatt gave her that gift made his blood boil. It wasn't the fact that he gave it to her or the fact that she loved it. The sketchbook was a reminder of what was lost between them and what she had given to the human. A piece of herself. Just a little fact. But it was more than that and he knew it.

Damien guessed that Lukas had known, had thought to ask during their card games. Not for the first time, he wondered exactly how much his friend had learned about her, how close they had gotten even as she retreated into herself. There had been so many times he had walked in to find them laughing and talking, so comfortable in one another's presence. At first, he had been irritated at how easily Lukas had become enamored of her and didn't see her as Damien had. But after that, it had become jealousy as Damien saw how close they had become, how much she preferred Lukas to him.

"Let's talk." Elora glanced up before closing the sketchbook and crossed her legs in front of her, the very picture of anticipation. Damien didn't go to her side, didn't sit on the couch beside her, and he noted the flash of disappointment on her face as he took a seat on a barstool.

"I met with someone today to get supplies, and she gave me some news about the Ashcroft family that pertains to both of us." Elora inclined her head to continue.

"Darian is attempting to take over the Tower and the entire vampire family as well. He saw Killian's death as an opening and is trying to take it. The problem is the Ashcroft family operates by very specific rules, and he didn't earn the right to lead them." He read the confusion on her face before explaining the process. "The Ashcroft family, as well as Radcliff and Ravenwell, operate based on power. Whoever is the strongest leads, and that was Killian. He killed the previous head vampire for the position and only the vampire who killed him gets the position, no matter what bribes or promises Darian gives out."

"I don't want it." Damien shook his head at her declaration, her voice shaking. Her hands clenched into fists before releasing once more.

"I know. The problem is that there's no proof of who killed him, so Darian is taking the opportunity to combine his own family with Ashcroft." Again, only a nod as she listened to him.

"An accumulation of power. Killian talked about the same thing sometimes, before I escaped the first time. He said it would be better if all vampires were under one leader, one person who called the shots. For him, it was the best way to deal with the humans." Damien studied her for a second.

"I thought you didn't remember anything." She shrugged.

"It comes back. Or some of it. Pieces of information, bits of memories. Sometimes something triggers it, and I get glimpses. Honestly, it would be better if it stayed forgotten." Since accepting that her memory loss was real, Damien had often wondered if it was better for someone to forget their worst memories, their most traumatic events of their lives. It would mean he didn't remember when his father handed him over to Killian to pay his own debts, wouldn't remember stabbing him in the chest and watching him die, wouldn't remember finding his mother's body.

But to live with fragments of memories, whispers of experience that you can never latch onto, never fully understand or remember must be torture of the worst kind. It wasn't a true forgetting, not how she experienced it. It was constant teasing, a constant anxiety knowing that at any moment something could trigger a memory, that she could remember another instance of abuse at Killian's hands or the hands of those he gave permission to. And the question always lingering in the back of her mind about what else she didn't remember, wondering if it was worse than what she did recall.

"I'm going to be blunt, Elora, because I don't know how else to be." She huffed a laugh at his comment, and Damien grinned despite telling himself not to. "Darian offered me a role in the Tower as his second-in-command, the same role I had under Killian."

"In return for what?" He could hear the shift in her tone, could see the change in her body language, the way she was poised on the couch to stand and run based on what he said next. She knew exactly what Darian requested and was only waiting for him to voice it.

"You, but you know that." As he knew she would, Elora jumped to her feet and rushed towards him, hands fisted at her sides, fury carved into her features. Her green eyes that always held that strange luminescence burned as if her entire being was made of fire and all he could think was he would let her burn him without a single thought.

"And? What was your response?" He met her gaze, refusing to cower from the violence he saw there. Before him was a woman who would not be used again, who would never be tied to another bed and drained within an inch of her life. It was beautiful, mesmerizing, and he couldn't look away even as he wondered if he was going to be stabbed again.

"I didn't give an answer because I don't want retaliation yet. I'll give him one when we have you safely with Silas. No one knows where his group lives and won't be able to get to you once we get you there. Then, I'll tell him no." Her shoulders relaxed and her eyes softened slightly, relief washing over her features. Cold fury ravaged his chest as he realized she believed he was going to say yes, that he was going to accept Darian's offer and hand her over.

"Did you think I would say anything else?" Damien didn't want her to answer, didn't want to hear her say it. Elora threw her hands in the air, a growl of frustration sounding as she turned away from him.

"Yes." She took a breath and twisted to look at him. "It isn't—. It isn't you, Damien. Please believe me when I say that. But there's only so many times you can be betrayed before expecting it from everyone, even those who have given you no reason to think they would."

And just like that, the pain in his chest was gone as he watched her defeated face turn back around. It wasn't about him, but about what the world had shown her and the role they had forced her into.

"I understand." She shook her head at his statement and settled back onto the couch, pulling her legs close. "No, I do," he repeated softly.

He paused for a moment, chewing the inside of his cheek, choosing his words for what came next.

"Do you want to know the rest of it?"

"Do I have a choice?"

"Of course you do, Elora. From now on, you have a choice." She was quiet while she weighed his words, his proclamation.

And then she met his eyes, hardened in determination, and nodded.

"Darian wants you as his bride." He heard her breath hitch, tracked the way her hand went to her neck, her collarbones where her scars were. Damien saw her sometimes, tracing them when she thought he wasn't looking. Her mouth moved slightly as she counted them, running her fingers down each one. It was methodical. Ritualistic.

"Of course he does. Nothing quite like taking the girl you watched grow up, the girl you fed from as your wife." Her eyes moved across the floor, as if frantically searching for something hiding there. With jerky movements, almost robotic, Elora's hands rubbed at her arms, and he finally saw the panic in her eyes, the fear that she was once again in that room with him.

Damien rushed and crouched in front of her so he could see her, so she could see him. He didn't touch her but called her name as he had done when she was trapped in her nightmares, trapped beneath their bodies.

"Elora, come back to me." Her eyes flicked to his, confusion clear on her face. "Come back to me, love."

"I won't do it, Damien. I won't go back to him or anyone else like him. Do you understand me?" Her voice was all broken pieces and rage, fear and determination.

"I know. And I'll help you make sure you don't. Every step of the way."

"How? Once I'm with Silas, you're leaving." He smirked at her as he stood, enjoying the way her eyes tracked him, the way they followed his every move.

"Who said anything about me leaving? Silas offered for me to join him, to stay with you." Elora's lips quirked, the smile there just below the surface that promised mischief.

"Can't leave me, huh? Can't bear to be away from me for too long?" She drawled, and he leaned in.

"Exactly." Her eyes darted to his mouth, and he flashed her a grin even as his pulse quickened, as he watched her bite her lower lip before meeting his gaze. She stood and stepped forward, closing the space between them and tilting her head slightly towards him. An invitation, a silent gesture of consent. And he wanted so desperately to give in, to cup her face in his hands and bring her close enough that there was no space left between them. He wanted to find out what her lips felt like, the way she would ruin him and leave her mark on every part of him. Silently, she did what he had only considered and took a step forward. He felt her now, her body barely touching his, her breath on his face as she searched his expression, and her eyes traveled down his face to his lips once more.

Without a word, knowing the agony it would cause her, he shook his head and stepped back.

"Why not?" Damien flinched at the anguish, at the anger in her question.

"You deserve better, and you need time, love." Suddenly, she pushed him, her hands flat against his chest as she forced him away from her. He grunted slightly as he fell back against the counter, the edge of it striking his back.

"Don't you dare! Don't you dare tell me what I deserve or what I need. I'm offering myself to you. After years of everyone taking and taking from me, stealing from me, I am giving you me. You say I get to make my own choices now, but you refuse the one I am making." She turned away in a flurry of crimson hair that settled around her shoulders, but not before he saw the betrayal, the tears rushing down her cheeks from those deep green eyes.

"I'm sorry," he whispered, as she furiously wiped away the wetness from her face and laughed bitterly.

"Don't fucking bother. I'm the one who's sorry. You're right, Damien. I have horrible taste in men." Elora didn't look back as she grabbed the sketchbook and pencils, clutching them to her chest as if they would absorb everything she was feeling. She straightened her spine and forced her shoulders back as she once more wiped the tears from her face, erasing any evidence of the pain he had caused. And that was the problem, even if he couldn't or wouldn't explain it, Damien knew that he would only bring her pain, either because of something stupid he would end up doing or because Silas would arrange his niece's marriage considering the archaic bastard that he was. Either way, it would be anguish, would be torture.

He wished she had stabbed him again. Maybe that would hurt less than the look on her face.

Chapter 20

Viktor

Elizabeth was awake and waiting for him when Viktor approached her cell. Her eyes were bright and feverish, skin flushed, cheeks rosy, and lips a deep red. If she had been human, he would have thought she was sick.

"Excellent timing. I just fed."

"I can tell." She giggled and ran her finger along the corner of her mouth as if there was some remnant of her food there.

"Do you think it feels this good for her?"

"And how does it feel?" He scolded himself for the question before it even finished leaving his mouth. Elizabeth arched back against the bed, her chest rising as she let out a moan that sounded distinctly sensual.

"It feels euphoric, like an orgasm coaxed by expert hands. Not like the boys in school, children who didn't know what they were doing and only cared about themselves. No, feeding is bliss. It's addicting, something to lose yourself in when it happens."

She watched Viktor's face, searching for any reaction to her description as he thought back to the party and the moment Elora drank for the first time since the medication left her system, since her urges returned. There had been hesitation in her expression, concern and fear, but also something more akin to gratification. Maybe not the bliss or euphoria that Elizabeth was describing, but something like it. If the experience hadn't been marred by the environment, by everyone watching, by her utter terror of what she was, would it have been similar to what Elizabeth felt? Or did Elizabeth simply take pleasure in it, something that was unique to her?

Viktor cleared his throat as Elizabeth stood and started moving towards the bars, her fingers curling around the cold metal, an inviting smile on her lips.

"No, I never saw Elora react like that." She gave him a curious look, as if she didn't believe him, before leaning back, hands still clutching the bars.

"Disappointing." She pulled herself back up, hair falling against her back in a pale haze. "What are you here for now? More blood? More questions?"

"A field trip." Her brow quirked and her eyes moved over his body, no doubt searching for any sign of a lie.

"To where, exactly?"

"To get your sister. I know where she is, or roughly where she is, and I want you to help me find her."

"And how would I do that?"

"We both know how. It's all you talked about when you were first admitted. The invisible tie between you two. Screaming at the therapists that you could feel her, sense her nearby. Let's test that."

"Don't pit us against each other. She's my maker, and I belong to her. We are one, sisters by blood and by choice."

"And here I thought you despised her. You said as much the last time I was here." She waved her hand in a dismissive gesture.

"Emotions are complicated. Our relationship is even more so." Elizabeth's fingers traced her scars as she sat back on the bed. Her eyes darted to him, fierce and hungry. "But never doubt my devotion to her." Viktor cursed silently. This obsession and loyalty would only cause problems, if not now, then down the line.

Maybe it was a mistake to bring Elizabeth in, to use her to get to Elora.

"But I'll help. I want to see her again. I want to feel the sun on my face and smell air that isn't filtered and pushed through a vent."

"There are, of course, stipulations. We can't have you running around outside, can't risk you attacking and escaping." With an eye roll and sigh so dramatic it was comical, she flopped onto the mattress.

"Taking all the fun out of everything." Viktor held up one of the syringes Thorne gave him and nodded towards it.

"This is the only way you're coming with me." He gave her a moment to consider the options, weighing the medication in his hand with her desire to find Elora. Viktor knew which one would win, that her single-minded obsession would force any and all thoughts away.

"Fine." With slow, almost hesitant steps, she came back to the bars and pulled up the sleeve of her shirt. Viktor shook his head.

"Neck. Quicker that way." She grinned, canines bared, and pulled down the collar of her shirt, exposing the pale skin there. Now it was his turn to hesitate. He knew he should have had someone restrain her or at least use handcuffs to keep her from grabbing him. The smile on her face was positively feral as she watched him.

"I promise I won't bite. I just fed, remember?" Elizabeth's assurance did nothing to assuage his fears, and he held the side of her neck, forcing her head to the side to draw the skin taunt. He told himself to not remember the way he had done this with Elora, how he had touched her the same way when he changed the bandages on her neck.

"Unfortunately, you won't feel the sun." He sunk the syringe into her neck and pushed down the plunger until every trace of the medication was in her system. She rolled her neck as her lips turned downward and gave him an assessing look.

"And why's that?" Viktor grinned as he handed her a large jacket and she shrugged it on.

"It's the middle of the night. We're going to surprise them with a visit." Viktor had decided that waiting until morning was a bad idea. Elora had seen him, probably heard his voice as he spoke with the old woman. And she would have told Damien, who would have made a plan to get her out of there. Waiting until morning was a risk he couldn't take.

"My sister never liked surprises," Elizabeth commented as Viktor reached into his pocket to make sure the other syringe was still there.

"I remember," he responded as Elizabeth pulled her hair over her shoulder, arranging it into a messy braid before holding her hand out for a tie. He shook his head, and she huffed before tossing the braid over her shoulder.

"Exactly how close were you two? You seem to know quite a bit about her." Viktor said nothing, just gripped her elbow and led her up the stairs.

"Close enough."

"You were meant to collect information about her, right? It's the whole reason you were there." He refused to respond as he stopped and opened the front door as the sound of her giggle found him.

"Yes. She was a mission. Someone I was meant to get close to." And he had succeeded. He had talked with her every day, listened to her anxieties and complaints, absorbed her darkest thoughts and fears only to repeat them back later to the council. Until he had stopped. Until reciting what she had told him in confidence had felt like a betrayal, and guilt had ravaged him like a disease.

"Tell me about her time there. I've always been curious." Viktor led her to the passenger seat of the car before getting in on the driver's side. He wasn't sure how to answer that, wasn't sure how to describe the person he had spent four years with. Even on his days off, Elora had been his focus, cataloguing and repeating each word she said like a recording in his mind. At first, he considered not answering Elizabeth at all, not sure how much he would unintentionally reveal concerning himself. But her obsession was what made her useful, made her cooperate.

"She was like most residents, I guess. She took her medication and went to therapy. She had already been there a while before I was sent in to gather information. At first, she was distrustful and avoided me like she did with the other nurses. From what I gathered, they had been cruel to her. Comments about her scars and gossiping about how she got them." The words dried up as he turned onto another street and away from the house.

"But I helped her after a bad therapy session. Talked her through a panic attack or something. After that we became close, and she would find me during the day to talk. She saw me as a friend." He hesitated as they grew closer to their destination. It wouldn't take long to get back to the Garden View apartments.

"Elora was fierce. She fought what they were telling her. Hell, she fought some of them physically and scared off quite a few nurses. She was also prone to depression, where she lashed out at herself instead of those around her. But she never lost her fire, no matter what they told her. Your sister was strong. A force of nature filled with all the destruction that came with that."

"Yes. She was definitely a mission. Nothing more." Viktor's face became stone as he watched the road. Too much had been revealed in his tone, his words, and Elizabeth had caught it. Yes, he could admit he respected her. She had lived through a nightmare and then had been dragged back. Elora wasn't to blame for what her father had done or what he had created her to be. Killian thought he had created the newest product for the market, a replacement for humans who had become too aware to be a submissive food source. All he had done was create a sacrificial lamb. And it had been Viktor's job to deliver her to the slaughter.

Chapter 21

Elora

She couldn't sleep and, for once, it wasn't because of night-mares. Instead, she kept replaying the scene with Damien in her head, trying to figure out exactly what had gone wrong, what she had misread. She had never let anyone touch her before, not even the so-called relationships she had in high school before they would see her scars and run away. Her first girlfriend had tried to kiss her after a movie, softly pecking her lips before try-ing to move to her neck. It had ended with Elora in tears as she curled into a ball, scolding herself for believing she wasn't cursed only be seen as a damaged item that brought revulsion. It had always ended with more sweaters as she grew more and more reclusive, no matter how hard Elizabeth tried to draw her out. But she had been willing to risk that with Damien, had be-lieved that he would reciprocate.

She had walked away furious at her own stupidity, at her delusion that she wasn't broken. Thoughts whispered cruel words into her ear as she tossed and turned in the scratchy blankets.

Dirty. Defiled. Guilty. Over and over like a broken record, re-peating constantly until she jerked herself out from under the blankets and yanked her sketchbook to her, ignoring the book lying beside it. It had appeared yesterday, had been there when she returned from a shower. There was no need to ask where it came from. And yet, despite the small act of thoughtfulness, Damien stepped away.

Her hand reached to her chest and scratched at her sternum as her brows furrowed at the strange sensation. It felt like a pull, a tug that made it feel like thousands of tiny bugs were scurrying across her skin. With a soft sigh, Elora turned to a blank page and started to sketch, line after line, until something began to take shape, something she hadn't planned.

She recognized the eyes first. Soft and wide, giving an innocent appearance framed by long lashes and crowned by arched brows. If she had any means of adding color, the irises would be ice blue with a ring of navy around the pupil. Then the lips took shape, full and turned up in the corners in a perpetual smirk that only left in the darkest of moments. Elora put the pencil in her mouth and scratched her chest once more, nails digging in through the cotton shirt. With a huff, she pulled the collar out and peeked down, wondering if one of the bugs that had to live in the carpet had somehow made it down her shirt.

Nothing. Just redness from where she had scratched at it. But the feeling did not abate, simply grew stronger, a tugging feeling that made her want to leap to her feet and walk towards the door.

"No." Elora whispered as she recalled the last time she had felt this. There had been only one other experience of the inexplicable sensation of being pulled towards something. Or someone.

"Elizabeth," she whispered before she tossed the sketchbook from her legs and jumped from the bed, rushing towards the door. Her heart was in her throat as the sensation grew with each step, her pulse racing as she felt her sister grow closer. It was like a warm breath on her neck, a gentle touch on her cheek.

Elora threw Damien's door open to find him perched on the edge of his bed, arms resting on his knees as he stared at the carpet. His hair was more disheveled than normal—messy, as if he had also spent his night tossing and turning. The navy shirt he had been wearing was in a pile on the floor beside him, and she took in the tattoos along his muscular chest and arms as his focus darted to her.

"She's here." Damien leaped to his feet, grabbing his shirt and pulling it on.

"What? Who?" Her hand went to her sternum once more, rubbing and scratching as the sensation became all-encompassing, the only thing she could focus on.

"Elizabeth. I can't explain it, but I can feel her. I could feel her at the hospital before the therapy session and I can feel her now. She's close, Damien." He nodded and grabbed the car keys from the bedside table. No further questions. No doubt that she was wrong. Trust. He trusted her completely.

"Shoes. Now. We need to leave," Damien ordered, and for once, she didn't argue. Her steps were heavy as she spun and ran to her room, grabbing the journals, sketchbook, and letter from Denise, which she had hidden away. Her hands trembled as she zipped up the bag and raced into the kitchen, pulling on her boots and lacing them.

Elora let out a sharp hiss as the sensation grew until it felt like someone was ripping her heart from her chest, pulling it through her rib cage. Damien shot her a look, his strangely calm face contorted in concern, while she simply shook her head. Describing the feeling was impossible, and she knew she finally sounded as crazy as Denise always tried to convince her she was.

"Elora! Where are you?" She froze as Elizabeth sang her name, drawing out each syllable as she did so until it was almost a song. The ache in her chest finally started to subside now that Elizabeth was so close. Both Elora and Damien listened as two sets of unhurried footsteps finished coming up the stairs before making their way down the hallway.

Damien took a step towards her and crouched down, meeting her eyes. His face was empty and his dark eyes were devoid of any emotion as the tiny flecks of gold disappeared while his lips tightened into a thin line. Was this who he was for Killian? Was this the mask he wore each time he was sent on a mission? It was terrifying and intriguing all at once and she repressed a shudder she wasn't sure was caused by fear. He held his finger to his lips and handed her a knife similar to the one she used on her father. But the blade on this one was thicker and shorter and she gripped it in her hand, feeling the weight of it in her grasp.

"Stay behind me," he whispered, and she inclined her head despite knowing that she had no intention of doing that, of allowing him to put himself at risk for her. Lukas had already sacrificed himself for her, and she wasn't letting it happen again. She didn't want to be protected. Every part of her vibrated with the need to fight, to draw blood if necessary.

Two sharp raps sounded against the plywood door, echoing down the empty hall. Elora said a silent prayer that Connie was a deep sleeper, that she wouldn't be drawn out by the noise.

"Elora," once more, Elizabeth sang out her name, elongating each letter. "Come on out, big sister." Damien stood once more and checked his own weapon — a knife similar to hers in his hand. He gave her a curt nod that she returned before standing, waiting for instructions.

The door burst open in a flash of splintered wood and shouts. Damien threw his body over Elora as the pieces flew across the room, revealing a strength neither of them thought Elizabeth had. Arms wrapped around her, holding her to Damien's chest as both their hearts pounded from surprise. Slowly, Elora and Damien stood to watch Elizabeth saunter into the apartment, appearing very much the same as the last time Elora had seen her. Her cool blond hair hung down past her tailbone, resting against the plain grey jacket she wore on top of what looked like a white shirt and jeans. Not the hospital attire Elora had ex-pected.

"I like the new apartment, Elora. A little old and needs some paint, but it works." Elizabeth's eyes roamed over the space, ig-noring the door that was now on the floor. "It's like the one we talked about sharing before everything happened."

"A bit overdramatic, don't you think?" Damien replied, and she grinned at him, revealing her dulled canines. Elora watched her sister move, tracking how she wandered over to the kitchen counter and leaned against it like she was waiting for something.

"Maybe so. But I was worried when she didn't answer."

"Why are you here?" Elora took a step towards her sister, but Damien grabbed her arm, pulling her back once more.

"I've made friends, and they needed help. Honestly, it's get-ting annoying helping people deal with you." Elizabeth jerked her head towards the doorway that was now filled with a body that caused Elora to take in a harsh breath before darting for-ward.

"You fucking prick! I—" Once more Damien grabbed her be-fore his eyes settled on Viktor.

"Are you here to try again, Viktor? Did the Resistance tell you to fix your failure?" Damien taunted, and Viktor tensed before stepping into the apartment.

"She's coming with me this time. Don't make me kill you, too." Elora's grip on her knife tightened as she once more saw Lukas kneeling on the garage floor with Viktor's gun against his temple.

"I will kill you." Her words were a vow, a promise, and Viktor shifted slightly towards Elizabeth as if she would protect him. But he didn't contradict her, didn't even glance in her direction. Elora could feel the rage radiating from Damien as he stood completely still beside her.

"Let me understand. You brought my sister, thinking it would encourage me to cooperate. And if I still refuse? What's your plan? Hurt her? I doubt you could. Hurt me? We both know that isn't an option." Elora took a small step forward, savoring how Viktor moved away from her. Before she learned the truth about him, his fear of her had broken her heart, had left her hating her very existence. Now, it was absolute perfection, and all she wanted was to drink it in, bottle it so she could replace the memory of the Viktor she had believed he was.

"If you ask me, I don't think he actually had a plan beyond using me to find you." Elizabeth arched slightly and cranked her neck one way and then the other, before meeting Elora's gaze. The blue in her eyes was now bright, as if there was a light shining just on the other side, illuminating them with a curious gleam that felt inhuman.

"Did you feel me? I know you did. I can feel you, too, if I get close enough." Elora nodded slightly at her sister as her hand went back to her sternum, rubbing gently at the spot that had hurt only minutes ago.

"Yes," Elora whispered. "It's the strangest feeling. Like a burning and itching and tugging all at once. I felt it in the hospital before our meeting and then until I left, but I never realized what it was."

Elizabeth nodded along with each word, her smile growing impossibly bigger as she pushed herself off the counter and clapped her hands together. Elora forced herself not to think about every other time she had seen this very action, every memory of excitement and joy that was now marred.

"I knew it! I knew it. The doctors told me I was imagining it and then gave me more pills. But I knew." The words were more for Elizabeth than anyone else in the room, a vindication that Elora understood all too well. For a second, her heart went out to her sister before Elizabeth fell silent, the light gone from her eyes. Being told that your entire reality was wrong, that what you were feeling was a figment of your mind was like being suspended without gravity in pure darkness. There was no way to know which way was up or down, left or right. No anchor to hold on to.

Witnessing that ever-present smile on her sister's lips disappear was jarring, and Elora reached for her, wanting to hold her in her arms like Elizabeth had done for her after the nightmares woke them both up. She would pull Elora into her lap, brush the damp hair from her forehead, First, one side then the other, Elizabeth would wipe away her tears before pressing a kiss to her forehead. She would hold Elora tightly as Elizabeth hummed softly until the shakes receded and her eyes began closing once more. Back then, Elizabeth was safety and warmth, a constant presence, strong and steady in everything she did. Now, Elora wasn't sure this was still the person she had known.

"Anyway, I don't know how he plans on making you go with him, and I don't care." Elizabeth shrugged slightly before pulling herself up to sit on the counter. A tension settled between the four of them as they waited for the other to speak. Damien stepped up next to her as Viktor eyed the two of them, watching each movement closely before glancing at the knives in both their hands.

"I don't want this to turn violent."

"You're a fool, Viktor. A complete and utter fool. At every moment, you've messed up and now you're trying and failing to fix it. You want to know the funniest part?" Elora paused as she noted the shift in his expression, the hardness that had settled into his features. It was the version of Viktor who had been in that garage. A sense of stillness filled her being, slowing her heart rate, stopping the trembling in her hands. She gave him a small, bitter grin as she shook her head.

"The funniest part is that if you had done things a little differently, I probably would have willingly gone with you. I was so sure you cared about me, so sure that you simply wanted to protect me and wouldn't care what I actually was. I was an idiot. I was the affection starved patient who latched onto the one person who showed me kindness and I would have followed you anywhere." She shrugged once more.

"You showed your hand too soon and now you're stuck here cleaning up your mess like the pathetic piece of trash you are." Viktor darted forward with his hands clenched into fists, but Elora held her ground even as her sister held her arm out.

"I think she's earned the right to express herself, considering what you did, Viktor. You should at least hear her out."

"That wasn't the plan," Viktor ground out through gritted teeth in response before his glare returned to Elora.

"Look, everyone. This has been a wonderful reunion, but we were just heading out." Damien adjusted the bag on his shoulder and nodded towards Elora. "So, unless you have something up your sleeve that you're hiding for some reason, we'll be leaving."

Elizabeth chuckled slightly before she glanced between Elora and Viktor.

"I never agreed to make you go with him, Elora. Only to help him find you." It was an apology even as Viktor's curses filled the space and Elora let out a soft laugh. He had nothing to use, had nothing that would force her to follow him.

Then—a knock on the door frame followed by one word that shifted everything.

"Elora?"

Chapter 22

Elora

"Wyatt, leave now. Run!" Elora's frantic screams filled the room as Elizabeth pushed herself from the counter and pulled Wyatt into her arms within a single heartbeat. She was quick, her movements a blur as she dragged a confused Wyatt into the middle of the room.

"Elizabeth, don't. He has nothing to do with this."

"But he looks like such fun. You're just collecting men like nothing, aren't you?" Elizabeth smirked at her sister as she forced Wyatt to his knees.

"If you hurt him, I will kill you." Elora's words were harsh and quiet as she glared at her, hand gripping the knife tighter, pulse racing. She could feel her blood pounding through her. Before this moment, she had never hated her sister. Elora had pitied her, had felt guilt for what she had done to her, and had loved her. Every image of a smiling and laughing Elizabeth flashed through her mind. But that version of her sister was dead, and she understood that now. The person—no, the vampire before her now was no longer the sister who had beaten up a boy for telling the school about her scars, the sister who had told her horrible puns until she started laughing again.

Elora wasn't sure who she was looking at, but it wasn't Elizabeth.

Wyatt groaned as he tried to adjust his position, the linoleum digging into his pants. His panicked eyes moved from Elora to Damien before craning to see the owner of the fingers digging into his shoulders, holding him in place.

"What's happening?" Wyatt's question was directed at Elora, his eyes wide in panic and something like anger. His voice wavered slightly as her hand clenched by her side.

"Yes, Elora. What's happening?" Elizabeth parroted the question as she bent down closer to him. "Tell me, did you get close to my sister? Did you fall in love with her, too?"

"Elizabeth, stop." Her sister cackled and ran one of her hands through Wyatt's hair before gripping a handful and yanking his head back.

"I'm just having a conversation. Nothing wrong with that. However—" she inhaled deeply and closed her eyes, "—he does smell exquisite." Elora waited for the panic to set in, a feeling that had become a friend over the years. She watched Wyatt's confused face as Elizabeth caressed his cheek and waited for the pounding heart, the shallow breaths, the shaking limbs.

They never came. Only calm and cold determination. Wyatt wouldn't be a sacrifice.

"You really brought a vampire to use. Genius plan, Viktor." Damien finally spoke, his voice coming from his spot beside her. He had been silent, as if allowing her space to do and say what was needed.

"This wasn't the plan. Let him go." Viktor fumbled for something in his jacket pocket before pulling out a syringe.

"No, no. Did you really think I would let you give me the second dose? Maybe my sister is right. Not the brightest member of the Resistance, are you?" Elizabeth studied each of them in turn, noting the weapon and syringe. "Drop them. Maybe I'll let him go."

"Let him go or I'll kill you," Elora responded, each word coated in ice and Elizabeth hesitated.

"That is an interesting thought. I do wonder what would happen with the whole tie between us part. If you kill me, would that hurt you?" Elizabeth shrugged slightly as she waved a hand through the air. "But I have a different theory I want to test. Want to know what it is?"

"Elizabeth, enough." Viktor took a step closer, and Elizabeth dug her nails further into Wyatt's shoulder, causing him to jerk slightly. Elora moved towards him, but stopped at the smile on her sister's face, at the feeling of Damien's hand on her arm. She turned her head and nodded to him before returning her attention back to the person who was once her sister.

"Tell me, Elizabeth. Then let him go." Elizabeth sighed deeply and leaned her head back, as if she was asking for strength. She kept her focus on her sister, not allowing herself to even glance at Wyatt. The confusion and betrayal there was too much for her. This was his reward for an act of kindness, for pulling a stranger out of a spiraling panic attack. Elora knew better than anyone that no good deed goes unpunished.

Denise.

Lukas.

Wyatt.

All punished for good deeds.

"You turned me with a single bite. Quite unheard of, from what I understand. And it made me wonder, does that extend to me as one of your created?" A slow and deadly grin carved itself across her face as the question hit Elora. She didn't know the answer, but it didn't matter. Not right now. Not when Wyatt was still kneeling at Elizabeth's feet, neck so close to her fangs.

"Okay. Now let him go."

"I never agreed to that." As if in slow motion, Elizabeth sank her teeth into Wyatt's neck, and Elora listened as his cry of pain echoed in the ancient apartment, felt the moment something surged inside her and filled her with something horrifically empty and cold.

"Stop!" Two things happened instantaneously at the sound of her command. The first was that Elizabeth went completely still, as if frozen in place, every limb and muscle hard as stone. The second was that Wyatt fell from her arms, collapsing in an unconscious heap on the floor. For a heartbeat, no one moved. Not even Viktor. They all stared at the vampire who seemed stuck in time, whose face betrayed nothing. It was as if reality had ground to a halt.

"We need to go." Damien stared at the scene in front of him as Elizabeth seemed to regain control of her limbs and fell to her knees, eyes glazed over and face slack. It was the same expression Connie had worn, but this time it didn't fill Elora with guilt. Viktor seemed to be in some type of shock as he stared at Wyatt's body on the floor, face scrunched in absolute disbelief and horror. This couldn't be how he saw this happening. When Wyatt appeared in the doorway, Viktor had probably expected to use him to force Elora to leave with him and then he would be the hero by bringing her to the Resistance, the very people he was supposed to deliver her to in the first place. Elizabeth's actions had changed everything.

"Elora, now," Damien commanded softly as he gripped her arm, pulling her away from the three figures before them. All she wanted to do was pull Wyatt into her arms and beg his forgiveness, apologize for causing any of this to begin with. It all traced back to her and a new weight settled heavily on her shoulders along with the others she already carried, even as she nodded and began to turn away.

"Don't. Come with me or he dies." In a strange sense of Déjà vu, Viktor pulled the gun from his waistband and pointed it directly at Damien, who merely smirked at him. Unless he managed to hit him somewhere vital, it wouldn't cause any lasting harm.

"Just stop," Elora pleaded softly and watched the confliction on his face. Elizabeth hadn't moved, only stared at her hands as if something was fundamentally different about her world. A gentle tug on her arm and Elora turned, arranging her body so Damien was blocked. Viktor wasn't going to shoot her, wasn't going to risk messing up this mission any more than he already had.

"Stop!" Viktor's shouts filled the room even as Elora heard him adjust as she followed Damien into the hallway. Despair flooded her system, and she felt her shoulders slump. A part of her had held out some level of hope that Viktor wouldn't be able to do this to her again, wouldn't be able to betray or hurt her. Silently, she berated herself for her softness, for her attachment to someone so determined to drag her kicking and screaming to her destruction.

Another step followed by a series of whimpers from Elizabeth and Wyatt.

"We need to take him with us, Damien. Please." Elora stopped and turned back, studying the body on the floor. Wyatt's skin had gone pale, all traces of the beautiful golden tone gone from the blood loss. His features were twisted in pain and his mouth was pressed into a line until his lips disappeared entirely. She turned her focus back to Damien, who only shook his head before gesturing for her to follow.

"I can't leave him here. It's my fault—" Elora froze as Damien rushed her and threw her to the side as a series of pops echoed down the hall. Each one was followed by a grunt and curse until Damien finally sank onto the floor. Time stood still for a moment as screams erupted from her mouth and tears formed as she crawled towards him, fingers digging into the floor, nails breaking as she frantically rushed towards him.

As she grew closer, Damien pushed himself to his knees, glaring at Viktor, who still held the gun in his hand, aimed directly at his chest. Elora gripped his arm, eyes searching his body and noting the three wounds on his chest. The scent of his blood hit her, and she whimpered. There was so much. Why wasn't he healing faster? Her fingers wrapped around his forearm, and she followed as he stood, hunched over slightly.

"Don't, Elora. Stay or I shoot him again." She darted a glance at her sister on the floor, whose own focus was locked on to Viktor and the gun in his hand. Elora struggled to understand her expression, the desperation and rage lining her features. Slowly, their eyes met, and Elizabeth nodded, understanding flowing like an electrical current between them. Elizabeth shifted and rushed Viktor in a haze of color, grabbing his wrist and squeezing until his scream erupted from his lips and the gun fell to the floor.

"Now!" Her sister's command rose above Viktor's shouts and Damien's grunts of pain as Elora grabbed Damien's arm, throwing it over her shoulder. Inch by inch, she dragged him down the stairs, cursing each time he fumbled. Behind her, she could hear bodies hitting the floor, could hear Viktor shouting at her to stop, could hear her sister's cackling laughter.

Blood dripped onto the dirty linoleum as they moved and she peeked slightly at Damien, the lack of color in his face and the way his arm wrapped around his chest. His breathing became shallower, erupting in rasps as her heart raced in her chest. Flashes of Lukas kneeling on the ground before Viktor raced back, the look of silent acceptance that he would die to protect her. Her face tightened into an expression of pure determination as she threw open the back door to the apartment building and rushed out into the darkness. It was silent. The only sound was Damien curses and grunts of pain mixing with car horns and late night traffic. No one was out as Elora moved them both into the alleyway and let Damien rest against the dumpster.

"My pocket. The keys," he forced out between breaths. "We need to go." His hand trembled as he reached into the front pocket of his jeans and pulled out a set of keys, jerking his head in the direction of a grey four-door car—basic and nondescript. Elora nodded, not trusting herself to speak, to not fall into a weeping mess at the sight of him bleeding everywhere.

"Can you drive?" She tossed his arm back over her shoulder and started to pull him towards the car as she considered his question. Before graduation, she had taken driving classes with Elizabeth. It had been a few weeks of practice driving on side roads where the damage they did would be minimum.

"Yes. I can do this." Elora didn't give him a chance to ask questions as she yanked open the passenger door and helped him slide into the seat. His face rearranged itself into one of anguish as he cursed loudly. Sweat lined his brow from the effort of adjusting himself against the leather seat while her own shaky hands lingered on his chest before closing the door. Behind the fear of Damien's bleeding body, she vowed Viktor would meet his end at her hand. There would be no feeding from him. There would be no mercy or pity. Anything she felt for him was gone the moment he pulled the trigger. It just took time for the rest of her to catch up to what her mind already knew—he was dead to her, and she would make sure his end was painful.

Her body trembled as she slid into the driver's seat and she started the car, pulling out onto the road. Damien muttered directions between rasping breaths, forcing them out between clenched teeth. Turn by turn, they eventually found themselves beyond the city limits. The car was silent as they rode down the empty road with her glancing at him so frequently that she was surprised she managed to stay in the lane. But she needed to see him, hear him breathe to know he was still alive. By this point, his healing should have started, and his breathing should have evened out. The gunshot wounds didn't seem like they were anywhere vital, but she wasn't sure she would even know. It wasn't like she had seen many people get shot or had witnessed vampires heal after something like this. The only experience she had was her own healing after Killian's visits, and that seemed minor in comparison.

Another shuddering breath from Damien and she shook her head. She needed to check on him, needed to see the wounds, and figure out what was happening. But there didn't seem to be any turnoffs or side roads to be found. Merely row after row of trees, of shrubs, and dirt. Not a single sign of life other than the birds that flew overhead and the one rabbit she saw darting across the road.

Finally, after another curse from her mouth, she spotted what looked like a turnoff, a dirt driveway or road. She wasn't sure and didn't care which one it was as she turned the wheel and forced the car off the asphalt main road, wincing when she heard Damien hit the car door from the harsh movement. Trees lined the dirt path, and the car jerked with every bump and dip. She flinched each time, imagining that it had to be agony for him as he slumped in the passenger seat. Only the seatbelt was keeping him upright.

"I'm sorry," she whispered as she leaned forward, trying to see anything beyond a never-ending sea of leaves and bark and the dirt road. "I'm sorry." Nothing. Not a sound from him.

She wasn't sure if this would lead to a house or something else, but she turned slightly and slammed on the brakes as the car skidded to a stop, deciding it didn't matter where they were as long as she saw him. Around her, reality seemed to fracture, tiny cracks working their way through her barest amount of control. Her thoughts fought against each other, all of them screaming at her to do different things—keep driving, park, go for help. All combined as the center of her world continued to bleed out on the busted leather seat. The scent of blood filled the car as she crammed her panic into the recesses of her mind, in the space where her repressed memories used to be housed. Panic would be of no use here.

Instantly, the car was in park and turned off before she leaned over the center console, pulling at Damien's jacket. He didn't make a sound as she adjusted his body so she could pull one arm out of its sleeve and then the other. She sucked in a breath at the sight of his drenched shirt, of the complete lack of color in his face, and the fact that his skin was impossibly cold. None of the warmth she so desperately craved.

"Fuck," she shouted as she threw the driver side door open and ran to the other side, opening his. None of this was meant to happen. They were supposed to leave and end up on Silas's doorstep where she could decide what to do next. She was going to move on from him and try to figure out how to live when everyone kept looking for her, kept hurting people to find her.

"Get him in the back seat," she whispered to herself. "Get him comfortable." Step by step, she talked herself through it. Desperately hoping it would help ease the growing dread in her gut when he didn't respond or even twitch.

Damien winced as she pulled at him, trying desperately to get him out of the car and into the back seat. But his body wouldn't budge, as if he was bonded to the leather.

"Damn it! Please. Come on." She kneeled down and wrapped his arm around her shoulder before standing back up, grunting slightly as he moved with her. Inch by inch, Damien slid across the leather and out of the car until his body almost dropped into the dirt. Only Elora's grip kept him from collapsing. Her heart raced and her muscles screamed as she dragged him to the back door, his boots dragging in the dirt beneath them. His pulse was faint. So horrifyingly and terrifyingly faint.

She turned and backed into the seat, pulling him along with her as she slid to the other side. Inch by inch, he moved with her as she fought to keep her grip. The arm rest and handle on the door pressed into her back as she adjusted, positioning him between her legs in an effort to keep him on the seat. One leg fell off, resting on the floorboard, and his arms hung limp on his stomach, while her heart raced in her chest as she felt him grow weaker. His head fell to the side as blood still seeped from the wounds. It was slower now, but it didn't matter. So much had been lost, and he shivered in her grasp as tears finally began to race down her cheeks. She cradled his head in her arms and arranged them both so she could study his relaxed features—cold and smooth as if carved from marble. Dark locks of hair fell against his face, and she brushed them away, kissing along his cheekbone as she wept.

He needed to feed. Maybe if she could replace what he had lost, the wounds would close, and he would wake up. He would have a smug smirk on his lips and would joke about her holding him and nursing him back to health.

A bolt of lightning struck her, forcing every other racing thought from her mind even as she fought to accept what this course of action would mean.

"No," she whispered as she sat up a bit straighter and adjusted him so she could see his face completely. "I won't lose you."

Elora didn't allow herself to think about what she was doing or what the consequences could be. None of them mattered as long as he lived, as long as he woke up. Even if he didn't want her, even if he denied her, she wasn't willing to live in a world without him in it. No one knew her so intimately, saw through each mask and recognized each nervous tick. No one else made her *feel*. Yes, it was anger and irritation and pain at times. But it was also acceptance and peace and safety. She was more than willing to feel the bad if it meant also feeling the good. He was the anchor of her reality, her tie to everything beautiful. She wouldn't force him to be by her side even if it meant the worse type of torture, because it would be better than nothing, would be better than the hole that would be left behind if he was gone.

She felt her fangs grow longer, and she sank them into her wrist, resulting in a rush of blood flooding her mouth. Quickly, she forced the wound against his lips, bringing his head to the crimson liquid like helping a child drink. His brows furrowed slightly as the taste hit his tongue and he latched on. His own teeth crashed into her skin, and she felt him drink, each pull no longer painful. It didn't feel like burning, like being lit on fire from the inside out. It felt like ecstasy, like bliss, so reminiscent of the first time she drank blood at the banquet.

It had never felt like this when the others had drunk from her.

Pull after pull, Damien drank deeply until Elora wrenched her wrist away and watched the wounds on his chest, hoping and praying that they would close. Slowly, so painfully slowly, Damien's breathing grew stronger, his pulse more consistent, and the bleeding stopped all together as the bullets were pushed from his body. She felt him stiffen as his body rejected the foreign items and then relaxed as the metal rolled onto the floorboard of the car.

Softly, she ran her fingers through his hair and rested her cheek on top of his head, inhaling the scent of blood and gunpowder mixed with something that was undeniably him, a scent she had grown to crave. Elora lost herself in the rise and fall of his chest, in the steady sound of his breathing, before they both fell asleep.

Chapter 23

Viktor

His head was pounding when he woke up with his face plastered on the floor, breathing in the scent of mold and blood. A groan sounded and pain reverberated through his body as he rolled over onto his back, feeling his shirt snag slightly on what he assumed was dried blood.

"Fuck," he whispered as he draped his arm over his eyes, trying desperately to shield the fluorescent lights. Slowly, he pieced everything together. Elizabeth had bitten the human, and then Viktor had shot Damien. A sense of pride rushed over him at the memory, at the brief flash of surprise on the vampire's face. With any luck, Damien would be dead. The bullets he used were made by the Resistance, coated with a substance that made it difficult for vampires to heal and made them easier to kill. A small grin played at the corner of his lips as he considered the potential success before reality came crashing down around him. Thorne and the Resistance wouldn't care that one vampire was dead. Instead, they would care about his two monumental failures—losing Elizabeth and letting Elora escape again.

"Are you okay, boy?" Viktor's eyes snapped open, and he lurched up, ignoring the pounding in his head and the unsteadiness of his feet. He closed his eyes for just a moment, desperately attempting to steady himself as he waited for the world to stop twisting.

"Yeah, I'm good." He glanced down at his shirt and winced slightly at the blood littering the fabric, the tear along the front that exposed his bleeding stomach. It didn't seem too bad, nothing life threatening. A part of him wanted a mirror to see what damage had been done to his face this time and discover if the scars Lukas had given him now had friends.

"Do you know what happened here?" The voice behind him was gruff and impatient, as if asking these questions were a waste of his time. Viktor took a breath and turned around, despite not knowing exactly how horrible he looked. A middle-aged man in a large sweater and jogging pants stood there staring at him from behind bushy gray brows and a large beard. Viktor surveyed the damage from where Elora's apartment was wide open, and he could make out the remnants of the door in the center of the dining room. There were dried puddles of blood along the floor right inside the doorframe, with a trail of it disappearing behind the figure who was still standing there scowling at him.

"Home invasion. Robbery. They got away." He forced the words out, figuring that the lie wasn't far-fetched based on what he knew about the area. The man in front of him nodded and peeked inside the apartment, shaking his head as he surveyed the damage. Viktor followed this attention before wiping his hand down his face, noting the red flakes left behind.

"Did you see anyone else leaving?" Viktor glanced at the man before looking up and down the hallway once more, searching for any sign of how long he had been out. Hours based on the light that he could see trying to get into the apartment from around the curtains.

"Nope. I was coming up to check on Connie, but saw you lying there." The man darted a look at the other apartment door. Was that the old woman's name? Wyatt's aunt or grandma. He wasn't sure exactly what the relation was. Viktor rolled his neck, trying to loosen the tightness in each muscle and ligament as the man stepped forward and knocked on Connie's door. He shoved his hands in his pockets as he waited, and Viktor only watched the scene play out. Not out of any desire to see if the woman was there, but maybe if he gave it a few minutes, the pounding in his head would ease and he could think a bit clearer. After a moment, the man turned to him and shook his head, brows furrowing together.

"They take anything?" He asked, and Viktor shrugged.

"Not sure. I was going to go in and check." A slow nod before the man stepped back, eyes roaming over Viktor's face and body. Was he trying to figure out if Viktor was the home intruder? The thief? Was he trying to figure out if he was a criminal? But the man said nothing, just turned and walked away as if this were nothing more than a friendly visit. Viktor wasn't even sure who the man was, but he brushed off the interaction and entered the apartment. Two discarded bags lay on the floor in the kitchen, surrounded by pieces of splintered wood. Blood had pooled on the linoleum. Wyatt's blood, more than likely.

Viktor kneeled down beside the bags and unzipped the first one, digging through the items there. Clothing, it looked like. Jeans and shirts mostly. A knife and a small stack of money. Nothing important. Viktor tossed it aside and grabbed the second one. This one had more girth to it, and he unzipped it, smiling softly as he took in the items. Elora's things, from what he could tell. Shirts and a couple of dresses. A sketchbook and a collection of three leather-bound diagnosis manuals. Viktor's heart leaped into his throat as he ripped one of them from the bag, opening to the first page to find Elora's name and a set of years.

Denise's journals. For a moment, he couldn't believe his luck. Another consolation prize to bring Thorne, he supposed. It wouldn't be enough to save him from the punishment that he would no doubt be handed, but it was something. He didn't flip through the pages or read the entries, even though he wanted nothing more than to do so. The man from the hallway may have contacted the police, and he didn't want to be there if they showed up. Instead, Viktor dumped the other bag out and put the journals in it, leaving behind the rest of Elora's items. He felt a small tinge of guilt that she had left behind the sketchbook. It had been the one thing she had wanted in the hospital, the one thing she had asked for that had been denied over and over. She wasn't allowed art supplies outside of art therapy, and he had seen how defeated she had become after each refusal. When they finally did give her materials, she had a breakdown, triggered by something in her past. It had been early in his time there, when she hadn't gotten close to him yet. This was a sign that she had healed enough to engage in her passion. And now she had to leave this one behind.

Viktor made his way down the hall, searching the rooms as he went. Damien and Elora had obviously packed as they prepared to run, but that didn't mean nothing hadn't been forgotten or left behind. He went for the back bedroom first, finding nothing but a crumpled shirt and a messy bed. Nothing in the closet or the drawers. Nothing was hidden under the mattress. After a moment, he moved on and glanced in the bathroom, finding discarded bottles of shampoo and toothpaste.

The last room he entered was Elora's. He knew it instantly in a way that he couldn't fully articulate. There was no outward mark that this was her room, no glowing neon sign with her name or picture of her on the desk. Maybe he had just come to know her well enough to sense her, could recognize her in the most mundane of things. Slowly, he went through the same motions he had with the first bedroom. The closet yielded only a jacket that he doubted she wore while under the bed revealed dust and a couple of spiders. The dresser still held a few articles of clothing that must have been left behind. Finally, a fantasy book sat on the nightstand next to a pile of discarded pencils and an eraser. She may have packed the sketchbook itself, but had missed those.

The bond, he realized. It's how Elora knew they were there. They had only focused on the fact that Elizabeth could feel her, that she could lead him to her. Viktor hadn't considered it would work the other way around as well, would warn her that someone was close.

With a soft sigh, he left her space behind and wandered into the living room. He let his eyes roam, noting the torn and stained couch, the coffee cup that had the logo for the cafe down the street. His steps were slow as he moved across the room and stopped in front of the window, in the very place she had been standing that day. With a single finger, he pushed the curtain aside and stared down into the street. Even through the dirt and grime on the window, Viktor had been able to see the conflicting emotions on her face, could practically feel the rage and pain radiating from her. And he deserved it. Every single tiny particle of her hatred and betrayal was warranted, even if he had tried to tell himself that it didn't matter.

He hadn't wanted to kill Lukas. There had been no sense of satisfaction when he pulled the trigger or saw the dead body. It was simply another vampire life he had taken. That sin could sit right next to the others, right next to the one where he killed Jaime.

Viktor let the curtains close and headed towards the door, grabbing the bag with the journals off the floor before opening the refrigerator to see if there was any blood stored. Thorne would expect him to have searched each and every inch of this apartment to ensure he didn't miss anything. This would fall un-der that umbrella.

There were three collection bottles in the front, along with coffee creamer and milk. Elora, he guessed. She had always had a love for coffee. Flippantly, Viktor moved the bottles aside and noted the two collection bottles behind those, each one stamped with a symbol, something like a crest that included a K surrounded by a rose. It was Killian's crest, a marker that these bottles were unique or special. And Viktor could guess why, as he shook his head in disgust. Either way, he grabbed each one and laid them in the bag, hoping they would stay cold until he got back to Thorne. This could be his best bet to remain in their good graces. It wasn't enough by any means to do what they needed to do or to fully test what they needed to test. But it could be enough to start.

With a sigh, he swung the bag over his shoulder and took a final look around the room, eyes lingering on each item as he fought off the sudden attack of nostalgia and grief. The apartment he shared with Jaime had been smaller than this but had looked the same. Theirs had only one bedroom, but other than that, the layout was exact. Side by side, they would study for their courses, teasing one another to elicit laughter as they grew frustrated with whatever the material was. Jaime would help him with his flashcards for nursing terms, while Viktor did the same in return while eating microwave food to ease their stress. It hadn't been perfect by any means, but they had been happy. Until they weren't.

Then, as if Jaime's ghost was there haunting him, Viktor turned and fled.

Chapter 24

Damien

They rode in a strained silence through Silas's front gate after Damien used the keycard on the panel. Elora seemed distracted in a way that put him on edge. Once more, she pulled at her sleeves and tried to curl up on the passenger seat—all moves he had become intimately familiar with, all signs that she was retreating again. He couldn't decide which part of that night had caused this or if it was a combination. There had been an immense rage in her voice when Viktor came through the door and demanded that she go with him. The hatred in her eyes would have been enough to kill anyone with a single glance, and there was the devastation that came when Elizabeth sunk her teeth into the human. And her screams of fear when Viktor shot him.

The healing process from the three bullet wounds was a bit more difficult than he thought it would be. He hadn't expected to pass out from blood loss and thought he would have healed up before that happened. But he had woken up in her arms, cradled against her chest as she held him tight, which was somehow worth losing consciousness for. For a long moment, he hadn't moved despite knowing they needed to leave. He kept perfectly still, controlling his breathing so he could keep them suspended in time. It took everything in him to not turn and look up at her, to not trace the lines of her face as she slept with an arm wrapped around his chest. It was a window into a different reality. One where he could give her what she needed and what he felt for her wasn't something to be suppressed but allowed to blossom.

But when she woke and her cheeks turned pink before shifting away, opening the door behind her and crawling out from underneath him with muttered words, Damien hadn't known what to do. The connection was broken, and he could no longer pretend he hadn't rejected her, hadn't seen the agony in her eyes as he did so. Instead, she curled into the passenger seat and waited for him to start the car, and all Damien could think was that something felt different, felt fractured.

Silas stood at the entrance to the manor as they pulled up, hands in the pockets of his beige slacks. His hair was combed back away from his face, though it still looked slightly messy, as if he had tried to tame it moments ago. Concern lined his features as Damien and Elora exited the car and approached him. For hours or maybe minutes, the three of them stood at the entrance to the manor in silence, each one of them considering what to say or what to do. Damien didn't know how to even begin. He was an outsider and an intruder staring at two people who had a shared history that only one of them remembered. Silas's eyes roamed over his niece, taking in the blood on her clothes and neck, the tangled mess of her hair, the distant expression on her face. His lips twitched slightly before he spoke, breaking through the anticipation lingering between them.

"I have a room ready for you, if you want it. You can clean up and then we can talk when you're ready." Elora nodded at her uncle, her appraising gaze moving from his eyes to his lips to his hands as if she would be able to discern any lie he may be telling. "Is there anything you need?"

"Blood," Damien interjected quickly. Due to her sped up hunger cycle and the last time she fed, Elora would be in dire need. He had heard her whimpering slightly, spotted her hand pressing into her stomach as if to suppress the hunger and pain that came with it. Silas nodded before turning back to his niece, his expression the very picture of concern and warmth. It wasn't faked as far as Damien could tell. He seemed to be a vampire who knew a type of reckoning was coming, a demand that every truth and failure be brought to light. It was as if he were preparing to be deconstructed and then hopefully put back together again. Damien wasn't sure she would be gentle with him.

"Thank you. I would like a shower and blood before we talk." Silas nodded and turned so she could enter while Damien followed in step. He wasn't sure what his role here was. Nothing had been established besides him becoming a part of the Corvin family. As far as Elora was concerned, everything was still unsettled. Was he still meant to be her guard? Or would he be sent from her side to do whatever Silas wanted of him?

"I assume there were issues getting here," Silas muttered softly as Elora gazed up at the portrait that held a rendering of her mother. Damien froze for a moment, watching emotion after emotion flutter across her face. Despair and anger and regret mingled with broken and incomplete memories. He wondered if she was remembering the lights on the ceiling that she had told him about.

"Obviously. Nothing we couldn't handle." Silas nodded and closed his mouth, waiting until later to ask more questions even as his gaze dipped to Damien's shirt that was stiff from the dried blood.

"Is that my mother?" Her question tore Silas's attention from Damien as he made his way to his niece. He smiled softly as he looked up, something almost remorseful displayed in his eyes.

"Yes. Her name was Iris. We were adopted together by our parents since vampires don't reproduce." Elora shot him a look and Silas simply shook his head. "Naturally. Vampires don't re-produce naturally."

She only made a noise as she continued to stare at the paint-ing. It was like she was tracing her mother's features, identifying each similarity, each difference. Now that he saw them side by side like this, Damien had to admit the resemblance was there, even if Iris's features were softer, almost duller.

"We were picked to be turned once we came of age and agreed to it. During our childhood and such, we were trained to take over the family, to lead it once our parents retired, so to say."

"And she didn't turn?" Her eyes still never left the painting, but there was a distant quality to them. Like she was trying to conjure up memories of her mother.

"No. At first, she had every intention of doing so and we were going to run the family side by side. But a rift occurred between us, and she left. I didn't see her again until her marriage to Kil-lian and then once a month or so after you were born. The last I saw her was when she came to me for help protecting you." Elora's focus snapped to Silas as her eyes narrowed.

"When? When was that? How old was I?" He raised his hands in a placating gesture and stepped towards her.

"I will answer every question you have. Every question you have ever had. I promise. But let's get you settled." His voice was soft, and Damien watched her physically relax before inclining her head.

"My bedroom?" Silas grinned at her question and gestured towards the staircase in the middle of the room. Damien knew the door to the office he had visited was to the right of the stairs, and he considered waiting in there for him to return. But every part of him commanded that he follow her and so he shifted into position. Step by step, they made their way to the second floor, where the manor branched off into two hallways leading in opposite directions. Silas turned towards the left and opened the first door.

"These will be your rooms. There's a sitting area, a bedroom, and a bathroom for you." Elora nodded and stepped through the door, sucking in a slight breath. Once Damien followed her through, he understood. It was all neutral colors, almost pale by comparison to the room at the Tower. The walls were sage green, and the carpet was a light beige. There was a couch along the wall and a line of bookshelves. An assortment of tables and armchairs were scattered around the room—all covered in grey fabric. If her room at the Tower was meant to be ominous, this was meant to be welcoming, meant to inspire hope and exude warmth. Damien smiled softly as she wandered through the space, fingers touching the furniture and the books that lined the wall, almost like she was proving to herself that this was real.

"Fantasy?" she asked, and Silas grinned.

"They were your mother's favorites. I heard you enjoyed them as well. Though from what I understand you would read anything," Silas hesitated, something calculating and almost fearful in his eyes. "That you would even read a cookbook if it caught your interest."

Elora's steps pounded across the floor, ricocheting within the room as Damien struggled to understand what had happened. Her hands were clenched into fists as a terrifying fury warped her features. He had only seen this type of reaction once—when he had called her by that pet name in hopes of forcing a response. And he had gotten one that had left bruises for days.

"Who told you that?" Silas gave her a sad smile and shook his head.

"You know who told me." A choked sob fell from her lips and Damien was sure he saw tears on her cheeks as she turned from them both and pushed through to the bedroom.

"Well, I don't. Would you mind filling me in?" Silas watched his niece for a moment longer before turning to him.

"Lukas. He reported to me towards the end after I contacted him and asked for information about her in hopes of convincing her to come here. I heard what happened to him. You have my condolences."

"Bullshit. Lukas would have told me." But the denial felt hollow. There had been so much in those last days that had been rushed, and he knew not everything had been discussed. They had assumed they would have time once they got out, that they would be able to sit and reveal everything in that apartment with Denise at their side. Silas gave him a small smile before strolling towards the open bedroom door where they could hear her moving around.

"How do you like it? You can change anything you don't like or want. I want this to be your space." Elora's eyes roamed over the bedroom, taking in the bed covered in linen sheets and a large green comforter. There were no posts on the bed. No silk. No black. Windows with the curtains pulled back lined one of the walls, giving her a full view of the garden below and the trees out in the distance. This room was everything her previous one had not been. Bright, warm, and inviting. A place where she could hopefully heal.

"It's beautiful. It's almost like someone told you what I would like." She let her accusation hang between the three of them as she opened the closet door and studied each article of clothing. It matched what Damien had suggested perfectly, though the colors were more varied and there seemed to be other options as well. Choices. Silas had offered her choices. He saw her exhale and then turn to them both.

"Thank you, Silas. Please have the blood brought to my room. I'm going to take a bath." Her words were cold, robotic, and directed only at her uncle. Damien reined in a flinch at the formality of the dismissal.

"Of course. We can talk as soon as you're ready." She nodded and turned from them both, entering the bathroom and locking the door behind her.

Damien stood there at a complete loss for what to do next, where to go, or what to say. He didn't want to leave her, but Silas gestured to him to do just that, and he did as he felt the vampire fall into step beside him. They only made it outside the room before Silas jerked his head at the door across the hallway.

"Your rooms. Same design as hers. I don't feel the need to give you a tour." Damien huffed a laugh even as his eyes lingered on her door. Something was wrong, had shifted, and it wasn't just the scene at the apartment.

"Do you think you can tell me what happened before she gets out? I want to know what we're dealing with." Damien opened the door to his new home, leaving it open for Silas to follow. A part of him was surprised that Silas hadn't been lying. His room was almost identical to hers, though the color scheme was darker, almost like the colors were colder. They both collapsed into chairs and Silas reclined into his while Damien found himself leaning forward, arm resting on his thighs. His eyes kept darting to the door, to the room beyond it. It was almost painful to be away from her, like there was something tugging him back in her direction.

"They found her. It was that fucking missing person's alert. Someone in the building knew she was there. Viktor showed up. He was the nurse at the—" Silas cut him off.

"I know who he is. Continue." Damien fought against asking exactly how Silas knew who the nurse was and decided it was a question for a later time.

"He came with Elizabeth, her foster sister. They have a tie between them, from what I understand. Elora said she could feel her. That it felt like a burning sensation in her chest. Like there was a tugging there until Elizabeth threw the door halfway across the apartment." Damien watched the slight twitch of Silas's brow, the flash of curiosity in his eyes.

"Viktor demanded she go with him, and Elora had a few things to say in response. Then it all went to hell." He ran his fingers through his hair and stretched his back slightly, wincing at the dried blood still stuck to his skin. "A neighbor she had gotten somewhat close to tried to intervene and Elizabeth bit him. She called it an experiment to see if her bite would turn him, like Elora's did for her. After that, I was shot three times, and we escaped."

He let out a breath as Silas seemed to mull over his account while he tried to remember if he left anything out.

"Elora. She was able to compel Elizabeth, another vampire. I've never seen it done before." A hum sounded from Silas's lips as he considered everything.

"We know that she's unique, that she's basically a brand-new creature. All of this is both surprising and not surprising at the same time." Damien lifted a brow and waited.

"Since we don't know what the changes made to her means, we can't anticipate anything. We can't be surprised if we are already expecting to be surprised," Silas explained, as if he has made some grand statement or revealed the secret to life.

"And you were wounded? Shot three times?" Damien nodded at the questions.

"Yeah. She drove for a while but stopped when I passed out from blood loss. I didn't realize he had hit me anywhere important, but I guess he did. The wounds didn't seem to heal like they usually do." Another hum as Silas thought through something.

"But you survived and brought me my niece." Damien winced at the familiarity of those words, could almost hear Killian's voice uttering a very similar phrase when he arrived with Elora unconscious in his arms.

"I suppose so." It was the only response he could think of as his eyes darted once more to the door, to the vampire just across the hall. Silas let out a slight chuckle and stood.

"Take a shower and change clothes. There are things in there for you as well. We had to make some guesses on what we bought, but it should work. I'll have some blood brought up for you as well. I have to imagine you're hungry after losing so much and healing at the same time." There was an edge to Silas's words, as if he thought Damien had lied somewhere in the story. Damien simply nodded and waited for his new vampire head to leave. He didn't want to have to admit he wasn't actually hungry. At least, not like he should be. Instead, his only thoughts were on getting back to Elora, to see her and know that she was okay, to bridge whatever the newest gap between them was.

Chapter 25

Elora

She took longer in the bath than she needed to, picking and choosing from the shampoos and soaps that lined the marble counter. A large mirror hung on the wall with tiny lights along the edges, but she refused to look at her reflection. There was nothing worth seeing—only tangled red hair that had grown too long and shadows under her eyes. Their brightness was diminished once more as she drowned in her guilt over not just feeding Damien her blood, but over Wyatt and Elizabeth. Without Elora's presence in their lives, neither of them would have ended up in that apartment. Elizabeth would have completed college and gone on to have an amazing future with a career and love somewhere down the line. Wyatt could have dated the cashier at the cafe and continued taking care of his aunt. Their mistake had been welcoming her into their lives, and now they were paying the price.

There was more of Damien's blood on her than she had thought. Her clothes had stuck to her slightly as she undressed, the fabric stiff and itchy where it touched her skin. After sinking into the tub, Elora drained the water that had turned dark pink and filled it back up, dumping in the lavender oil in hopes it would relax her as the bottle claimed. The feeling of him feeding from her rushed back and her eyes closed, letting her head rest on the back of the tub. Being fed from had never felt like that.

Enjoyable. Almost euphoric. It had always been agony until she fell unconscious from the drugs or pain.

And then there were the unknown consequences of it. Elora didn't want to consider those. She didn't want to consider how Damien would react if he found out he fed from her after vehemently vowing to never do so. Would it matter that she was trying to save his life? Would that factor into his reaction? Then, there was the question of what her blood would do to him. Would he become obsessed like Killian and Jonas had? Like Darian had? Would he come to crave it, become addicted to it? She had wanted him to crave her the way she did him. Not her blood, but her touch, her warmth. Her smile. That was what she sought out every time she saw him, even when they fought.

Elora wiped a tear from her cheek before sitting up and hugging her knees to her chest as the water grew colder by the second. She couldn't tell him. That was all she knew. He already thought he had healed without any type of intervention and there was no reason to shatter that illusion. Instead, she would follow his lead and take a step back, allowing the ties between them to fray and snap until there was nothing left. He would live his life, and she would live hers.

The knock on the bathroom door pulled her from her thoughts and she jumped, the water splashing against the edge of the tub.

"Yes?" Her voice was loud in the bathroom, seeming to bounce off the tile.

"Your blood is out here in the sitting room when you're ready." Damien's voice filtered back to her from the other side of the door, and she groaned slightly. Being around him was difficult. His very presence was a reminder of the betrayal she had committed in the back seat of that car. Even meeting the eyes she would have willingly fallen into made her heart twist and turn, made the memory of holding him in her arms while he drank rush back.

"I'll be right there." She winced at the sterility of her words, of her tone. It felt wrong, artificial even. There had been a rift between them before Viktor and Elizabeth appeared at the door. A chasm created the moment he stepped away from her. She felt it so deeply that it was now a part of her even as she still fought to put together all the shattered pieces of her psyche.

After a deep breath, she stood and wrapped a towel around her body and wrung out her hair before adding another towel. Damien wasn't in the bedroom when she walked out and put on a plain dress. Most of the options had long-sleeves, but this one didn't. Instead, they stopped right before her elbow and the neckline came to a point between her breasts, while the skirt fell to her knees. She knew her scars were on display, but maybe Silas needed to see them. She pulled the towel off her head and tossed it back into the bathroom before running a comb through it, grimacing at the length.

Damien stood up as she entered the sitting room and made her way to the desk, where two glasses of blood stood waiting. The image was so reminiscent of how she fed at the Tower that she hesitated for second, fingers outreached and trembling.

Not drugged, she reminded herself. Not here.

Finally, she swallowed down her fears and memories as she took one of the glasses before curling up on the couch, pulling her feet underneath the dress. She could feel Damien's eyes on her, tracking each movement, lingering on the exposed skin that she had never willingly displayed before.

One sip and then she waited before taking another. She didn't believe Silas would drug her, but old habits die hard, especially when self-preservation was a factor. It wasn't paranoia if the shadows in the depth of her mind had been proven real at every opportunity.

"Thank you." Elora still didn't meet his eyes, even as his words reached her.

"For what? I didn't do anything worth thanking me for," she responded before taking another sip. Every part of her wanted to finish this glass and ask for another, and then another. The hunger was overwhelming, agony as her body warmed and her muscles contracted. She hissed softly and felt him move closer, sitting on the other end of the couch.

"For taking care of me. For dragging me out of that apartment. For making sure I didn't die. Take your pick." He huffed a laugh, and she felt the cushion move as he shifted once more. Finally, she finished off the glass, holding the blood in her mouth for a second before swallowing. It moved down her throat and into the cavernous pit of her stomach. Slowly, it worked its way through her body, trailing through her veins and enveloping each and every nerve.

"You would have done the same for me." Cold. Detached. A simple statement of fact. Elora sucked in a breath as his hand reached out and took the glass from her. For a moment, he disappeared, and she listened to the sound of liquid pouring into the glass and his footsteps returning. She waited for him to sit down beside her, for his weight to sink into the couch cushion as he kept his distance once more.

Instead, his face filled her view as he kneeled in front of her and held out the glass of blood. She met his eyes long enough to see the anxiety and concern in every line, every feature.

"Talk to me," he pleaded, and she closed her eyes, not bothering to care that he would see the way she tried to put up a wall between them. The way the deep breath she took was to steady her body and thoughts that always turned chaotic whenever he was near.

"About what? About Viktor and my stupidity? About Elizabeth and how I turned her into a monster? How about Wyatt and the fact he was only turned because he tried to help me? Which one of those do you want to talk about?" She finished the glass in two swallows and set it down with more force than she intended, the sound of it hitting the side table filling the room as she pushed herself to her feet. She felt Damien tense and stand, squaring his shoulders and planting his feet as if preparing for a fight. Her arms crossed over her chest as she walked away, not able to look at him as her mind gained a will of its own, releasing thought after thought without her permission.

"Or about you rejecting me? About how you almost died in that car? About how Viktor almost killed you, too? That you were shot because you protected me?" Her voice broke as she forced out the last of her questions. None of those words were meant to come out. Those questions were never meant to see the light of day. But he had a special ability to break down whatever barrier she attempted to put up, to melt away any ice with just a look. Her memories had once been a weakness, attacking her and tearing her down with each one that resurfaced. Damien had replaced them, filling the voids within her. But he didn't respond, and she listened as he approached her with hesitant steps, as if he expected her to lash out.

Gently, he touched her arm, his fingertips like the cure for every wound she had. She sucked in a breath and felt herself shudder slightly as her eyes closed and her head tilted back.

"I'm okay," he whispered as he moved to face her and cupped her cheek in his hand, bringing her face down until all she could do was meet his eyes. "We are okay."

"But they aren't. Wyatt isn't, and I don't know what happened to him. We left him there with them. With her." He didn't move or look away as she let the guilt within her free. It seemed to cascade from her lips, pouring out in hopes of purging her of its poison.

"Silas can send some vampires to find him. To find Elizabeth, if you want." He wiped a tear from her cheek before pulling her close and she felt every muscle stiffen, felt her thoughts stutter. This was too close. And yet it wasn't enough and would never be enough.

"He'll protect you. You'll be safe here." His words were lost in her damp hair as he pressed his lips to the top of her head. Her eyes fluttered shut, and she let out a sharp exhale. This was where she felt safe. Not with Silas. Not surrounded by a dozen bodyguards or anyone else. But in his arms, feeling the warmth of his body as he held her like something precious. And she had destroyed that, broken it down and threw a match until it burned to ash. Even now, she could sense her blood in his system.

Elora allowed herself one more heartbeat before pushing back and gathering her hair over her shoulder, paying immense attention to braiding the strands.

"You're right. He'll protect me now." She turned back to Damien, noting the confusion there as he tried to understand what had changed.

"Elora, I don't know what happened, but this—" He stepped forward, hand outstretched as if to touch her, as if to pull her back into his arms.

"Nothing happened, Damien," she interrupted before wandering into the bathroom and grabbing a hair tie off the counter where a pack of them sat. Silas really had considered everything, either from guilt or fear of her reaction to him and everything he would say. After a deep breath, Elora returned to the sitting room, hair braided and tossed back over her shoulder. It took every ounce of strength she had to not return to Damien's arms, to not confess everything.

"I'll take you to Silas." The cold expression she had grown to know so well in the Tower slipped back into place and she told herself it was for the best that he grew to hate her again now. Knowing he was alive would have to be enough.

Chapter 26

Elora

It wasn't Silas's office that she and Damien were directed towards once they exited her rooms. A young male vampire stood outside the door, hands behind his back and blonde hair falling into his eyes.

"This way," were the only words he said as he kept his focus on anything other than her. Slowly, they went back the way they had come—down the hallway to the stairs and into the entryway where they turned right. The silence was painful and the urge to grip Damien's hand for support made her fingers tingle and twitch at her side. Instead, she allowed herself to study the décor of the manor she now called home. It was everything the Tower was not—bright and welcoming with warm colors and furniture. Even the art felt hopeful with bright landscapes or bouquets of flowers. Lilies and daisies and tulips. Not a single rose, and she couldn't decide if it was just a happy coincidence or a deliberate choice.

Damien kept in step behind her, slowing and stopping when she did. Her gaze lingered on the paintings, on the gardens beyond the windows that lined the wall. The view was everything she had dreamed of while at the hospital, while locked inside the sterile ward with a measly hour of obstructed sunlight a day. Nature was never a part of it. Only stone walls and concrete, which squashed any hopes of grass or flowers, leaving weeds to peek through the cracks. And in the Tower, there had been no sunlight, no windows, nothing. A fitting prison cell for a prized animal.

"In here, miss." The vampire gestured towards the doors that now stood open, and she inclined her head before entering the room, eyes instantly locking onto Silas waiting in the center. It felt like what would be called a parlor in the shows she watched though she had never been in one. A collection of couches and armchairs, a bar in the back corner, and a large fireplace in the center of the back wall. It was cozy despite the tall ceiling and open space, the type of room where secrets were told and kept, hidden in the cushions of the furniture and grains of the wood floor.

Elora took in several deep breaths, holding them in her chest as she roamed the room. She couldn't sit, couldn't be still because it meant this entire conversation would begin and pieces of her life would be unearthed, expertly excavated and held up for inspection. Truths that could turn her reality inside out would be revealed.

"I'm glad to see you're feeling better." Silas's voice filled the room as she took in the line of photos on the far wall. It was a collection of professional-looking portraits and snapshots, moments frozen in time. With trembling fingers, she picked up one of the silver frames and stared at the image there. It was her at around eight—all toothy smiles and innocence. Her hair was in two braids and her skin was unmarred by the scars that told the world she was broken. Clutched in her hand was a small bouquet of white flowers.

"Is this me?" Silas made a slight noise of confirmation as he approached her and noted the frame in her hand.

"Yes," he responded. "The majority of these are. For a while, you were allowed here along with your mother. Even though she decided to never turn, we stayed close for a while. At first, I was upset, and it did cause a divide between us. But when she got pregnant with you, we became close again. I had grown-up a bit and was able to accept her choice. It also meant you would visit for days or weeks, running all around the grounds and causing chaos everywhere you went. It was the most life the manor saw in those days."

He picked up another frame and handed it to her as she returned hers to its spot. Another one of her, but this one was she was older and none of the joy in the previous photo was present. Haunted eyes and slumped posture and just above the high collar of her green shirt was part of a scar. The first of many, as she knew.

"This is from the last time I saw you until your mother showed up asking for help. You had come over for a week. Iris always wanted you to have a relationship with me, with this part of her life, and we did have a wonderful dynamic. You were my world." He sighed heavily as he stared at the photo. "You were different. I had noticed changes before this and had asked questions that were not well received."

"The rift with Killian?" Elora had completely forgotten that Damien was there with them. He stood a few paces away, far enough to respect this moment, yet close enough to be involved in the conversation. She noted how his eyes kept darting to the photos beside her, along with the one in her hand. Without saying a word, she offered the photo to him and he hesitated before taking measured steps towards her and took the frame, careful not to let their hands touch as if he somehow knew that she couldn't bear the contact right then. Of course, he knew. He always did.

"Yes, exactly," Silas answered before returning his attention to her. "I asked about your change in demeanor, in personality. You were always so full of life, fierce to the point it drove Iris insane at times. And then, one day, you came over, and it was all gone. Only pale embers where there was once fire."

He gave her a sad smile before turning from the line of memories that she could not bring forward. Despite being surrounded by the very place where she spent so much of her childhood, not even fragments rose to the surface. Even the happy memories or the ones full of sunlight and laughter, were hidden away with the rest. Collateral damage to everything else.

"How old—" she hesitated before swallowing and following Silas towards the sitting area in the center of the room. "How old was I when that photo was taken?"

Her palms grew sweaty as the words left her mouth. A part of her didn't want an answer, screamed at her for asking such an incredibly stupid question. Why did she need to know that? Why did she need to know when it all started? Silas seemed to understand the struggle, the reason for the question and exactly what it would reveal because he waved a hand towards the chair beside him and sat.

"Eleven. I didn't see you again until you were fifteen and I had you brought here." Flashes of a large figure gathering her up from her bed, unlocking the chains on her wrists, and carrying her out of her room filled her mind until it was all she could see, all she could hear.

"You sent someone to get me." Silas nodded slowly, as if giving her the space she needed to remember. "I can't see their face, but they got the chains off and carried me out. Then—I don't remember anything after that."

Another nod as she reclined back in the chair and pulled her legs underneath her. She could feel Damien standing just behind her, a silent sentry as he listened to every word. He had shifted when Silas revealed how old she had been, had exhaled sharply when she recalled how she had made it out of the Tower.

"I kept you here for roughly a year before I sent you to a foster family with certain assurances that you would be taken care of."

"Why?" she forced out, denying the burning in her throat, the tears beginning to gather. "Why throw me away like that?" Again, she felt Damien shift, taking a single step towards her as if to comfort her.

"Not throw away, Elora. Never that." Silas moved closer, sliding across the cushion, complete and utter devastation carved into his face. "Killian sent out scouts. Vampires who were tasked specifically with finding you. We were able to misdirect him since his focus was on other vampires, who he believed wanted you for political reasons. But eventually, he turned his attention this way. I couldn't risk you being taken back, and I knew he would never think to search among humans."

She closed her eyes for a moment, feeling the honesty in his words. Not a single part of her believed he had willingly sent her away, had tossed her aside when she grew to be too much trouble, too much effort. Question after question raced through her head, and she desperately tried to latch onto one of them.

"I—" she began before words left her once more.

"Didn't she need to feed while she was with them? It seems like it wasn't an issue until her foster sister." Damien's question filled the silence, taking the words from her mouth. He knew exactly what she would ask, what she would want to know, as if he was in her head.

A brief flash of fear raced across Silas's face and her brows narrowed as she guessed at the answer. "The medication?" A nod. A single, solitary nod.

"We gained access to it when we infiltrated the Resistance years ago. I knew they would grow to be a problem even if the other vampire heads didn't believe me then. At the time, they were more of a nuisance than anything else. But they had potential, and I had warned the other vampires not to underestimate them. As a result, I was able to have them steal some and once I found out what it could do and reverse manufacture it. I didn't originally intend to use it on you. I only wanted to research it and develop countermeasures. During your time here, you fed like everyone else, though never from anyone directly. I gave your foster family a prescription, for lack of a better term."

"What changed?" Again, Damien.

"I honestly am not sure. It could be you grew out of the dosage, and it wasn't enough anymore."

"It was expensive," she whispered, remembering Elizabeth's words in that hospital room during their doomed therapy session. "They couldn't afford it anymore. Did they know what I was?"

"No. It was safer that way. They took you in willingly, at my request." He shook his head. "I wish they had told me if that was the case. I would have helped or brought you back."

"Well, you didn't. And I ended up attacking my foster sister and being sent to that hospital before ending up back with Killian." Both males flinched at the same time, simultaneous reactions to the guilt they both felt. And they deserved it. So many secrets. So many betrayals.

"And my mother? I only remember her disappearing."

"Killian killed her in his rage at you being gone. I wasn't able to get her out in time after she chose to go back to try to keep him distracted. Iris believed she could return and pretend she knew nothing of your disappearance. He didn't buy it and made an example of her." There was a slight glistening in his eyes as he recalled what happened to his sister, what was sacrificed to save her daughter from the hands of a monster.

She chewed the inside of her cheek to force herself not to cry, to not spiral into a pool of self-hatred. Life after life had been sacrificed and stolen simply to protect her. And what was she doing with that sacrifice? Hiding in her uncle's manor, hoping and praying no one would find her. Her nails dug into her thigh as she tried to center herself, anchor herself in reality. A hand gripped her shoulder, the heat from his body seeping through her dress, burning her skin, and it took every ounce of her restraint to not lean into it, to not rest her cheek on it. Silas clocked the movement meant to comfort as the news of her mother's death hit her, and despite her best efforts, she felt her body relax just the tiniest bit.

"I have so many more questions, but they all disappear as soon as I try to ask them," she confessed, and Silas gave her a smile that looked painful.

"I understand, Elly. I truly do. And I'm here to answer them to the best of my ability whenever you are able and ready to ask them." He paused, as if considering his next words carefully. "I won't ask what happened and you never have to tell me, never have to relive a single moment of your time there."

"Thank you," she whispered softly. Two warring factions resided side by side inside her. One wanted to reveal every dark and disgusting thing that had been done to her. The way she had been shared and offered up as a reward. That part desired nothing more than to see him flinch, to see him recoil from what had occurred after he noticed something was wrong. The other never wanted to allow those words to escape her lips, wanted it to stay nestled inside her where only she would know the full extent since the other person who knew was now dead by her hand.

"Why—" she swallowed roughly, her throat dry and constricting around the question she forced herself to ask. "Why didn't you get me out of there sooner? You said you knew. You fucking knew." The wince and regret on his face did nothing for her, didn't bring her the satisfaction she thought it would.

"I have no excuse for not stepping in sooner. I could tell you that I didn't know the full extent, that I trusted my sister when she said everything was fine, that he had backed off, that you were safe. I could tell you that it is the single greatest regret of my life. But none of that would be enough. I failed you, Elora."

Every word she had planned on saying instantly evaporated. The vulnerability, the anguish that took hold of Silas, was heartbreaking to witness. He seemed diminished, as if the weight of his failure was crushing him as they spoke, with each part of his confession. A small corner of her heart understood his lack of action, his desire to simply trust his sister, but in no way was she able to forgive him. Not yet. Maybe not ever. Everything was raw and festering under the surface, infecting every thought, every emotion, every decision. All she wanted was for it all to burn to the ground so she could dance on what was left. She would destroy the world if it meant they begged for mercy, pleaded for her to stop, just as she had.

She cleared her throat, straightening as much as she could, and met Silas's gaze. "I assume there is more to discuss." Elora knew there was, had seen the looks he and Damien had shared when they appeared, and she remembered Darian's demand for her to be turned over to him.

Silas nodded and jerked his head for Damien to sit with them. She hadn't even noticed his hand was still on her shoulder, fingers clutching her as if he could protect her from the truth. After barely a heartbeat, his hand disappeared, and she felt the absence instantly. Only coldness was left behind as he took the seat beside her and leaned forward as if preparing for something horrific.

"Darian has renewed his request for a meeting, claiming it is simply to solidify his claim to the Ashcroft family and gain permission to join it with his own. This would give him more power, more authority within the council, which was always a goal for him, as well as Killian. He also claims the meeting is to discuss the growing Resistance, who he says are the problem at this point." It went unspoken that she was meant to play a role in that, and her blood was meant to replace humans. Or the blood of those turned by her. Like Elizabeth and potentially Wyatt, if her sister's theory had been proven true.

"And what will you say?" Damien's question was voiced before she had a chance to do so herself.

"I will attend, as requested. However, what you do is up to you, and you will have my complete support in whatever you choose." She nodded and stared at her hands, tracing the various scars and lines in her skin.

"How long until I need to make a decision?"

"Within the next day or two. The meeting is four days from now and I will need to give him an answer." She nodded slightly before standing.

"Am I confined to the manor?" Silas's eyes widened in horror at her question.

"Of course not. The entire grounds are open to you." Without a word, she left the parlor and darted out the door to the gardens.

Chapter 27

Damien

Both he and Silas merely watched as Elora left the room and turned towards the doors that led outside. Every part of him wanted to follow her, to shadow her steps, to ask if she was okay, even though he knew the response was no. She had been given answers to so many questions that she had, but he was sure that it only brought forward more. And so many of them probably couldn't or wouldn't be answered. Killian was dead, as was her mother, so there would be no answers given by them. Even if he had the wildest and most creative of imaginations, he could never imagine what it was like to know that the burned holes in her memory would now never be mended or filled in. He didn't believe there was a worse torture than that. Despite everything that had come with his upbringing, at least he knew it. The memories may be painful, but at least he had the option of forcing them away.

During the entire exchange, Damien had tracked every movement, every flinch or twitch, every time her voice broke. He had felt it as she relaxed under his hand as he fought to comfort her. He knew intimately the death of a parent. Not a parent who didn't deserve the title or who had been nothing but a poison that attempted to infect everything and everyone. No, he knew what it was to lose a parent who had tried to protect you, who had held you when you cried and told you stories in the middle of the night when you couldn't sleep. There was nothing like that agony, like the open wound that it left behind. It never truly healed, always waiting to force pain to radiate through your body at the slightest recollection of them.

"You're expected to come as well. To the meeting with Darian." Damien forced his attention to Silas and away from the doorway, breathing in the smell of lavender left in her wake.

"Do I have a choice in whether I attend?" The edge in his voice was unintentional, but Damien couldn't make himself regret it. He wasn't sure how long he would last in a room with Darian, how long he could control himself before he ripped the skin from his bones, removed each finger that touched her. And if Jonas was there, then it would only end in a bloodbath. He didn't care if he was part of the casualties, as long as it meant she was safe from them.

"I want to say that you do. But I think the best course of action is for you to attend, whether she does or not. Your presence will be needed when I deny Darian his claim to the Ashcroft group."

"On what basis?"

"That he didn't murder Killian, as their customs dictate." Damien scoffed softly at the explanation, at the confidence in Silas's words.

"There's no proof either way."

"According to whom, exactly? You? Darian? Do you really think I didn't have eyes in the Tower, especially during the last few months? I thought you were smarter than that." Silas shook his head softly as if disappointed, but Damien simply stared at him in shock. So many groups had managed to infiltrate the Tower, but Killian had been too distracted or complacent or both to notice. Silas had always been a wild card of sorts since no one knew much about him or the vampires he was in control of. But the more Damien learned, the more he realized Silas had always been more of a threat than Killian ever gave him credit for. Not only did Silas have cameras in the Tower, but he knew Resistance members and had infiltrated their organization. He had managed to take Elora from a sealed room where she was chained to a bed and had Lukas working for him towards the end. Silas was everything Killian had aspired to be.

"You have footage?" Silas nodded and Damien swallowed. "Have you watched it?" Another nod and Damien hung his head. He didn't need to see the video, didn't need to relive what already played on repeat in his mind. Every time he closed his eyes, he saw her panic, distrust, and rage. The only reprieve came when he was forced to witness the pain on her face when he moved away from her, denying her in that decrepit apartment.

"She doesn't want it," he revealed, and Silas simply hummed slightly. "We discussed it before when I told her about Darian's offer to me."

"It's her choice, as I said before. But I want to give her the opportunity."

"It would put a target on her back. Even more than she already has. Every vampire who wants that seat will come after her." Rage crashed into him, replacing the hesitation and concern that had been there a moment ago. Silas was putting her in danger, once more a potential pawn in a game she didn't seem to want to play.

"It's why I have an alternative plan, should she say no. And it's one that I and the other head will agree on, which will render what Darian wants null and void. Dismantle the Ashcroft family and allow their members to be absorbed into the groups left. Corvin, Ravenwell, and Radcliff would each take any vampire who desires to join them. It would do away with any power grabs." The plan made sense, and Damien was willing to admit that. It would work as an alternative when Elora denied her position. Her reaction to the news that she was the rightful head of the Ashcroft family had been visceral. There had been disgust lining her denial, as if the thought of being anywhere near the Tower and everything there was repugnant, as if she would rather remove a limb than step foot there again.

"What do you think she'll pick?" Damien knew what he thought but was curious about Silas's opinion of his niece.

"I don't know. I see traces of the girl I knew, traces of her fire and desire to bend the world to her will. But I'm not sure if there is enough of her left." Regret lined each word, a pain so immense it felt like a tangible thing.

"What was she like?" Damien almost whispered, voice low and soft as he glanced up at the photo of Elora as a child, flowers clutched in her fists, neck free of any scars. "Before everything."

Silas reclined back on the chair, a wistful smile playing on his lips as if it couldn't find enough footing to stay around. A soft chuckle left Silas's mouth as he shook his head.

"A terror. A force of nature in the most wonderful of ways. She was her mother in every sense. They shared their love of nature, of art, of stories. She destroyed more than one floor in this house with paint. Elora was kindness, confidence, and defiance wrapped up in one unique package. I never knew so much life could exist in a single person." His eyes shuttered slightly, as if he was comparing the child he knew with the woman she had been forced to become. Two sides to the same coin. Damien had seen everything Silas had described, caught glimpses of it between the arguments and fights and darkness.

"And how was she at the hospital? At the Tower?" Silas tilted his head back, staring at the ceiling as he waited for Damien to answer. Silently, he searched for words to describe who he had seen. He ran his hand through his hair and swallowed.

"She was—" He hesitated briefly, picking the right words. "A contradiction in every way. Fierce and violent when pushed. It was like seeing a flash of lightning in a sky without any light. She handed my ass to me on more than one occasion. Stabbed me more than once." Silas huffed softly and nodded, as if he knew that side of her all too well.

"But there were so many moments of her retreating, hiding from everyone and everything. It was like she thought if she tried hard enough, she could cease to exist, her very presence eradicated from the world. It was heartbreaking and at the time, I didn't understand it. Not until the Tower and the night of the banquet."

"I heard quite a bit about that from Lukas. He was deathly afraid she wasn't going to survive, that she was falling into a place she wouldn't come back out of." Damien swallowed, once more ignoring the rush of guilt that came with Lukas's name.

"He was telling the truth. We watched her after that night, and I know Lukas tried desperately to keep her above water. But in the end, she was ready to die. And almost did. The night she killed him, she had planned on slitting her throat. She never meant to come out of that room." Silas inhaled sharply at the revelation, and they fell into silence. Damien could only assume her uncle was buried in guilt, in shame just as he was.

"You love my niece." Damien's eyes snapped to Silas, who was still staring at the ceiling as if there was something uniquely interesting up there. His arms were spread across the back of the couch, but his body was rigid as he spoke.

"I care for her." The words felt wrong on his tongue, felt like they didn't fit correctly in his mouth as he forced them out. An understatement. She was the center of his world, the anchor that held down his reality. Without her, both would cease to exist, and he would be left in a void with nothing to bring him back.

"We both know better than that, Damien."

"It doesn't matter. She needs time to heal, needs time to come to terms with everything, and she deserves someone who is better equipped to help her through that. I'm not the man for her, not after everything I did."

"Maybe so. But is that your choice to make? Or hers?" Silas stood, smoothing out his shirt and adjusting his sleeves as he glanced down at Damien, a calculating gleam in his eye. "Would you mind checking on her? I would hate for her to get lost on the grounds."

A scoff left Damien's mouth even as he stood and forced himself not to rush to the door, to not throw it open and find her. Every part of him itched to be near her, to simply be in her presence because it meant being in the light. She wasn't fire and heat like sunlight even though she had been before. No, now she was starlight. Cold and beautiful as she shined in the darkest of nights. She was a fucking beacon that called him home.

Damien didn't say a word but turned on his heel and finally listened to the part of him that had screamed at him to leave with her earlier.

He found her quickly enough. The gardens were to the left of the main door, just around the corner of the manor. Hedges lined the space, creating pathways that were lined with stones. Flowers grew in the beds and nestled the benches between them as if they could comfort whoever hid there.

Her knuckles were white as she clutched the stone bench beneath her and stared directly ahead at the collection of rose bushes in the center of the garden. Red and white and yellow blossoms intertwined with thorny stems seemed to reach out towards her, as if to touch her. Damien kept his steps light as he approached, desperate not to startle her as she continued to exist in what seemed to be a daze.

"Elora," he whispered as he drew closer and he tracked the way her hand brushed away the tears, removing any evidence of what she seemed to perceive as weakness. The mask that had become so common since they arrived shifted into place. It was like her features frosted over, like ice was injected into her veins until there was nothing left of the laughter he had heard before or the smile that made him want to eradicate anyone who tore it from her lips. Her spine straightened, and she shifted her attention to him.

"Did he send you to check on me?" Even her words were stilted and monotone.

"He did say something about making sure you didn't get lost." He grinned, hoping with everything he had that she would smile or laugh or something.

"As you can see, I didn't. No need to worry," she responded before returning her attention to the roses. "Do you think he would remove them? Replace them with something else?" Damien sat beside her, perched on the very edge of the bench to give her space.

"I think Silas would do anything you asked of him." She hummed softly in response and the sound joined the bird calls and insects off in the distance, creating a distinct melody to their conversation. They lapsed into silence as Damien fell into his own thoughts, his own obsessions. He needed to be near her, see her, breathe in her scent in a way that felt all consuming.

"Do you want to talk about any of that?" She shook her head before glancing over at him, searching his face for something he didn't understand. Her brows furrowed together as her focus moved from his eyes to his cheekbones, to his lips. It felt like being studied, and he desperately wanted to know what she was looking for. Finally, after what felt like hours, she stood and gave him a sort of sad smile, one that felt like a goodbye, before returning to the manor and leaving him to once more regret backing away from her in that fucking apartment.

Chapter 28

Viktor

"Failure again. And a monumental failure at that," Thorne stated in a matter-of-fact tone. No bitterness. No anger. Her eyes wandered over the kitchen instead of Viktor, lingering on the paintings along the wall behind him. "Not only did you lose the target, who may be beyond our grasp now, but you also managed to lose Elizabeth and allow her to potentially turn someone else. Did I miss anything?"

Viktor said nothing because there was nothing to say. No defense for his actions, or lack thereof. No excuse that he could give that would make any of this better. He had been overconfident in his control of Elizabeth, in her desire to work with him. Elora had been correct when she called him a fool, had laid out the reality of his situation in exquisite detail, even if it had been painful. This was his mess once more, but he doubted Thorne would allow him to try to fix it yet again.

With a grunt, he placed the duffle bag on the kitchen table between them. He had shown up at headquarters with a nasty gash on the back of his head, a large cut across his abdomen, bad news, and consolation prizes. Yet again, his true mission was failure, but at least he had something to hand over.

"Yes, I failed in my mission and allowed Elizabeth to escape. I underestimated her and her connection to the target. As soon as the target was in front of her, Elizabeth became single-minded in her focus on her sister. However, I was able to obtain some items that may be useful and gained crucial intel." Thorne raised a brow before pulling the duffle bag towards her.

"Explain," she commanded as she unzipped it and began pulling out items. A collection of what appeared to be medical texts except for the tiny symbol on the spine and four collection bottles with Killian's crest.

"The journals are Denise's. They contain her notes about the target, including their sessions and all changes to her medication while there," Viktor outlined as Thorne sat back and stared at the items before her. "The bottles are for Killian's personal use. That is his symbol there on the bottle."

"I'm aware of what his crest looks like. Get to your point." Viktor nodded at the command and swallowed down the immense disgust that always came when he discussed this.

"The blood is from the target. My guess is that Killian was collecting it for personal use. He also could have been selling it or giving it out to others." Viktor couldn't help the disdain that entered his voice, the repulsion he felt when Killian's actions were brought up. Thorne studied the bottles with a renewed interest, picking them up as she seemed to weigh them in her hand. It wasn't enough by any means, not if they wanted to produce anything on a large scale, but it would be a start. With what they had, the Resistance scientists could experiment and test with Elora's blood and not Elizabeth's, which had proved less than fruitful.

"My theory is that he stopped feeding directly from her and began draining her instead." He noted the visible flinch from Thorne as the words left his mouth. Despite what Elora was, it seemed no one was able to stomach what she was put through.

"And this theory is based on what?"

"The night she killed him, Killian had stated that he didn't believe she planned on making it out of the room, that she planned on bleeding out before she could heal. Her response was that it helped that she had been drained."

"Quite the reasonable theory, and I'm inclined to agree. Though I do wonder at the change in his behavior." Viktor snapped his focus to her, struggling to understand how Thorne would know so much about not only Killian, but what occurred in the Tower. The knowledge seemed beyond what would be expected as the head of the rebellion.

"As for the intel, something strange occurred during the altercation with the target. When Elizabeth bit the human, the target had shouted at her to stop. And Elizabeth did. Instantly. It was like she was frozen in place." A dark expression passed through Thorne's face, and Viktor stood a bit straighter.

"She compelled her? Another vampire?" Her questions were almost frantic, tripping over one another to be voiced.

"It seemed that way." She simply nodded and reclined back in the wooden chair. Her brow furrowed as she grabbed the top journal and began to flip through it, stopping every few pages to read whatever was there.

"Your failure cannot go unpunished, Viktor. I'm sure you understand that." Viktor stared directly ahead of him, noting the chip in the paint on the cabinet. He was fairly certain that particular one held the coffee mugs but couldn't remember. All he knew was he couldn't meet Thorne's eyes, couldn't bear to see the disappointment there. He owed everything to Thorne and the Resistance. They had helped when Jaime had returned home, freshly turned and in the midst of bloodlust. The vampire who had turned him had left him in an alleyway to make his own way home. Viktor had only protected himself. And when the Resistance members showed up and found him holding Jaime's body, they had taken control. Now, he had failed them.

Through it all, he heard Elora's words repeating in his mind. Calling him a fool, a failure. Outlining his mistakes, declaring she would have gone with him if he had done things just a bit differently. He had known that even before she spoke the words into existence.

"And it certainly must be dealt with, since your failures are resulting in questions about your loyalty. It's quite the coincidence that the woman you spent all your time with for four years, the woman you took care of, whose trust you earned, has managed to escape you twice. Many are wondering if perhaps you are protecting her. Purposefully keeping her from us." She let the accusation linger between them as if it was a spiderweb and Thorne believed he would get himself stuck in it. He shook his head, panic rising as he finally understood exactly how this all appeared.

"I can assure you that's not the case." Thorne only hummed slightly before looking through the journals.

"I'm not sure a person can spend that much time with someone without gaining some feelings. By your own admission, you were kind and comforting to her. You gave her little gifts and even convinced her that you cared for her beyond simple friendship. That type of behavior leaves a mark, no matter how hard you may have fought against it." Viktor felt himself bristle at the accusation even as his mind conjured memories of holding her when she broke down, of cupping her face in his hands, of brushing his knuckles along her cheekbone. Had he developed feelings for her? Was Thorne correct?

"I don't blame you, Viktor. Nor do I think you did it on purpose or that you're weak. But I do think it's possible those emotions are getting in the way, whether you realize it or not." He shook his head once more, denying what he knew could actually be very true. At the apartment, he could have shot Damien in the head and left with her. He could have scooped her up and brought her back here, kicking and screaming. At the first sign that Elizabeth was turning on him, he could have drugged her and neutralized her as a threat.

"Thorne, I don't feel like I've been compromised despite any feelings I may have gained for her. I won't deny that I came to care for her while doing my job, but it was a necessity. I needed to see her as my patient in order get close to her and that meant learning about the darkest parts of her past that she remembered." Thorne's gaze was scalding as she forced him to avert his eyes, unable to handle the danger lingering there. Her green eyes had turned dark at his confession, one that he regretted instantly. Originally, he had promised and vowed that he harbored no feelings towards her, that he had simply done his job by collecting intel and getting close to her. Thorne now knew that it had been a lie he fed to the entire council.

"You're not to have any other part in obtaining the target. Effective immediately, you're removed from that mission, and I'll be putting you on another one that hopefully you'll be able to fulfill." Her tone felt like someone had taken a whip to his back, each word a lash that spoke only to his failure. He was exactly what Elora accused him of being—a useless member of the Resistance, whose actions resulted in taking two steps back for every step forward. Irritation and rage coursed through him, heating his blood and forcing him to stand more rigidly.

"And what will that be?" He forced his tone to remain neutral, to not reveal just how deeply Thorne had managed to cut him.

"Fixing your fuck up. Find Elizabeth and whoever she bit back at that disaster of a mission. We cannot have her biting people left and right if she is able to turn them that easily. Do you understand? She is the most dangerous thing we have dealt with."

He wanted to ask why he would be trusted with this if Elizabeth was so dangerous, if she was so crucial to finding and stopping. Instead, he forced his lips together to keep himself from asking the question he was sure he already knew the answer to. He had messed up one too many times and was now disposable. If Elizabeth killed him in the process, there was no real harm done.

"Of course. I won't fail you," he vowed as he nodded his head, accepting the mission without complaint.

"Make sure you don't, or you will be demoted to a grunt worker taking care of internal tasks. Am I clear?" Again, only a nod because he didn't trust himself to speak, didn't trust that what came out of his mouth would be a simple acceptance.

Thorne continued to flip through the pages, stopping at one and taking a moment to read through it. With each second that passed, her features contorted into something Viktor couldn't read. It seemed like concern or regret, but that didn't seem correct. Maybe it was a dark fascination with the story occurring within those pages.

"Where do you think you'll start looking?" Thorne didn't look up as she asked her question, and Viktor repressed the deep sigh he wanted to exhale.

"Her family's home is the best place to start. It is still listed as her address on all her identification documents. If she isn't there, hopefully it will give me a clue as to where to go next. I also plan on checking in with the relative of the person Elizabeth bit. She's an aunt or grandmother. I can check if she is okay and look for them at the same time. It would also be useful to find out if he's with Elizabeth, his relative, or somewhere else entirely."

"We need to know if he turned, Viktor. She could eradicate the human race in this city if turning has become that easy. Hell, it would wipe out the original vampires or at least render their numbers pointless. She could effectively take over this entire city if she wanted it."

"Elizabeth? Or the target?" Viktor wanted to believe Elora would never do that. She had lived with humans and respected them, even believing she was one until only weeks ago. Elora had never shown an ounce of cruelty or ambition to be in control of anything or anyone. She could be violent when pushed, but that wasn't the same as allowing or causing entire groups of people to be destroyed.

"Both, I believe. Elizabeth is utterly unhinged and insane. And Elo—" Thorne sighed softly and shook her head. "I know the target does not seem like the type to hurt or wipe out anyone. But trauma and revenge can warp a person, can twist and manipulate until all they want is for their enemies to burn and are willing to sacrifice anyone else in the process. Do not discount her just because she doesn't seem like the type."

Viktor got the distinct feeling that Thorne wasn't only speaking about Elora, that her explanation included someone else as well. Once more, he saw the way Elora kissed Killian's forehead and moved the strands of hair away from his face before she plunged the knife into his neck. He recalled the way she seemed to grin when his blood hit her face and she stabbed him again and again, only stopping once Damien grabbed her wrist.

Maybe Thorne was right.

Maybe Elora had become exactly who he thought she was incapable of being. And maybe they had all forced her to become the villain they were so desperately trying to avoid.

Chapter 29

Elora

"I would like to speak with you, please." Elora's request interrupted the two vampires as they pored over security plans. A schematic of the manor was laid out on the desk, along with a map of the grounds. They were more expansive than Elora had thought. Both Damien and Silas glanced up and her uncle nodded before muttering something to the vampire beside him. Slowly, she walked through the office, giving them time to finish up their conversation. Her eyes wandered over the framed photos, similar to the ones in the parlor she had already seen. More of her as a child in what seemed to be a dream, a fairytale in which her innocence was her own. Her red hair flowed out behind her as she ran towards the trees, eyes flanking back at whoever was taking the photo. Another where she sat with Silas, a book in his hands as he seemed to read to her. With a harsh intake of breath, she shook her head at the moments trapped in time, memories that she still did not possess, and turned her attention back to her uncle.

Her eyes remained on Silas as he finished pointing at something on the map, refusing to even risk making eye contact with Damien. She could feel him watching her, peeking up from the papers on the tables before returning to what he was meant to focus on. Elora knew if she looked, she would see the cool indifference that had become the norm between the two of them.

There was a rift between them, and even Silas had noticed it. Damien believed it was from him rejecting her and she was willing to let him believe that if it meant the truth was kept hidden. He had fed from her even if he didn't remember, meaning she had forced him to break his promise, his vow. And she knew he would never forgive her for it.

Silas came around the desk as Damien headed towards the door. Still, she refused to look at him as Silas reclined against the edge and waited until the door clicked shut. He watched his niece flinch slightly before she sat in the armchair in front of him.

"Are we going to discuss what's happening between you two?"

"I'm not sure what you are talking about." She met his eyes, forcing her expression to empty, but Silas only sighed softly.

"You've been avoiding him. I'm aware your relationship with him is complex, but this seems different from being simply complicated."

"Lukas had a big mouth," she snapped before closing her eyes and taking a breath. "After I tell you what I came in here to talk to you about, it may make more sense."

Silas crossed his arms over his chest, the perfectly ironed dress shirt wrinkling slightly with the movement. She had thought out this conversation so many times. Rehearsed in her rooms when she was alone, while she bathed, while she wandered the gardens with Damien just a few steps behind her.

"I have a plan, and I want your help to execute it." Silas nodded and waited. She let out a breath and began the speech she had prepared. "There are two things I want, Silas. I want to take over the Ashcroft family and I want Darian dead. And I have an idea on how to accomplish both."

"I was under the impression you wanted nothing to do with the Ashcrofts. Not that I wouldn't support you, but this is a bit of a surprise." Elora nodded. She had told both Silas and Damien she wanted nothing to do with her original family. And at first, that had been the truth. But to claim her position was to claim resources and power, all of which she had earned. The humans had also fueled this decision. She wanted the Resistance gone, wanted them to leave her alone. In the deepest pits of her heart, Elora also knew she simply wanted revenge, even if she wasn't quite ready to admit or embrace it.

She shrugged. "Things change. I want a position that will allow me to protect myself, be in charge without relying on others to care or die for me. I've done enough of that."

"You aren't responsible for those deaths, Elora. And no one else is going to die." She chuckled darkly at his confidence.

"I am the root cause, Silas. My mother died to protect me. Lukas and Denise are the same. It's only a matter of time before I'm found and everyone else that I love is sacrificed. I know that your location is secret, but it's only a matter of time and we both know that. I won't let it happen. I won't look down at another dead body knowing I could have prevented it." Despite the breaks in her statement and the sobs she barely held back, she knew she had made her point in the way her uncle seemed to relent.

Silas made a low noise. "Fine. How do we achieve that?"

A grin stretched across her face as she answered. "I attend Darian's meeting with you."

"Is that all? I imagine there's more to this."

For the first time since she walked in, Elora hesitated. This was the part she had a feeling Silas would be less than supportive of. Every time she rehearsed it in her head, Silas had refused to help. Even her own thoughts knew this plan was risky. She adjusted her sleeves before meeting his eyes.

"I intend to take Darian up on his offer. Or demand, I suppose." Silas's expression turned calculating as he watched her.

She could see the wheels spinning as he connected the dots, trying to identify each of the threads she was weaving together.

"You intend to marry him." Elora shrugged, forcing down the bile and the feeling of Darian's hands on her skin.

"Yes. I do." She smirked. "He won't survive past the ceremony. That I can promise. And when he's dead at my feet, no one will question my control of the Ashcroft family. My two desires fulfilled in one ceremony."

"You don't think he will be a touch suspicious?" She waved a hand in a dismissive gesture.

"If I came straight to him and offered myself, then yes. That's why you're taking me and offering me to him in a show of solidarity. He claims he wants to deal with the humans by joining together. I'm the price you're willing to pay to show your commitment to that."

"And if he asks why I'm handing over my niece?" The question was a formality, and they both knew it. Silas just wanted to hear her say it, give him permission for what he would have to voice later.

"I'm your niece in name only. And survival is worth more than one female vampire. One abomination." The words tasted foul on her tongue, and she saw Silas flinch as she said them.

"I see why you sent Damien away. Even with things complicated, I can't imagine he would be supportive of this plan of yours."

She chuckled before falling silent. "No, he wouldn't. He would probably try to get me to leave the city or something like that." She paused, refusing to let herself think what a life with Damien where she wasn't being hunted looked like. "But—"

She wiped a tear away she hadn't even noticed appear on her cheek.

"He fed from you. And you're afraid of what that might mean." Her eyes snapped to his. "He shouldn't have survived being shot with those laced bullets, Elora. I knew from the moment he explained what happened."

She didn't say anything, couldn't say anything. If Silas had figured it out, how long until Damien did?

"Shortly after he brought me back to the Tower, he vowed to never feed from me. At first, it was his hatred for me. He had said that he had standards, and I didn't meet them. But then it became more about everything related to it. At least, I think so." Elora stood and walked over to the bookshelves, trying to keep her thoughts and emotions under control.

"He was dying, Silas. In my arms in the back of that ugly car on a dirt road in the middle of nowhere," she choked back a sob and swallowed, forcing her voice to not break again. "I didn't know what else to do. I didn't think about the consequences, or how he could hate me after. Or what my blood could do to him."

"I understand, Elora. But—" Silas pushed off the desk and approached her, searching her face for something. "I don't think he would hate you. He deserves more faith in him on your part. However, your concern regarding what your blood will do to him is valid. But it's also a large part of why you should tell him."

"And if he does end up hating me for it?" He smiled softly down at his niece.

"Then you'll be leaving soon anyway, and nothing will have changed that much. But I don't think he will. He's utterly devoted to you." She huffed a laugh to drown out the pain. Devotion was not the same as love, and that had been what she wanted from him.

"Either way, you'll tell him nothing about the plan. Only that we're attending Darian's meeting to deal with him head on. He doesn't need to know more than that."

"Darian will expect to see him there."

She sighed deeply before glancing at the door Damien left through. "I know"

Chapter 30

Elora

She avoided Damien successfully for three days, but now that the meeting of the vampire heads was only a few hours away, it became impossible. Somehow, he had already found out she would be attending, and she was willing to bet that Silas was to blame for that. Every conversation they had circled back to talking with Damien, to revealing what had happened in the back of that car. Or at least letting him know the plan. Silas argued that the shock of hearing him offer Elora to Darian could have disastrous consequences, specifically for him. Her argument had been it was necessary for that to happen, for it to appear real. They had no idea what Darian knew of their relationship, and they couldn't rely on him to not know anything, especially since Damien protecting her was well established rumor to some and a fact to others. His reaction needed to be genuine despite the threat of bodily harm it posed to Silas.

"Why are you going?" His voice filtered in from the bedroom into the bathroom, where she stood at the counter, running a comb through her hair while dozens of thoughts spun through her mind as she readied herself. She needed to look appealing, but not so much that it was suspicious. Every single detail needed to be fully considered, fully thought out, or everything would fall apart. She shot him a brief glance in the mirror, noting the perfect fit of his dress shirt and slacks. His hair had been trimmed once more with the sides shaved down, while the rest fell in waves around his face. He was achingly gorgeous in a way that made her plan that much more difficult and her hand twitched with the desire to run her fingers through his hair, touch his cheek.

They could always run. She could grab his hand and drag him from the manor and into a car so he could drive them as far away as possible. It was so tempting, the fantasy so real she could touch it. But it would curse him to a life with only her as company, hiding in a tiny town or shack somewhere. It would fall apart so quickly from either running from threats or him growing tired of her.

His dark eyes roamed over her face, the way her hair hung down her back like waves of blood, the tiniest bit of red on her lips. Instantly, his brows narrowed in what she assumed was suspicion. He had probably believed she would refuse to attend the meeting, would stay here in her rooms where she was protected. But being shut away in a psychiatric ward with guards and locked doors had done nothing to protect her. She learned the hard way that if someone wanted to find her desperately enough, they would.

"It's my decision and I have my reasons," Elora responded as she returned her focus to her reflection, where she struggled to arrange her hair. Should it be up to expose her neck? Should she leave it down to cover the scars since there would be others? She bit her lip in thought as she pulled part of it up and held it there, surveying how it looked from every direction.

"That doesn't answer anything. What're you planning, Elora? What did he get you to agree to?"

"I know that you think I'm easily manipulated by the men in my life since I don't have the best track record. But I can promise you that this is one time that I'm fully aware of what's happening." With a scoff, she dropped the long locks and stood.

Down would work. If she needed to show off her neck to get Darian's attention, she could simply move it. Elora had a feeling that he wouldn't be too difficult to manage.

"Do you understand who will be there? Jonas? Darian? Potentially others who did exactly what they did? Are you prepared for that?" There was an edge to his questions, as if he were walking a very thin line between rage and fear. Then again, maybe the two of them were so intertwined that it was impossible to know where one ended and the other began. She met his gaze for the first time in days. Dark shadows hung under his eyes, and he looked exhausted. Was it because of her? Because of her blood?

"Are you trying to scare me into not going? Seems like a childish tactic for you."

"If it works, then it doesn't matter if its childish!"

"I'm aware of who will be there. Trust me, Damien." He shook his head and sighed as the hand at his side twitched slightly, as if he wanted to reach out and touch her. She almost wished he would, even if it would make this all so much worse. There wasn't a single moment that she didn't crave his presence, didn't want him to touch her even if it was a hand on her shoulder.

"I don't," he called out as she pushed past him, heading directly towards the closet to finalize whatever this costume would be. The disguise of an angry and betrayed niece, of a gift wrapped up in pretty ribbon. Maybe a silk dress or shirt, she considered briefly. To imply that Silas knew exactly what happened behind the Tower walls. Elora made a small sound at his declaration as she felt him follow her, rooting himself in the center of the closet doorway. There was no escaping the conversation.

"I mean, I do trust you. Usually." He smirked softly at her. "But you can agree that you make irrational decisions, that your sense of self-preservation isn't the best. If you thought it would protect someone you cared about, you would do anything. Even offer yourself to Darian." She glanced at him long enough to see the sharpness in his features, the underlying anger in his eyes. He knew she wasn't telling him the whole story, that Silas was keeping it from him, and it was driving him mad.

"I can promise you I'm not offering myself up to protect anyone else. I simply want to be there with Silas since I'm sure to be a topic of conversation.

He huffed a laugh. "Of course you will be. He's obsessed with you. He wants you under his thumb, there for him to have access to at any time. And you're walking right into it." She felt her body react to his words, to the truth in each one. Damien was right, and they both knew it. It was just he didn't know that she was counting on Darian's obsession, on his determination to get her back in his grasp.

"I know better than anyone the depths of his obsession. You don't need to remind me."

"Which is why I don't understand why you are doing this."

"It's my choice. Aren't you the one who said I would always have one?" Elora despised herself for throwing this back in his face, for using his own words that were uttered in such a moment of vulnerability on both of their sides against him. She forced her attention back to the clothes hanging in front of her but still caught the way he winced.

"You know that you have a choice, even if I don't agree with the one you're making." She bristled at the wording as her mind raced back to him stepping away from her, of her placing herself on a platter and handing it to him. Like a fool, she had believed he would gather her into his arms and accept her despite everything he knew about her. In her nightmares, he raged against her, called her dirty and weak, laughed at her when she screamed at him to stop.

"That seems to be a trend for you." Slowly, she pulled down a dress with long sleeves and a high neck, exactly the type of clothing she would have requested. It was Damien who told her uncle of her preferences, who knew her so intimately. But that wouldn't work for the role she was attempting to play.

"This is different." His words were almost a whisper, and she shrugged, forcing herself into the state where she became ice, became stone—completely cold and unfeeling. She moved towards the closet door where Damien still stood, feet planted on the ground and arms crossed over his chest. He only watched her, noting the dress in her hands and the red on her lips. A flash of fear crossed his face before he could hide it.

"I shouldn't have done that, Elora. I shouldn't have told you that you have a choice and then stepped away like that. I just—"

"No, you shouldn't have. But you also shouldn't have led me to believe I was important to you, that you cared for me beyond helping me escape." She sucked in a breath and turned away from him, prepared to change with him there. It wasn't anything he hadn't seen before.

"Whether you care about me or not, I do care about you. I have for a while. Probably since you helped me through that nightmare the first time. And it's fine that it's one-sided. I'm an adult and can handle it. I will work through it and move on." She felt him step closer, and she clutched the dress in her fists as words started pouring from her mouth in a cascade that she couldn't control or stop. Her heart raced with a fierceness she hadn't experienced. It was as if she was watching herself from the outside, a scene playing out on television. Her eyes were wide as they moved over the room, not seeing anything but her own panic as words simply gushed forward.

"It's why you don't need to know why I'm going. I won't let anyone else die for me. Not Silas and not you. Not when I almost lost you once." With that, she clamped her mouth shut and closed her eyes as she prayed that he wouldn't ask any questions, wouldn't ask what she meant. It wasn't supposed to come out. She hadn't planned on saying those words or revealing anything. Her pulse pounded in her ears as the silence stretched between them.

"What do you mean, you almost lost me? I've never left your side." Elora sighed and took in the hesitant tone, the anxiety and fear that ran through each syllable and word. Maybe it would be better if he found out now. If he hated her, it would make what had to happen at the meeting easier.

"Silas said the bullets were laced with something. A coating of some sort meant to damage a vampire, meant to slow down their healing," she explained as she turned towards him. His face was empty as he listened, simply his eyes displaying the rage she knew he felt.

"You almost died on the way here. We stopped, and I dragged you into the back seat. I thought you would heal if I just took care of you. But the bleeding never stopped, and your heart was so weak I could barely feel it. All I kept thinking was that you were dying, and I couldn't let that happen."

"You gave me your blood." A statement and she nodded, tears rushing down her face. A single nod from him as his jaw clenched.

"I'm sorry. I am so sorry. I didn't know what to do, and I figured that even if you hated me for it, at least you would be alive." Her voice had gone quiet as she let word after word spill out into the closet. Her apology wasn't enough. Would never be enough and she knew that from the way he stared at her before glancing at her wrist where his teeth had been, where she had bitten open her skin for him.

"You succeeded. I'm alive." He said nothing after that. Instead, he left his emotionless and monotone statements behind as he turned. Only once the bedroom door clicked shut did she collapse to the carpet and sob.

Chapter 31

Viktor

The childhood home had been a pointless waste of time. He had known it the moment he parked along the sidewalk and saw the boarded-up windows beyond the dead lawn of overgrown weeds and dirt. After he broke in through a back window, Viktor had found nothing except dust, graffiti, and pieces of broken furniture. No childhood photos. No journals or glowing signs that outlined Elizabeth plans. And so, he had moved on, leaving the abandoned home behind and went instead to Wyatt's relative's apartment.

There were no sounds behind the door after he knocked and glanced up and down the hallway. It was strange being back there. The door behind him had been repaired since he was there last. A new one put back on its hinges after Elizabeth threw it across the apartment. He had been a fool to think she was going to work with him. But Thorne had been one as well. Taking Elizabeth had been her idea, and Viktor was just meant to execute it. Maybe that was the issue. Both he and Thorne had failed spectacularly, and now he was simply taking the fall. He bore the blame so Thorne could remain in her place of power.

He shook his head slightly as his fist hit the wood, listening closely for any sound. The last time he had knocked on this door there had been shuffling as the old woman made her way to him and then lied to his face. She had claimed that Elora

"

wasn't here, wasn't in the apartment behind him. With a bit of irritation in her voice, the woman had said she hadn't seen her at all. Once again, Elora had a strange ability to bring people to her side. Not only vampires who sought what she could offer, but humans. The man that Elizabeth had turned into collateral damage was proof of that. There had been a sense of desperation in Elora's voice as she begged for his safety. Wyatt, his name was. In a matter of a few short days, both Wyatt and his relative had been won over by her.

Viktor wished he could say it took longer for him to fall under her spell, but it would be a lie. It had been almost instantaneous. Her smile in the dayroom while she watched her reality shows, her resilience after meeting with Denise, and her view of the world that was still bright. Somehow, despite everything, she managed to keep a warmth about herself that only disappeared for variable spans of time, always reemerging like a creature at sea rising up for air. A part of him wondered if the pull she had was part of what made her special, part of what Killian had done to her at a cellular level.

His hand wrapped around the cold metal of the door handle and turned. Unlocked. It inched open as he pushed it, carefully peeking inside. The old woman who lived there wouldn't hesitate to bash him in the head with a rolling pin if she thought he was an intruder.

Nothing. Silence. Not even the sound of a television or clock. It was the type of quiet that was unnatural and put a person on edge, like holding one's breath before plunging into the depths. As he stepped inside, it was the smell that hit him first. Something rancid or rotten, like something had been left out. Viktor's eyes roamed over the living room, which was filled with various knickknacks and trinkets, framed family photos, and paintings that looked like they had been done by an amateur.

And then he spotted it. The turned-over chairs, the shattered teapot, and the shards of ceramic lodged in the carpet. The cups were nowhere to be seen and the spots where the tea had probably spilled had long since gone dry. How long had it been since he was here last? Days? He had lost track of time as he sunk into his failure and cocooned himself in it like it would protect him from the disappointment on Thorne's and every other Resistance member's face.

It had to have been at least a day since this had occurred. Whatever it was.

His steps were cautious as he moved deeper into the apartment, eyes roaming over the chairs in the dining room that were overturned and the wooden table that lay on its side. In the kitchen itself, the refrigerator had been left open and part of the rancid smell assaulting his senses was emanating from there. Using only his fingertip, he pushed the door closed and hoped the smell would dissipate before moving to the hallway behind where the couch was, a short corridor with two doors opposite each other.

Viktor opened the first one on the right and found a bathroom that smelled of vanilla. It was as if everything in that room was meant to radiate that scent — from the air freshener on the back of the toilet to the soap by the sink, to the bottles of shampoo and body wash along the side of the bathtub.

But there was nothing. No sign of a human or even a struggle. This room had been left untouched by whatever violence had occurred here. Viktor closed the door and turned to the other, ignoring the way his hand trembled as he reached for the handle. It was as if somewhere in him, he knew what he would find. He had experienced this already a long time again, back when his world ended in a flurry of tears and screams and vows of revenge. Images of blood-stained gold hair and ripped body parts rushed back, and he could only close his eyes in hopes it would disappear.

After a deep, shaking breath, Viktor turned the handle and pushed the door open, not caring about the sound it would make when it hit the wall. It reminded him of his grandmother's room before she died. Another assortment of trinkets and framed photos. A bedspread of flowers and leaves in a pale pink color. Underneath the smell of dried flowers coming from the bowl of potpourri on the dresser, there was an underlying smell of blood. His feet sunk into in the carpet as he continued to enter, eyes searching for the source of it. Small droplets of something red lined the floor, leading around the bed to the space between it and the wall. His heart raced in his chest as he prepared to see her body lying there with bite marks on her skin and blood surrounding her gray mass of hair. He imagined the frozen expression on her face, along with her empty eyes and limbs stiffened into whatever shape they were left in when she fell. The old woman's face would be drained of all color, flesh left ashen and cold, just as Jaime's had been when his body had been pulled from Viktor's arms.

He rounded the corner of the bed and found — Nothing.

No body. Only a set of blue scrubs drenched in dried blood bundled into a wadded mess against the wall. He couldn't help the relief that washed through him, the exhalation of the breath he had been holding. His knees cracked slightly as he kneeled to the ground and picked up what he thought was the shirt with two fingers, pinching it as he brought it up to view it better. And there was his answer.

Blackwell Psychiatric Hospital was embroidered right above the chest pocket.

"Damn it," he whispered as he let it drop back to the ground and stood. It answered one question but opened so many others. Each one raced through his head in a continuing stream of fear and anxiety. His limbs froze as he became paralyzed with hesitation, unsure where to go or what to do. The hospital seemed like a fair place to start, but how would Elizabeth manage to hide herself and potentially two others there? Viktor looked out over the bedroom once more, searching for any other clues about where the old woman may have gone. It was obvious she wasn't killed, at least not here. But she may have been turned by Elizabeth or Wyatt.

He retraced his steps and left the apartment, closing the door as softly as possible. Drawing attention wouldn't be productive since there were at least signs of a struggle in there. If the police showed up and he was identified, that could create a whole world of problems. It was only after the door closed and he started down the stairs that he heard someone behind him.

"Looking for Connie?" A gruff voice erupted from the hallway behind him. He hadn't heard anyone as he descended the stairs and stepped into the lobby area of the apartment. Viktor schooled his face into something he hoped looked innocent and concerned before he spun around to face them. A man in maybe his late forties stood with his hands on his hips, a tool belt pulled tight against the denim coveralls with a nametag pinned to his chest. The name was smeared and looked worn away to the point Viktor couldn't read it.

"Yes, sir. Have you seen her? No one answered the door." He tried to play the part of a concerned relative or family friend. The man, a maintenance worker from the look of his outfit, nodded slightly.

"She left last night with her nephew. They didn't say anything. But she seemed slightly upset. I think something happened to one of her family members," he explained softly, as if he were afraid to be overheard.

"Was there another woman with them?" The maintenance worker gave him a strange look, and Viktor realized how his question sounded. He sounded like someone simply seeking information, asking questions that didn't need to be answered.

"My sister. She had been visiting, I think." The false explanation fell off his lips so quickly even he was surprised. The man's face relaxed slightly, the lie settling between them.

"Yea. A blonde. She looked a little rough. So did the nephew."

"Did they say anything about where they were going?" Again, a hesitation as the man's gaze raked over him, trying to find some hint that he was a threat to the old woman and those with her. Viktor trained his face into an expression of worry, of desperation, and the man sighed.

"Something about a warehouse in the industrial district and that what they needed was there. That's all I heard." Viktor nodded and considered the options. The industrial district was huge, and there were roughly ten or so warehouses. It would take time to figure out which one. But maybe, if he looked at what types were there and what they were close to, he could narrow it down. His mind started racing through options even as the man continued to stare at him, waiting for a response.

"Thank you, sir. I appreciate your help." A single nod as the man glanced down the hallway, probably planning his next maintenance request visit. Viktor simply turned from him and marched back to his car to try to find maps of the district.

Chapter 32

Damien

Her fucking blood. She had given it to him. Was that why he had been so obsessed with her since they reached the manor? Or had he been that way before? Had his mind always been filled with nothing but thoughts of her, or was that a byproduct of her saving him?

If someone had asked him only hours ago if he loved Elora, he would have said yes without a single moment of hesitation. But now? He wasn't sure, and he hated it. Damien used the mirror in the visor to glance back at her where she sat side by side with Silas. A long black gown, similar to the one she had been holding in the closet when his world came crashing down around him, clung to her frame. Despite the turmoil in his mind, he could admit that she was a vision, even with her face set in that cold way that reminded him of a sculpture. Her features were twisted until they became sharp lines and hard edges, her eyes dark green shards that revealed nothing of her thoughts or why the fuck she was with them.

He had asked Silas over and over again, demanding to know why she was accompanying them, and why he would drag his niece to the very people who used her. Silas merely claimed that it would make sense eventually, that she had made a choice, and that was what was important. A curse had come from his mouth each time Silas denied him any clear answers, any details. When she had emerged from the manor, Damien had sucked in a breath before sliding into the car. As much as he wanted — no, needed to look at her, he couldn't. It always came back to whether or not her blood had infected him the same way it had Killian and all the other vampires who fed from her. He wanted to say that he had always been obsessed with her, that she had always been a permanent fixture in his mind. But he wasn't sure. Instead, doubt created a film over every memory, every interaction they had. At least now her behavior made sense. Her guilt had been eating her alive.

"Is there a plan here, Silas?" He met the vampire's gaze through the mirror and tracked the way Silas's eyes darted to her, as if seeking her approval for whatever he was about to say.

"We attend the meeting and hear Darian out. I'm sure he has a case he wants to make for him taking over the Ashcroft family and merging it with his own to consolidate power."

"And what are your thoughts? What are you planning to say?" Silas shrugged slightly while he seemed to consider Damien's question as if he were handpicking each word and deciphering every meaning it could have before connecting them in a sentence.

"Depends on what he offers. What he demands. We adjust accordingly." Damien's eyes darted to Elora, who only stared at her hands lying in her lap. Her red hair fell in waves around her face, hiding her expression from him.

"We know exactly what he will demand. And we are taking her directly to him."

"Again, we will adjust accordingly." A noise that distinctly resembled a snarl ripped through the car as they entered the city, and the buildings grew taller and closer together. Damien took a deep breath, regretting the sound that came from his mouth, unsure why he seemed to have no control over himself now. Again, his mind went back to the fact he fed from her, the possibility that every reaction and emotion stemmed from that. Would he get the same hungry look that Killian had in her presence? Would he become so desperate for another taste that he would do anything for it?

No. He would rather rip his canines from his mouth. If his mind even hinted at those urges, Damien would do what he needed to in order to protect her.

"And if he demands her? If he demands your niece? What then?" Another glance at Elora, who said nothing, simply continued to stare at her hands in a way that put him on edge. It was too close to her stillness, to the shadows she retreated into while in the Tower. Then, subtly, so much so that it was barely perceptible, she shook her head. Silas turned back to Damien and gave him a deadpan expression.

"We will adjust accordingly." There was a coldness to his voice that Damien hadn't heard before.

"You plan to give her to him. Plan on sacrificing her to what exactly?" He watched as Silas became stone, every muscle clenched and contracted as if he were in physical pain. Something like regret flashed across his face, the only emotion displayed so far on the car ride.

"I'm not a sacrifice, Damien." Her voice was so low at first that he thought he imagined it. His focus snapped to her where she was still staring at her hands, picking at the skin around her nails as she always did when was nervous or agitated. He wanted nothing more than to clutch them both in his hands, stop her from ripping herself apart.

The three of them lapsed into silence as the car drove down the streets where vampires and humans wandered up and down the sidewalks. Cars passed by them and the entire time Damien struggled to piece together whatever this plan was. Was she aware of Silas's plan? Is that why she was here willingly? There were too many questions and not enough answers.

The driver pulled up along the curb outside The Rose Hotel, which he could only assume was a joke on the part of Darian. An insult to the vampire who sat behind him, waiting for her door to be opened so she could be led to the slaughter. Damien stepped out of the car and onto the sidewalk, glancing down either side of him, assessing for threats and identifying any guards. He spotted two on either side of the hotel entrance, probably belonging to Darian. The two male vampires met his eyes and nodded as Damien opened the back door and held out his hand for Elora to exit.

He refused to look at her even as the heat from her hand seared his own, as if she was branding him as hers. She had marked him in so many ways by now that it seemed unnecessary. He still had marks from where the fork had been lodged in his neck and the stem from the wine glass that had been stabbed into his chest. And that was only physical. The others were too deeply ingrained for him to fully disentangle himself from them.

The Rose Hotel, from what Damien could see, was the type where people didn't worry how much the items in the mini-bar cost. They didn't worry about room service and ordered massages in their room after doing yoga or drinking mimosas for breakfast. Pristine white walls and gold framed windows traveled up all seven stories. The design rendered it old and modern all at the same time and screamed opulence.

Elora released his hand as soon as she stood upright, using both hands to smooth out the fabric while he shut the car door and Silas appeared beside her. His face was the very image of polite disinterest, as if this entire meeting was beneath him. With a small smile at his niece, he extended his arm, and she placed her hand on his forearm as she had done when Damien escorted her to the banquet. And now here she was once more being hand-delivered to those who wanted to control her. The parallels were not lost on him. Silas nodded to him and Damien took his place behind them as they entered through the doors that the guards held open. Eyes lingered on Elora, questioning and hungry as she kept her focus on the path before her. Not once did she allow her attention to waver and look out over the hotel lobby, despite its grandeur.

It reminded Damien of Killian's aesthetic in a certain way. From the frames of the paintings and portraits to the vases that held fresh flowers, gold trimmed every item or covered every piece of metal while the marble floor gleamed as if it were freshly polished. Light instrumental music played in the background as they moved toward the elevators that would take them to the top-floor suite where Damien knew the rest were waiting. The click of Elora's heels on the marble mingled with the music as they stepped inside, and Silas pressed the button for the top floor. Each wall of the elevator was covered in a mirror and Damien tried and failed to keep his focus from her as they rode in silence. Her attention was on the floor, as if she couldn't bear to look at herself, another behavior he had noticed during the time they spent together. She would only look at herself long enough to fix her hair or check her scars. She didn't seem to understand exactly how beautiful she was, exactly how indescribable she was to see in the flesh.

Damien's attention moved away from her as the doors opened into a large room that mimicked the design of the lobby — marble flooring inlaid with gold while flowers covered up the smell of blood. Voices floated in from a room to the left, snippets of conversation as if deals were already being made. It caused Damien's body to tense and prepare for the attack that was sure to come.

Another nod from Silas before their trio entered the side room that contained a large rectangular table with a chair at the head and three chairs along both sides. Already, Darian sat at the head furthest away from the door. Damien recognized Korina reclining in a chair towards the end of the table and a vampire with silver hair sat to the left of Darian — Chloe, head of the Radcliff family. He wasn't sure what Korina was doing there and what role she was to play at the meeting. She tossed him a sultry smile that he turned from to glare at the vampire seated beside her. Jonas, that asshole, sat at Darian's right. Already his eyes were greedily searching for her, boring holes in Damien as if it would make her appear faster, give him a better view of her.

Damien listened to the sharp inhale of breath from Elora as she entered and heard the way she tried to force herself under control. Was she back in that room once more? Was she reliving her darkest memories, as he knew she did when something triggered it? Sometimes it was a smell, he noticed. Other times it was a phrase or a touch. And every time he wanted to banish them all, wanted to destroy Killian all over again. Maybe Darian or Jonas would have to do.

Chapter 33

Elora

She knew every face in the room except for one. A vampire with long, light brown hair that fell in waves over her shoulders. A burgundy button-up blouse matched her dark skin perfectly and her eyes practically sparkled in the light. She was beautiful in a way that dragged even the most loyal of partners away from their lovers just for a taste of what she offered. And it wasn't lost on Elora the way the stranger's eyes went instantly to Damien and clocked every move, every step, every flinch or twitch. A flirty grin spread across her face before her eyes met Elora's. Only then did the smile falter, disappearing in a flash of disgust and thinly veiled hatred.

Elora felt him as he stood behind her in a way that was so reminiscent of their time in the Tower when she was the captive, and he was the guard charged with keeping her in line. A hand touched her arm, drawing her attention to Silas before she dragged her gaze over the rest of the table. Jonas, with his thin hair that hung limp around his shoulders, sat beside Darian. Both vampires wore twin expressions of greed and hunger as they watched her from their seats. Elora could have sworn she heard them both inhale deeply.

The vampire with the silver hair arranged in a messy bun at the nape of her neck was familiar, and it took Elora a moment to place her. She had been at the banquet when Elora's true nature came out, when she had fed for the first time since she attacked Elizabeth. The current look on the vampire's face mirrored the one from that night. Revulsion and rage lined each sharp feature of her face, and her plump lips curled into a sneer as Silas led Elora to her seat at the other end of the table. To her right sat Silas and to her left was Damien with the female vampire, who smiled so wolfishly at him in the next seat between him and Jonas.

"Introductions should be made, correct? There are some new faces here." Silas's suggestion, which was more of a demand, ruptured the tense silence as everyone at the table studied the other, and Elora kept her hands clasped before her on the table. The wood was cool and radiated through the sleeves of her dress, causing her to shiver slightly.

Play the role of the submissive niece, the voice in her head reminded her. She could feel their eyes settle on her like she was an attraction at a fair, kept behind ropes as she stood on a pedestal.

"Of course," Darian's voice reached her, and she felt her nails dig into her palm at the sound. With a slight shrug, she forced away the feeling of his fingers on her skin that acted as a reminder of who he was and what he wanted.

"Darian, head of both Ashcroft and Ravenwell families," he announced.

"Presumptive head, you mean?" Silas's voice was smooth as he smiled at Darian, whose mouth twitched slightly at the reminder.

"Of course." Darian gestured to his left. The female with the silver hair glanced around the room, her assessing gaze meeting each of them in turn before lingering on Elora. She felt the hatred radiate from the vampire's eyes, a centerpiece on the otherwise empty table.

"Chloe. Head of the Radcliff family." Her voice was a surprise with its light, almost musical quality. Elora had imagined something harder, like ice cracking in spring.

"Silas. Head of the Corvin family." He gestured to Elora. "My niece and Killian's daughter, Elora." There was a brief moment of silence as words wrapped around them. Everyone in that room knew who she was, yet the statement of her identity left them all frozen in place.

"Damien," he announced to the table. Elora noted the strain in his voice and forced herself to keep her eyes on her hands, picking slightly at a bit of skin around her fingernail.

"Korina." Seduction laced her declaration of her name and Elora peeked at her slightly, noting the way her sultry grin was aimed at Damien. Slowly, Elora slid her hands off the table and into her lap, hiding the way they curled into fists at the display. It shouldn't bother her this much, and yet it did. She held no claim to him and never would. If he wanted Korina, she wouldn't interfere, no matter what it did to her in the process.

"Jonas." His eyes went directly to Elora, and she felt the weight of them, the greasy tendrils of his desire and obsession reaching across the table to caress her cheek.

"Introductions complete," Darian stated blandly, and Elora listened as his chair scooted back and he stood. "Now, for the reason that I asked you all here. I'm seeking to claim the role of head of the Ashcroft family in combination with my own. Already, I've been acting as such in place of any other claimants."

"And were you the one to end Killian?" Silas's words were almost lazy as he spoke, and Elora finally glanced up in time to see a shadow pass Darian's face.

"I was." Elora stifled a laugh as his words left his lips, as he claimed ownership of her crime.

"I'm afraid, Darian, that your word simply isn't enough when we are discussing the joining of two families together, rendering you the head. That much power would require more than a simple declaration of what you did." Once more, Silas's words were almost bored and uninterested as he spoke. But she knew her uncle was tracking each twitch of Darian's expression, and she had the distinct feeling her uncle was enjoying this greatly.

"I heard that's why you're having trouble gaining support, Darian. Isn't that right?" Damien's voice came from beside her, and she smiled slightly at the sound. She knew if she looked at him, there would be that sneer on his face that she had seen directed at her so many times.

"Gaining support has been a slow process. But with the support of the other vampire heads, I know that I would be able to gather more and take my place."

"Or we can simply dissolve the Ashcroft family and allow the vampires to join any of the three remaining." The suggestion resulted in Chloe nodding along with Silas's words.

Elora watched her uncle grin in the face of Darian's simmering violence. "Unless you can prove you did it?"

"I can't," Darian forced out. "But with the human resistance becoming more and more of a problem, we need to show power and strength."

"Silas's suggestion would allow for that as well. There's no need for you to take control. We would each remain the head of our own respected families and welcome in any vampire who's displaced." Chloe's gaze snapped back to Elora, who simply sat in her chair and studied the swirls in the wood, taking in each word in order to fit it into her fairly non-existent plan. She knew her goal, and she wasn't sure that it mattered how she got there. Either Silas offered her as a show of cooperation or Darian demanded her and her uncle agreed.

No, it didn't matter how she got there.

"I would like to address the glaring issue in this room, Darian. If you don't mind taking a little detour from your obvious power grab. It seems to me that there are more important things to discuss."

"Such as?" It seemed as if Darian were forcing the words out through gritted teeth, as if his jaw was clenched so tight he could crack a tooth. It was satisfying, in a way.

Chloe gestured towards Elora and raised a brow. "That." Only a single word, but Elora felt it deep in her core like a vibration that radiated through her until her hands gripped her gown in her fists to prevent her from doing or saying anything stupid.

"And what about her, Chloe?" Silas's tone held an edge to it. The easy and lazy disguise was shattered at the mere mention of her, and Elora felt her heart warm just a bit.

"She's a problem, and we all know it despite any feelings or obsessions we may harbor." Chloe gave a pointed stare at Darian at the end of her sentence, as if there would be any confusion about who she was referring to before she continued.

"Killian played with things he shouldn't have, and now we are dealing with the aftermath. I'll be blunt. That's an abomination that could destroy everything we have built."

A silence fell over the table as they all absorbed her accusation regarding who and what Elora was, and she wasn't sure she could argue against Chloe. Killian had acted as a god and altered creation when he built her gene by gene. She was sought after by humans and vampires alike, and her blood seemed to cause something dark to rise in the vampires who tasted her. Yes, Chloe was indeed correct.

"What would you suggest?" Darian this time as he stared daggers at the vampire seated beside him.

"Removal from the equation. Again, to put it bluntly, execution." The response was almost instantaneous. It was like Chloe had already called for a vote she had to have known would fail. Darian was obsessed or addicted to her blood at the very least, and Silas would never let her be harmed, even if they didn't know that. Elora knew, and that was all that mattered in the end.

Silas's and Darian's voices merged together in a single word: "No."

Elora watched the female vampire sit up straighter in her seat. Had she not expected this outcome?

"It seems I'm outvoted. But I promise we will come to regret this. When her progeny have overrun the city and have eradicated the human race, we will regret this."

"I'm not sure that the elimination of humans is necessarily a negative thing, Chloe. They have become bland and rebellious. It's resulted in more live feedings, which in turn led to knowledge of us spreading like wildfire. Now, they have formed what they call a Resistance. If keeping her alive leads to their eradication, as you called it, then I see no real loss."

"And the fact you and Killian were addicted to her blood makes no difference?" Darian allowed a cruel smile to spread across his face as his focus moved from Chloe to Elora, and she stiffened under his scrutiny.

Play the submissive, she reminded herself and hunched her shoulders slightly as if the weight of his gaze was too much, as if she was not worthy to meet it.

"If she can help create a new and improved food source, I can't see how that would be a bad thing." Darian's eyes never left Elora as he spoke, the dark hunger never clearer in his normally pale green eyes. Chloe shook her head as if she was cursing the folly of males, and Elora couldn't help but agree with her. Once again, it was about her use and her blood, and it took every ounce of self-restraint to not scream in rage and defiance. That opportunity would hopefully come soon enough.

Throughout the entire exchange, Damien had not once moved or even twitched at the demand that she be killed. She stole a glance at him to see him staring at Jonas, eyes blazing in a way that would make her want to retreat if they were pointed at her.

"Back to the matter at hand," Darian announced as he nodded slightly at Jonas, whose smile only grew to reveal his fangs. She couldn't stop the shiver than ran through her, the instant feeling of their hands once more. Coming into the meeting, she had been so sure that she could do this, that she could face them and fulfill the only goal she had. Now, under their scrutiny and knowing glances, Elora wasn't as confident.

"Silas. Chloe. I have a slight proposition for you. A trade, if you will." Damien shifted in his seat at Darian's words. They had both known this was coming, and she had practically bet on it, had hinged her entire scheme on their overwhelming need for her blood. It was finally about to pay off.

"Let's hear it," Silas drawled, once more playing the role of the uninterested vampire head who was inconvenienced by this entire thing.

"I'll agree to stop my ploy to take control of Ashcroft. I'll agree to dismantling it and accepting vampires into my own family should they wish to join. In return for her." Darian pointed at her from across the table, and Elora darted a look at Silas.

"She's worth more than potentially controlling two different families? Are you serious?" Chloe stared wide eyed at Darian and Elora almost snorted in response. The head of the Radcliff family had no idea how valuable she was to him. Just how much he was willing to give up for one more taste.

"Yes, she is," he responded in a cold tone even as his eyes never strayed from Elora, who was once again staring at her hands. She could feel his focus on her as if it was searing a hole in her chest, in her neck where she was willing to bet that he was focusing his attention.

"I, for one, vote yes. Having her under control is the second-best option besides executing her. And since that is apparently off the table, I can agree to this. Silas?"

Elora's attention shifted to her uncle and noted the detached assessment in his eyes, the disgust as his lips curled slightly. Damien's breathing had quickened, and she could sense how stiff he had become. It was as if he was prepared to defend her, to step in and destroy every vampire in that room to make sure she didn't go with Darian. And she loved him for it even as she wished his newfound hatred for her ran just a little deeper.

"Agreed. My niece for the disbanding of the Ashcroft family. Obviously, terms will need to be set." The screech of a chair being thrown back was the only response to Silas's agreement. Damien jumped to his feet, palms flat on the table, as he leaned over toward his current vampire head. Elora glanced at him, absorbed the hard lines of his face where they had contorted in a rage that was terrifying to behold. Every emotion was on display and each vampire who sat at that table could hear them in his voice, see them etched into his face.

"Are you fucking kidding me? If I had known you were such a cowardly prick--"

"Sit down, Damien, if you wish to leave this room unharmed." Silas managed to match Damien's energy, mirror the anger radiating from every part of him.

"No! You know what he did to her and will do to her again. And you're going to hand her over like that?"

"Damien, please stop." Her words were a whisper meant for him, but she noted the way every pair of eyes focused on the two of them.

"Elora, you can't possibly —" She held up her hand to stop any further words that would break the fragile hold she had on her ability to follow through. Getting Darian to this exact place was meant to be the difficult part of the plan. Elora never thought it would be facing Damien's pain and fury, the hurt in his voice. She knew what he was thinking because she had considered it as well. It had kept her up at night, plagued with nightmares full of accusations and curses. Every time she closed her eyes, she saw each person who had sacrificed themselves to get her out of Killian and Darian's hands. Lukas. Dr. Montgomery. Her mother.

"We both knew this was going to happen. That it was inevitable." His face hardened, and she watched as it happened. Each feature, one by one, became set in stone as if he were carved from marble, rendering him terrifyingly beautiful. But his eyes, those dark pools with flecks of gold, revealed only pain and betrayal.

"Lukas died for nothing then. Denise died for nothing. I hope you can live with that." Damien paused for a moment as he seemed to study her face, probably searching for any hint that this was some horrible joke.

"Don't expect me to save you a second time." He let his words linger between them before stomping out the door. The last thing she heard from him was the elevator chiming as he left.

Chapter 34

Elora

"So, about the terms?" Silas's question broke the oppressive silence that had settled over the room, and Darian smirked.

"I always knew you were an intelligent vampire, Silas. No matter what Killian believed," he explained as he reclined back in his chair. "I knew that you wouldn't want the thing that single-handedly led to your sister's death under your roof."

Elora tried to stifle the flinch she felt at his words, but from the chuckle she heard from the head of the table, she had failed. She had always believed that she was to blame for her mother's death, but hearing it was different. It was a slice across her flesh, a stabbing in her ribs. Silas said something about Killian not always understanding the bigger picture, always being blind to the motivations of others as she attempted to force away the sensation. Her mother had died trying to protect her, to keep her hidden from Killian as long as possible. And those lies and deceptions had resulted in Killian murdering her like he had so many others.

"What are your terms, Silas?" Darian drawled, as if this whole matter was of no consequence now that he had what he wanted almost in his grasp.

"You'll disband the Ashcroft family. Announce it and retreat to your own headquarters. We can sell the Tower and split the money between the three of us," Silas gave her a quick glance, smooth disgust in his features. "And you nor anyone else will not touch her until after everything is signed, once I know you have held up your end of the bargain. But my niece will not be your consort or your blood whore. I still have standards to uphold."

Darian's lips curled slightly at the stipulation that he not touch her, and she said a silent thank you to her uncle. It would buy her time, keep her safe from Darian's greedy hands and teeth until the last pieces could be put in place. She watched Jonas shift in his seat, suddenly uncomfortable, as if he knew Silas was referring to him as well.

"I think that sounds fair. To be honest, Silas, I planned on having the girl marry me. I have been open about my desire to claim her. It would grant her protection as well." Silas nodded along with Darian's words, while Elora turned her attention back to her hands once more and reminded herself that it wouldn't happen. That he would never get to touch her if everything went correctly.

"Here's the timeline I'm imagining, if it's amendable to the two of you." After a gesture from Silas, Darian continued explaining his plan. Chloe hadn't moved, hadn't said a word as the two males discussed Elora's fate.

"We wed in a week. At the ceremony, I'll also announce the end of the Ashcroft family and inform them that they need to pick a different vampire group to join. After that, she's mine without any interference from you or any other vampire." Silas nodded along with each step as a smile crept across his face.

"Agreed. Shall we write up the terms and sign?" Darian grinned at Silas's question.

"She will stay here in the meantime. In this suite, if you like. At my own expense, of course. However, allowing her to return to your home is out of the question, since no one knows where it is. I can't risk that."

"Of course. But I will post a guard to protect her in case anyone decides to break the deal." Jonas and Darian exchanged a look before they both nodded as their silent conversation ended. Elora had no doubt that there had been some unspoken plan to use her presence in the hotel to their advantage. Feeding from her, no doubt, at the very least.

"That's smart, Silas. Since there are so many people seeking her." Silas merely nodded in response to Darian's pointless observation and stood, holding out his hand for Elora. She took it gratefully, determined to get away from the room and the vampires in it. Neither Korina nor Chloe had said a word throughout the discussion of the terms, and Elora darted a glance at both of them. Chloe only stared at her in disgust, the same expression she wore the night of the banquet. The unhappiness with how the pieces had settled was clear, as if she was screaming it into the room, forcing them to listen to every word of her disapproval. And Korina watched her with a strange type of interest, like she was assessing her, trying to figure out if Elora was worth anything.

"I will be getting my niece her own room with two keycards. One for me and one for her guard. Any interference or attempt to break these stipulations will have consequences. Am I understood?" Darian smiled slightly as he nodded and watched her. It felt as if he were trying to find a way around Silas's rules and find a way to her without breaking them.

"Chloe, can you draw up the contract? You were always so talented at legal language," Silas asked as he drew Elora's hand into the crook of his arm. She wondered if he could feel her trembling, feel the way her heart raced in her chest as she tried to escape her body or even reality. It had all become too much. Too many memories. Too many sensations. Too many voices and sounds and smells. Was this simply hunger? Or was it the past coming back to torment her?

"Of course, Silas. I'll have it by morning, and we can sign it before parting ways. Darian can prepare for his wedding, and you can continue to use your niece to our advantage. It's good for her to have a use outside of her blood, isn't it?" Silas said nothing to Chloe's declaration, only inclined his head and pulled her from the room. Neither of them said a word until the elevator doors closed.

"Did you accomplish what you set out to?" There was a strain in his voice, a weariness that made him sound ancient. It was as if trading her, or appearing to, had drained him of every bit of energy or life he had. She watched as he ran a hand along his face before thrusting it through his hair.

"I did. And I thank you for the part you played. I'm sure it wasn't easy." She gripped his hand in her own, hoping he could feel the gratitude, the appreciation she tried to force from her body to his.

"No, Elora, it wasn't. I admit that. But I'm worried about Damien." She tensed as if her muscles had turned to stone and rendered her completely still.

"It was important that he didn't know. His reaction needed to be genuine since they're aware of his protecting me in the past," she rationalized even though the words felt bitter on her tongue. They tasted of lies and delusion and guilt.

"I understand that. I do. But will you tell him now?" She considered it for a moment, sorting through the various avenues, the ways that her plan might go awry if he were to be told. To her immense relief, she was saved from answering by the elevator chiming and opening into the lobby. Once more, she nestled her hand in the crook of his arm and let him lead her to the desk where a young man in a grey suit sat. His blond hair was brushed to the side, and it looked like it had been glued to his head, as if he were worried it would move from the slightest bit of air.

"Two rooms, Jason. The small suites on the fifth floor if they are open." Elora lifted a brow at her uncle's knowledge of the man's name. There was no nametag that she could see, and Silas grinned like a child with a secret.

"Of course, sir. We have rooms four and six open on that floor. Both have a bedroom, ensuite bathroom, and common area. Will that work?" The man's voice was slightly high-pitched as he spoke. His eyes never left the computer in front of him as his fingers moved over the keyboard and the mouse clicked. Elora watched as his face scrunched and then smiled slightly after his explanation.

"Perfect. Put both in my name and only in my name. There will be no notes about who is in which room. All four key cards will be given to me, and I want someone to monitor the cameras on that floor. No one but myself and the guard I will introduce you to are allowed anywhere near those doors." A hard edge entered Silas's tone as he dictated his orders, and Jason simply nodded along.

"Which will I be in?" She asked softly, but Silas put a finger to his lips in a signal that said they would discuss it later and she returned her attention to the receptionist. With a soft grunt, Jason stood and entered the room behind him, where she could hear him moving around. In a few moments, he emerged with a small stack of keycards in his hand.

"These two are for room four and these two are for six. Do you have anyone specific you would like to watch the cameras?" Silas took the keycards from Jason's outstretched hand as he seemed to consider his options.

"Richard and Emily. Richard will take the first shift of 12 hours and Emily will take the rest. Don't tell them anything when you bring them in. I'll give them their instructions."

"Of course, sir. I'll call them now. Emily should be on her way in, and Richard is usually on call in case someone doesn't show up."

"Exactly why I picked them," Silas responded with a small smile on his lips as if he were speaking to a child and letting them in on his secret. She could only watch the exchange, note the way her uncle moved from stern commands to soft explanations at will. He appeared to know everyone who worked there. Or at least the important people. This was meant to be neutral ground from what she understood. No one claimed this hotel or the area surrounding it. So, what was going on?

"I'll alert you once they arrive." Silas simply gave him an indulgent smile before turning away and wandering back to the elevator. The tenseness of his limbs had returned now that the interaction was over. It was as if Silas had donned a mask and now it was gone, revealing the distraught and guilt-ridden vampire underneath. She wanted to pull him into an embrace and promise it would all work out, that she would be fine when all was said and done.

The elevator doors closed, and they traveled to the fifth floor. Silas gestured towards room six and used the keycard to open the door before allowing her to enter first. The smell of dried rose petals assaulted her senses, and she cringed, recoiling back just a step from the way it called forth every emotion and thought she forced down during the meeting. A warm hand landed in the middle of her back, and she shuddered slightly.

"We'll have them removed as soon as we get you settled. I promise. I forgot they were in all the rooms to cover up the smell of cleaner." Each word was lined with regret as she nodded and took a step into the room. First one and then the other until the small hallway opened up into the living room. Cream walls were framed by dark wood with a lush beige carpet along the floor, which somehow drew the room together. It was inviting in a way that made her want to keep going, to not stop until she collapsed on the tan couch placed before a large television mounted on the wall. Generic pictures of the city skyline and the hotel were framed and she had to imagine that every room like this was basically the same.

"The bedroom is through there, as is the bathroom." Silas inclined his head to the right where there was an open door. She spied the large bed covered in pillows and blankets that matched the couch.

"Who will be my guard?" Her question sounded too loud in the room, as if it had filled it to capacity and she and Silas were only intruders in this space. He sighed softly, and she watched something like hesitation rush across his features.

"Damien. I know that it's complicated and messy, but I trust him and him only. You don't need to interact or speak. He just needs to make sure no one gets in here. Darian and Jonas are both problems, which you know better than anyone. Hopefully, it'll take time for them to figure out which room you're in."

"And how did they know you?" She was reminded of the question she attempted to ask while downstairs.

"I own this hotel under a different name to keep myself anonymous, and it worked when I suggested it for the meeting. Everyone believes this is neutral territory, which worked to our advantage." Elora couldn't help but appreciate her uncle's cunning, the way he had shifted so many pieces into position for this to occur. She wasn't sure if it was guilt that motivated him to strategize, to allow her to claim what she wanted, or if it was simply his love for her. Maybe a combination of the two, both feelings tied together in a complicated knot that she wasn't sure could be undone.

Elora huffed a laugh and shook her head. "Amazing," she whispered. "Absolutely amazing, Silas." The expression on his face told her that he wasn't sure if this was meant to be a compliment or an insult, a comment on his ability to lie and manipulate the chess pieces she didn't realize he controlled.

"I need to contact Damien. Take a look at the bedroom and such while I do. I'll also have clothing brought to you, if you like. But there should be a few things in there." She nodded as she turned towards the bedroom, trying her hardest to ignore the way her stomach had turned to concrete, the weight that had settled over her as she waited for Damien to appear.

The bedroom was small compared to the one at the manor, but it was cozy in a way that felt like safety. There were curtains along the glass doors that led to the balcony and a long dresser along the wall just below another television mounted to the wall. At least Damien wouldn't be subjected to her reality shows as they shared this space. She smiled softly as she remembered the expression of horror when he watched a brief moment of the wedding show before everything fell apart at the apartment.

Maybe she should watch it now for research purposes. To know what a wedding included, what would be expected of her. Elora had never planned on getting married, not before the hospital and certainly not after. She had never imagined herself in a white gown with her face covered by a veil. On the shows she watched, white dresses were always said to signify innocence, and that had been ripped away from her years ago. It felt like a lie to wear one now.

Elora peeked into the bathroom, noting the bathtub along the wall with a shower head towards the ceiling. A long mirror lined the other wall with bright lights surrounding it while stacks of towels and tiny bottles of soap and shampoo sat on the counter. She could hear Silas's voice filtering in from the other room as Damin's the name was muttered in an exasperated tone. Once more, her stomach clenched, and she felt her entire body contract as she imagined all the things Damien was probably saying or yelling at her uncle. His declaration as he left the room had been agony, a sharp stab to the heart.

A loud exhale followed the curt goodbye from Silas, and she cautiously stepped back into the common area, as the receptionist had called it. Her uncle's face was tilted up towards the ceiling and his eyes were closed, lips thinned into a line. He seemed so close to breaking apart right there in the room and she knew it was her fault, that she had asked him to say and do things that probably brought back the day he lost her, the day her bright eyes had darkened, and her light was extinguished.

With slow steps, she approached him and wrapped her arms around his chest, resting her head against his shoulder. He tensed for only a moment, as if the shock of her willingly touching him had rendered him motionless.

"Thank you, uncle," she whispered into his perfectly pressed dress shirt, and she felt his arms encircle her. He smelled of something so familiar, a scent that she vaguely remembered coveting as a child when she came to see him. Even then, it had forced her muscles to relax, every feature falling into something like peace when he had been near. She heard his breath hitch at her use of his title. Not once since they were reunited had she used it in this way, never with affection or gratitude. The pain and betrayal had been too close to the surface in those moments, resulting in the word sinking its claw into her tongue, refusing to emerge. She felt it as he seemed to press a kiss to her head before squeezing her once more. On the surface, she was a woman in her mid-twenties, but now, she was simply the little girl who had been stolen from him. They had been ripped apart.

She wasn't going to allow it to happen again.

Chapter 35

Damien

People moved out of his way as he darted out of the lobby and onto the sidewalk. A few cursed him, called him an asshole or prick, but it didn't matter. Nothing fucking mattered. Not anymore. Silas had given her up, and she had allowed him. Rage rushed through him, made his blood boil and pound in his head until he couldn't hear the sounds around him. No cars honked at the stoplights, no drivers shouted at people to move, no conversations about pointless things penetrated the wall of pure wrath that enveloped him. Betrayal was what it was. Just another one from her. First, her blood. Now, she had walked back to Darian and, by extension, Jonas. She had saved him in that car, but for what? To watch her leave him behind? To see her become a shell once more?

Damien didn't bother to check if he had the signal to cross the street and darted into the crosswalk. Vaguely, he heard cars honk, and more people cursed at him. It didn't matter. He didn't care. A sharp ache erupted in his chest as he considered why this had destroyed him so completely. Was it her blood? Chloe had accused Darian of being addicted, and she was correct. Killian had been the same. But both had survived without it for years, roughly a decade. They hadn't needed it. Only coveted it, desired it to the point they were willing to tear her apart piece by piece to drain every last drop from her.

His hand clenched by his side as he stopped and glanced around him. The amount of people had thinned, and Damien guessed he had to be almost five blocks away from the hotel. Some of the initial rage had eased, leaving him with an empty feeling in his chest, a hollowness that reminded him of his days before turning. It ached in a way that made him want to return, to ask questions and demand answers from either Elora or Silas. He had a feeling that Silas would be silent, giving vague responses that left a foul taste in Damien's mouth.

Every word out of Silas's mouth in that meeting had been torture. Every look of disgust and repulsion he gave Elora, every reference to her being a thing to be traded. Damien hadn't truly thought Silas would give her up to them, would hand her over. If anything, he thought that she would at least fight, would destroy everyone in that room. Where was the vampire who stabbed him on multiple occasions, who had destroyed Killian until she was drenched in his blood?

"Fuck," he muttered into the darkness even as he turned around and started wandering back, steps heavy and slow as if he were dragging himself along the sidewalk.

He hadn't expected things to be easy when they left the Tower, but he hadn't foreseen this. Not a single second of this felt real. It was as if reality had faded away and left behind a cruel joke where everyone was laughing except him. No, in this version, he was the joke. Part of him, the side that had been turned to stone while working for Killian, screamed at him to not care, to allow her to give herself to Darian if that was what she seemed to want. He had promised her choices, but never in his wildest dreams had he thought this would be one of them.

The other part of him, the part that had been thawed by her fire, wanted to drag her away from that hotel and hide her again. She had said they both knew this would happen, but why did it need to? Damien could take care of Darian and Jonas if necessary, and he would savor each moment of it. Once more, his thoughts went back to drinking her blood, an experience he didn't remember. When he was near her, it wasn't her blood he craved, but her smile. He didn't want to feed from her, no matter how addictive it was meant to be. He wanted to soak up her laugh like it was the very substance of life itself. If he didn't hear it, his world would crack and shatter piece by piece until there was nothing left.

Even after feeding from her, it was only her he wanted. Not her blood.

The realization stopped him dead in his tracks as he approached the hotel. The outside lights were blinding as he stared at the front door, struggling to find the courage to go in and find her. His parting words to her echoed in his head, and he cursed once more. He had told her Lukas's and Denise's deaths meant nothing now, that he wouldn't be there to save her again. It had been a lie and even then, he knew it. There wouldn't be a single instance where he didn't save her.

"Damien." The feminine voice that caused him to take a deep breath came from the alley between the hotel and whatever the building next to it was. A restaurant? He didn't know and hadn't bothered to look. Damien turned towards it as he strolled into the area that was lit only by a few external lights. Korina stood near the door that probably led to the kitchen or the laundry. Her face was arranged into the same sultry grin she always wore, but there was a gleam in her eyes that never meant anything good.

"Korina." His curt greeting was met with a slight flinch from her before she reclined against the wall in a show of nonchalance.

"That was quite dramatic, don't you think? Especially over her." He tracked the way her fingers twitched before she shoved them in the pockets of her black slacks. There was no weapon he could spot, but that didn't mean anything.

"I don't remember asking your opinion." Her smile faltered, and she glared at him.

"Don't you want to know what happened after your little outburst?" He did, and she knew it. Her lips curled slightly at the edges as he waited. Damien's thoughts raced in a dozen different directions, but they all ended up at the same place. Elora gone and him staying with Silas. There was no world in which Darian allowed him to go with her, to remain at her side.

"It was all a bit boring, to be honest. Chloe was still angry about it being left alive and not executed like she wanted. But she was fairly stupid to think it would happen either way, wouldn't you say?" Damien stiffened as Korina called Elora an *it*, rendering her a thing. He didn't speak, didn't move. Nothing good would happen if he did.

"However, there's happy news. A deal was struck. The Ashcroft family will be disbanded in a week and now I need to figure out where I want to go." She arranged her face as if she were considering the pros and cons of each one, and Damien had to bite the inside of his cheek to keep his temper in check.

"All in return for that thing. The ceremony is in a week. I bet she'll need to go dress shopping and cake tasting. How fun." A wedding? A fucking wedding? Did Darian think marrying her would make it better? Make his desire and addiction somehow okay? Korina chuckled at whatever she saw on Damien's face, and he took a step towards her. Once more, her smile faltered, and her laughter faded away to a tense silence.

"And why were you there? I wasn't aware you were considered that important." Her expression darkened at his words, just as he knew they would. If she wanted to tease him, then he could reciprocate. They knew each other's weaknesses like no other, knew exactly where to hit, and he knew he had struck an exposed nerve. It had always been the vulnerable part of her armor. She had been turned decades ago and had never moved on beyond being Killian's side piece. It had driven her insane, turned her bitter and cruel.

"Darian thought you might want company, a distraction. I was chosen to do that." His skin crawled at the idea of being distracted by her, that Darian would offer her like a consolation prize.

"Is that all the use he sees for you? I would have thought you learned your lesson with Killian." He saw her flinch as if he slapped her and he regretted the cruelty of his words. Korina was worth more than being handed over like this. After a moment, she stared down at the ground, the dirty concrete where years of liquids had been spilled as the trash was taken out. Damien watched her as her eyes darted one way and then the other, as if she were processing something difficult.

"Why, Damien? Why does she matter?" He raised a brow even though her attention hadn't left the ground.

"You were in the meeting, Korina. You heard the answers to that." His voice was soft, hoping to ease whatever pain she was obviously in. He could understand her turmoil, her potential hatred for Elora. For her entire time as a vampire, Korina had sought only status and respect, sought to be desired for more than what her body offered. And in her eyes, Elora could claim all of that despite the meeting making it clear that Korina had all that in spades when compared to the vampire she was so viciously jealous of.

"Why does she matter to you?" Regret radiated from each word in such quantities that Damien felt it in his core. He had never looked back when he and Korina had gone their separate ways. There had been no sign that she had harbored anything for him, any lingering affections.

"I don't know what to tell you. I know you want me to say that she doesn't matter. That she's just someone I was protecting and that I can walk away from her now," he explained before swallowing, debating on exactly what to tell her. Darian had raised her up, and he knew that she would report back to him if she thought it would improve her position. But the look in her eyes was so broken, so shattered that he struggled to find anything but authenticity in it.

"You were the only one who treated me well, Damien. Who respected me. Who cared about me." Her words were quiet, as if she thought if she whispered, they would dissipate before they reached him. He was left speechless at her confession despite having known how she had been treated by the others. But he hadn't thought he was the only one who granted her a shred of decency.

"I'm sorry, Korina. I am, but there's nothing left between us." His phone began vibrating and he pulled it from his back pocket as she wiped away the tears that had started to run down her cheeks. He had never seen her cry. Not when she had walked away from him. Not when Killian had tossed her from his office with a sneer on his face.

Damien answered without bothering to look at the name.

"Yes." He heard Silas clear his throat before speaking. Once more, that anger that had seeped into his core rose to the surface and he turned away from Korina. He couldn't handle them both.

"I need you to do something, but I'm not sure you'll like it," Silas explained, and Damien stiffened. He had known this was coming, but had hoped it wouldn't. Silence lingered between them before Silas spoke once more.

"I need someone to guard Elora until Sunday. Stay with her and make sure no one tries to get into her room."

"Why would that matter, Silas? Why keep her protected after trading her like a bargaining chip?"

"In the deal we made, neither Darian nor anyone else is allowed to touch her. I don't trust them to keep their side of the bargain. I need someone I can trust to not hurt her, to not touch her." There was validity to Silas's fear that they would find out where she was and break in. Their obsession knew no boundaries, no limitations. If she was left on her own, could she fight off them both? Could he even leave her to find out?

"Silas, I don't know if I can." Damien wasn't sure what his response would be when he was in her presence once more. Her betrayal hurt more than anything he had experienced. Worse than every failed promise from his mother. Worse than his father leaving the first time. It felt like a piece of him was missing now, like she had excised the part of him that trusted her and tossed it on the table before him. He couldn't imagine it growing back, couldn't picture that hole filled up once more.

"Damien." His name only. A plea from Silas, from an uncle. "Please." And just like that, Damien crumbled. Every part of him that had planned on denying him disappeared in a single instance.

"Where am I going?" He heard a sharp exhale, followed by a room number. With a final curse for his own inability to leave her, Damien hung up and went to her room, where he was sure she was waiting.

* * *

The room was on the fifth floor, room six. He knocked and waited, glancing up and down the hallway in an effort to identify any blind spots, searching for potential threats or problems. He noted the camera on both ends of the hallway plus one that faced the elevator. The door inched open to reveal a vampire who looked like he had aged decades overnight. Silas's hair was a mess, and his shirt was wrinkled and twisted as if he had been gripping it in his fists. But it was his eyes that displayed everything. It was sheer exhaustion and defeat mixed together to create who was now standing in the doorway.

Silas moved aside and let Damien enter before shutting the door, instantly locking it behind them. "Here. The room key. I have the other one."

"Were any other measures taken to protect her?" All business now. No emotions. No fear or concern for her wellbeing beyond keeping her safe. He wanted to ask how she was, if she had gone silent after the meeting, if she was still in this reality or if she had been dragged into her memories.

"I have people loyal to me watching the cameras at all times and have two rooms rented under my name. Anything else I should consider doing?" Damien grinned slightly at Silas deferring to him as if it would fix anything. Even now, it was taking every bit of restraint he had to not beat the vampire senseless.

"No, that should be fine. It's only for a week, right?" Silas nodded as his mouth moved like there were words he needed to say, but couldn't.

"Yes. She's in the shower or bath. I'm not sure--"

"The bath. She's in the bath." The statements were out of his mouth instantly. He knew where she would be, where she would have ended up after that meeting. Silas gave him a sad smile.

"I have clothes being brought up. Jason, my assistant and the receptionist from tonight, will be bringing them along with better toiletries. He's aware of the precautions being taken."

"And what are the plans for this week? I hear there's a wedding to prepare for." There was a harshness to his tone, something that was a mixture of rage and jealousy.

"Dresses will be brought in a day or so. I'll have her pick pictures of ones she likes tomorrow and then we will move forward with fittings. She's not to leave the room for anything. Any other preparations will be taken care of."

"Understood." Once more, he was her guard. Once more, the good soldier following the orders of the vampire head. It was as if history was repeating itself, like he was trapped in a loop that forced him to repeat every mistake he had made with her, forced him to lose her once more.

Silas let his hand rest on Damien's shoulder in an act of what he thought was comfort, but there was none to be had.

"Protect her, Damien." He merely nodded in response as Silas left and Damien locked the door once more. His steps were achingly heavy as he walked to the bedroom doorway and listened to the water slosh in the bathroom. He had been correct, and he could almost imagine how she was scrubbing her skin raw in water that was too hot to not be painful. She would wrap a towel around her body and then her hair before she wandered out. Silently, without understanding what he was doing or why, he moved through the room to the small pile of clothes on the dresser. Nothing that was hers, from what he could tell. A hotel issued bathrobe. A nightgown. Sweatpants and a shirt. A set of undergarments.

He stifled a curse and placed each item of clothing on the bed. Slowly, he laid out the undergarments, then the nightgown, and finally the bathrobe. He had never seen her wear one, but that didn't mean she wouldn't want to wrap herself up in it. The robe itself was plush and soft, and he could imagine her trying to disappear into it like she had before with the throw blanket he had given her that first day in the Tower. She never knew he had bought it for her, had left it in that room in case she needed it. Even then, he had protected her without realizing he was doing it.

No, the blood wasn't to blame for his own obsession. It had taken root in him before any of that had even happened, before she had stabbed him with a fork, had pushed and goaded him, had rendered him hopeless. It had been like that for both him and Lukas, though he didn't believe his friend had felt for her like he did. Lukas had seen his sister in her. The same desire to bend reality to their will along with the same exhaustion from trying to stay alive, from battling a mind that wanted them to give up and surrender to their darkest thoughts. And Lukas had helped her fight in an effort to save her when he wasn't able to save his sister. The same pain that came each time he thought of his friend ripped through him and he almost doubled over. Lukas hadn't deserved that end, and Viktor would pay for it.

Damien heard her pull the plug, followed by the water rushing down the drain. Her whimper as she stood and the sound of water splashing on the floor reached him as he gave himself a moment. He allowed himself a single moment before returning to the common area and sinking into the couch, feet on the table in a probably pointless attempt at appearing unbothered by it all.

Stone. When she came out of that bedroom, she would only see a statue of him. A hollow husk that simply followed orders and nothing else until she was gone, and he was left behind.

Chapter 36

Viktor

Every person he had spoken to said that this warehouse in particular had a lot of foot traffic lately. It was rarely used according to the locals, which is why they had noticed the change in the first place. The woman in the secondhand clothing store that was only a few doors down said there had been people wandering in and out at all hours. Usually, the workers wore overalls or thick jeans along with khaki work shirts. It was a uniform of sorts, but these people seemed to come from all types of professions. Sometimes she thought she heard screams but couldn't be sure. Screams, shouts, and gunfire were normal to the point most locals didn't hear it anymore. They didn't ignore it, but it melded in with the sounds of cars and honking and loud music from the teen drivers.

Normal. It was just normal for them.

After the third person reported the same thing, Viktor decided it was time to investigate himself. That was how he found himself with a set of binoculars on the roof of the building across the street, shivering in the cold despite his jacket and long sleeve shirt. He had underestimated how close it was to winter.

The building appeared fairly deserted, but he knew that could mean nothing. Elizabeth was unhinged, absolutely insane, but she was also cunning in a way that made this entire mission feel pointless. She would know how to hide them, probably already had some type of escape route planned. A back or side entrance covered from prying eyes. One man he spoke to said he had seen people go in, but they never seemed to come out. Then the man had shrugged and rationalized that maybe he just hadn't seen them leave, as if that version of events helped ease his potential guilt at not intervening or calling the authorities. People here had learned to mind their business, to keep their eyes down and only gossip to themselves.

He let out a harsh breath that became instantly visible in the air before him. This was giving him nothing. No people. No vague cries of pain or anything else. Not even any lights shining through the few windows on this side of the building. Had they converged here and then left, migrated to another spot somewhere in the city? If so, his search would have to start over, and Thorne would be pissed off again. She would probably accuse him of letting Elizabeth escape as well. It seemed that it was his fate to repeatedly disappoint her.

With that thought in the forefront of his mind, blocking any tidbit of common sense, Viktor stood and left the binoculars behind. He could always come back for them after checking out the warehouse. With a slight grunt, he pulled his jacket closer around him and zipped it up before running his hand through his increasingly long brown hair. Jaime would have loved it. He would have threaded his fingers through as they lay in bed, just as he had the day he told Viktor he wanted to be turned and that Viktor should as well. A fierce denial had swiftly fled Viktor's mouth, each word full of disbelief and anger and fear all wrapped up in one cold moment that resulted in a rift between them that was never fully closed.

He gripped the flashlight in one hand before using his other to pat the spot where the gun was waiting to be of use. With movements that felt more confident than he truly was, Viktor made it down the fire escape and across the street, swiftly glancing around him to make sure no one had shown up while he was moving. He hesitated when he reached the front of the warehouse and let his focus rake over it, searching for any lights or sounds that would tell him he needed to be careful.

Nothing. Not a single difference, and he darted down the alleyway, searching for a window he could fit through. The area was filthy, filled with the sound of the rats scratching around in the overflowing dumpsters that lined the far end of the alley. But other than that, there was no movement, no hint that anyone else was here standing guard.

His heart raced slightly as he forced himself to ease his breathing, to keep himself as quiet as possible. If they were here — Elizabeth or Wyatt or the aunt — then he needed to draw absolutely no attention to himself as he moved through the rooms. And if there were others here, those who had been turned by Elizabeth, then he needed to become invisible or simply accept his fate now. A few windows lined the wall, all darkened from the lack of light inside, and he approached the first one. His hands gripped the bottom of the frame as he tried to lift it. The window didn't move an inch and he flattened his palms against the glass, pushing up. Again, it didn't move.

"Damn," he muttered before moving onto the next one, which didn't budge either. Finally, the third window slid up, creaking and protesting the entire way till it was a little over halfway up. Barely enough room for him to squeeze through. It would be tight and probably painful, but it would work.

Viktor shined his light into the space beyond the window and searched every spot he was able to illuminate. It was empty as he expected, but there were items thrown among the crates and boxes that looked ready to be moved. Discarded clothing, shoes, cups, along with what looked like wallets and purses. Not the normal things that one found in a warehouse.

He entered headfirst, keeping his flashlight pointing ahead of him. Or slightly ahead of him as it shifted once his hands reached the cold concrete of the floor. It was smooth under his fingers as he pulled himself in and felt the frame of the window scratch and yank and dig into his skin despite the jacket and shirt he wore. For a second, he thought he had miscalculated and wasn't going to make it through. He would be stuck there until someone wandered down the alley and spotted his legs jutting out from the random window in the discarded and supposedly unused warehouse. Or he supposed he could try to call Thorne, maneuver himself until he could reach his phone and dial her number. But that would be admitting something close to failure, and he didn't want her to see him in this position. He could almost picture the blended look of disappointment and anger he now knew so well.

A soft grunt of triumph sounded from his lips as his waist finally came through and then the rest of him without another snag. With a crash, his legs hit the ground, and he cursed at the pain that radiated from his knees, which had taken the brunt of the impact. Viktor kept his flashlight trained on the empty space around him, on edge and listening for even the slightest noise. A crash. Light footsteps. Breathing, even. Anything that would warn him that someone was there with him. But now that he was inside, it was silent. Not even the sound of rats surrounded him. Instead, it was almost unnerving how quiet it was. The walls seemed to block out the noises from the street, the cars driving past, the horns that honked even this late at night, the music from the bars a few buildings down.

His steps were slow and measured as he inched further into the room, flashlight shining in the pitch-black corners where nothing, but empty space and walls were waiting. Finally, after a long moment, Viktor let out a breath, satisfied that the place was abandoned, and he approached the first pile of items closest to him. A dress—a pale pink thing that was dirty and covered in what he hoped was dirt. To the left of it was a small leather purse, and he picked it up to search inside. A wallet had been left behind despite there being nothing else inside. He opened it and shined the flashlight on it to reveal a young woman with black hair. Twenty-one, according to the license. From a few streets from here, if he remembered correctly.

"Shit," he murmured. There was only one reason someone left behind something like this. He dropped it to the ground and moved onto the next pile. Another dress, but much smaller. Blue with pink flowers and lace around the bottom hem and sleeves. A child. With a noise of disgust, he moved on yet again, cataloging each and every item he found. People from the industrial district as well as some from the more affluent areas, places like the city center and the suburbs. Some were the discarded clothing of entire families.

Finally, he spotted another pile of familiar blue scrubs, and his steps grew faster as he all but sprinted towards them. This was a clue, a hint as to what happened, or at least where to go next. Despite knowing what the bundle of items were, Viktor still cursed heavily when he lifted it up with his fingertips. These were covered in blood. There was no evidence to the contrary, nothing he could latch onto in hopes it was dirt or dried mud. Maybe even oil or grease from somewhere in the area. He held the garment up as he pinched the shoulders before he laid it out flat on the floor in front of him. With the flashlight, he searched for it—the thing that would cement his fears in reality.

Blackwell Psychiatric Hospital.

"Fuck," he whispered as he moved through the rest of the bundle, finding no less than four shirts with name badges discarded within the folds of the rough fabric. One by one, he looked through them, searching for names he recognized. Maybe two of them? He vaguely recalled their names, but he hadn't exactly made friends while he was there. Sometimes, he had met with some of the other nurses at the bar after their shift, but that had been mostly to gain information and gossip. After the first couple of years, he had basically stopped going. Only once in a while to try to keep up professional relationships in hopes no one would question how much attention he gave Elora.

These two, if they were who he thought they were, had worked in the medium security ward, but on a different shift. The other two he didn't know. Probably another ward, but which one? There was the maximum-security ward where Elizabeth had been held and then there was the low security one where residents were able to get passes to visit their families. Elora had been in the mid-security unit. Families were able to visit, bring treats or gifts, but no one left, and any visits were closely monitored for any sign of violence or hostility. But only a few residents had anyone who even called, and even less had visitors. There was no children's ward. That was an entirely different building on the other side of the city, from what he understood.

Questions raced through his head as he pocketed the name badges and stood to look through the rest of the warehouse. Why nurses from the hospital? What was this place? A meeting ground? A place to turn humans? Was it Elizabeth doing it, or had she recruited others, like Wyatt? And if so, for what purpose? Viktor had a terrifying feeling that the answers to these questions would be catastrophic and that they could be summed up in a single truth—annihilation for humans. But again, why? Elizabeth was insane, that much was clear. But this appeared so organized. If she had systematically turned nurses, then there had been some rational thought behind what she was doing and that was utterly blood chilling. Insane and intelligent were never a good combination when bloodlust was involved.

Viktor walked through a doorway that led to another space. Cots lined the room in neat lines. Restraints were tied to each one, but he doubted that they had done much good since there were quite a few cots that were completely destroyed. Bits and pieces of the frames lay strewn across the room along with pieces of the thin mattresses, which looked suspiciously like the ones at the hospital. This was getting too coincidental to ignore.

Deciding he had seen enough and that he needed to make a phone call, Viktor left the way he came. His focus lingered on the child's dress, the dark spots along the collar, and shuddered. Children. They were potentially turning children. This was why he had refused to turn to begin with, no matter how much Jaime had begged. Viktor knew of their cruelty, their desire for blood that seemed to overshadow anything else. Jaime had only seen some romantic version of it all, had explained they could be together without worrying death would separate them. That had been the beginning of the end for them. After that night, they never truly looked at each other the same. Love that had shown so brightly in both their eyes had dulled even though they were desperately trying to latch onto each other, to save what they had shared in hopes the other would change their mind. Maybe that was why Jaime had turned even after their fight. Maybe that was his solution to the death of so many years of dedication and love.

It was easier to get back out this time, as if the window had shifted since he came through the first time. Once he was back in the alley, he sent Thorne a message that he had an update and then reminded himself to wait to call the other person he needed to see, reminded himself it was probably the middle of their shift.

Thorne, however, returned his message instantly with the demand that he report back now.

* * *

She was waiting when he walked through the door to the main headquarters, standing at the foot of the stairs. Her graying hair was tied back in a low bun and her eyes were cold, almost frigid. Viktor instantly stood straighter as she studied him. He was sure she tracked the dirt covering his jeans, the small tear in his jacket that he hadn't noticed before then. Probably a gift from the window as he forced himself inside. No welcome. Just a jerk of her head towards the kitchen that seemed to be their unofficial meeting place. Either that, or she simply wanted her cup of tea that she drank in almost unholy amounts.

"Well? Don't wait to start on my account," she demanded as she did exactly what Viktor had anticipated and pulled a mug from the cabinet before moving onto the kettle and tea bags.

"I think it's exactly what you were afraid of. I found the warehouse where they seemed to be staying, but it was empty. Only clothes and such. I checked a few of the wallets and purses I found. I also found some cots in one room with restraints and broken frames, ripped up mattresses." He paused as Thorne sat down in front of him and reclined back in her chair. Nothing on her face revealed any sense of surprise at his words. It was as if she had been prepared for this the entire time and was just getting confirmation.

"She's turning them. Or has set in motion turning them. A perfect system. She turns a few who then turn a few. So on and so forth until there's nothing left." Thorne sighed as he finished explaining his theory and took a drink from her mug that read "Cat Mom," despite there being no cats on the premises.

"You're right. I was afraid of that. It was the worst-case scenario, but it was the one I thought was most possible. Is the target a part of it?" She watched Viktor closely, probably searching for any sign that he was protecting Elora or hiding information.

"There's no evidence that she is, but I don't know. If you want my opinion, I think Elizabeth is working alone."

"Why do you think that?" Viktor was shocked at first that Thorne even wanted to hear what he had to say, was interested in his insight into Elora at all. He had already been accused of being a traitor because of his feelings for her.

"It's difficult to explain. She—" Viktor considered his words. "She has a respect for humans. She truly thought she was one for years and when she realized she would have to drink blood, it was repulsive to her. And she was haunted by what she did to Elizabeth. That she bit her and turned her. I just don't see her being part of it."

Thorne leveled a cold, assessing gaze at him, taking in each feature of his face. He didn't bother to hide his emotions or his thoughts. It was pointless now.

"You truly think that? Based on what you know about her?" Viktor nodded and stared down at one of the scars along his wrists from his stay at the Tower.

"I do." Thorne's lip twitched, almost like she was holding back a smile, and Viktor shifted. Was it because he had revealed something he wasn't meant to? Was it because she now realized how much attention he had paid to Elora? Was it the proof she needed to get rid of him?

"What else did you find?" The abrupt change in topic unsettled him, gave him the feeling he had missed something crucial in the exchange.

"Scrubs from the psychiatric hospital. I plan on talking with a friend in the morning to see if anything strange has been happening and then I would like permission to do a recon trip. See what is going on over there." Thorne shook her head and set the cup down, leaning forward until her forearms rested on the table.

"Speak with your friend or colleague. See what they know, if anything. But do not go there alone. If she's using the hospital as some type of base or has turned people there, it's too risky. Understand?" Her words were cold, edged with a command Viktor knew she expected to be heeded. He just wasn't sure that he would. Since his loyalty had come into question, every fiber in his body had screamed at him to find the secrets, identify the leads, to do anything to prove himself. Over and over, Elora's voice filtered into his thoughts, calling him a fool. They mingled with Thorne's revelation that he was no longer trusted. A whirlwind that left him with a single thought, a single desire. Prove himself once more. To the Resistance. To Thorne. Even to Elora.

Chapter 37

Elora

They spent almost three days in absolute silence. Only the sound of the television filled the space. Not even a muttered "good morning" or "good night." Nothing. It was absolute agony, and she felt herself falling back into the dark place she knew all too well. And it wasn't just that she and Damien weren't speaking, that he was ignoring her existence beyond making sure she was safe. It was all of it. It was her impending nuptials where so many things could go wrong. It was being locked in the hotel suite because there were too many vampires who wanted her, namely Jonas and her husband-to-be. History was indeed repeating itself, and the nightmares were once more tearing her sanity apart piece by piece.

Every night she saw Wyatt forced to his knees in front of Elizabeth. But when it came to the moment when Elizabeth bit him, it was Elora's teeth in his neck. She felt Damien dead in her arms in the back of that car before Killian returned from the grave to drag her back, all decaying flesh and crawling maggots in the stab wounds. She heard Lukas screaming at her that she had killed him, that it was her fault.

Each time she woke with a start, the pillow soaked through with sweat and tears. The first night there had been holes in the blanket where she had gripped it so tightly. Just outside the door, she thought she could sense someone standing there as if they were afraid to come in. Not once did Damien comfort her, and she knew he never would again. He wasn't saving her from the mess she had created. Hopefully, when all was said and done, he would understand. After all, hadn't she finally understood why he goaded her that night, why he told her about Viktor's blood, pushed her until she lost control, and stabbed him in the chest with the stem of a broken wineglass?

He hadn't even said a word while she flipped through the catalog of wedding dresses brought by Silas. Instead, he had excused himself and left the room, only returning once her uncle called him back before he left. She had picked three dress options. Each one was carefully chosen to send a message, one that couldn't be ignored by anyone in attendance.

And now he was gone again to help whoever was delivering the dress options. She was to pick one and then it would be adjusted as necessary before Sunday. It all felt too quick, too rushed. Time needed to stop moving for a few hours, needed to allow her to catch up and come to terms with everything. It had been her plan, but she felt like she was barely staying afloat, barely keeping herself from drowning. Elora was meant to be the puppet master, but she felt like anything but that. Someone was pulling her strings, but she didn't know who.

Just as the date that was occurring on the reality show she was watching started going downhill, a knock sounded at the hotel door. The dresses. A bitter taste coated her tongue as she questioned it all briefly. Would the dresses feel like shackles? Would they make her want to remove her skin, like she had at the banquet? As she pushed herself up from the couch and turned off the show, Elora shook her head. It didn't matter if it did or didn't.

Another knock. This time was almost aggressive in how hard the fist hit the door. Damien. He was probably already irritated about being dragged into this, forced to do more than simply sit on the couch and ignore her very existence.

"Alright," she called out as she opened the door. A scream erupted from her mouth as the door was thrown open and hit her face. She felt her nose twist, followed by her blood gushing down her face, dripping onto the sweater and then the carpet.

Elora staggered backwards, steps uneasy and stilted as her hand went to her face to try to stop the blood. Only then did she glance up and see the sneering face staring at her like she was a feast, and he was a starving man. Bile rose in her throat as she took one step back and then another.

"No! Silas! Damien!" She screamed their names over and over as Jonas shut the door behind him, leering at her as he started to step forward.

"Your uncle thought he was clever when he made those stipulations, didn't he? He really thought we would follow them. That I would follow them when you're being given to Darian?" Jonas tutted his tongue as he continued to step forward towards her. For each of his steps forward, she took one back, over and over.

"We're going to have such fun," he promised, and his tongue darted to his lips as he ran it over them. Her heart pounded in her chest with such intensity she was sure it would simply cease beating at any moment. All she could think was that she had messed up, that she had opened the door without checking who was there, and now he was here with her.

Jonas's grin grew until she could see his fangs that seemed to protrude from his mouth, and he tipped his head back. His eyes closed as he inhaled and moaned slightly, the sound forcing vomit to rise to her mouth. Finally, he glanced back down at her and his eyes grew darker until there was nothing left but blackness.

"Perfection." Before the word was out of his mouth, she ran. Her feet pounded on the carpet as she twisted and raced towards the bedroom, the bathroom, anywhere with a lock. If she could barricade herself, then Silas and Damien would have time to get back. They would deal with Jonas, toss him out and send him back with his tail between his legs. Jonas would be on the list after Darian, if she survived this. Killing him now would only cause problems. Her illusion of the submissive niece, the broken woman who had been given as a gift was paramount to her plan. To show her own teeth, to reveal the violence beneath the surface, would be to undo everything.

Fingers wrapped around her loose braid and yanked back, dragging her body back before she managed to make it to the bedroom door. A scream erupted from her lips, tore from her throat even as tears rushed unbidden to her eyes. She didn't want to cry, didn't want to give him something she knew he loved to see. He savored it almost as much as her blood.

"No, no. Don't do that," he purred cruelly as she hit the ground, his hand still wrapped around her hair. Slowly, so slowly, he dragged her to the living room. Her screams never stopped, neither did the thrashing of her body and the kicking of her feet. Her hands grabbed at his own as she tried to pry them off of her.

"Stop! Please!" The words were on repeat, a chant, a demand that was met with only dark laughter as if he was soaking up the sound.

Once more in the center of the main room, Jonas's hands released her hair, and her head bounced off the floor. The pain swept through her as she cried out before turning over onto her knees, trying to force herself to her full height.

Just stand up. Stand up and run.

The hungry look in Jonas's eyes was worse than anything she remembered seeing. Flashes of him cornering her in the Tower rushed back, visions of him leaning down to touch her face before whispering violent promises to a child. She had been a child.

Her hands gripped the carpet as she stood and was given a brief moment to draw air before a hand clenched around her throat, blocking her airway as he maneuvered her where he wanted her. The carpet caused her to trip, feet never finding enough traction to stand up straight, to gain some semblance of balance. She whimpered as her fingers dug into his hand, nails digging into his skin until she drew blood. He was in control here and he knew it. He wanted her to know it as well.

Her back hit the wall, and she tried to scream again, but nothing came out. She tried to inhale, to breathe, but his hands simply gripped tighter. Her hands struck out, hitting his cheeks as she clawed at his face until he hissed in pain and grabbed her hands, pinning them together in one of his. Three slashes appeared on his cheek, but healed instantly before her eyes. The skin pieced itself back together, leaving only three pink marks behind.

A grin that promised everything she was terrified of spread across his flushed face. Jonas leaned in and ran his tongue over her face, from her chin over her lips and onto her cheek before licking his lips once more and moaning at the taste. She could smell him, the scent of her blood and his cowardice. Her vision started to darken slightly, tiny dots appearing as her head grew light and her body relaxed. He wouldn't kill her. Darian would destroy him if he hurt her too much. It was the only consoling thought she could latch onto as her eyesight began to dim.

His fingers loosened and oxygen rushed into her airway as she regained feeling in her limbs. The room came back into focus, and she prayed that maybe that was all, that he just wanted to scare her and show her that she was his. Yet, she felt him breathe as he leaned forward and ran his nose along her jawline and down her neck before placing tiny kisses along her collarbones.

"Silas! Damien!" Her screams erupted once more, and his hand released her wrists before moving over her mouth as irritation raced across his features. Would they make it back? Would they get here before his teeth sank back into her neck?

"Shh, now Elora. That isn't necessary," he scolded softly as the hand on her neck tightened just enough to keep her from moving too much. The other wrapped around her wrist and gently pulled it up to his mouth. Revulsion and understanding slammed into her and she tried to shrink, tried to pull her arm from him, but he shook his head and gripped her neck tighter. Once more her airway was constricted so she could only take shallow breaths that did nothing for her. Her lungs screamed for oxygen as her heart pounded faster and faster with each second that passed.

She had escaped this once but had walked back into it exactly as Damien accused her of. Jonas's lips kissed the flesh of her inner wrist and lingered on the raging pulse there. He met her gaze as his teeth sank into her skin and her own eyes squeezed shut, not wanting to see what she knew was coming.

The sound that tore from her wasn't human or vampire, but something else. Something shattered and condensed and all-consuming. It caused the mirror beside her on the wall to shake and Jonas drank even as she wept and screamed and begged and prayed. Or maybe she hadn't? Maybe all those sounds were trapped in her mouth, her vocal cords cut as he took and took. Maybe this was a nightmare, and she would wake up at any second.

Elora's eyes snapped open to see Jonas's own closed as he clutched her wrist to his face and the sounds of feeding filled the room. With a quick jerk, her knee shot up and hit him between the legs where all men were weak. She felt his grip on her neck and wrist loosen, felt his teeth slip out of her skin. With every ounce of strength she had left, Elora shoved him with her hands flat on his chest while blood rushed down her arm and poured onto the carpet.

Jonas, satiated and almost drowsy, toppled to the ground, his head bouncing off the carpet. He didn't make a sound, simply licked his lips once more and smiled. How many times had she seen that look on Killian's face once he was done? They sat there in the room for a second, a strange silence falling between them as if time had stopped and this was the moment they were both stuck in. Elora pressed herself against the wall, watching him as he groaned and then chuckled, the sound was an ice pick stabbing into her ears and she could only hope she would go deaf.

"You're going to be so much fun," he forced out between laughs. Still, he did not move to stand or do anything other than savor the blood that now filled him. Her thoughts were frantic screams and demands to hide and run as she pushed off the wall and darted past him, leaping over his outstretched arms before slamming the bedroom door shut and turning the lock. Tears came back, merging with the blood as they fell to the floor. Her head was throbbing from where he pulled her braid, where he dragged her by it like it was a leash. Pain radiated from her wrist, and she wasn't sure if her nose was broken or not. The blood there had dried a little, but she could feel it across her face, caked on her cheeks and chin. She knew the rest of her looked just as horrible, just as bloody.

Jonas groaned slightly and then there was movement in the room. She could hear it as he seemed to stand and walk towards the bedroom door, towards her. Her hands latched around the handle as if it would help, as if it would do more than the lock she had already put in place.

"A few days, Elora. Then you're ours to do with as we please. No one will be able to save you. Not your uncle. Not Damien. No one." She felt him on the other side of the barrier for a second more before he moved through the room again and the door opened and closed. Only then did she sink down to the floor, clutch her knees to her chest, and allow herself to fall apart and weep. Her body trembled and shook like something was trying to break free from inside her, ripping her apart in the process. Elora would welcome it if only to escape the feeling of his hands on her, his tongue on her skin. Vomit rose in her throat, and for a second, she feared she was going to ruin her uncle's carpet in a different way.

What she knew was that Jonas was wrong. She wasn't going to be theirs. Never again would she be someone's possession.

Chapter 38

Damien

The three drinks he had thrown back so far had done nothing to dull the ache in his chest. There had been only emptiness when they had been informed by the front desk that the gowns were there for her to try on. She had nodded and said to send them up before the voice on the other side claimed they needed assistance with them.

And he had jumped on the opportunity like it was the last drop of water in the desert. She would be fine, he told himself. Silas was on his way up, and they would simply switch places. He would help get the dresses into the room and then disappear once more. Watching her look through the catalog had been torture, or maybe it was a punishment for rejecting her, for his words to her before he left that meeting. Either way, he couldn't face it. He couldn't watch as she stared at each dress with a cold calculation that felt out of place, felt wrong for what was happening. Was she going to make a statement? That would be like her. Nothing she did was subtle or without purpose. She may have been forced into this position, but the rest would be on her own terms.

But he hadn't thought they would be in this place at all. In his mind, they had continued to live at the manor. He would work for Silas and spend his time with Elora while they tried to see where their—

Their what? Relationship? Friendship? He wasn't sure what to call it or if he should even attempt to label it. Their past together was too complicated for a single word. But they would have stayed together, and that was what mattered. That wasn't an option anymore. On Sunday, any delusions or dreams he had harbored would truly disappear, vanish into a void where all broken hopes went.

Damien lifted his hand at the bartender for another drink. The woman, pretty with dark hair and darker eyes, only shook her head sadly before taking his glass to replace it with another. He would simply drown her out and if that didn't work, he would cut her out of his chest himself. Light music filtered through the room, some type of orchestra symphony, which felt very much like something Silas would have played at a bar in his hotel. Were they up there right now, picking and choosing from the dress options? Were they pinning it to make it fit her perfectly?

Fuck, that drink couldn't come fast enough.

A body settled onto the barstool beside him, smelling of something so familiar he would know it anywhere. It was a part of him now, and not simply because he had consumed its source. He spun his entire body to Jonas, who lifted his own hand for a drink. Messy hair fell flat against his face and there was blood down the front of his cheap button-up shirt.

Her blood. Damien glared at the vampire beside him, debating his options. He could kill him. Smash his head into the bar top and then stab him with a broken glass. It would be poetic in a way, since Elora had done something similar to him not too long ago. Damien could drag him out into the alleyway and beat him until it would take weeks for him to heal completely. Each option felt better than the last.

The bartender set a glass down in front of both of them, but Damien's eyes never left Jonas even as he grabbed his cup and downed it, savoring the amber liquid before swallowing. He needed to calm his heart rate, ease the tension from his body before he did something stupid. Not something he would regret, but something that would more than likely cause problems.

"Damien," Jonas said before taking a drink from his own glass.

"Jonas," he mimicked back before he turned back to the bar. Maybe he was overreacting. Maybe Darian had a supply of her blood from Killian, and that was where the crimson on his shirt came from.

"How are you feeling about this wedding? I imagine it's hard for you." Jonas's tone was too light, too easy and Damien felt himself tense once again.

"Not my place to have any feelings about it." Jonas chuckled loudly at Damien's response, as if he had told a joke.

"We both know that isn't true. You helped her escape. Everyone knows it. I also remember the banquet."

"I protected her on Killian's orders. From what I heard, you were scolded for touching her."

"Maybe so. But believe me when I say I got to do that later." Damien felt his hand clench into a fist as he fought desperately to keep himself in control. He took a deep breath and exhaled slowly as his hand loosened.

"I've heard the stories" was all he could force out between his teeth as they ground together.

"Her taste really is something unique," Jonas grinned widely at Damien, twisting on his stool to fully see him. "It's hard to go without for too long."

Damien simply sipped at his drink and peeked a glance at Jonas in the mirror behind the bottles of liquor.

"I wouldn't know. I prefer when those I feed from give consent. Or maybe that isn't something you're able to get?" Damien watched the flash of rage on Jonas's slightly warped features in the mirror.

"She was created to be fed from. Consent isn't necessary when she's a walking blood bag." Jonas sneered before turning to the bartender to order another drink. There was nothing for Damien to say. Nothing that wouldn't reveal too much to the prick beside him who would run to his master hoping for scraps. Instead, the words screamed inside his head, throbbing against the confines they found themselves in.

She is more than that.

She is more than you will ever be.

She deserves more than this.

And we are not worthy of her.

But the words remained unspoken, a repetitive chant that continued on and on in the tense silence between them. Jonas took another drink and smirked.

"Sometimes you just can't wait, you know? Sometimes you have to find a way to get what you want." Damien's eyesight went white and then black as Jonas's words reached him. His nails dug into his palms as the implications of those words hit him like repeated blows to the gut, the jaw, everywhere.

"I'm not sure what you mean. I've never had to find a way." He was goading Jonas now, and he knew it based on how the other vampire had grown almost sullen as he nursed his drink. The blood on his shirt had dried, but the scent still lingered in the air between them. It brought to mind visions of violence and a smile so beautiful he would tear stars from the sky to see it only once.

"I'm sure she gives it to you willingly. But some of us have to take it," Jonas drawled slightly as he licked his lips like there was something left there for him. As if there had been something there to begin with. His body vibrated with unspent rage, with the understanding that something had happened. And he needed to be with her. Jonas would be dealt with later.

Damien finished his drink and marched away from the bar, his hand in his pocket where the keycard was. A harsh chuckle followed him like a rabid dog as he darted to the elevator, no longer bothering to keep himself contained. His steps were fast and heavy on the marble flooring as he ran through every scenario in which Jonas had gotten to her. How could he? How did he find out where she was? Where had Silas been? Too many questions and no answers. At least not yet.

He didn't hear the elevator chime as he got off and stomped towards her room, using the key card in his pocket to open it. Silas stood in the center of it, hands limp at his side, staring at the closed bedroom door. The scent hit him first, heavy and all-consuming. Lavender and copper. Damien's eyes shot around the area, lingering on the small puddle of blood that had soaked into the carpet and the droplets scattered around the furniture. Instantly, he was torn from this time and place, from this reality and sent back to the night she came to his room completely covered in blood and bites and wounds.

"What happened?" Damien's voice echoed in the room and Silas jumped, as if torn from a dream.

"I—" Silas stopped and swallowed before shifting his attention back to the door. "I don't know. I just got here."

"You were supposed to be up here! It's the only reason I even left to help that woman with the dresses," he shouted as he moved frantically through the room, eyes lingering on every drop of blood.

"I helped with the dresses, Damien. They're over there." Silas gestured to the couch where a stack of garment bags was thrown across the cushions. Damien stared at them for a long moment as he waited for reality to catch up.

"But they called up here. Told her they needed help with them, and I agreed because I thought you were going to be in here. When I didn't find the assistant, I assumed you were with her." Damien felt his heart drop through his stomach and out through his feet, sinking into the carpet beneath him. None of this made sense. Jonas couldn't actually be that intelligent. At no point had that vampire given even the slightest hint he could do more than follow orders. And if it was orders, why would Darian not partake as well?

"Who was here?" Damien was certain Jonas had been there, but was he the only one? Silas shrugged and jerked his head towards the bedroom.

"She's in there. And she won't talk." Defeat laced each word, and if Damien didn't know better, he would think Silas actually cared about his niece. But he had already given her up, traded her in exchange for the division of power to remain the same. For Silas, it was nothing more than an insult. Jonas had blatantly thrown the terms in his face despite what had been discussed and agreed on.

"Leave. Find out who managed to fucking trick us." Silas simply nodded at Damien's order before leaving the room. His shoulders had sagged as he seemed to drag himself away, as if he were carrying the weight of the world on his back.

Damien locked the door and rested his forehead against it as his eyes closed, taking in a deep breath. Control. He needed to be levelheaded for this. A single sign of his rage could frighten her and send her in the opposite direction. He had seen how Elora sank into herself as a means of protection. It was as if she thought by cutting off every emotion, she could avoid agony and fear and everything else that plagued her. The risk of disappearing into the darkness was worth it if it meant no more pain.

And now she had been hurt again.

Slowly, he made his way over to the bedroom door and sat down in front of it, leaning back and resting his head against the wood. Some part of him knew she was in a similar position. Only her knees would be pulled up to her chest and her face would be buried in them. His suspicions were partially proved correct when he heard her sniffle through the door, and he closed his eyes. In almost complete detail, he could see her curled with her hair a mess that fell around her face and shoulders. The blue sweater she had been wearing when he left would probably be torn and covered in blood. Would there be any wounds? He had to imagine there was considering how much blood was on the carpet.

"Elora," he whispered through the wood. Would a louder voice startle her? Scare her?

Nothing except the sound of someone shifting.

"Elora. I need to see you. I need to know—" Damien stopped himself before he said something stupid, like needing to know she was okay. It was dangerous on two fronts. On the first, he knew without a doubt that she wasn't and that if she said she was, it would be a lie. The second was it was too vulnerable, too honest, and that was gone between them. But he did need to know. The very idea that she was there bleeding or crying was too much.

"Please, Elora. I just want to see you." Damien hung his head, fully prepared to hear no response. Even just the sound of her voice would be enough.

"Is it only you?" His heart leaped into his throat at the sound as he twisted his body towards her voice. Yet he couldn't even enjoy it as he noted the fear and uncertainty there.

"Yeah, just me. I promise." She seemed to hesitate for a moment before he heard the door unlock. His moments were clumsy as he jumped up and stood as the door inched open, then stopped. A blood splattered face peeked out from the space between the door and the frame. Her eyes darted across the room, searching for any sign that he was lying, that someone else was there. He heard her exhale before she pulled the door open and stepped aside.

Damien entered the room, focusing instantly on the large crimson spot on the carpet in front of the door before looking over the rest of the space. Nothing else had changed since he left only a few hours ago. The bed was messily made, like she had just tossed the blankets up towards the pillows. A large suitcase sat open on the dresser with her clothes spilling out. He heard the door click shut, followed by the lock moving into place behind him, and he spun back towards her.

"Damn it," he whispered harshly as he took her in. Her hair was a wild, tangled mess that was somehow shorter. Instead of resting down her back, it fell into knots around her shoulders. His eyes searched the floor and found the pile of her hair thrown across the room. Damien returned his attention to her face, noting that it looked like something struck her nose, resulting in the dried blood that now covered her lips and cheeks. There was a piece of fabric wrapped around her wrist, but the blood had seeped through.

"I put my nose back in place," she murmured as she pointed to it with trembling fingers. Their eyes didn't meet even as he silently pleaded with her to look at him so he could see that she was okay, could see if she had retreated to her dark place.

His steps were slow and cautious as he moved towards her, hands held in front of him. Still, she didn't move, simply stared at the spot on the carpet that was drenched with her blood. Finally, they were face to face. Only a few inches separated them as he touched her arm with his fingertips. He didn't know what had happened, how far it had been taken, or if she would even want to be touched.

"I thought it was the woman with the dresses. I thought it was you," she explained, voice cracking. Tiny shards of each word fell from her chapped lips and lingered between them as he struggled to form any of his own. It didn't matter who she thought it was when she opened the door. It never should have happened. And he decided then that it never would again. Jonas's hands would never touch her again.

"It's okay. It doesn't matter." He laid his palm flat on her arms before squeezing slightly, hoping to still the trembling that was threatening to shatter whatever semblance of calm she was managing to hold together.

"No, if I had just looked before I open—"

"No. No. None of that matters. You did nothing wrong." He felt her shoulders shake as tears raced down her cheeks.

"It was Jonas," she muttered after a long moment and took a step closer to him as if asking him to hold her. He didn't move at first as he felt the heat from her body. How much contact would be okay? What would be too much? His arms hesitated as he encircled her and pulled her against his chest. She buried her face in his shirt before resting her cheek on his shoulder. All at once he felt her muscles relax, her shoulders lower, and her breath come out in a single shaky exhale against the side of his neck.

"I know. Was it just him?" He felt her nod against his shirt, and he squeezed a bit tighter.

"I opened the door before I knew who it was and before I could stop him, he was inside—" She fell silent and Damien lowered his head to hers, pressing his lips to the mass of red hair. He could smell the blood that covered her, but below that was the smell of who she was—lavender. His mother always said that particular scent was used to ease anxiety, used to calm racing thoughts and diffuse spiraling fears. And that was what she was for him. Even now, the fury that had filled his entire being was gone, settled into a corner of his mind until it was needed once more. She was the song that lulled the beast crawling beneath his skin, and he was powerless against her.

"You don't need to tell me what happened, love," he murmured into her locks, and he felt her shake her head as he tried to ignore the fact he had once again called her love, once again blurred that line between them.

"I need to. Please."

"Okay. Whatever you need." She moved away from him, and he let his hands fall down to his sides. He felt the loss of her like a removal of something vital, something would render him complete once more if he only gained it back. His eyes ran down the length of her, noting the slight limp as she walked and the way she seemed to hold her head impossibly straight, neck a steel rod. Slowly, she crawled onto the bed and crossed her legs in front of her before patting the empty place beside her.

Damien sank into the mattress and faced her instantly before clutching her hand with his. Words began to spill out of her mouth as she explained what had happened. How Jonas had forced his way in, and the door had slammed into her face, breaking her nose. How she had run but couldn't move fast enough and he grabbed her hair, pulling her behind him with her braid. How he had licked at the blood on her face before sinking his teeth into her wrists. After she had managed to lock herself in the bedroom, she had cut off her braid with the dull scissors in the bathroom.

It was as if she needed to purge it all from her system like a toxin, like maybe if she gave it words, it wouldn't be able to hurt her anymore. His blood boiled at each sentence from her mouth and visions of the fate Jonas had designed for himself threatened to consume him. Her head dropped down to her chest now that she had said what she needed to. Every trace of who she was had slipped away, and he cupped her cheek in his hand, forcing her to meet his eyes. The depth of the darkness in her eyes was so vast he could get lost in it. It was the type of darkness that snuffed out the light around it, absorbed it into a black hole where nothing could exist. He knew he would willingly throw himself into that void if it meant bringing back even just a touch of her light.

Elora cleared her throat and pulled herself away from him, schooling her face into something that felt detached and artificial. A mask that he knew too well. Whatever closeness they had only a second ago was now gone.

"I think I need to take a shower. I'm sure I look like a disaster." She chuckled harshly before scooting off, but Damien's hand shot out and gripped hers.

"Are you okay?" She smiled sadly and nodded.

"I'm sorry," he said softly. "I should have been here." The guilt he felt was etched into his very bones, infecting the marrow and spreading through him. But Elora only stood and glanced down at him with complete indifference.

"Don't worry about it." She gave him one last lingering look, a split second before everything shut down once more. For a second, he thought he could see pain or hurt that wasn't from Jonas. It was almost as if his words to her were lingering between them. His vow to never rescue her again and his heart clenched as he wished he could erase them from existence, go back in time and stop himself from being such an asshole, from speaking in anger.

Instead, he said nothing as she went into the bathroom, closed the door behind her and locked it. He stared at it for a moment, savoring the lasting feeling of her hands on his skin that was fading much too quickly, before he stepped into the common area and contacted Silas. Together, they needed to plan.

Chapter 39

Viktor

After a few hours of sleep, he sent the message to his ex-colleague early the next morning. The meeting with Thorne had left him feeling unsettled. The knowing gleam in her eyes as he explained why he felt Elizabeth was working alone lingered in a way that made him question every choice he had made since joining the Resistance, since agreeing to work in the hospital to gather intel on Elora and Denise. He had seen the questions in Thorne's eyes as he spoke, probably considering why he felt so adamant about it. And the truth was that he wasn't sure why he was so certain in his assertion concerning Elora's possible involvement. Even now, as he drove to the restaurant, he dissected each word he had said to Thorne and attempted to trace it back to its origin. Why did he believe that? Was there a chance he would be proven wrong and once again look like a fool? He shook his head slightly as he turned down a side street, following the familiar path that led to the area near the hospital.

He wasn't going to be proven wrong. Somehow, he knew that without even the slightest hint of doubt or hesitation. It was possible that Elora could still turn into the villain he knew Thorne feared she would become, but this didn't seem like the way she would go about it. If Elora were to become the enemy that they all believed she would be, it would be in a different capacity. He had seen what she could and would do when she stabbed Killian over and over until Damien stopped her. But he had also witnessed the absolute horror and devastation when Elizabeth attacked that human. If anything, Elora would seek revenge on those who wronged her. If anything, she could be an ally in stopping her foster sister.

Thorne and the Resistance would never see her as such. They would always see her as a tool. A weapon. An enemy.

The diner Viktor met Ethan at was just down the road from the hospital, which was part of why it was such a popular spot for the nurses and other staff. The other reason was the cheap food and strong coffee. Viktor locked the car as he approached the nondescript restaurant nestled into the strip mall with a thrift store and a pawnshop. The sign for the diner was ancient and falling apart, but Viktor knew it was referred to as *The Blackwell Diner*. A bell rang out as he pushed the door open and looked over the decor—the booths with cracked leather and wobbly tables, the bar with a line of stools. The kitchen was partially shown behind the counter, where an overly energetic waiter was moving between the four people sitting there. Viktor nodded at them before searching for Ethan. He was there already, relaxing against the back of the booth, his shaved head resting along the edge. The hospital-issued blue scrubs were covered in various spots and fluids, and his name badge hung from the front pocket. The night shift had just ended, and Viktor had a sudden rush of guilt at the fact he was keeping Ethan from a shower and some sleep.

With a slight grunt, Viktor slid into the booth and watched as Ethan signaled for the waiter.

"Long shift?" He asked as Ethan downed the mug of coffee before him, and Viktor wondered how many that had been since he showed up.

"You left at the right time," was Ethan's only response as the waiter approached and waited patiently. "Cheeseburger and fries, please."

"How would you like that cooked?" The response from the waiter sounded almost robotic, like the question came out of his mouth without thought or understanding of what was actually going on.

"Medium rare." The waiter nodded, his black hair falling around his young face, and turned to Viktor.

"The same. And a coffee, if possible." They fell into silence punctuated by the low chatter of people as the waiter spun and returned to the kitchen. Viktor had never seen this particular one before, but he usually wasn't here this early in the day. This was when he would be already clocked in for his shift and preparing the morning medication for the residents. Elora's sarcastic grin flashed in his mind, a reminder that his feelings for her were complicated. A tangled knot that he had been struggling to unravel. All he was sure about that that he didn't love her in a romantic way, despite the strategically placed lingering hands or moments that felt too close. But he had played on her obvious attraction to him, the way she latched onto him like he was the only stable thing in the hospital.

The thought once more made guilt churn in his gut. It was the realization that Damien had been completely correct when he accused Viktor of preying on her and her desire for a connection of any type with someone who was kind to her.

"Why did I leave at the right time?" Viktor asked as the waiter brought another mug and filled both his and Ethan's with the strong liquid. A hand covered in small cuts and bruises reached out and grabbed three sugar packets, ripped them open, and dumped them into the mug before stirring quickly with the spoon.

"It's just weird there now. I know they say to not read too much into the resident's behaviors, but the patients in the wards are acting strange. More hostile sometimes. Scared and not sleeping. Most have had to up their sedative in the evening because they either won't sleep or wake up screaming about being attacked." Ethan's blue eyes darted to the window beside them, eyes tracking over the cars in the parking lot as if he were looking for something specific.

"We both know that residents go through phases. Sometimes there are no issues, and they're perfectly behaved. Other times, it's like they were drugged and went wild." Viktor shrugged as if this was simply a fact. There was truth to it. Residents were notoriously sensitive to their surroundings. A new nurse or doctor or change in routine could cause the entire ward to descend into another realm, another dimension where everything was shifted onto its side. Other times, it became outright chaos.

"Normally, I would agree, Viktor. You know I would. We both have worked there the longest. This is different. Trust me." And they had. Ethan had worked there for roughly six years, beating Viktor by two. While Viktor had only worked in the medium-security ward to get close to Elora, Ethan had worked in all three and had spent the most time in maximum security. When he had started, Ethan had been placed in the first ward, where residents came and went based on their progress and behaviors. After a year or so, he had been moved to maximum security, which is where he had been when Viktor saw him last. From what he understood, Ethan had been moved once more.

"Why did they move you? I thought you were staying there for a while longer." Ethan shrugged before drinking his coffee.

"No idea. But that's part of the problem. No communication. Not with the max unit, anyway. No one goes in without permission. Only certain nurses are allowed to escort residents down there. It's almost like a little island all by itself." The waiter returned with two identical plates, one in each hand, and set them down in front of them. A large pile of greasy-looking fries sat next to the cheeseburger, with the lettuce, onion, and tomato placed off to the side of the plate for the diner to add if they wanted. Ethan grabbed the knife from the table and started cutting the burger in half, and Viktor couldn't help but question when the last time the nurse had eaten. It was hard to find time to have lunch or eat a snack during a shift. The residents, especially those in the maximum-security unit, required every bit of focus and attention they had. It was almost impossible to send them off to eat while the other one held down the fort. For Viktor, it had been small snacks at the nurse's station during group therapy or quiet time.

"Anyway, where did you disappear to?" Ethan's question came between bites as Viktor prepared his own food, placing the onion and lettuce under the bun.

"Couldn't do it anymore. The screaming, the medication, the depression. It was too much," he explained, ignoring the way the lie fell from his tongue. In a way, Viktor rationalized, it wasn't a true lie. Eventually, if Elora hadn't been part of the equation, he would have quit eventually for exactly those reasons.

"It wasn't because your favorite resident was released?" Viktor almost choked on the fry he had taken a bite of before Ethan spoke. There was a small curve to the nurse's lips as he watched Viktor's reaction. After a quick drink of coffee, Viktor chuckled softly in the hopes of playing it off as nothing more than gossip.

"Is that what the rumors say?" He kept his tone light, but he felt his muscles tighten slightly. Had it been that obvious to everyone? Then again, Damien had noticed almost instantly, so Viktor wasn't sure why he was surprised.

"It was the gossip, yeah. I think it was more jealousy than anything. There were a few nurses who were looking your direction, and there was plenty of talk about Elora being the best option in the ward." The last part of the sentence held a tinge of disgust as Ethan explained the conversations that had been going on behind closed doors. It was an irritation Viktor should have shared, but was he really that different from them? Those nurses saw Elora as something to covet and play with. Wasn't that what he had done? Sure, he had orders to get close to her, but it didn't make it okay.

"Well, she isn't why I left. Just got tired of being spat at and called names for hours." Viktor shrugged as they both began eating, and he fell back into his thoughts. Yes, he had grown to care for her during that time. He hadn't wanted to see her hurt or upset and had helped her whenever she fell into her nightmares and became trapped in her memories. But he wasn't sure it was love. Not in that way. It wasn't what he had felt for Jaime, no matter how much he had pretended to be. He had wanted to simply be in her orbit, protect her, and hear her laugh.

"Anyway, the max ward has all new guards, and residents are being taken down there for little things. I may be quitting soon. Can't deal with whatever craziness is happening. It isn't worth the pay." Ethan forced the words out as he started working on the fries, resting his elbow on the table as he dipped them in ketchup. Viktor forced himself to listen, to not leap at the opportunity to bombard the nurse with questions.

"Really? Usually, they have to do something fairly violent to get moved." His mind went back to Elizabeth and how she had been dragged down there after the disastrous therapy session with Elora. Her screams had echoed through the halls as she cried out for her foster sister, screaming that she would kill them all. The nurses had talked about it for days after that, even though they were ordered to say nothing in Elora's presence. Denise had worried there would be repercussions for her favorite patient. Viktor hadn't understood exactly why Denise had been so hesitant and secretive about Elizabeth, but now it made sense. If she had known about the tie between them or what effect Elora had, then every choice Denise made was to either hide or protect her. Probably both.

"The requirements for being moved have been decreased. Now the smallest act of aggression ends up with them gone. There are only a few left in your old unit. Even the one who killed her daughter got moved. Just for ripping up a drawing during art therapy and screaming at the therapist," Ethan explained before taking another bite of his hamburger. "And she was set to be released soon."

Viktor recalled what he remembered about that resident and could only conjure images of a fairly docile and depressed woman in her thirties. She had been admitted by court order until she was fit to stand trial, from what he remembered. But she was also going to be released to the guardianship of her elderly parents during the trial itself. Never once had she shown signs of violence or even hostility. She quietly moved through her day, took her medication without question, ate whatever they gave her, and attended therapy. There was no reason for her to be in the max ward unless she had been triggered somehow.

"That's weird, Ethan. Fucking weird." The nurse merely grunted as he finished off his food, and Viktor struggled not to lapse into his own thoughts, his own spiraling suspicions that he itched to investigate.

"But I doubt you asked me just to chat since we barely saw each other, even when we were working the same ward," Ethan commented as Viktor finished off his own food and leaned back in the booth.

"New job isn't working out how I hoped. I was thinking about going back." As good of a lie as any. It wasn't like he could say he was investigating a new type of vampire who might be turning humans at an uncontrollable rate. Ethan nodded absentmindedly as he signaled the waiter for the check.

"Well, I would pick somewhere else. That place is going to hell, and I wouldn't suggest being there for it." Ethan looked him over slightly before handing the waiter his credit card. "I'll pay for both. You look like you've seen better days."

Viktor wanted to be insulted by Ethan's comment and moved to grab his own check from the waiter, who twisted away with a detached air about him before he could. He couldn't imagine that he truly looked that bad. Then again, since the last time Ethan had seen him, his hair had grown out, and he had gained a scar along his face and more on his neck. Was this how Elora felt whenever she realized someone had noticed her scars? The sensation of being completely perceived was unsettling, causing him to squirm and fidget in the booth.

"Thanks. I appreciate that." It was the only thing Viktor could think of saying. Ethan nodded and stood, giving him the universal sign that this lunch was over, and they were going their separate ways. The nurse across from him would be going home to a shower and sleep. And Viktor would be preparing to infiltrate the max ward tonight.

Chapter 40

Elora

"We are moving your room until the ceremony," Silas announced as she left the bathroom, the towel wrapped around her hair. She had changed into one of the long dresses he had bought her during her time at the manor. All long sleeves and high necklines. Once again, she focused on how much her uncle appeared to have aged. There was darkness around his eyes, that somehow seemed darker than before, along with deep grooves around his lips. She shook her head, scolding herself for bringing him into this and asking for his help. After all, she could have simply lived her life at the manor, hidden away until Darian or Jonas or the Resistance found her. They would, and she knew that. No, this was better. Facing it on her own terms and not hiding behind Silas or Damien, even if they would prefer for her to do that.

"When?" The question came from the figure sitting on the couch, as far away as possible from the dress bags hanging over the armrest. Damien didn't glance in her direction, but kept his focus trained on her uncle, whose own eyes darted between the two of them as if he could discern what had happened while he was gone.

"As soon as you're ready. I have taken some extra precautions and did a little digging into what happened. If you'd like to hear about it, that is," Silas amended quickly, and she gave a curt nod before pulling the towel from her now shorter hair that fell un-evenly around her shoulders.

"Compulsion, unfortunately. And so incredibly basic that I foolishly didn't consider it. The woman who delivered the dresses had an assistant come with her. She was put under Jonas's spell, so to speak, and claimed they needed help to bring them up. That was the phone call you received," he explained as he turned to Elora.

"His desperation is truly monumental," she commented as she settled onto one of the chairs near the door. The slit in the dress she wore parted slightly where she crossed her legs, re-vealing the scars that lined her flesh. Somehow, they felt larger, longer, and more prominent after Jonas's visit. As if him touch-ing and tasting her again had forced her body to put each mark they left behind on display. No one would miss seeing them if they only glanced at her.

She darted a quick look at Damien, whose focus was still trained on her uncle. His face was contorted in anger as if he were barely holding himself back from doing something stupid. She had seen this particularly dark look only once before—the night he drugged and tricked Killian, giving her the opportunity to kill him. It didn't bode well.

"I'll pack up my things, and we can move." Elora didn't wait for a response from her uncle and didn't expect one from Damien. They had returned to their roles. Hers was the willing sacrifice, and he was the silent fixture in the room. If he didn't move around, she would think he was part of the furniture. A beautiful work of art meant to be admired along with the rest of the decor.

She didn't shut the door all the way, leaving it just the tiniest bit cracked as she started moving through the room to gather her meager belongings. As she began putting her clothes in the suitcase, Elora listened to the heavy footsteps growing nearer.

Damien's. She knew the sound better than anyone else's, had memorized his gait and the rhythm of his steps. They stopped, and she heard his voice, low and indecipherable, as he spoke to her uncle. She only caught a few words, with 'Jonas' and 'key-card' being the clearest. They were discussing it yet again when all she wanted was to forget. At the very mention of his name, he was back in the room with her, licking the blood from her face, whispering terrorizing promises in her ear. She shuddered slightly at the thought, at the reminder, and tossed her clothes inside before grabbing the bottles of shampoo and such from the bathroom.

The hotel door opened and closed before Elora made it out to the living room, where only Damien stood waiting for her. His hands were shoved in the pockets of his jeans, and he glanced at her before holding out his hand for the suitcase.

"I can carry it." She stated, and he sighed softly.

"I'll carry that, and you can carry those," he responded as he jerked his head towards the three garment bags on the couch. She forced down the remark that sprang to mind. It was sarcastic and borderline rude, perfectly designed to goad him like he had done to her so many times. But she had a sinking feeling it would do nothing now, and she wasn't sure she could handle the lack of a response. The chasm between them was too wide, and it was her fault. Was this worth it? Sacrificing whatever was growing between them for revenge and the ability to protect herself and those she loved?

Elora handed him the suitcase and hung the garment bags over her forearm before waiting for him to tell her where to go. Silas had failed to share that tiny bit of information before he disappeared.

"Where did my uncle go?" she asked as Damien opened the door and stepped out, head turning to study each side of the hallway. Probably checking for threats, for Jonas, for Darian.

"Downstairs. The lobby. He was checking on a few things." His response was curt, each word sharp as it left his mouth. It stung in a strange way.

"For?" Elora could have sworn she heard him sigh at the question, as if even speaking to her this much was a punishment for something. He pushed the button for the third floor and glanced at her with eyes that never looked so empty. Not even the slightest hint of emotion.

"Probably something about your wedding. Two days now, right?" She straightened at the dark tone, at the jab it was meant to be.

"Three, actually." Damien simply made a slight noise, as if acknowledging her response as he stepped off the elevator, and Elora followed. This hallway was much plainer than the ones further up. The walls were painted a dark red with cream accents. There were mirrors at the end of the hallway opposite them. The corridor itself was lined with at least a dozen doors, each with their own gold numbering. Room 303 was just to the left of the elevator, and Elora followed him, waiting patiently as he unlocked the door to her new room.

This time, she wasn't met with the scent of dried roses. Either Silas had already had it taken care of, or these rooms didn't receive the same treatment as those further up. Damien tossed her suitcase onto one of the two beds in the room as she wandered in, fingers trailing across the dresser that lined the wall with a television mounted right above it. It was placed strategically between the two beds, lining up perfectly with the large nightstand that held a clock and a phone. It reminded her of every hotel room she had seen on TV growing up. It even had a slightly musty and stale smell, despite the open small balcony.

Elora placed the garment bags on the only armchair in the room before turning to Damien, who stood perfectly still near the entrance, right next to where the door for the bathroom was.

"Which bed would you like?" she asked him and noted the way he seemed to tense at her words. Or was it the sound of her voice that caused it?

"I don't care. You pick." He kept his eyes on something behind her, refusing to meet her gaze. She huffed softly at the response and shifted her position to block whatever he was focused on. Just as she suspected, his eyes automatically moved, picking something else at random to stare at.

"You aren't looking at me or speaking to me." It wasn't meant to be a question, and they both knew that. She knew that he understood that as he finally glanced at her, eyes still empty. It was worse than the sneers, the revulsion, the hatred. She would take any of those over whatever this was.

"Your uncle's orders don't require me to do that."

"I understand. If that's the case, I'm going to start trying on the gowns. I might need your help, if that's in line with your orders." She struggled to keep the irritation from her voice. It wasn't just the disconnect between them that caused it to rise to the surface. His parting words during that meeting played on repeat in her mind when she gave herself a moment of silence. She heard the anger in his voice, the heartbreak in each word when she laid down to sleep, when she took a bath, and could think of nothing else. Would he forgive her when the time came? Would he even be around long enough for that?

Damien said nothing as she started separating the bags, laying them out one by one on the bed furthest from the door. Three total. It seemed pointless to her to try them all on. The dresses were all chosen for very specific reasons. Her hands reached down and gripped the bottom of her dress, pulling it up and over her head before she tossed it in a heap towards the top of the bed. Her bra came next, since all three gowns had their own built in.

The removal of her dress was met by the shuffling of feet as Elora assumed Damien turned away from her. Slowly, she stepped into the center of the gown's skirt and pulled it up to slide her arms into the straps. This one was her least favorite due to its square neckline that covered most of her chest. But it had been one of the few in the catalog that didn't have sleeves, so it was picked. Keeping her hands and fingers gentle with the lace and beading that seemed unnecessary, Elora adjusted the bodice before turning to the mirror.

A frown was instantly on her face as she took in the view and let the gown hang on her frame. It was simple, which she supposed was good. It didn't detract from what she wanted to be on display. And if her hair was up, then there would be even less to draw the eye away from the scars along her neck and chest. The only issue with the square neckline was that it started just below her collarbones, covering up the rest of the damage.

"No," she muttered slightly as she removed the dress and placed it back in the garment bag. Her hair fell down around her shoulders in long strands that still somehow managed to get in the way of her movements. Quickly, with Damien standing guard and his eyes secured to the door, Elora tried on the second dress. A gown with a halter neckline that clung to her form all the way to her feet before flaring out somewhat comically. The catalog called it a "mermaid" gown, which she supposed was an appropriate name. The halter top of the gown covered more than she had expected, and she sighed softly before grabbing the third.

Once again, she slowly slid into it, waiting for the reaction she knew would come when she chose it. The catalog had said the dress was an A-line gown with a strapless, sweetheart neckline and she hadn't understood a word of the description. All she saw was the gown from the banquet, only slightly more elaborate with its beading and appliques. The line of tiny buttons traveled up the back from her tailbone to just above the bottom of her shoulder blades. There was no cream or pink this time. Instead, the gown was called "dusty rose," which felt appropriate somehow. White or ivory would be a joke that she would have no choice but to laugh at.

"Would you mind helping?" She swallowed down the Déjà vu of it all. Only this time, Damien would be helping her into the dress, not helping her escape it. Elora refused to even glance in the mirror or at him, who hadn't responded or moved. Her hands held the bodice to her body as she fought to ignore every memory that came rushing back from that night. Jonas cornering her when she had escaped Damien. Darian's knowing smile when Killian reintroduced her. And then there was what came later that night when she was drugged and left to their mercy. She bit her lip and blinked away the tears that were forming in her eyes as her constant, internal mantra repeated itself.

Ignore it. Push it down. Not now.

"Seems cruel to have you wear this as your wedding gown." She hadn't even heard him move as she fell into her own thoughts, her own memories of that night. He stood directly behind her, and she could feel his presence like it was the only thing that could keep her rooted in this moment in time. His hands threaded themselves in her hair as he gathered it up and moved it over her shoulders despite the fact it wasn't long enough to be in the way. Her eyes closed at the contact, at the feeling of his skin on hers again. She had become addicted to the sensation. Even before things became this complicated, before the manor, before they left the Tower. Elora hadn't lied to Wyatt when she said she understood hatred better than love, explained that hatred didn't expect anything in return. Maybe that was why she latched onto Damien so tightly even before she realized she had. She knew he would never ask or demand anything of her.

"He didn't pick it," she whispered as his fingers started to work at the dozen or so tiny buttons along her back. Her body broke out in goosebumps when his knuckle grazed her skin, and she shivered slightly. Would he be wearing that infuriatingly smug smirk because of her reaction? Or were they too far gone for that?

"You did?" There was a hint of anger in his voice, almost like she was pulling a reaction from him against his will.

"I did." Another couple of buttons were done, and she felt the dress grow tighter, holding onto her frame. Her hands dropped to her sides. "You don't like it?" Her question was a whisper, unsure and anxious and terrified. She wanted him to say yes as much as she wanted him to say no. The question rendered her so vulnerable before him. She would rather strip down naked and be put on display than ask him something like this. And yet, stupidly, the question had filled the room.

"Don't ask me that." His words were tight, forced through the jaw she had seen clench so many times because of her.

"Is that a no?" She tried to laugh as he finished the last couple of buttons. If she pretended long enough, maybe everything would be fine. They could pretend together. Ignore reality and disappear into whatever world they created. Fingers slid into her hair once more and brought her hair back behind her shoulders. His hands worked through the strands as if trying to comb it or work out non-existent knots. She leaned back against him, hoping that he wouldn't move away from her.

"Why are you doing this?" His voice came from just beside her ear, so close she could feel his body against hers, feel his breath on her ear and cheek.

"Which part?"

"The wedding, Elora," he whispered softly, and she licked her lips.

"I have my reasons. I only ask that you trust me."

"How? How can I do that when I watched you offer yourself up?" She spun around and faced him. His brows were furrowed together, but whether it was from anger or something else, she couldn't tell.

"I don't know, Damien. I just hope you can." His face contorted into something akin to pain and confusion, something that seemed like agony as he looked down at her. Dark brown eyes flicked between hers, searching for something she couldn't give him right now. Not yet.

Elora finally turned to the mirror and studied the gown. The color was beautiful, as was the rest of it, she supposed. If she was going to get married, this would work. The important part was how much was showing. Her fingers traced along the scars on her chest—stretching along the swell of her breasts, her collarbones, and her throat. More trailed down her arms until they grew in number towards the crook of her elbow and then her wrists. In those places, skin was indistinguishable from scars.

A sharp breath passed her lips as Damien stepped up behind her and joined his hand to hers, tracing the scars along with her. For her, it was an almost ritualistic process that she engaged in. Denise always said it was a coping mechanism of some sort. Touch them. Count them. Anchor herself in reality. And that was how Elora always viewed the act. Damien's touch felt different in a way she didn't quite believe possible. It was almost like reverence, like he was touching them as a form of worship. It was too much and not enough all at once. Her breathing grew shallower as his fingers traveled from her neck down to her collarbones, along the skin there. Elora's eyes fluttered closed as he continued to move across her exposed skin, causing her body to flush and grow warmer and warmer by the second. Every single nerve ending in her body was alive and screaming for him.

Damien's fingertips reached the top of her breasts that were now on display thanks to the corset in the bodice. A shiver raced through her even as she grew so hot she was sure she would spontaneously combust, taking the gown and the hotel with her as she turned to ash. She pushed her body back until she was flush with his own. But it wasn't enough. Not enough touch, sensation, or skin.

"Damien," she whispered, though she wasn't sure she was capable of words or even coherent thoughts at this moment.

A wave of coldness slammed into her as Damien's fingers left her and he stepped away. Her eyes snapped open and met his through the mirror. There was something dark but heated there. Like fire burning in the middle of the night where there is no other source of light. She wanted to be consumed by it. He shook his head slowly, and she wasn't sure if the movement was meant for her or himself. Before she could ask what happened, the lock at the hotel room door clicked, and Silas returned, destroying any chance she had at demanding an answer.

Chapter 41

Damien

The key card he had gotten from Jason worked perfectly. Before heading to the second floor where the room was, Damien had made sure Jonas was otherwise occupied. As he strolled past the bar, he spotted Silas, Jonas, and Darian tucked away in a booth, a bottle of either red wine or blood on the table in front of them. It looked like Jonas had changed from the bloody shirt he had been wearing after he tried to break her again. Silas met Damien's gaze and gave an almost imperceptible nod of his head. Technically, Silas had no part in this. No, his hands would remain clean, while Damien's wouldn't. Not if he had his way.

Jonas's room was bland in an almost sterile way. The same pictures on the walls as Elora's. The same couch and aesthetic. Just a single room, a bed, and a bathroom. The scent of her blood lingered in the air, reigniting his wrath and his itch to remove each of Jonas' fingers before moving on to bigger body parts. The vision of her bit wrist and her broken nose was all he could see, crowding out anything and everything else. The shirt Jonas had been wearing was folded neatly and placed on the desk in a strange sort of shrine. Damien could picture him sniffing it, inhaling her scent, and promising himself that very soon he would get his fill of her. He felt his hands clench around the strap of the bag he carried once more.

No. Calm. Collected. It would last longer that way. As long as his emotions didn't get the best of him, this could last hours. Silas promised to have guards on her at all times while he was gone. Vampires who had been ordered to not let anyone near her. Even the receptionist had been replaced to prevent a repeat of the trick played by Jonas. This could take as long as he wanted. A savage grin cut across his face, distorting his sharp features into something almost feral.

Damien tossed the bag onto the desk beside the shirt, vowing to take it with him when he left. One by one, he pulled his supplies out and set them side by side. There were only a few, each one sharper than the last. The last item he grabbed was four large plastic tarps. With meticulous care, Damien arranged the room to his liking. The tarps were spread over every part of the carpet, and a part of him wondered if he should have brought more to cover the walls. At the thought, another grin.

He was going to enjoy every moment of this.

In the center of the protective cover, he placed one of the chairs that sat at the tiny table meant to mimic a dining room. The finishing touch was the handcuffs he prepared, procured with Silas's help. It wasn't chains or shackles, but it would have to do considering the time restraints on putting this plan together. Preparation done, Damien took the other chair in the room and waited, just off to the side of the door. He couldn't risk Jonas spotting him and running like a coward.

It was only now that he wondered if she would want to be here. If she would want to take part, exact her own revenge against him. He hadn't even considered it, and a part of him felt guilty about that. The vision of her covered in Killian's blood played out before his eyes. The sight of her with the knife in her hand, the soft kiss she had pressed to his forehead after she pushed aside a strand of his hair. Her darkness matched his own, but he was selfish, and he knew that.

Jonas was his.

And he didn't have to wait long. When he heard voices outside the room, a drunken slurring of indecipherable words and sounds, Damien stood and moved into a dark corner of the room. The stun gun waited in his hand while the other flexed impatiently. What could two obvious drunks have to say to one another?

The lock finally clicked and the door opened. The scent of expensive whiskey and blood assaulted Damien's senses as Jonas entered the room and locked the door behind him. Both locks moved into place—the deadbolt and the door lock—and Damien grinned. Jonas was trapping himself without any help from him.

With growing impatience, Damien watched Jonas stumble further and further into the room, tossing his own key card on the desk. If the drunk idiot saw the arrangement of knives and the plastic on the floor, he said nothing. But Jonas had never been too intelligent. It was why Killian avoided asking him to do anything too difficult. Check on a blood bank or collect a payment. Nothing that required too much thinking. But Killian had kept him as almost a friend. Or maybe Jonas had known things Killian couldn't risk getting out.

"What the fuck?" Jonas's words stumbled over each other as he spoke and stared down at the plastic tarp. With a few quick steps, the stun gun was pressed to Jonas's neck, and a surge of electricity shot through him. He barely had enough time to cry out before he fell to the ground in a crumpled heap. It was too similar to how she had looked on his floor that night.

Calm, he reminded himself. Control.

But it was becoming increasingly difficult as scenes rushed to the surface, teasing and taunting any ounce of restraint he had. This would probably be over quicker than Jonas deserved. Damien grunted as he gripped the body by the arms and lifted

Jonas up just enough to place him on the chair. His head hung to his chest, face covered by that black hair that always looked greasy and stringy, like thin pieces of wet thread hanging from his scalp. The handcuffs clicked closed around his wrists and ankles, securing him to the armrests and legs of the chair. Finally, as a finishing touch, Damien tied him to the chair itself, securing his torso with an entire length of rope. He didn't need any surprises.

After a tug on each part of the restraints, Damien dragged his own chair to sit and wait for Jonas to wake. He leaned forward and rested his arms on his thighs, letting his eyes move over the vampire still passed out in front of him. Jonas had always been a weasel, managing to integrate himself with vampires in power, leaving him with an unearned sense of importance. But at his core, Jonas had always been a coward, too stupid and oblivious to recognize himself as one. Damien's interactions with him had been limited. Killian seemed to keep them apart, and he wondered now if that had been purposeful. Killian never seemed to want anyone to know about what happened behind closed doors, anything to protect the façade of a distraught and loving father. Damien had fallen for it more than anyone else.

He didn't think it would take too long for Jonas to wake, and he was correct in that assumption. Roughly twenty minutes later, a harsh groan spilled from Jonas's lips, and Damien straightened in his chair, the anticipation making him almost giddy. He had fantasized about this for so long that it was almost unreal to actually be there with Jonas at his mercy.

With another groan, this one louder, Jonas's head rose, and his inky hair fell over his face. With the very tips of his fingers, Damien moved them out of the way and savored the immediate flash of fear. No, not fear. Terror. The expression of a vampire who knew what was coming. Jonas should have realized that he wouldn't let hurting her again slide.

Quickly, Jonas tried to hide the fear under the guise of anger, and Damien chuckled softly at the attempt. With a series of sharp jerks of his hands and legs, Jonas fought against the restraints and tried to yank himself away from the chair itself. There was no one to protect him, no one for Damien to worry about. Killian had protected him by simply being alive, and that wasn't an issue now. Jonas had been lucky so far. There had been other concerns, issues far more important than him. Getting Elora out of the Tower had been the first and then keeping her safe had been the second. She had always come before his revenge, but Jonas's luck had officially run out.

"Don't bother, Jonas. I made sure you weren't going anywhere." Damien's assertion was met with shouted curses.

"You can curse my name. Scream for help. Whatever you want. I made sure the entire floor was cleared out. Not a single living person is anywhere near here. Do you understand?" Jonas only growled in response, baring his teeth as if it would change anything about his situation.

"Now, Jonas, I'm curious. Did you really think there wouldn't be any consequences to your actions? I know thinking isn't your strong suit, but even you can't be that stupid."

"That's what this is about? A blood whore?" Jonas spat the word out as if he wasn't obsessed, as if he wasn't the problem here.

Damien tsked in faux disappointment and shook his head as he stood. "Language like that won't do you any favors."

"If you hurt me, Darian will come for you." Jonas's voice shook slightly, as if not even he believed that.

"We both know that isn't true. If anything, he'll thank me for getting rid of someone who touched her. After all, the whole point of this entire wedding is to claim her for himself. I'm just pruning the unwanted weeds." Damien wandered to the desk and picked up the first of the instruments he had lined up there as he spoke. He could hear Jonas' labored breathing and the sound of the handcuffs moving as he twisted around to track Damien's movements.

A scalpel. The metal was smooth and almost glittered in the fluorescent lights above them. It wasn't necessarily the best tool for the job he intended, but it would work. Time had been an issue and Silas had done the best he could when gathering the supplies. There was no way that Damien would be ungrateful for what they had managed to find. Damien kept his steps slow and measured as he came back around and crouched in front of Jonas. The vampire's face paled when Damien held up the blade and lazily glanced at it.

"Is this similar to what you used on her? Probably not. Killian always had a flair for the dramatic. I assume it was very elegant and maybe even detailed with vines." Damien stopped and met Jonas's eyes. "It's the closest I could get."

"It was all Killian. Damn it! I just --"

"Shh, Jonas," he cooed softly and placed the blade against Jonas's lips. "You only took what wasn't yours. You only stole and beat and hurt and claimed. Now, are you going to be quiet, or do I need a gag? I really don't want to hear you speak again."

Jonas spat at him, and Damien felt the wetness on his cheek. A wave of rage threatened to overtake him before he wiped it away with the back of his hand and chuckled darkly.

"Let's begin." Damien's hand wrapped around Jonas's right wrist and anchored it to the chair. Fingers twisted and reached as Jonas squirmed and jerked his body one way and then the other.

"Which one should we start with? The pinky? The thumb? The ring finger?" Damien savored the slight whimper that came from Jonas, at the sound of a scream lingering right behind his teeth, stuck there exactly like hers had been.

"I guess I'll pick if you don't have a preference."

And just as a stuttered "no" bumbled from Jonas's mouth, the blade hit flesh and then something hard before turning sideways until it was flat against the bone. The blade met no hesitation as it sliced its way through until it reached the other side, emerging from underneath his fingernail. The meat that had once been his index finger slid to the floor, joining the blood that had started to puddle there.

"Fuck! Please. Please, just stop. I'll never touch her again. I swear. I promise. Please!" Jonas's screams reached a crescendo as Damien went back in and removed the rest of the meat and skin from the finger, leaving him only the bone from the knuckle to the tip.

"One down. Nine more to go," Damien announced as he stared into Jonas' tear-stained face. "Should we take bets on how long it takes until you pass out? My money is on four based on experience."

"I'll heal. You can do this over and over, but I'll heal."

"Now, there's that lack of intelligence I mentioned. Yes, the skin will heal, and you will stop bleeding. But there is something I've learned from doing similar activities for Killian. Skin doesn't regrow. Muscle doesn't regrow. Not to this extent. You'll be left with only pale white bone." He shot Jonas a feral grin, one that hadn't fully left his face since the blade hit the vampire's skin. "If you were going to survive, anyway."

With those words, Jonas renewed his efforts to get free. Wrists yanked out in an effort to break the armrest as his ankles did the same. Pointless. And insulting, if Damien was honest. He had earned his reputation, and this felt like Jonas didn't believe it.

"Another finger then?" Without waiting for a response, Damien flayed another one and then another until there was only bones for fingers. And he had been correct. At the fourth finger, Jonas' screams had ended, and his head had slumped forward as he passed out from shock. Damien shook his head and waited, watching as his skin did indeed piece itself back together around the bone, stopping the bleeding.

As he waited for Jonas to wake back up, he debated whether to finish the other hand or start bleeding him first. He could start with incisions along Jonas's chest and arms, deep but barely enough to make it take time for it to heal. Finally, after a few minutes of silence that felt much too loud, Damien slapped him across the face. Once. Twice. Three times and Jonas sputtered back to life like an old truck.

"Please, Damien. Please. I'll give you anything you want. You want secrets? I can give them to you. You want to know what Darian is planning for her. I'll tell you. Please." The begging was starting to become irritating, and his head began to throb slightly, as if it would drown out the sound of Jonas' blubbering. For a moment, he almost discounted the desperate promises, but the part about Darian having plans caused his hands to hesitate, for the blade to hang just above Jonas's collarbone. He had a fair idea of exactly what Darian had in store for her, but what if it was worse than he thought? What if he needed to get rid of two problems tonight? The idea had already crossed his mind more than once.

"What's he planning?" he asked gently, as if he were speaking to a child who had done something wrong and needed to be coaxed into admitting guilt. The blade traced Jonas's neck and collarbone, drawing small streams of blood that slowly trickled down into his shirt.

"Don't hurt me anymore, and I'll tell you. Promise me you'll let me go." Damien made a show of rolling his eyes dramatically and sat back on his heels.

"I promise to let you go if you tell me."

"Bloodlust. He plans to drain her and then starve her until she loses control. She will bite anyone who comes near her. Turn them."

Damien reined in the disgust that appeared in the pit of his stomach before he let his grin return with renewed vigor. Playtime was over. He had planned to draw this out a little longer, but now all he wanted was to see the life leave Jonas's eyes, watch his body go limp.

Jonas screamed again, the sound tearing out of his throat and mingling with the tears and sobs as the knife slid into his forearm. The cut was vertical, starting at the crook of his elbow and ending at his wrist, just before the start of his palm. Meat and flesh and blood raced forward, spilling out into the hotel room. He stunk of cowardice and greed, of arrogance and fear.

"You said you would let me go!" Jonas screamed and spittle shot from his lips, filling the air between them. Damien shook his head with a soft smile as the blood drained from Jonas's face and he grew paler and paler with each passing second.

"I never said when. You should really be more specific when setting terms. One more, Jonas." Another incision along the other arm. Crimson liquid spilled out and onto the plastic beneath them both, spreading into a pool that Damien was thrilled to be kneeling in as he watched Jonas grow weaker, as his features grew slack, and the fight drained out of him. Not from fear this time, but from blood loss. The skin wouldn't be able to piece itself together quickly enough for Jonas to stay conscious much longer. And he had one last thing to do. One last item to take. A trophy.

He stood and the drenched fabric of his jeans clung to his skin as he moved behind the unconscious body. Damien's hand clutched a handful of Jonas's greasy hair, damp from sweat, and yanked it back. His mouth opened impossibly wide as a weak whimper sounded. With his free hand, Damien reached back towards the table and grabbed the pliers.

"She deserves a souvenir, don't you think?" Jonas didn't speak. He couldn't. The blood loss had rendered him unable to do much beyond sobbing quietly, his eyes flickering open and closed.

The pliers wrapped around one fang, and he pulled, gritting his teeth as the stubborn thing refused to be moved. Then, a loosening, a tug, and finally the canine was free, erupting from Jonas' mouth with the most comical popping sound. And then the other. Damien tossed Jonas's head forward, where it hung down on his shirt, soaked through with sweat and blood.

The dying vampire moved, twitching as life continued to seep out of him. The bleeding from his forearms had slowed, and the cuts were a bit smaller but not enough to save him. Blood covered the bones protruding from his hand as Damien took a step back and stared down at his handiwork. It didn't feel like enough, would never feel like enough.

In a swift movement that was almost a mirror image of Elora on the night of Killian's death, Damien plunged the scalpel blade into Jonas's neck where his pulse had grown so weak it was almost nonexistent. He heard a soft inhale of breath that could have been a gasp or an attempt at another scream before he dragged the blade to carve a chasm across Jonas' throat while what was left of Jonas's blood flowed out and down his shirt. Only then did Damien move away. One step, then two, then three, until he was far enough back that he could view his handiwork. It was almost like gazing at a work of art in a museum, analyzing and scrutinizing each brushstroke and color choice.

This was his painting. An ode to her.

He watched the life finish draining out of Jonas before checking his pulse. Nothing. Damien's grin grew as he texted Silas that he was finished and that a clean-up was needed. With a soft chuckle, he grabbed the teeth and shirt with Elora's blood and left his artwork behind.

Chapter 42

Viktor

Blackwell Psychiatric Hospital looked exactly as it did the day he left, the day he returned to his apartment and was hit over the head. It was only when he woke up that he discovered it was Damien and understood the role he was meant to play. The collateral, the control mechanism. Viktor hadn't actually thought it would work after how he left things with Elora. He really should have listened to her when she first came to him about Damien. Maybe things would have turned out differently. She would have ended up with the Resistance, and wasn't that what he wanted?

It didn't matter anymore. That was all over and now he was drowning in failures that he needed to rectify, which was why he was here without informing Thorne or waiting for back-up as he was ordered to do. The plan was to simply sneak in and see if there was anything here to even report. Ethan said things were strange, but the board members could have simply changed how things worked. It had happened in the past and he wouldn't doubt that they would do it again if it meant increasing their profit margins.

The iron gate was wide open as he approached. He had been fully prepared to either jump over it or find a space wide enough he could try to fit through since it was usually locked. Maybe that policy had changed as well? Maybe someone had left recently, and the gate hadn't closed like it was meant to? He pushed the questions aside and carefully walked up the driveway, staying in the shadows offered by the trees that blocked the lights along the front of the building. It was the same brick facade, the same lines of flowers and hedges along concrete walkways. There were bars over the windows, but there didn't seem to be any security. Usually, they roamed the grounds during the night to make sure no one managed to get out of their room. Those in the lowest security ward had a tendency to try to go for strolls at night. Or that is what they said when they got caught.

There were a few lights shining through the windows, dim and subdued, as if they were attempting to push past a fog. The hallway lights, if Viktor was guessing correctly. Instinctively, his eyes went to the window he knew to be Denise's office. Would everything be boxed up and removed? Had another doctor taken over her place within the hospital, just as she had been replaced in the Resistance? He had never meant for her to die that night in the garage, hadn't even known she was working with Damien and Lukas. Even if he hadn't been the one to pull the trigger, Denise's death still weighed on him, a brick that was tied around his neck that he dragged around every second. Body after body was piled on top of him, and he wasn't sure he would be able to pull himself out from underneath them.

His steps were as quiet as he could manage as he approached the building and checked the main entrance. Faint lights filtered through the large windows, revealing the reception desk and leather chairs. Not too long ago, he had escorted Elora through the lobby to the waiting car, counting down the seconds until she was no longer his mission. He had thought that maybe once she was gone and living what he hoped was a better life, the guilt that perpetually ate away at him would cease. When she had attempted to open the door to him visiting her outside the hospital, he had slammed it shut and refused to witness the pain on her face. Just one of his many betrayals.

Despite the red blinking light on the keycard sensor, he tried the door, only to find it locked, and he cursed slightly. Damien had taken his badge when he kidnapped him from his apartment and probably used it to break in to steal Denise's journals. Even so, he highly doubted he would still have access since they thought he had quit.

Viktor turned from the front entrance and started around the side of the building, sticking close to the flowers that lined the wall. There were cameras that recorded footage of the grounds, but the closer a person was to the actual building, the more hidden they were. It was a blind spot that had been used more than once by nurses who snuck out to smoke. Slowly, he rounded the corner as he tried to force his heart rate and breath into submission. His eyes darted around him, searching for any sign of a security guard or rogue patient. Nothing. Not a single soul. Only the sound of the wind in the trees and an owl somewhere in the distance.

Finally, the door he was aiming for came into view. It was technically a delivery entrance, but was used by staff and nurses who forgot their keycards or who didn't want to be seen getting back into the building. His hand had a slight tremble to it as he reached out towards the knob and turned. Unlocked as he had expected and hoped. Inch by inch, he pushed it open and peeked inside. A storeroom of sorts greeted him. Boxes filled with other boxes were stacked on the floor, and a line of aprons hung from the hooks from where the cooks and cafeteria workers left them when they clocked out. Along the wall were shelves full of cans and bags of cereal bricks, ground coffee, and tea bags. This was the overflow storage. Items kept separate in case a delivery was late or missing certain items.

The door clicked closed behind him as he entered and exhaled. So far, everything had been going smoothly. More so than he had anticipated. Even at this time of night, there were the late-night workers who did the stocking and preparation work for the morning staff. His pulse jumped a bit at the thought, at the realization that this should not be going so easily, that he should have run into someone by now. With a thick swallow, he forced down his suspicions and attempted to steady his shaking hands.

Just check, he told himself. Just check to see if there is anything worth investigating. It would be easier for one to get in than the group Thorne would be sure to send. This was his chance to prove himself. To rectify all the mistakes that he had made in the last few weeks. He had failed Thorne and the rest of them, who took him in and gave him a purpose after his reality fractured in a flurry of blood and teeth. He had to fix this. If not, Elora had been right.

There wasn't a soul in sight as he left the storage room and found the stairs that led to the bottom floor. His hand grasped the railing as he steadily made his way down, heart pounding so hard in his chest he was surprised it didn't echo in the stairwell. Silent steps descended one by one until the path ended at a single door at the bottom. This was the very bowels of the hospital, the space where residents with no chance of being released were sent. They were the ones nurses whispered were without hope, those whose violence could never be cured by modern medicine. They would joke that maybe the older, more barbaric methods should make a comeback, that some residents could use a lobotomy to silence whatever drove them to violence and to rid them of whatever demons resided in their minds. All poor taste, in Viktor's opinion.

The door opened with a light click and chime of the lock coming undone. Viktor cursed as he held perfectly still, listening for any movement or noise coming from the silent hallway. His brow furrowed in confusion. Usually, no matter what time it was, there was chatter or cries or screams of some sort. It was never truly silent. Every instinct in his body shouted out in warning, begging and demanding that he turn around and forget about this incredibly stupid plan. Did it really matter that much if he found out the information before going to Thorne? Did he really need to prove himself that desperately? The answer, unfortunately, was a resounding yes. No matter how stupid this was, no matter how unformed this plan was, he needed to fix this after two catastrophic failures.

The nurse's station to the right of the door was empty, rendering his entire practiced speech useless. He had outlined an explanation for why he was there, had planned on claiming he was looking for something that had been left behind when he last visited Elizabeth. But no one sat there charting, watching the monitors, prepping medication, or even looking at their phones. Viktor bit the inside of his cheek as he rounded the nurse's table and started sorting through the piles of papers thrown around.

Care notes. Appointment times. Incident reports. Transfer forms made up the majority of the documents, as Ethan had mentioned. He sifted through them, reading the reasons given for each one. Threw a chair during group therapy. Yelled a threat to a staff member. Threatened another resident. Refused medication. Nothing that would warrant this type of reaction. That would simply be a sedative and a few hours in the green room, maybe an extra session with their primary psychiatrist. Then, his blood ran cold when he spotted transfers from the low security ward. There was a progression to this type of thing. Low security went to medium, and medium went to high. Not once during his four years had someone gone from the lowest level to maximum. There had never even been a case in the history of the hospital as far as he knew.

A creak sounded from the hallway beyond the locked door made of reinforced plexiglass and his eyes snapped to it, expecting to see a returning nurse or even a staff member. Maybe even a resident who had managed to get out of their room. It was known to happen, even if it was rare. But nothing. No one was standing there, hands pressed to the door, eyes wide and dead from the sheer amount of medication. Viktor let out a breath and started to search through the papers once more. New badges from nurses he didn't recognize were stacked off to the side, all bearing a single mark in the right corner. A red star. He had never seen them before, and he had to imagine this was what Ethan had referred to when he mentioned the need for special permission. Viktor grabbed the stack and started to look through them, tossing them one by one back onto the desk as he did until he stopped and focused on the one in his hand.

Wyatt Chandler. Nurse. Maximum Security Ward.

And off in the corner was the little red star. Viktor squinted down at the picture where the human Elizabeth had turned stared up at him. His eyes were full of cruel mischief and his lips were turned up in the corners. This was not the same man who had rushed to check on Elora, who had earned her trust and affection despite every betrayal she had endured, including the one by his own hand. It was all the proof he needed, and he shoved the badge into his pocket and turned back to the others. Were they all turned? Were they human? He knew where his money would lie if he were asked to make a bet.

"Excuse me? You're not supposed to be here." A feminine voice rang out and Viktor snapped straight, hands clenched instantly into fists, as if in preparation for an impending fight. He took in the nurse in front of him. Blue scrubs and mousy brown hair framed a round face. Confusion and something like fear lined her soft features, and he attempted an awkward smile that said that this was all a silly misunderstanding.

"I'm sorry. I was looking for someone." He chuckled softly at the end and watched the nurse's eyes dart to the space behind him.

"We know who you're looking for," a dark voice whispered behind him and his body tensed, muscles contracting as something struck him, hard and fast. Pain burst from the spot at the nape of his neck and a shocked cry erupted from his mouth even as he crumbled to the filthy linoleum, and everything went dark.

* * *

He came back to reality mere moments later. Or maybe minutes? Hours? Viktor wasn't entirely sure. The only truth he knew was that his head felt like it was fracturing into a thousand tiny shards, burning from the inside out. The arms that gripped his torso released him and his knees hit the concrete. The sound mingled with his own cry as the pain radiated throughout his legs and into the rest of his body. His eyes squeezed shut as mutters and snickers reached him, along with the overwhelming scent of blood. It filled every part of him, becoming almost inescapable as he forced his eyes open to survey the room. At least a dozen figures dressed in an array of outfits surrounded him in a semi-circle. Some wore the blue scrubs of the hospital while others were in dresses and suits and jeans and T-shirts. It was a strange collection of what the city had to offer, and each person was watching him like a predator tracks its prey. Vampires. They were all vampires and here he kneeled among them. Was he meant to be food? A sacrifice?

"It isn't nice to sneak into people's homes, Viktor." A horrifyingly familiar voice reached his ears, and his attention snapped to the area in front of him where a single woman stood with a man just to the right.

Elizabeth watched as Viktor tried to adjust the way he was positioned, attempting to take some of the weight off his knees. She was dressed in what he imagined was a formal gown, which was shockingly in sync with whatever this was meant to be. It was almost cartoonish, like a scene out of a comical horror film. Nothing that one would take seriously. The gown was silver, with a slit up the side that stopped in the middle of her thigh while her white hair fell in waves around her bare shoulders, and Viktor couldn't help but think she was a beautiful monster. She was the type who lured people to their deaths, convincing them to go into alleys or abandoned buildings with just a smile. It was everything movies claimed vampires were—seductive and sensual. Dangerous, and he wondered exactly how many of the vampires surrounding them were lured in by her.

He tried to push himself to his feet, but the figure beside him pressed down on his shoulders. The signal was clear. Stay on his knees before their leader, because that was what Elizabeth was. Wyatt, at least that was who he thought it was, stood a few paces behind her. A guard, perhaps. Or maybe he was given a position of honor, considering how Elora cared for him, had demanded his safety. A tinge of guilt hit him as he studied the vampire, dressed exactly how he had been that night at the apartment. Jeans and a T-shirt that stretched across his frame. If Viktor hadn't brought Elizabeth that night, Wyatt would still be human and caring for the aunt, lamenting Elora as the woman who got away.

"Didn't know anyone was home," Viktor responded as the pain in his head subsided to an ache and words were once more forming. A smile stretched across her face, dark and cruel in a way that made the hair on the back of his neck stand up. He had messed up again. In his desperation to prove himself, he had run face first into yet another failure. At this point, if he survived, he would take whatever punishment Thorne and the rest of the Resistance gave him. Failure was his old friend, forever haunting his steps and poisoning every decision and move he made.

"Understandable. But now you get to be our guest! Isn't that exciting? We don't usually have them, so forgive our meager accommodations. I'm sure you're familiar with the room options." Elizabeth seemed to watch every twitch and shift on his face as he tried to settle his features into a blank expression. He would give nothing away. She thrived off of reactions, of anger or fear, and he would give her neither.

"Take him to cell five," she announced before meeting his eyes. "You'll remember that one well, I think." Viktor shuddered. She was right. He knew exactly what room that was. It was the room he took her from, the room she had destroyed except for the mattress on the floor. The message that reached him was clear. He was now her prisoner, and he could only guess what she planned for him.

Chapter 43

Elora

She was awake when he came back. The clock on the bedside table read three in the morning, and she froze as the door clicked open. Voices proceeded it, hushed words that were too garbled to understand. But she knew Damien's voice like her own. It was her personal melody, a symphony that only she could hear. It eased the tension from her bones and allowed her muscles and limbs to become languid, as if she were melting into the plush mattress beneath her.

There was a part of her that wanted to remain unnoticed, for his eyes to move over her as he performed his tasks. Simply seeing him, being in his presence, dragged forward the way he helped her with her gown, the way his fingers had lingered, how his knuckles had brushed her bare skin. To be touched in a way that was almost hesitant. It was like there was something about the act that rendered him nervous. It was strange to see him unsure, to feel that in his touch. He always exuded confidence, almost arrogance, in every move he made and word he said. She had never seen him anxious about his actions, his intentions, and how they would be received. The way he was always cognizant of ensuring she was in control, that she consented to his touch, was something she had become addicted to.

He didn't believe he was good enough. And she understood that so intimately it was as if they shared the same toxin, which had poisoned them both. He was more than she ever thought she would deserve. When he looked at her, she felt exposed in the most intoxicating of ways, like he could see each and every dark and twisted corner of her and accepted them. He may not share her feelings, but he knew her inside and out and never flinched.

Yet, even as the door opened and she heard him enter, Elora didn't make a sound or move a muscle. She didn't twitch as he turned on the bathroom light, illuminating a form covered in a dark substance. At the sight, her desire to remain unnoticed disappeared in a wave of fear and concern and anger. Her heart pounded as the blanket flew from her body and she leaped to her feet, darting across the room.

"What happened?" Her voice was loud and demanding, forcing him to stop in his tracks as his head hung against his chest. The light illuminated the stains across his navy t-shirt, making the color darker. His skin was stained by drying blood splatter across his limbs and she could see even more along his face. Whatever had happened had been violent. Bloody. She only hoped the other person looked worse.

"Took care of a problem." His words were cold, as if ice had been injected into his veins to create a shadow of the vampire she knew.

"And who was the problem?" she responded, tone just as harsh despite knowing exactly who it had been. The scent radiating from him was all too familiar, causing her body to stiffen, and she took a step back from him in hopes it would disappear, that she could somehow escape it. His head twisted to her instantly, clocking the movement, and his features shifted from icy rage to guilt.

"I think you know," was all he said before he entered the bathroom and closed the door. For a moment, all she could do was stand there in complete shock. She had known he was angry, that he blamed himself for not being there when Jonas tricked everyone and pushed his way in. In that way, they were mirror images of each other—both blaming themselves for something that was not their fault, something that was not in their control. Jonas had planned each part of it, moving each player into place, picking his timing perfectly. He was nothing if not an opportunist.

Elora debated charging in there even as she heard the shower turn on and wet clothes fall to the floor. She could demand details. There was a craving in her to hear each and every sordid minute of what happened, of what Damien had done. She wanted him to paint a picture so vivid it felt as if she was there. So visceral that she could feel the blood, the satisfaction that she was sure he felt with every injury he bestowed on Jonas. But the thought of seeing him in there was too much, causing something to clench low in her stomach, and she sighed heavily, spinning on her heel before returning to bed. She turned on the main light, sunk down onto the mattress facing the bathroom, and crossed her legs to wait patiently for him to return.

Fingernails dug and picked at the skin on her hands, pulling at the cuticle as she listened intently for any change, for the shower to turn off. The scent of Jonas's blood was fading away, replaced with the hotel soap that didn't seem to really smell of anything in particular. Her eyes darted to the small pile of papers on the bedside table, the list of terms she was meant to read by tomorrow. Silas had brought them shortly after Damien had left for the night, a yellow envelope that held the legal language for her wedding and everything that went with it. According to Darian, only Silas needed to sign them. Her wants and desires didn't matter in this scenario.

Elora let out a small noise of disgust as she grabbed the small stack and returned to her spot, resting the sheets on her legs. The legal language was difficult to understand as she tried to decipher what it said. Something about both parties agreeing to everything that was outlined below, and a part of her wished Silas had walked her through it. She flipped to the second page where the actual terms began, divided between the three major parties. First were the terms outlined by Darian, then the terms from Silas. The last part of the document was the terms for Elora. Not dictated by her, but a list of what she would be expected to do as his wife. She almost didn't read them, told herself that it was a horrible idea, that it would weaken her resolve and thrust her back into her nightmares.

Yet her eyes moved across the page until they latched onto the heading: Terms for Elora. A list of five from what she could see. As she read the first one, Elora choked back a sob, which grew more and more difficult as she continued.

Each term was more horrifying than the last, but they all boiled down to possession and control. A part of her appreciated the fact there were no lies or smoke and mirrors about it. Everything was laid bare in black and white to anyone who read it. It was a declaration on Darian's part. The action of a vampire who feared no one, who was secure in his position. It made what was to come that much better.

"What're you reading?" His voice startled her, and she laughed softly as she jumped. The papers fell from her hands and onto her lap. She hadn't heard him get out of the shower or even leave the bathroom. Reading the terms had threatened to rip her away from reality, and every bit of her focus had been on staying in the present.

"I think you know," she responded, mimicking his own answer in hopes of irritating him. From the way his face sharpened, she had succeeded and took a moment to savor getting anything other than emptiness from him.

"The terms? Are you going to sign them?" She shook her head at the question and turned her attention back to them. It was the only thing that occupied her thoughts right then despite the fact he stood in front of her. His t-shirt was tight across his broad chest while his damp hair fell into his face and tiny droplets of water rested on the moth tattoo along his neck and the others along his arms. Flowers, she realized. A collection of various types in black and grey. His dark eyes seemed to radiate so much light it was almost blinding.

"My signature isn't required." He huffed and stepped forward, grabbing the papers from her lap before swiftly turning away.

"Seriously? That was rude." Damien said nothing, but she tracked the way his steps ceased and his shoulders tightened. She knew exactly which part he was reading, and which part would cause him to react this way. The sound of harsh breathing filled the otherwise silent room before he spun back around towards her. She had never seen him like this. His entire body seemed to tremble and vibrate as if physically containing whatever he was feeling was nearly impossible. As if he was one single moment from becoming the embodiment of wrath. Words of remorse sprung forward. Her entire plan waited on the tip of her tongue, waiting for her to reveal it and take away just a tiny bit of his pain. Not a single one of the terms he was reading would come to fruition.

"One, she is to obey any and every order, request, and command given by her husband." He spat the last word as if even saying it was toxic. She gave him nothing when he glanced up from the paper to gauge her reaction, even as she wondered if he still needed to be kept in the dark. As distasteful as it was, the answer was yes. After the reaction in the meeting, it would be suspicious if he was suddenly calm and collected at the wedding itself. His reaction and demeanor needed to be genuine.

"Two, she is to provide blood upon request, either by direct feeding or by allowing it to be collected." Again, a pause and a searching look. Again, she gave him nothing.

"Three, she is to allow the use of her body upon the request of her husband. Four, she is not to leave the Ravenwell residence or have guests outside of her immediate relatives. Well, that's kind of him." It was the first comment from him, but he didn't stop.

"Five, she is not to be touched in any way without the permission of her husband." He tossed the papers onto his bed, hands clenching at his sides as she watched him struggle to collect himself. Elora said nothing. What was there to say that wouldn't reveal everything? She waited for him to continue, waited for him to comment and rant and whatever else he needed. Every word, no matter how cruel or harsh, she would take without question or complaint. The least she could do was let him scream and vent and be the vessel that received it all.

But he did none of that. Instead, his body fell in defeat as he dropped onto the edge of the bed opposite her. One final look before he placed his elbows on his knees and lowered his face into the palms of his hands.

"I can't do this, Elora. Don't ask me to do this." His voice broke and every part of her shattered at the sound.

"Damien, I—" she swallowed, considering each and every word. This was too much. The sheer agony and defeat in each word that came from his diminished form was torture. She wasn't going to keep doing this. Genuine reactions be damned. Only hours ago, she had asked him to trust her. It was her turn to trust him. Despite everything between them, the lies and betrayals, the hatred and cruelty, he earned her trust. She had to be a fucking idiot for not simply explaining everything, for not sparing him this. Silas had been right from the beginning.

She dropped to her knees and crawled forward until she was in front of him. Her hands reached out to his and drew them away from his face, revealing the sheer anguish underneath. A breath caught in her throat at the sight as she sat back on her heels, preparing her words.

"I should have told you from the beginning. None of that is going to happen. I promise you. Okay? That piece of paper won't matter." She let her words sink in as confusion filled his eyes before moving to the rest of his face. His mouth opened and closed as if trying to form words or questions but couldn't.

"I asked you earlier to trust me, but I should have trusted you. After giving you my blood, I was terrified of what I did to you and didn't want to drag you into anything else. You've done enough for me. But believe me when I say Darian will never touch me again." Something was working behind his eyes as his hand came to her face and cupped her cheek. His thumb ran along her cheekbone and her eyes closed at the sensation.

"I don't think you understand how scared I am for you; what I would do for you."

She shook her head slightly, not wanting him to move his hand, not wanting to lose his touch. "You've already made up for Killian." Her thoughts went back to his words at the apartment when he said they would be even soon enough, that he would fix what he had done.

"It's not about that anymore. You deserve to be safe, to be protected. You deserve to be touched when you allow it, not when others demand it." His words were soft, as if speaking them was a confession he never planned on making. She couldn't think of a single thing to say in response. Every thought and sentence stuck in her mouth, stumbling over one another. Each one was a declaration, a confession that he could once again reject. Caring for her and ensuring her safety was different from what she wanted from him. Instead, she simply sank into his touch and let herself savor it for as long as he allowed.

His hand left her cheek and tears formed in her eyes from the loss. A small smile graced his lips as his face brightened slightly, and he stood and pulled the blankets on his bed down. Only then did he turn around and offer her his hand. There was a vulnerability in his face, a nervousness in his movements. It was adorable, and she giggled slightly at it, the sound strange after their conversation. He pulled her up and gestured for her to get into the bed he had claimed. Wordlessly, Elora did as she was bid and crawled in, scooting until she was on the far side. Her heart jumped into her throat as he followed suit and pulled the blankets up over them, causing the papers with the lists of expectations to fall to the floor. Thought after thought hit her as her anticipation grew with each second that passed while she waited. This was uncharted territory. Outside of him comforting her, they had never shared a bed.

Damien laid flat on his back and extended his arm. She wasn't sure she was breathing as she nestled into the space he opened for her, resting her head on his chest, her hand over his heart as it seemed to race as quickly as her own. His lips met her hair, and she exhaled slowly. If she pretended enough, this was normal. If she pretended hard enough, they were simply a couple on vacation, cuddling in bed after a long day of shopping and sightseeing. Inside this room, everything could be different.

"I killed Jonas," he whispered into her hair, voice heavy as if every word was a fight.

"I know," she responded before they lapsed into silence and then slept.

Chapter 44

Viktor

As far as he could tell, the cell had not been cleaned since he took Elizabeth out of there a mere couple of weeks ago. Had it really only been that long since everything had fallen apart even more? He let his head rest against the concrete wall and closed his eyes, trying not to breathe in the scent of blood that seemed to radiate from every possible inch of space. Shouts and cries of pain punctuated the silence that seemed to settle throughout the ward. Each time the doors opened and closed, his body stiffened as he prepared for the end that never seemed to arrive.

The first time they had come, it had been Wyatt with someone Viktor recognized. She had been a nurse in the low-security ward, and he had searched her face for any sign that she recognized him. But there was nothing. Not the flicker of an eyelash or twitch of her lips as his sleeve was cut off at the elbow and his blood was drained once more. It was a process he was intimately familiar with. Only this time, his blood wasn't being given to Elora as some type of cruel trick by Killian. This time, he had no idea what was being done with it.

He rubbed his cheeks with the palms of his hands, wincing slightly as the feeling of grime and whatever else laced his skin. In the distance, a door opened and closed, followed by the girlish giggles he had expected to hear before now. Muffled words filtered down the hallway, and he shifted slightly, trying to decide if he should care how he appeared. No matter what he did, he couldn't hide the dirt that coated his skin and clothes, couldn't hide the dried blood from where they had been draining him.

"Do you like your room?" Her voice felt like sandpaper against his skin. It was its own special form of torture, a unique reminder of his most recent failures.

"I've been in better, but the decor is fantastic," he responded dryly before glancing up at her. She looked exactly how she did before he was dragged down here. The same silver gown, though it seemed to have lost some of its shine, and there were splatters of blood along the bodice. A few steps behind her stood Wyatt, dressed in a black shirt and jeans. His hands were thrust into his pockets as he watched the scene with a strange sort of detachment. There was nothing in his expression as he stared at Elizabeth. No animosity for turning him. No anger or even adoration. Viktor couldn't help but wonder if Wyatt's aunt was somewhere in the ward. Maybe in a cell similar to his own. Or had she been turned?

"Unfortunately, this is the best we have to offer at the moment. Though I'm sure our fortunes will be changing soon." Viktor sat up a bit straighter at her words, at the hint that there was, in fact, something coming. He hadn't been sure if he would be kept here as some sort of toy, a blood bag for those she turned. Their numbers had been increasing from what he could tell. More and more voices filled the ward, arguing about space and hierarchy. If they weren't careful, they would destroy themselves from the inside out. Thorne had been correct. Elizabeth was the bigger threat, the problem they needed to focus all their resources on. Even if Elora became what Thorne feared she would, Elizabeth was still the one turning humans at a rapid rate. It was a plague, he realized. An incurable disease that Elora had started, but that Elizabeth was purposefully spreading. In a matter of months, if not less, the city would be overrun by those connected to Elora. Her own personal army, in a sense. The question was whether she would use it.

"I have news about our favorite vampire," she sang into the cell, hands gripping the bars as she met his eyes. Her own were almost luminescent as she gave him a wide smile. It was difficult sometimes to differentiate the vampire he knew her to be with the innocent, almost girlish woman who stood before him. He simply raised a brow in response, waiting for her to continue.

"My sister's getting married!" Her declaration ended with a piercing squeal that somehow made it more difficult to fully comprehend the words she had said. The idea of Elora marrying felt strange, like there was something that didn't quite fit within the equation. Was it Damien? He was the only option he could imagine, but it didn't feel right either.

"Congrats. To who?" He tried to keep his tone calm. That protective urge he felt whenever Elora's name was brought up raced to the surface, and he forced his hands to relax on his thighs as she waved her hand dismissively.

"Some vampire head. The Ravenwell group, I think. I wasn't exactly educated in vampire customs and such." Luckily, Viktor had been. He recalled the meetings from when he first joined that felt more like a job orientation where they threw information at a person in hopes they would remember it. They had covered everything—the Accords, the vampire families and their heads, how power and influence worked in those circles. Viktor remembered being absolutely amazed by how much information they had on a race of people who were supposed to be a secret.

"Darian," he said to no one in particular, and he heard her make a small noise.

"I guess it makes sense that you would know that. You are part of a group that wants to kill me and my sister." She chuckled softly at her own observation, but there was an edge to it. The laughing vampire who had come to his cell had disappeared and left the unhinged one behind.

"I take it we weren't invited." He watched her flinch at his words, and he knew exactly why her entire mood had shifted the longer they spoke. The foster sister hadn't been asked to be a bridesmaid or maid of honor. She hadn't even been told of the wedding. Instead, she had probably found out about it through gossip or rumors. Viktor glanced back at Wyatt, whose own expression seemed pained, like someone was stabbing him in the ribs with a small knife. Not enough to do damage, but enough to hurt.

"No, we weren't." There was a sadness to her tone, and he studied her, noting the longing and despair that was painted across her face. Her eyes seemed darker, and her lips were a thin line. Every part of her was impacted by this, as if being away from Elora was causing her body to deteriorate. Viktor shuddered as he considered what would happen if they were brought back together, if Elizabeth was allowed to flourish in Elora's presence.

"Maybe the invite got lost," he offered before shifting his attention back to the wall in front of him. She made a soft noise as if she were considering his explanation and latching onto it like a life raft in the middle of the ocean.

"Perhaps," she responded after a moment. "It does seem all very rushed from what I understand. Only a day from now. Barely any time to prepare." Viktor let out a soft breath and considered the facts as they stood. A rushed wedding between Elora and a vampire head. The entire situation was off. She had never seemed like the type to marry, but maybe that had changed since she had escaped Killian.

"Are you saying you don't believe your sister is actually marrying?" Viktor let the question hang between them as he darted a look at her, finding a smirk on her face.

"No, I don't. And you don't either. You know her better than that." She leaned away from the bars and whispered something to Wyatt, who merely nodded in response before leaving. His footsteps seemed to echo in the hallway as he left, and Viktor tensed at his departure.

"I think my sister has a plan and that it will be utterly glorious." Elizabeth raised her face to the ceiling and closed her eyes as she spoke, as if she were praying. It was strange to see this level of reverence or worship for someone he had gotten so close to, someone he cared for. Elora would hate it, and he wondered if Elizabeth remembered enough of her foster sister to realize that. After a moment, a peaceful smile spread across her face, and she lowered her head, meeting his eyes once more.

"Either way, I do plan on bringing her a gift." Her voice was back to light and playful. It was whiplash, off-putting in a way that made him want to shift further into the cell. She wanted him to ask what the gift was. He could practically feel her screaming at him to do so. But he wouldn't, not when he instinctually knew.

"It seems like they have been careful draining you." Again, that drastic switch and the resulting second of confusion as he tried to keep up with her, tried to anticipate what she was going to say or do next. He focused on the wall before him, not sure if it mattered if he read her expression. There were long, deep scratches in the concrete and dark stains that he was fairly certain were dried blood.

"They've been gentle while they steal my blood, yes." The biting sarcasm wasn't supposed to make an appearance. Her giggle bounced off the walls of the ward, filling the space until there was nothing else. He flinched at the sound and realized he would never get used to it, would always react to something so terrifying.

"I can't have you dying or turning." Her words came out as something akin to a song, each syllable drawn out and somewhat whimsical. A part of him was relieved that she didn't want him dead or turned, but that didn't mean much when she was this insane. She seemed to be turning everyone, so why was he off the table?

"I would have guessed both those options would be appealing to you," he responded as he continued staring at those gouge marks on the wall in front of him. Were they created by Elizabeth? Or a patient before her?

"You would have guessed wrong. I have a very special use for you." Viktor felt his body tense up at her declaration. It was what he had figured was the case. He was once again some type of bargaining chip or toy that she was playing with. First, it was Killian using him to keep Elora in line. Now Elizabeth had plans of her own. The only question was what they were and if he would survive them. He opened his mouth to respond just as footsteps echoed down the hallway and Wyatt stepped up beside Elizabeth. His face dipped, and he whispered into her ear. The whole time, she nodded and grinned as if the secret was the key to everything she had planned.

"Good news! You'll be getting out of that cell sooner than I thought. Get some sleep, Viktor. Tomorrow is a busy day."

Chapter 45

Damien

The pit in his stomach that morning was so vast he was certain it would swallow him whole, drag him down into its depths until there was nothing left of him. And maybe that was for the best. At least then he wouldn't have to see her in that gown, watch her walk down the aisle with Silas at her arm to give her away to that prick. But instead, he was to stand up there with her, a guard even as she exchanged vows and gave herself away.

Trust me. Elora's voice rang inside his head again, a whispered plea that he felt in every nerve of his body. He wanted to trust her, to believe that she knew what she was doing. But every time he got close to surrendering to her request, Damien saw her on the floor of his room once more. He heard her broken voice as she tried to pull herself back together, felt the clumps of hair that fell into his hands as he washed the blood away. Damien swallowed as he waited for her to appear in the small side room of the hotel's conference room that had been transformed into a makeshift chapel. He peeked through the cracked door and scoffed slightly at the sight. The chairs were placed in two sections, each row four chairs long and six rows deep on either side of the aisle. Flowers lined the walls, and an archway was set up at the front of the room. Again, flowers. Roses, in particular. A deliberate choice, no doubt.

He sighed deeply and ran his fingers through his hair, shifting slightly as he watched the door. Damien had never been to a wedding, and it was some type of sick joke that this would be the first one. It had to be the universe punishing him by forcing him to see her in her gown with a veil over her face as the reality of what Darian wanted hung over their heads.

Trust me. Once more, her words were a caress against his ear, an attempt to ease the tightness of his muscles and jaw.

"I can't do this," he whispered before peeking into the chapel once more. The chattering and laughter had grown steadily as vampires and humans alike piled into the room, mingling and gossiping. He heard her name a few times, spoken with either disgust or amusement.

"Finally getting what he wants," came one comment, followed quickly by another. "First, she was Killian's blood whore, and now she is his. Just moving from one to another."

Damien's hands clenched into fists as he restrained himself from rushing into the room and shutting up every person who dared to discuss her, who was stupid enough to let her name pass their lips. He memorized each face, each sneer, each expression of disgust. If he could, every person in that room would meet the same fate as Jonas. Dispatching him, taking his time, removing the fingers that touched her, the teeth that bit her, had brought him a sense of peace. The process had been calming, a balm for a turbulent soul. The smell of Jonas's blood and fear had sustained him even once he returned to the room and was met by her concern. He hadn't expected her to be awake and had hoped she would sleep through his shower before he slid into his own bed, reminding himself over and over that he couldn't slip into hers. That he couldn't pull her close, breathe in her scent as his eyes closed, and he fell asleep with her in his arms.

Then, they had done that anyway. He had invited her in, and she had crawled under his blankets and moved in close as if she knew what he needed. Just as he always knew what she needed, what she was thinking. Even before the blood, they had understood each other. Broken people understood broken people in a way no one else could understand. And their shattered pieces fit together to create something cohesive and strangely beautiful despite the sharp edges.

Now it was being destroyed once more. Their pieces were being torn apart, leaving only gaping wounds behind. He wasn't sure they would heal this time. He had given too much of himself to her, had gift wrapped individual slices of his soul, left his heart in her hands. There was nothing for him to keep when she left in a matter of hours.

The door behind him opened and he spun around, sucking a gasp of breath at the vision before him. Elora was in the gown from the other day, the one he had helped her get in and out of, the one she wore when she begged him to trust her. Her hair was up from what he could see, with crimson spirals that fell down around her face, framing lips covered in dark red, and eyes lined with black. Somehow, they were brighter. The green was almost luminescent as they peered out from dark lashes. The veil that would eventually cover her face fell in waves of lace from a small crown of silver vines and jewels. She was a goddess, the embodiment of rising from the ashes, of wearing her pain and scars as armor. She was something to be regarded only with reverence. No one in that room deserved to even lay eyes on her.

Elora met his eyes for just a moment, just long enough for him to see the anxiety there, the hesitation and fear before it shifted into the mask he knew so well. Blank. Empty. But there was steel in her spine as she stood up straight and pushed her shoulders back. Damien tracked the way her hands clenched, how she fidgeted from foot to foot as they waited for Silas. He could hear everyone in the main room chattering and assuming their places. In his mind, he could picture them getting into their seats, gossip and vitriol still spewing from their lips. Darian would be in his place in front of the archway. It was a joke, something that was like a bad plot line from an equally bad show.

"You look nice," he muttered into the silence, and he felt her attention snap to him as he glanced at her. Elora's brows were knitted together as if trying to understand the words he said before she nodded slightly.

"Thank you," she whispered softly. "Trust me, Damien. Please, just trust me." She must have seen his own fear on his face, an emotion he wasn't used to. At least not for years now. Fear used to be his best friend, along with hunger and defeat. Before, it was always for himself and his mother. Now it was for her, for what would happen to her once this was all said and done and he was forced from her side.

"I'm trying," he bit out, intending to stop speaking with that. But his mouth had a mind of its own as he continued, thoughts rushing past his lips even as he told himself to shut up.

"Do you understand how hard it is to do that? To watch you do this? And what? Hope that you know what you are doing? That he won't hurt you again? I can't, Elora. I—" His words broke off as Silas entered their tiny room dressed in a dark suit with his hair brushed away from his face. There was a darkness lacing his features, and Damien once again noted how much older Silas appeared, how much this entire fiasco had aged him. He wouldn't have been surprised to see streaks of gray in his hair.

"Are you ready?" Silas's words were not directed to him but to Elora, who seemed to stand up a bit straighter. Every scar was on display in a dazzling show of strength, but he could already hear the whispers that would rise like a symphony when she walked down that aisle. He had heard them before at the banquet, the assumptions and cruel jokes that they made. But she was making a statement this way. She could have worn something that covered every inch of skin that had been marked by them. It was what she had done in the past when she had been unnecessarily ashamed of them. Looking at her now as she owned each and every one of them was like seeing something sacred, something not meant to be seen by humans or vampires. He had told her she looked nice, but that wasn't a strong enough description. Every word that came to mind was an understatement that refused to suit her. Beautiful, gorgeous, stunning, heavenly. No, none of them fit her. She looked indescribable in a way that felt like a dream he didn't deserve to have.

Elora nodded at her uncle and seemed to study him for a moment before her arms wrapped around his chest. She pulled him close, burying her face in his shoulder while Silas's arm closed around her. He pressed a kiss to the top of her head before whispering something in her ear. Damien shifted slightly at the scene. He felt out of place, like he was witnessing something he wasn't meant to.

"Damien, you should take your place at the front. I want you near her during this." He nodded at Silas's command and allowed himself one last look at the scene before him. Elora hadn't moved away from her uncle, her arms still enclosed around him as if locking him in place. Silas returned his attention to his niece and moved back, staring down into her face. Damien wished desperately he could see what Silas saw, could read the emotions there in hopes it would give him the slightest hint of what was happening.

Trust me. Her words seemed to return over and over again. A repeated melody in his mind as he finally turned from them and left the room, closing the door behind him. No one else needed to witness the tender scene between an uncle and his niece, even if Damien couldn't understand how Silas could hand her over, could appear so stoic while sacrificing her in the name of power. Only one thought repeated in his mind, mingling and colliding with her plea for him to trust her.

I shouldn't have taken her to him. We should have fled the city. The thought was bitter as he surveyed the room once more. The smell of roses assaulted him, and he glanced around, noting the dozens of vases full of them. Red and white and pink and yellow. All colors and types mingled with leaves and baby's breath to lend the appearance of this being a normal wedding, where the groom and bride were in love and wanted to dedicate their lives to one another. But that was not this wedding.

Darian was already in his spot, along with a young man with a priest's collar, standing in front of the archway. Sweat lined the priest's brow as he fiddled with the papers in his hand. Human, Damien guessed. But did he know who surrounded him right now? Or was he nervous for another reason? Humans could sometimes tell when they were in the presence of something not entirely human. They felt uneasy and on edge around them as the sense of being prey swept over them.

As he strolled to the front where Darian stood, Damien adjusted his shirt, pulling the sleeves down to his wrists and straightening the buttons along the front. A smirk lined the vampire's face as he watched Damien take his place directly across from him, hands clasped behind his back in an attempt at self-control.

"Aren't you going to say congratulations?" Darian's request lingered between them as Damien swallowed and felt his fingernail dig into the palm of his hand.

"Not until it is all said and done." Darian's smile widened at the response, and his eyes shifted to the door Damien had just walked through.

"Maybe I'll let you visit every once in a while. I'm sure Silas will want to know his niece is alive. You can be the one to check on her." Damien didn't react, refused to give Darian exactly what he was searching for.

"I'll follow whatever orders Silas gives me." The smile on his face faltered a bit before a light wave of music filled the room. Each voice was silenced instantly as bodies twisted in their seats, their eyes searching for the bride. And there she stood with Silas by her side, her hand holding his forearm in a death grip. Damien couldn't see her face beneath the veil, but his imagination ran wild. Wide green eyes full of determination and fear. Her lips pressed into a thin line as she unsuccessfully tried to force her mask of indifference onto her face.

Silas did not have the expression of a delighted uncle giving away his niece in marriage. His own face was pinched and somewhat pale as they made their way down the aisle lined with a pristine white rug. There was no bridesmaid, no maid of honor or best man. No flower girl, ring bearer, or anyone else he knew weddings tended to include. He had been forced to watch enough of that horrible reality show that Elora loved so much.

Elora held the large bouquet in one hand as they approached. Each step was slow, as if they thought they could postpone this a bit longer. She had picked the bouquet. Or Silas had. Not a single rose was included. Only carnations and hydrangeas, along with another flower he didn't recognize. There were strands of lavender in between the various flowers, giving it a somewhat messy yet elegant look. Finally, Silas nodded briefly at Damien before handing Elora over to the monster before them all. He couldn't look at Darian standing there, couldn't bear to see the grin and hunger on his face. Even picturing it, knowing it was plastered on his face, forced Damien to take a slight step back to put distance between them. His rage begged and pleaded to be let free, arguing that Darian had earned it over and over again.

Yet, all he heard, even over the music slowly coming to an end, was her voice.

Trust me.

Chapter 46

Elora

The grin on Darian's face threatened to make her ill as she stared at him. The blood she had drank before getting dressed lingered in the back of her throat as she swallowed, clutching her bouquet to keep her hands from trembling. Silas patted her hand softly and kissed her cheek before turning away to take his seat in the front row. She watched as he reclined against the back of the chair and placed his ankle on his knee—the very picture of an unbothered uncle watching his niece marry.

Damien stood behind her, a stoic presence there to protect her at Silas's request. As she left the room with Silas at her arm, she hadn't been able to meet his eyes. She knew exactly what she would see—a blank expression of angles and edges. Cold and focused, just as he had appeared whenever Killian was nearby. The soldier once more. But it would be his eyes that revealed the pain she was causing him. The swirling pools of brown with the hidden flecks of gold would illuminate every thought and urge he was holding back. He had the power to stop her in her tracks, to stop her from continuing her trip down the aisle and abandon this somewhat stupid plan. When they had spoken last, she had almost faltered, had almost begged him to save her from all of this and leave the city. Fantasies of them living some pastoral life of perfection in the woods or the beach or the mountains danced in front of her, disappearing into clouds of smoke every time she considered one too long. If it wasn't Darian searching for her, it would be Elizabeth. And if it wasn't Elizabeth, it would be the Resistance. Unless she removed every threat, those fantasies were out of reach. A fever dream meant to torment and tease, to chip away at whatever hope or sanity she had left.

Her fingers gripped around the bouquet as she straightened her shoulders and faced Darian. Even now, facing the creature from so many of her nightmares, she didn't want to be saved. The people who tried to save her had a tendency to end up dead, and that wasn't going to happen to Damien or Silas, no matter what she had to do. No matter how much regret and guilt she had to swallow in the process. And underneath the desire to protect herself was the darkness always at the periphery. She wanted revenge, wanted the rush of satisfaction and pure ecstasy she felt when her knife plunged into Killian's neck.

The priest cleared his throat, and Elora looked at him for the first time. A young man with blond hair and small lips gave her an apologetic smile, as if this entire thing was a minor inconvenience that they were both unfortunate enough to take part in. From underneath her veil that hung down to her thighs and cascaded down the back of her gown, she returned his smile for just a moment before turning back to her fiancé.

"We are gathered here to join together Darian and Elora in matrimony. They will now exchange the vows they have written themselves." Elora almost snorted at the words. Quick and to the point, she supposed. It was nothing like her shows, where there was a long-drawn-out speech at the beginning where they spoke of love and its everlasting nature. There would be none of that here, and she was almost relieved. No pretenses about this, no pretending that this was anything but a transaction.

"I vow to uphold my end of the terms and to protect my wife from all dangers, both inside and outside of our family. As long as we both live." The gleam in Darian's eyes was pure hunger and greed. She could practically hear his thoughts as she swallowed and forced her heart rate to calm, reminding her body that fear would not work here, not at this moment.

Darian slipped a small silver band onto her ring finger and let her hand drop down against her dress once more. She refused to look at it, to allow it to exist within the space of her mind as she fought against the reminder of his fingers and teeth on her skin, of the feral smile on his face leering over her as she passed out from whatever concoction Killian had given her.

"And now yours." The priest's voice broke through, and she nodded at him, thrusting the bouquet behind her. Hands instantly took it from her, and she turned to the crowd who were watching her with wary expressions, no doubt expecting a quick ending to what they all knew was a sham.

"My vows come with a story for you all." She felt Darian shift as if he were going to stop her, but she put her hand out. Her eyes never left the audience in front of her as they watched the scene unfold. "I will tell my story, and then I'm yours." A strange noise left Darian's mouth as if the delay was physically painful, as if being denied what he had bought for even another moment was devastating.

"Once upon a time, there was a little girl who was loved by her parents. They read to her, told her stories, and bought her everything she wanted. She drank her fill of blood and danced and played throughout her days living in the castle where she never knew pain or hunger," she began before pausing. Her eyes moved as she read each expression in the audience. Frustration. Irritation. Impatience. Curiosity.

She avoided her uncle's gaze as she took a single step forward and lifted the veil from her face before letting her hands drop to her sides. The skirt of the dress felt heavy as she watched some shift in their seats while others audibly gasped. Their collected reactions only encouraged her as she prepared for the next part of her story. She had planned every detail of this speech, excising pieces of her life for their consumption.

"But then it all crashed down. Her father told her she was special and took from her. Every night, he visited her, whispered promises and apologies and threats while she wept, and her body tried to recover. Her mother screamed and cried. She was kept away from her family, who noticed the changes in her. The way her body was now covered in scars. Cuts and bites left behind as a physical reminder of her role."

Another step forward, and she felt Damien follow suit. A single step towards her, mimicking her movement as she focused on those in front of her. Their whispers and gossip rang in her ears. Each accusation hung in the air between them as she told her story. Curiosity and impatience had been replaced with varying degrees of horror and repulsion, but she wasn't entirely sure it was aimed at her. Eyes shifted over her face and neck and chest, counting and noting each and every scar she described.

"And then her father decided to share her. He offered up her blood as a gift and reward for those loyal to him, for those he counted as friends," she continued as she gave Darian a pointed look and felt it as every pair of eyes followed hers, lingering on him. His face was contorted in rage as he listened to the story, as he heard her confession and accusation. There was nothing he could do now without showing his hand. If he demanded she stop, the audience would know her story was true and that he was attempting to silence her. If he allowed it to continue, all he could do was hope no one believed her. He was stuck, and she gave him a smirk before turning back to the audience.

"The girl grew older, and her skin became covered in more and more scars from their feeding and violence. Sometimes feeding was not enough, and she lost even more. Her innocence. Her light. Her will to live. And when she did try to fight, her mother was threatened, and the girl was drugged to make her more pliable." Elora turned back around and pulled the veil aside, giving the audience a full view of her back and the marks that lined the space there.

She took a step forward towards the priest, whose face had paled even further as if the story had rendered him ill, like the very sound of her words had run through him like a poison. Darian's face revealed his barely restrained fury, the promise of violence radiating from every feature. A hand reached out, and she took it, allowing herself to savor the feeling of Damien's skin against hers. It was an anchor that drew her back to reality. Voicing the story had been a crucial part of her plan, and from what she had seen on each face, it had struck in just the way she wanted. Yet with each word, each syllable, she had become increasingly unmoored from the world around her. The room had descended into a swirling void that merged with her old bedroom. The gown had shifted into something more akin to fingers and teeth, a grotesque covering made of flesh and pain. Each face morphed into a version of Killian's.

"Then the girl escaped, and her mind protected her. Blocked out all memories of her time there, only appearing in fragments in her nightmares. She was kept locked away and drugged to protect her. And when she returned, she was placed back in the same chains she had been in before. Except this time, she had grown her own teeth and claws and desire for blood and violence." Elora stepped towards Darian, who twitched slightly, and held his gaze, daring him to be the one to look away first as her hand sank into the pocket of her gown.

"And when she killed her father and left him in an ocean of blood in his own office, she decided to never be held against her will again."

Elora didn't give Darian or the audience a chance to react as she pulled the knife from her pocket and slashed through the air. Warmth hit her face at the same moment the collection of curses and shocked gasps filled the room. Darian's eyes widened in disbelief as his hands reached for his throat, desperately trying to hold in the blood pouring out through his fingers. His free hand reached for her, grabbing at her hair and face, seeking to punish her for this transgression while his mouth opened and closed as if he would scream or call for help, but no sound escaped. Only sharp attempts at breathing as the skin started to stitch itself back together. But she had planned for this. She had watched her own skin heal and leave scars behind.

The gore-covered knife pressed forward as it entered his chest, sinking past the jacket and silk shirt to the flesh beneath. His hands wrapped around her neck, squeezing tighter and tighter until she could barely breathe. She pressed the knife further, until it met resistance when it hit his ribs. A grunt fell from her mouth as she pushed it forward and dragged it down towards his waist. There was a prize there, something she coveted just as he had coveted her. And she would not be denied it. The grip on her neck loosened as his hands fell to his sides, all the fight gone.

Vaguely, she heard the shouts of anger and fear erupting around her, heard Silas's voice rising above the rest as he commanded them to stand down. To her right, she felt the priest back away, papers clutched between his hands and pressed to his chest as if they would protect him from her. Darian sank to the floor, eyes so large it felt impossible, like a caricature of the vampire. His skin had paled, but his hands now moved from his sides to the jagged hole in his chest before grasping at her face and her hair, yanking the veil from her head as she gave him a savage smile. Did he know that his efforts were pointless? That this was his fate, no matter what he did? His mouth moved once more, forming the shape of words that were never given a sound. She was sure it was some type of threat or promise, a plea to spare his life. He would vow to leave her alone and to never touch her again. Elora shook her head, hoping but not really caring if he understood the meaning behind it. It was too late for promises and regrets.

The knife fell onto the marble floor beneath it, the sound of it muffled by the cacophony of voices all demanding she be stopped, that Silas do something about what was transpiring before their eyes. She felt Damien's heavy steps as he stepped in front of her, planting his feet on the marble as if to guard whatever this was. For a moment, she allowed herself to consider whether he finally understood, whether he would forgive her for keeping him in the dark.

Her hand slipped past the layers on Darian's body, past the jacket and shirt, past the ribs broken by the knife. The jagged edges of bone scratched her hand as her fingers wrapped around the organ that was now barely beating. Darian's eyelids fluttered softly as his breathing came slower and slower. Fingernails dug into the muscle and blood of his heart as she pulled, yanked, and tore it out of his chest with a loud grunt. His entire body moved and shifted as she ripped his heart from his chest and stood, leaving his body on the marble floor now covered in an ever-expanding sea of blood. The entire skirt of her wedding gown was now a deep red, the original color disguised and replaced by the visceral evidence of her revenge.

With the heart in her hand, blood dripping off the edges of her palm and fingers, Elora turned to the crowd. One by one, she met their eyes, absorbed the shock and anger and fear that pulsated from each one. She found Silas, who turned from his attempts to keep the crowd at bay. His focus shifted from the now red wedding dress to the heart in her hand to the savage smile on her face. Pride and satisfaction raced across his own before he nodded slightly.

"My name, as many of you know, is Elora Ashcroft, and I am the rightful head of both the Ashcroft and Ravenwell families. I have proof that I murdered Killian Ashcroft, and you have all witnessed the death of Darian Ravenwell." Mutters and shouts filled the room as she stood before them, her heart racing in her chest as she watched their reactions. The heart began to cool in her palm, and she twisted towards Darian, eyes raking over his body. A part of her feared him coming back like the villain in a horror film. He would leap to his feet and attack, seeking his own revenge. But there was nothing. Not a twitch or even the slightest movement of his chest. Only a gaping hole and a partially open throat. It was glorious.

Elora had heard people say that revenge didn't accomplish anything, that it wouldn't make someone feel better. But they were only partially correct. It didn't erase the trauma. The scars didn't magically vanish from her skin once Darian was dead, and his heart was in her hand. Instead, there was a weight that had disappeared from her when she had seen the light go out of his eyes. No longer did she need to fear him finding her or chaining her up once more for his own personal use. Jonas was dead. Killian was dead. And Darian was as well. The three demons from her nightmares were eradicated, their lives and threats extinguished.

"No. You cannot claim both seats. Darian gave the Ashcroft family up." Elora knew the voice instantly. It was the same one that called for her execution, that called her an abomination. She smiled at Chloe and stepped towards her.

"Darian agreed to dismantle the family once the wedding was complete, and we were legally married. That never happened, so the Ashcrofts still exist. And I am their head." Chloe's calm exterior erupted in fury as the truth of Elora's words hit her. She had been the one to draw up the contract and had been the one to outline the terms.

"And since the Ravenwell family operates on the same set of ridiculous rules, I am now the head of that family as well. I will be merging them together to make things simpler." She flashed Chloe a smile before turning to the room as a whole. "And that will conclude tonight's ceremony. Thank you for coming."

She let the heart fall to the floor, splattering on the marble as she pulled the ring from her finger, dropping it onto Darian's body. Silas nodded and stepped aside, content to take over the crowd that seemed poised to attack at any moment. But her part in this was complete, and he would take the lead now. Chloe seemed to tremble with rage as Elora picked up her skirts and marched forward, head held high and eyes focused in front of her. She arranged her face into a mask of strength—stern and cold as she forced herself to walk away from the scene. Whispers followed her as she moved. Declarations of hatred and loyalty, of respect and disgust, all mingled together. Chloe's shouts rang out, accusing Silas of planning this from the beginning, of playing her for a fool. Elora only chuckled and shook her head even as she felt Damien fall into step behind her.

Tomorrow, she told herself. She would deal with that tomorrow.

Chapter 47

Damien

Damien followed her out of the makeshift chapel and down the long hallway to the elevator. The blood-soaked train of her gown dragged along the marble, leaving behind streaks of red on the pale gray. He watched her move through the hotel, steps sure and steady as she led them to their room. Her spine was straight, and her chin tipped up in defiance of everyone who dared to meet her eyes. Warring thoughts and emotions rampaged through him, demanding that he forgive her while others argued she should have told him what was happening, let him in on the plan itself.

Both of them were covered in Darian's blood. The pale rose gown she had worn for the ceremony had turned crimson while strands of her hair fell onto her face and cascaded down to her shoulders. It had somehow come loose and undone during the ceremony, becoming a wild mess that only enhanced her feral beauty. He knew why she had chosen this dress, why she had demanded so much flesh be on display. When she ripped Darian's heart from his chest and displayed it before the entire chapel, she wanted them to see exactly why she had done it. When she had told her story in lieu of vows, she wanted them to see the evidence etched into her skin. Each scar. Each puncture wound.

Fuck. It was indescribable. Word after word evaporated on his tongue as he tried to give life to what he had witnessed. It had been something holy in the darkest of ways.

Damien's job had been to stand beside her at the ceremony while Silas gave her away. Even as his hands clenched at his sides, even as the very core of his being screamed at him to intervene, he had done as she asked him. Trust me.

"Unbutton my dress, please," Elora whispered softly as they returned to her original room on the fifth floor. He felt his entire body go stiff at the request and the sheer exhaustion in her voice. With trembling blood-stained hands, he grasped the white buttons and undid them one by one, just as he had with the ribbons the night of the banquet. His fingers trailed along her bare back, tracing each scar. He felt her skin bristle, felt the goosebumps that lined her skin at his touch. A soft moan escaped her lips, and his movements froze while the heat from her body seared his hands. He couldn't help the small smirk that curled at the edges of his lips, the satisfaction of witnessing what he did to her.

"I'm sorry." Another whisper as her head hung slightly. Step by step, he moved around her until he was directly in front of her. She didn't look up, didn't meet his gaze. The power she exuded at the ceremony had evaporated, drained from her, leaving only sheer exhaustion behind. Or maybe it was something else. Maybe she was finally able to simply be, simply exist in a natural state that didn't demand a performance from her. No forced smiles. No disguise of ice and brutality to craft her into someone else. Maybe she was simply Elora, a woman who had seen too much in her twenty-six years.

With the very tip of his finger, Damien lifted her face and brushed back the strands of hair obscuring her peculiar green eyes. They always contained a strange type of brightness that radiated from them, as if there was a light behind them that drew everyone in like moths to a flame. Except now, they were dimmed. That light was nowhere to be found.

"Never apologize to me." At his response, Elora closed her eyes and tried to lower her head once more, but he gripped her chin. "Never again."

"But I need to. I need to explain. I need you to forgive me."

"For what? Saving my life so I could see that? You don't need to apologize for that. I understand why you kept it a secret." He took a breath before continuing because if he didn't say this now, he never would.

"I was upset, angry even when you told me about your blood because I was terrified of what it meant when it came to how I feel about you. I thought I would become obsessed with not you but your blood like they did. And that was fucking terrifying—the thought of becoming them when all I wanted was to help protect you, help you build a place where you are safe."

"I—" Damien shook his head and placed a finger on her lips.

"I need to say this. Please let me," he pleaded, and she only nodded. "But I was obsessed with you before your blood, before Silas's manor, before the apartment. Hell, even before we escape the Tower. You are a distraction that I welcome every minute of every day. When I thought I was going to lose you in Killian's office, I was willing to sell my soul to make sure you lived. I would have destroyed every single person who put you in that position, including myself."

He brushed a tear from her cheek as she simply stared at him. Everything else had melted away, leaving the two of them in that room, rooted in a single minute in time when he had ripped his heart from his chest and handed it to her, fully prepared for her to do what she wanted with it as long as she listened, as long as she held it in her hands for only a moment.

"You—" He hesitated, searching for words to describe the hold she had on him. "Declaring, admitting, confessing that I love you is not enough. It doesn't do justice to what I feel for you. I want nothing in return. I don't expect you to reciprocate or feel the same after everything I've done. All I ask is that you allow me to remain in your world. Allow me to watch you bend reality and recreate it. Allow me to stand beside you while we watch them burn."

No more words were spoken as a soft smile spread across her lips, her eyes impossibly vibrant as she took a single step forward and allowed him to lift her chin. It felt like a second chance, a redo of the apartment, of when he denied her.

"Please," she whispered, and he felt her breath on his lips, her body pressed to his.

"Am I still your choice?" The question was terrifying. Never before had he been this vulnerable. Every thought and emotion were spread out on the table for her to study and dissect. Time stood still as he waited for her response, and he knew she could feel his heart racing in his chest, a physical testament to what he felt when she came near, when he saw her across a room, when he simply thought of her.

"There was never another one. Only you."

"Can I kiss you?" She smiled, the gratitude clear on her face before her lips met his. In a single moment, everything outside that door vanished, dissipating like it never existed. It was per-fection made physical.

His hand gathered her hair, grasping the crimson locks gently until he angled her face towards him, granting him better access to her. A voice screamed at him to be slow, to follow her lead, to let her have the control she had never been granted before.

Everyone had always taken, always ripped her apart to take the parts they wanted from her. And he was determined to never give her the impression he was doing so now.

Her lips parted, and he fought back a smile at her silent con-sent, her permission for more. His tongue slid into her mouth just as the kiss transformed from sweet and hesitant to demanding and feverish. Her hand gripped the front of his shirt where the blood had begun to dry and pulled him closer and closer as if they could become a single entity, an amalgamation of their collected sharp edges and chipped barriers and broken shards that were pieced back together. Neither of them was quite whole as they lost themselves in each other. Her other hand still held up her gown, the only barrier between the two of them.

Elora let out a slight whimper as he pulled away without releasing his hold on her hair near the base of her neck. With his other hand, he wrapped his fingers around her wrists and lifted them to his lips. His eyes moved over the flesh there, the lines of scars she had so desperately kept hidden. He met her eyes for a single moment and saw only fear. The kind that came with being on display, of someone seeing the past etched into her body. Each scar was a story of survival, of pain, of fear. But they were also a shrine to her strength, to her determination, to her ability to survive anything. And he was merely a penitent, ready to worship at her altar.

One by one, his lips met her skin. Each scar kissed with reverence, as they should be. He felt her shudder under his touch, heard her moan, and let out a harsh breath at the sensation. A grin spread across his lips as he moved from her wrist, kissing each scar as he worked his way up her arm to her biceps before reaching the collection on her shoulder and etched into her collarbone.

Her head arched to the side as her eyes closed with her mouth slightly open as her breaths came out in shallow pants. Every part of her body seemed to vibrate as he focused solely on her, on demonstrating exactly how sorry he was, exactly how devoted to her he had become in the moments between all the bullshit. He felt her pulse beneath his mouth as he kissed each scar. His nose nuzzled against her chin, along her jaw, and he felt her press her body against his in a demand, a plea that he wasn't sure he could agree to. Under the armor she wore, under the steel in her spine, and under the confidence of her words, she was still Elora, still pulling herself together and attempting to heal.

"Damien," she whispered, voice low and breathy.

"Yes," he responded, and her body shuddered at the huskiness of his voice, the promise of what could come.

"Touch me. Please." Desperation mingled with desire as she turned her face to look at him. He knew that her longing mirrored his own even if he fought to keep it contained, reminding himself that she was in control.

Words failed him, and all he could do was nod before the gown fell to the floor in a pile of crimson and rose—a wedding dress no longer. He swallowed roughly as his focus moved from her hesitant eyes, her collarbones, her breasts, her hips—every bit of her. Not a single spot was free of scars; not a single spot was anything less than breathtaking. He had seen her naked before—when he helped her bathe after Killian hurt her, when she had given up and undressed in front of him without a single thought.

This was different. It was an offering. Once more, she was giving herself to him, and this time he refused to step away, refused to deny her. Her arms shifted to cover herself, as if being on display like this was suddenly too much. Damien pulled her hands into his own and kissed each palm before cupping her chin, so she was forced to look at him.

"Exquisite." It was the only word that came to mind, the only word he could utter as her eyes widened slightly and her cheeks turned the most delicious shade of pink.

Chapter 48

Elora

No one had ever called her that. No one had ever looked at her scars, seen her laid bare and uttered anything even close to that word. She had always been a possession without autonomy, something to be consumed. Her body felt as if it would splinter apart and collapse into a heap on the carpet if he didn't touch her. And she was terrified that he wouldn't, that his desire to protect her and allow her to heal would stay his hand. She could feel the way he tensed as he held himself back, probably terrified of sending her back to a memory, a place where she felt nothing but pain.

"Tell me what to do. Tell me what you want," he whispered into her ear, his hands rubbing down her arm. Every nerve in her body was on fire as if lightning flowed in her veins, filled every crevice and shadowy place within her. She swallowed and met his eyes, noting the hint of hesitation there.

"Touch me." She gripped his hand and moved it to her breast, moaning slightly as he palmed it. He chuckled softly at the sound even as she felt every part of his body stiffen. Slowly, so slowly, he let her guide his hands over her ribs, her hips, and back up along the same path. Her lips crashed into his once more, desperate and all-consuming.

He was her choice. She wanted him in every way and step by step, she pushed him back, her lips never leaving his. His hands held onto her hips, fingers digging into her soft curves as if he thought if he let go, then this moment would cease to exist.

His legs hit the edge of the mattress, and she froze. Every bit of confidence was gone as she hesitated in what the next move was. She knew what she wanted, but wasn't sure how to ask for it, demand it from him. Never had she led, never had she been an active participant. It was strange and empowering all at once, making her feel like she was bursting out of her skin.

Damien had to have spotted the hint of uncertainty in her eyes because his hands cupped her face and he smiled, kissing her once more.

"I have something for you." He slid between her and the bed, leaving her standing in nothing but her undergarments. Instinctively, her arms wrapped around her middle.

"Now?" She joked and huffed a laugh as she watched him look through a small pile of clothes on top of the dresser they shared. Shirt and pants seemed to fly through the air until she heard a small sound of triumph before he turned around. His brows furrowed as he noticed the arms wrapped around her chest, trying to cover as much as possible.

"Yes, now." She tilted her head slightly as he approached her, steps soft and slow as he fiddled with something in his hands.

"Close your eyes and turn around." She raised her eyebrows at the command, and he chuckled slightly. "Please," he added.

Her body trembled as she followed his instructions and turned around, closing her eyes. Thought after thought raced through her mind even as she seemed to vibrate with anticipation, trying to guess at what was coming, what was worth stopping everything for. Every nerve ending was on fire as she waited for what seemed like an eternity for something to happen, as her skin demanded to be touched.

A gasp sounded from her lips as something cool landed against her chest, right between her breasts on her sternum.

Without thinking, she raised her hand and touched something smooth attached to a chain. Her fingers explored it as she tried to understand exactly what she was feeling and her brows narrowed as she traced the edges. Soft curses filled the air, and she giggled as she felt him struggle with the clasp. It was a pendant. She knew that much. A small round item encircled in some type of frame.

Damien's hands came to rest on her shoulders as he steered her, both of them laughing as she stumbled slightly. Only two steps, and his hands left her just as his voice reached her ears.

"Open your eyes." She did as he asked once more and met her reflection in the mirror. Her eyes refused to land on the scars, on the sheer amount of her that was exposed. Instead, they focused on the pendant now resting right below her collarbones. A dark gray jewel or pearl surrounded by what looked like two crescent moons, one above and one below.

"It's beautiful," she whispered, and he nodded.

"They did excellent work, given the material I gave them to work with." He positioned himself between her and the mirror, blocking her view, as if he knew how difficult it was for her to see herself covered.

"You deserved a souvenir." He let his words sink in as she searched his face for an answer. Her fingers touched the white frame around the jewel just as her eyes widened in understanding. A slow nod met her realization, and she grinned at him.

"A black pearl in the center, surrounded by fangs. I want you to wear it for what comes next." His voice had become husky as he led her back towards the bed. With each unsteady step, she forced herself to meet his eyes, to allow herself to drown in the pools of black and gold. Her fingernails dug into his forearms as she struggled to stay upright, her knees threatening to buckle as heat pooled in her stomach. But the smile never left his face.

"Did he suffer?" Damien's eyes widened in surprise as her legs hit the edge of the bed. Gently, almost hesitantly, he pushed a strand of hair away from her face.

"Yes." His words reverberated in her bones as her eyes closed. She felt his lips against her ear and his breath before he spoke again. "Should I tell you? Give you another gift?"

Elora didn't move as his fingers trailed up and down her arms, over her shoulders like she was a map he was trying to memorize.

"I removed the skin from his fingers, sliced away any part that touched you. One by one until there was nothing but bone from the knuckle down." She smiled at the soft purr of his words as he lifted her hand and pressed his lips to each fingertip as he spoke.

"I removed his fangs. Yanked them out before I slit his throat and watched him bleed out until I knew that he was dead." He grinned as he pressed a line of kisses across her throat, and she threw her head back to allow him better access. "Though I think your show today put mine to shame."

She giggled slightly at the fake irritation in his voice as he pulled back just enough to see her face. His eyes lingered on the pendant for a heartbeat before he met her gaze and swallowed.

"You've seen enough of pain, of those taking from you. Let me show you pleasure, love." He dropped his head so their foreheads met, the movement strangely intimate. "Let me worship you."

Elora swallowed and nodded once, a single incline of her head. She felt him exhale, as if he had been holding his breath as he waited for her answer. His fingers gripped her biceps softly as he gently laid her on the bed. Goosebumps erupted across her body as her bare skin touched the cool blanket, causing a harsh gasp to sound. Damien shifted slightly, sinking to his knees before her. Warm fingers wrapped around her ankles as she reminded herself that it wasn't the cold iron of the chains, but Damien's hands. For only a moment, he seemed to hesitate, as if he were giving her the chance to remind herself of reality.

"They're gone, love. It's only you and me now." A long sigh forced itself past her lips before it turned into a languid moan. Her eyes closed and forced away every memory that was desperately trying to resurface, to ruin what had to be a dream. Her reality was never this calm, never this beautiful, never this perfect. It was always shadows, pain, and blood. This was never meant for someone like her, someone always just on the edge of imploding.

He pulled her towards him until she was perched on the very edge of the bed. Fingers pushed under the band of her underwear before he slid them down over her thighs and legs until they laid on the floor beside them. Her breath hitched as she pushed herself up onto her elbows to find him watching her with a type of reverence in his eyes. No one had looked at her like she was worthy of love and pleasure, and everything that came with it. It was intoxicating, something that would be so easy to lose herself in.

Soft kisses trailed up her inner thighs, one for each scar that acted as evidence for what she had survived. He glanced up at her from between her legs as he sought permission, the gold flecks never shining brighter than in this moment.

A nod.

A single nod from her as she bit her lip, not sure what was coming. She only knew that she trusted him. If she asked him to stop, he would. If she asked for more, he would oblige without question. He was hers, and she was his. Her eyes focused on the faint scar where his shoulder met his neck in the form of three puncture wounds, the place where she had marked him without realizing what they would become. Finally, she relaxed and watched that smirk she had grown to hate stretch across his face before he began praying. All the while, the necklace made from teeth and blood lay amongst her scars.

Chapter 49

Viktor

He wasn't sure what time it was when Wyatt appeared with something dangling from his fist. There were no windows in this ward, and he couldn't fully keep track of time either. They had come twice since Elizabeth left him and drained more blood. Never a lot, not like at the Tower. But he could feel himself weaken just as he had there, and he kept dozing off, eyes fluttering shut even as he tried to stay awake. Elizabeth had plans for him, and he wasn't sure he wanted to sleep while under her control.

"Time to go." Viktor stared at the vampire on the other side of the bars, taking in the almost flat quality of his voice. It was devoid of anything that would render him alive. No tone. No inflection. No emotion.

"How can you work for her when she turned you?" The question had been on repeat in his mind since he first saw Wyatt standing beside Elizabeth like a soldier, standing guard over the vampire who had stolen his life. And what had happened to his aunt? Viktor hadn't seen her, but that wasn't necessarily a surprise. If she were here, then she would be with the rest of those Elizabeth had turned.

"I don't work for Elizabeth," he responded curtly. Viktor noted the way his voice wavered slightly and the way his eyes seemed unnaturally bright. Actually, he realized, all the vampires he had encountered while here exhibited the same trait. Elizabeth's looked like sunlight pouring through a blue stained-glass window while Elora's always reminded him of emeralds.

"This looks a lot like working for someone," Viktor explained as he shifted slightly, pushing himself further into the room against the filthy wall. Any bit of exposed skin was already covered in dirt and filth that he was sure would take multiple washes to remove. The only clean parts of him were in the crooks of his arm, where the nurses drew his blood after wiping the spot with an alcohol wipe.

"All of this is for Elora. You know that as well as I do."

"She does have a way of inspiring loyalty,' Viktor mused as he recalled the way he had come to care for her beyond what was necessary for his job. "How did you meet her?"

Wyatt's hands froze just above the lock in the door as he seemed to consider Viktor's question. Or maybe he was deciding whether to answer. Viktor had been curious about how he had been dragged into this scenario, beyond the literal dragging Elizabeth had done in that apartment.

"She moved in across from my aunt," Wyatt began, and Viktor tracked the way the vampire flinched when he mentioned the old woman. "Connie—my aunt—was always trying to fix me up with women who lived in the apartment, and Elora was her latest target after giving her a basket of something she baked. Muffins, probably, if I knew my aunt at all." The item in Wyatt's fist hung by his thigh as he seemed to lose himself in the memory, as if he were reliving it right there in that hallway. But all Viktor heard was the use of past tense.

"Elora had a panic attack, I think. I found her in the hallway, trying to bring herself out of it. I helped her and took her into my aunt's apartment, and she calmed down. Of course, my aunt put her plan into action. She accused me of forgetting something on her grocery list, so I would have to go back out. Suggested I take Elora with me. I was surprised she agreed since I had heard about a roommate." Wyatt studied the item in his hand, and Viktor followed his gaze. From where he was sitting, he could make out chains and leather, but nothing more. His stomach clenched as he considered all the possibilities, and Wyatt chuckled softly, fidgeting with the key in his hand.

"The funniest part is my aunt didn't need to do her normal routine. I would have asked Elora to get coffee on my own. Even then, I was drawn to her in a way that I hadn't been in years. And now I get to be connected to her forever. She is me, and I am her." That fanatical smile Viktor had seen on Elizabeth's face so many times stretched across his face as he shoved the key into the lock.

"Are you going to fight me?" Wyatt let the question hang between them as he gave Viktor time to consider the question. His options were practically nonexistent, yet Viktor thought them through, nonetheless. Maybe if he had done more thinking before acting, he wouldn't be in this mess in the first place. It wasn't the first time the thought had popped into his head uninvited since he was thrown into this cell. The way Viktor saw it, even if he did manage to overpower Wyatt, there was still an unknown number of devoted vampires to get through in order to even get out of this hallway. And then there was escaping the building and the grounds themselves. Plus, they had taken enough blood at this point that he wasn't sure he would be able to even walk farther than the end of the hallway before collapsing without help. But maybe, just maybe, if he waited, an opportunity would present itself.

"No," Viktor responded tightly as he prepared himself for what was coming and stared at the thing in Wyatt's hand. As he had moved further into the fluorescent light right outside the cell door, Viktor could see exactly what it was. A short length of thick chain with a large padlock on the end. A collar, he realized.

He was meant to be collared like a dog, dragged along behind Elizabeth like a pet.

"Don't move once I unlock this door. If you do, I will bite you. I know how you feel about my kind." Wyatt unlocked the door once he finished his threat and moved into the cell, steps firm as he advanced. Each muscle seemed tense, as if Wyatt believed Viktor would fight despite claiming he wouldn't. Viktor didn't even twitch as the vampire kneeled in front of him and the cold metal hit his neck, causing a rush of goosebumps. He shivered slightly from the contact as Wyatt sat back on his heels.

"You don't know anything about how I feel about your kind." Viktor couldn't stop the retort that fell from his mouth even as the padlock snapped closed, and its weight settled along his collarbone. Wyatt groaned slightly as he stood back up and extended his hand towards Viktor with a bemused expression on his face.

"I know you see us as missions to be accomplished. As tools for you to use. I know your little group wants to eradicate every vampire in the city and that you want to use Elora to do that. She told me who you were before I even stepped into that apartment and was turned." Viktor couldn't help the surprise that flooded his face at Wyatt's revelation. It wasn't the vampire's knowledge regarding the Resistance or even his analysis of why Viktor had acted the way he had. It was that Elora had told Wyatt about him.

"How?" Viktor forced out as he took the offered hand and stood, meeting Wyatt's grinning face as he did so. At first, the vampire didn't respond, only gripped his biceps and started to steer him from the cell. The ward had deteriorated since Viktor was here last to collect Elizabeth, which he didn't realize was even possible. This area got the least amount of funding for upkeep, and it had shown in the rusty bars, the chipped paint, the holes in the plaster, and the chunks missing from the floor.

"The day you visited my aunt. I was with Elora in her apartment when we heard you in the hallway. I had brought her coffee and a gift. Then, your voice ruined the moment. After you disappeared from the building and she watched you leave, she told me bits and pieces. I filled in the rest when Elizabeth told me more about the Resistance and their goals," Wyatt explained as he led Viktor to the door and unlocked it, pushing him through. Viktor had no words to say in response. He had known Elora was there just on the other side, but he never thought anyone other than Damien would be there with her.

Something tightened in his chest as he remembered the expression on her face as she peered down at him from the apartment window. There was so much rage and pain in her eyes, carved into her face. It was beyond anything he had seen from her before. Not even when Denise drove her to violence or when she shut down, when her release was denied once again. And he had caused it, had transitioned from helping her through those moments and emotions to causing them. The realization was shattering, and he felt his shoulder slump as Wyatt opened the main door that led outside.

A large black SUV was waiting a few feet away from the building's entrance, with Elizabeth leaning against the passenger side door. It was another prom dress or formal gown. The dark red silk was draped over her features, hugging her hips before falling into layers of fabric. Her skin seemed even paler than before, and her hair lay in soft curls along her shoulders and down the front of her gown. It felt fitting despite being almost cliche that the vampire would be dressed in crimson silk, and Viktor wondered if the display was for him or Elora, if she was playing a role.

"Ready? We're going to see an old friend," she explained before giggling. It was a sound that made him want to recoil and disappear. A sound that meant pain was coming, and he would be the recipient of whatever horrors she had schemed and plotted. Viktor had a fairly good guess about who the old friend was since there were only three people they both knew. Wyatt was currently holding his arm in a vice-like grip, which meant there were just two other options, and they were more than likely together.

He didn't fight as Wyatt pushed him into the back seat and slid in beside him, squeezing Viktor between him and another male vampire, who looked ready to bite him any second. Elizabeth took her place in the front passenger seat while a male Viktor recognized as a cook in the kitchen turned the key in the ignition and began to drive away from the hospital.

The drive was blissfully and unexpectedly silent as Viktor fell into his own thoughts, once more rethinking every decision that had led to this moment. His hand reached up and touched the collar, feeling the cold of the metal that had warmed only a bit since it was put on. The weight was almost unbearably heavy on his neck and shoulders, and he groaned at the discomfort, tugging and pulling at it in an effort to somehow render it more comfortable. But his efforts were in vain, and he settled against the seat, watching everything pass through the windshield.

They took multiple turns, leading to a part of the city he had never really been before. It was known for its expensive hotels and resorts, for high-end restaurants that cost more than his electric bill, and for boutiques with clothing that would pay his rent. Very few people, if any, were on the streets, and he had to wonder what time it was. Not a single shop or restaurant was open. The only light came from hotel lobbies and bright streetlights that lined the sidewalks.

Finally, the SUV stopped in a parking lot full of various vehicles, along with a large array of people. Most of the women were dressed in formal gowns or as close to it as possible. The men donned button-up shirts and slacks or jeans that looked brand new. It felt like the clothing he had worn to a winter dance in school or to his graduation when he finally got his nursing degree.

As he exited the car and Wyatt grabbed his arm once more, he realized with no small amount of horror that not a single individual in that parking lot was human. They weren't even truly vampires. The brightness of their eyes gave it away—the strange luminescence that seemed to radiate from the inside as if it couldn't be contained by something so weak as a body made of nothing more than flesh and bone. Viktor's gaze roamed over the crowd as he attempted to count every one of Elora's—

What were they, exactly? What would be the name for those Elora's bite had created through Elizabeth and those she herself turned? Elizabeth had referred to Elora as their mother, so did that make them her children? He wondered briefly if she would even claim them, if she would welcome them with open arms. Only weeks ago, he would have said no, but he wasn't sure now. Would they be the key to Elora's impending vengeance? He had no doubt it would come eventually and that he would be on that list.

He quickly lost track after a few dozen, and he felt every bit of hope he had held onto disappear in an instant. At this rate, the humans in the city had no chance of survival. Viktor gave it a mere month before they were wiped out, and Elora's offspring moved on to other food sources. And then how long until they were eradicated, leaving a city of vampires created by Elora behind? His breath hitched as he felt the overwhelming weight that came with knowing your species would not continue much longer settle throughout his body. It was rage and fear and hopelessness all morphed into one toxin that infected every bit of him.

"Let's go see our mutual friend and congratulate her." Elizabeth's voice dragged him out of his spiraling thoughts, and something clipped onto his collar. He didn't bother to look and see what it was. A leash, he surmised, and was proven correct when Elizabeth took the end of it in her hand as if she were casually walking her dog. After a slight tug on the chain and a giggle from the vampire holding it, he followed her with heavy steps towards a tall building with a sign that said The Rose Hotel in an elegant script above the front doors that no doubt led to an equally elegant lobby.

Elizabeth took the lead and stood on the sidewalk below the front of the building, eyes locked on a single balcony a few stories up. He craned his neck to watch the same spot as he felt the others fall into a chaotic collection behind him. His eyes darted to Elizabeth for only a moment, just long enough to witness the expression of pure rapture in her delicate features and watch the way her fingers rubbed at her sternum, nails digging into the skin there. It was as if she was waiting for a miracle that she knew without a doubt was coming.

Time seemed to stretch on as they waited, the tension growing thicker with each second until he was sure everyone in a five-block radius could feel it in the air.

Then, as if the clouds were parting to reveal an angel, she appeared dressed in a T-shirt, hair shorter than he had seen it in years. Damien quickly came to her side, and together they surveyed while Viktor tried without any luck to read her expression. A collected gasp filled the night air, and they all fell to their knees in supplication before her.

With a relief he didn't fully understand, he knew exactly what—or who—the gift for Elora was.

Chapter 50

Elora

She wasn't sure how much later she awoke with his arm around her waist, her back pulled close to his chest, where he lay nestled in her tangled hair. The heat from his body was better than any hot bath or ray of sun. It was the cure to every fear and worry and danger waiting just outside the door. Yet, she could feel it. That tugging at her chest. It was a warm breath on her neck, a soft caress across her cheek, a hand on her lower back. A drop of ice-cold water down her spine. She felt like a puppet whose strings were controlled by something or someone more powerful than her. A force beyond time and space. The gasp she let out was painful, a pair of fingernails dragging across her throat. The burning and itching and pulling as someone came closer. And closer.

"Damien," she whispered, and was met with a soft grunt or whimper that would be adorable, if not for the circumstances.

"Damien, please. Something isn't right." That seemed to pull him from his sleep, and he shot up as he had been shocked by a bolt of electricity. His wild eyes searched the room for whatever enemy he believed was there. They lingered in the shadowy corners and the places where threats would hide. His hand never left her body, but rested on her hip as his fingers squeezed the soft flesh of her hip.

"What is it?" His voice was thick as he forced himself to wake and wrangle his thoughts from where they retreated while he slept. She threw the blanket from her legs, reminding herself that she was in a T-shirt and nothing else. Clothing and dressing hadn't been a focus. As he helped her clean off the blood and gore, the only remains of Darian, Damien had put her in one of his shirts, claiming he didn't want to see her in anything else as they crawled back into bed.

Her steps were slow as she followed the tugging sensation. It reminded her of the game she had played with Elizabeth, where they would hide items and tell each other if they were warm or cold as they searched for them. As she moved around, it felt like she got warmer and colder depending on the direction she went. Towards the bathroom, the sensation went cold. Towards the hotel door, even colder. Yet, as she moved step by step to the window and small balcony, her body became an inferno

Elora looked out from the balcony on the fifth floor at the mass of people standing before her. The tugging sensation was agony now, as if her ribs were being cracked open and every organ removed. Her lungs, first one and then the other. Her heart would somehow continue to beat in her hands after it was removed, as blood drained from it.

She felt Damien beside her, his hand on her hip as he pulled her close to him, nestling her against his body as if he could protect her from this. Yet Elora had a feeling that protection wasn't needed. Not in the way he believed she would require it.

"What the fuck?" he whispered, and she only shook her head as she studied the crowd. How many were there? Dozens? No, more than that. A hundred?

Below her, standing a few paces in front of the crowd, was Viktor. His hair was longer and matted, as it had been when he was first held as collateral by Killian. Only cuts lined his exposed chest. No puncture wounds from what she could see. She made out the defeated daze of his eyes as he stared directly in front of him.

A collar, metal like the ones used for dogs, was around his neck with a large padlock clear on one side. On the other were the beginnings of a leash, and Elora tore her focus from Viktor and followed it. Inch by inch until it reached a pale hand gripping the leather handle. Elizabeth stood there before the crowd with the leash in her hand like a peasant seeking favor with their monarch. A gift in hand with a smile that screamed across the space between them, between the sidewalk and Elora's balcony. Everything about her expression said she knew her gift would be welcomed.

But was it? Elora didn't fully understand the hesitation she felt, the swirling mixture of guilt and anger that left her slightly nauseous. She wanted Viktor dead, wanted him to pay for Lukas, for Denise. Even if he hadn't killed her himself, it was on his orders, based on his plan. She felt Damien shift beside her, probably having spotted Viktor as well. His hand tightened slightly on her waist, as if it were trying to clench into a fist. She imagined a grin would be clear on his face.

Somehow, Viktor had gotten a message out of the Tower, had managed to scheme and plot from his cell while they drained him for her to feed. Killian's final act of cruelty in an attempt to force her into submission. In her darkest moments, the ones where she had fallen into the shadowy places inside herself that craved only blood and violence no matter who's it was, she had compiled a list based on fragmented memories. Killian. Darian. Jonas. Only Viktor was left. Elizabeth met her eyes, feverish and fanatical, before her voice erupted through the night air, silencing the murmuring of the crowd behind her.

"Elora. Our creator. Your children are here. We are many, and we are yours to command, to sacrifice, to lift up into your graces." It was like a sermon in church, a priest speaking directly to their god, praising them in worship. Elora could only gaze down in horror as her eyes traveled over the group. There were so many. So many bowed with their hands raised towards her as if asking for her blessing. She shuddered as understanding fragmented her thoughts, her sanity, and her entire reality. With a simple declaration from her sister, the peace Elora had found with Damien and the pleasure he had given her were eradicated, ripped away from her as her silent screams tore from her throat and chest.

Her foster sister had been unhinged the last time she saw her, but this was beyond even her wildest fears. Elora scanned the crowd, searching for Wyatt, finding him instantly where he stood to Elizabeth's right like a second-in-command. He gazed up at her with the same fanatical love. It wasn't the soft expression he had worn at the coffee shop or even the sheepish smile that had been on his lips when he gave her the sketchbook. His features were distorted by what was there now, and she drew her focus away, unable to look at him a moment longer.

Elora had no idea Elizabeth had grown this insane and become this disconnected from reality. She wasn't their mother, goddess, or creator. If anything, that was Killian. Elora was simply someone who had lost control and made a horrific mistake. She never expected this to be the consequence. With a strangled whimper, Elora turned away from the scene and the cries of worship erupting from the crowd below them. It felt unreal, as if she had somehow fallen through a portal, stepped into another dimension where chaos reigned supreme, where another version of herself held sway.

"We have to go down there," she whispered as if she hoped Damien would stop her, as if he would be the voice of reason because all rational thought had left her. Maybe if she just spoke to Elizabeth, maybe she could talk some sense into her, drag her back to reality and they could rebuild. Damien met her eyes as he seemed to try to read her expression. She knew what he saw, could feel every warring emotion seeping from her body, from her skin until it was on display for him and anyone else.

A single nod and she sucked in a sharp breath. His hands gripped hers, squeezing softly before he dropped it and went in search of clothes. Pants, she realized. She needed pants before she left this room, before she faced her sister and those she had brought with her.

A few short minutes later, Damien and Elora stood hand in hand as the elevator traveled down to the lobby. With each floor that passed, as the number on the tiny screen decreased, Elora felt the tugging in her chest ease even as her breathing grew into shallow pants, as if her lung capacity had been cut in half. Damien's hand left hers for only a moment as he turned to face her, back facing the elevator door. His brows furrowed together as he brushed back her hair, eyeing the shirt and sweatpants she would be wearing for this encounter.

"I'm with you. Always." Her lips pressed to his as the door chimed open, and she stepped around him to march towards the lobby door. Only a few people were still lingering—a couple who seemed to be checking in and the receptionist that worked for Silas. He gave her a quick puzzled look before turning back to his customers with a forced smile on his face, handing them the keys to their room. Had they seen the crowd as they walked in? Or had they made it inside before they gathered under her window? With each step, the door grew closer, and she felt her body constrict, limbs forcing themselves closer to her body, head sinking as if she could simply condense herself out of existence.

The warmth of Damien's hand settled firmly on her lower back, fingers pressing into the fabric of the shirt. She knew that the gesture was one of support, of loyalty, and not of urgency.

Elizabeth would wait out there for her forever if necessary, and Damien would do the same.

But is it for the same reason?

The thought barged in, and she hesitated. Elizabeth would remain outside in the rain until Elora emerged from the hotel out of obsession and fanaticism. She wanted to believe that Damien would do so out of love. But that seed of doubt crept in, took root, and began to invade every memory from when she forced him to feed from her. She suppressed the thought, shoving it into a tiny box, and vowed to leave it hidden in the deepest recesses of her mind where it had stored the worst of her memories. They could stay there and rot side by side, leaving only the barest amount of debris in their wake. Her hand gripped the door handle that would take them out to the crowd and to face whatever nightmare Elizabeth created. No, not Elizabeth. That Elora had created.

And there she stood, looking so much like the sister who had saved up to buy her gown for each dance in school. For a moment, Elora was transported back to the last one they attended together, arm in arm while her date trailed behind, grumbling something about Elizabeth being there with him. It had been them against the world for years, equal parts to the whole. Now, the balance had shifted.

"I guess I'm a little underdressed. I didn't expect company." Elora wrangled the trembling she felt in every inch of her body under control. Her voice came out exactly as she hoped, complete indifference and boredom. Elizabeth only grinned before bowing her head slightly in a gesture that made Elora tense and Damien's grip tighten.

"I dressed for a wedding. I see you already changed out of the gown." There was a flash across Elizabeth's face, and Elora wondered if it was disappointment or irritation.

"It was a little bloody. Sadly, my fiancé didn't survive the ceremony." The grin that spread across her flawless features was absolutely feral, as if Elizabeth wished she had been there, had been able to savor the blood and violence. Maybe they had more in common than Elora thought.

"I would expect nothing less from you." Elizabeth's voice rose as she spoke, erupting from her mouth to fill the night. The crowd seemed to shift, to move closer with their hands outstretched.

"And why is that?" Elora forced her body to ease despite the agony in the places where it had tightened.

"You are a part of me. You made me in your image. We are one and the same. And we always shared a slightly violent streak. Remember that kid who made you cry? His jaw and teeth were never the same, were they?" Elora vividly recalled who her sister was referring to. A boy in high school had taken pictures of Elora in the locker room and showed others. He had met his fate shortly after. His jaw had been wired shut. The details of what happened were hazy, but she remembered the blood and his fear each time he saw them afterwards.

Maybe they were one and the same. After everything with Killian and Darian, maybe they were equally dark.

It took every bit of her strength to not retreat, to not turn around and flee back into the hotel and the bed she shared with Damien. Every word she had practiced on the way down, every script she had written for how this would go, had evaporated in a single moment. There would be no convincing Elizabeth to stand down and send them all home. That had never been an option in the first place, and Elora understood that now. There was a hunger in each and every face staring at her like she was the only living creature in the world.

"We brought you a gift." Elizabeth's declaration was met with bowed heads towards Elora, who finally allowed her focus to shift to the kneeling figure beside her sister. Elora had been correct when she thought that his hair was matted and that there was dirt and blood on his skin. There were no puncture wounds that she could see, but that meant nothing. His golden-brown complexion was sickly pale. It was a miracle that he was even able to kneel. It was so reminiscent of the first time she saw him in the Tower, when he was brought in to be punished for her actions. It seemed like a lifetime ago, back when she believed that he cared for her and that she wasn't a mission to complete.

Wyatt stood at Viktor's back, the handle to what looked like a leash gripped tightly in his hand. Words sprang to the surface as tears filled her eyes. She wanted to apologize, to beg his forgiveness, to ask where Connie was. Had she been left in peace? How would she survive without Wyatt to help her? Her eyes darted to the crowd, praying that she didn't spot the woman's wrinkled face and messy gray bun.

"Forward," Wyatt demanded, and Elora flinched. Even his voice was different. Cold and harsh as he pushed Viktor to her, forcing him to crawl on his knees towards her. She watched the pain race across Viktor's face, and she waited for a sense of satisfaction to envelop her, for her to savor his discomfort and agony at this moment. Not even when he kneeled directly in front of her, his eyes seemingly locked on her bare feet, did that sense of triumph come.

"He's yours, Elora. You can do whatever you want with him. No one fed from him directly while he was under my care. I wanted him unharmed when I delivered him." There was a smug satisfaction in Elizabeth's voice, a confidence that revealed she truly believed Elora would support this. And she should. She knew that she should. After all, it wasn't that she was squeamish about pain or torture. She had ripped out a vampire's heart at the altar.

"We thank you," Damien responded as the silence between their small group continued to grow. Elora could feel his fingers press just a bit, as if to ask if she was okay. The answer was a resounding no. She doubted she would be ever again. She doubted she ever had been okay to begin with. The closest she had gotten to peace was with Damien, but it had been fleeting, and now she was back in a reality that grew more terrifying by the second.

Even as she kept her eyes on Viktor, Elora felt Damien shift to take the leash from Wyatt, muttering another thank you. It was too similar, too much of a reminder of everything that came before. Everything she knew she should be feeling was strangely absent, a void that refused to be filled by anger or satisfaction or even excitement that Viktor was now in her hands. Elizabeth's giggle finally broke Elora's trance, and she stared at her foster sister, attempting to reconcile the sound that had once brought Elora joy with the scene before her.

"It's only the first of many, Elora. We'll be back. If you need us, you simply have to call out. We can feel you. Just as you can feel us." Elizabeth bowed deeply at the waist, her pale blond hair falling in waves around her face, hiding her expression. As she straightened, Elizabeth spun on her heel and vanished into the crowd, leaving only Viktor and Wyatt behind.

"Please," Elora whispered as she met the amber eyes that had once coaxed her out of a panic attack in the middle of a hallway. Wyatt only tilted his head slightly, a confused expression settling quickly.

"Don't follow her. I'm sorry, Wyatt. This was never meant to happen." Elora knew she was begging and that her apology probably meant nothing. Something like a grimace crossed his face, and she felt her heart leap slightly as hope rekindled. If she could convince him not to follow Elizabeth, maybe she could fix whatever this was.

"There's nothing to apologize for, Elora. We're one now. I am you and you are me." A strange smile plastered itself on the lips she had once considered kissing before he turned and followed Elizabeth into the crowd. One by one, each vampire bowed deeply before following her foster sister into the night until she was left with Damien at her side and Viktor kneeling at her feet.

It was only then that she understood Chloe and her words at the meeting. She realized why Chloe called for her death and demanded her execution. Killian had not simply created a vampire or a food source. He had engineered a plague that was already rampaging through the city, and she was patient zero.

Chapter 51

Epilogue

Thorne

Thorne had picked this restaurant for their meeting for a couple of reasons. It was constantly busy, and they served decent food. It wasn't as fancy as some of the other places in the area, but that only lent it a unique charm that made it seem like a surprising discovery. After all, no one would look twice at the exterior when the other places were newly remodeled. The booths were cozy and created a perfect space for secret meetings. Yet, the two key reasons had nothing to do with the food or atmosphere. Instead, it was the fact that the majority of the staff worked under her as part of the Resistance and there was less of a chance of vampires hiding here. It was difficult to stick around if they didn't order or consume food. In her extensive experience, even being around human food was too much for most vampires.

The young man set the plate of pasta in front of her before taking a moment to refill her wineglass. Thorne had been nursing it for almost an hour now and still hadn't finished it. Being drunk or even slightly buzzed for this meeting was not an option, not when her guest was a vampire.

"She's arriving now, ma'am. Her car pulled up out front." Thorne nodded at the server's report and shifted slightly in her seat, pulling down her shirt sleeves and adjusting the collar. When the head of the Radcliff vampire family had sent her a message through one of Thorne's spies, she had been hesitant to accept. She had listened to the Resistance member explain what had happened, recalled how they had been approached and told to relay a message. It was a bold move, if Thorne was honest. It revealed that Chloe Radcliff knew exactly what spies were among her ranks and knew exactly who had infiltrated her businesses. It was admitting weakness, and Thorne had to wonder exactly what was so crucial that Chloe had risked that.

Then again, Thorne was fairly certain she knew. Rumors and gossip had reached her as various members made reports about people going missing, an increase in humans being attacked and turned without any thought or reason. And Viktor had never made it back to headquarters, had never sent her another message after mentioning the hospital. A slight twinge of guilt hit her as she took a small sip, barely letting the wine pass her lips. She knew exactly where Viktor probably ended up, knew that he had probably disobeyed her orders in an effort to prove himself once more. He had given nothing away when she took him off the mission of locating Elora, but she could practically feel the desperation and desire to prove her and the rest of the council wrong radiate off of him before he left.

Thorne shook her head sadly as she shoved down the feeling that she should have done more for him, should have recognized that he was in too deep long before the events at the Tower. She should have removed him from the equation as soon as his reports became more and more vague, as he said her name or referred to her with an increasing amount of affection. That was how Thorne had lost Denise. And now, it was how she lost Viktor.

It seemed that no one could resist the target, and Thorne had to wonder if it was simply who the vampire was or if it had something to do with what Killian did. Playing with nature, picking and choosing traits, amplifying certain genes had left behind a new creature. Not human. Not a vampire, not in the same way. No, Killian had created something never seen before in nature, and now they were dealing with the consequences.

Thorne knew the moment Chloe walked into the diner. It wasn't due to anything obvious. Conversations continued and laughter filled the room. Servers still performed their jobs, expertly weaving through the tables and customers. Sounds of cooking food and repeated food orders filtered in from the kitchen doors as they opened and closed. Instead, it was in the way the air seemed to grow heavier, as if something was pressing down on this plane of existence. Thorne could feel it in every part of her body, every limb, every nerve as she took another drink of her wine, taking in more this time in hopes of easing the growing anxiety in her gut. Chloe would sense and exploit it in a single moment if Thorne didn't get her act together.

It really shouldn't have been a surprise that Chloe looked exactly the same as the last time Thorne had seen her. The same silver hair and blue eyes. Thorne knew she had changed, knew that her eyes were framed by crow's feet and wrinkles, that her hair had gone mostly gray, and that her eyes no longer held any light like they had once upon a time when the world still held hope.

Chloe found her instantly, as if she knew where Thorne was before she even entered the restaurant. After a quick glance over at the other patrons and workers, Chloe wandered over with that easy grace that Thorne had always envied even when she was younger. The look on her face was somewhat distasteful as she eased down into the chair and crossed her legs, reclining against the back of the chair.

"I'm surprised you agreed, to be honest. I thought I would show up here and find a trap." Chloe eyed the wine glass and the plate of food before meeting Thorne's gaze.

"You said it was important. And I know you wouldn't reach out to me unless it was important."

"Between you and your brother, you always understood me best," Chloe chuckled softly before her expression grew grave and she leaned forward. "We have a problem, and I'm sure you have heard whispers of it already." Thorne only nodded. She wasn't going to give away details or information that she may or may not know. Let Chloe play her hand first.

"Vampires being created at an alarming rate. So quickly, in fact, that is would easily wipe out humans. And it all goes back to her."

"Elizabeth." Chloe nodded as Thorne spoke the name of the creature who was now potentially causing the eradication of not one, but two species if she wasn't dealt with.

"Along with another who is currently amassing a concerning amount of power within the vampire families." There was a hint of venom in Chloe's voice that made Thorne want to shift, made her want to fidget and finish off the glass of wine.

"And how is she doing that?" Thorne had heard rumors of a wedding, but that didn't equal amassing power. If anything, it would do the opposite.

"She is now the head of two families and the probable heir to a third. In one move, she became the head of Ravenwell and Ashcroft. Silas will name her his heir. I'm sure of it." Thorne's mind started racing as she considered each and every possible ramification of this. Having one vampire as the head of multiple families could prove useful. Kill one vampire and the families would fall apart. They would only need to kill two, and Chloe was one of them.

"And how did that happen? The last I heard, she was marrying." At Thorne's question, Chloe's eyes went dark, as if the rage inside her was barely contained. Thorne had seen that look before when Chloe had been denied taking a consort despite the fact Darian was famous for it.

"She killed him. Killed them both, actually. I always figured that she was the one to murder Killian, but apparently there's video proof. And she ripped out Darian's heart at the altar after he said his vows and she told everyone in the audience what was done to her. Jonas is also missing, and the rumor is he was done away with as well. Her enemies are dropping like flies, Thorne." A strange sense of pride ran through Thorne despite the edge of fear in Chloe's words that she had never heard from the vampire. Chloe had always been unwaveringly confident, no matter what was happening or what danger she was in. There had been fights with other vampires and with humans, and never once had she shown even a sliver of fear. It was strange to hear it now.

"Killing three vampires, two of which were known for cruelty to humans and vampires alike, hardly seems like a problem for my people," Thorne drawled as she watched Chloe stiffen.

"She's the reason for Elizabeth. She's the reason for every single creature who was created by Elizabeth. And she will be the reason this city falls." Desperation clung to every word as Chloe leaned across the table and Thorne finished off her wine, signaling for the waiter to refill it.

"And you want my help? The help of my group to stop this? To stop Elizabeth?" Chloe began nodding as Thorne asked her questions.

"Yes. Yes. All of that. But not just Elizabeth. We can't simply cut the weed at the stem. We have to rip it out from the root. We have to remove any chance of this happening again. Do you understand what I'm saying?" There was a frenzy to Chloe now, as if her very existence depended on what Thorne said in this moment.

"You want to kill Elora as well. Remove the problem at the cause." A statement and Thorne felt her heart constrict in her chest. This was exactly what she feared, exactly what she assumed would happen when Chloe asked for the meeting. She swallowed as she watched Chloe's smile be replaced with suspicion.

"Yes. Can you help with that?" Thorne considered the question as she studied the cloth napkin in front of her, along with the plate of food that had gone cold. Her appetite had dissipated the second this had gone from sharing information to planning someone's death. Elora had done nothing wrong, as far as Thorne knew. Other than the attack on Elizabeth, she had never hurt anyone else who didn't deserve it. But Chloe's point still held too much weight, too much truth to be ignored. Elora was the cause of the disease sweeping through the city, infecting every home and alleyway, as Elizabeth called them to her.

"How do we know she needs to be done away with? How do we know she wouldn't help deal with the problem?" Chloe scoffed softly and leaned back to study Thorne.

"They came to her. They called themselves her children. Called her their mother and goddess. There isn't really time to find out if she's willing to help. And asking her may only tip them all off and ruin our potential element of surprise." Thorne only nodded along, unable to deny the truth in Chloe's explanation despite how unsavory it sounded.

"Okay. You sold me, Chloe. What exactly are you proposing?" That shrewd expression Thorne remembered so well settled on her, indicating that what was coming was going to be a problem.

"First, there's something you have to tell me," Chloe explained before leaning forward once more, forearms resting on the linen tablecloth.

"Will you be able to watch your daughter die when the time comes, Iris?" Thorne recoiled at the sound of her previous name, at the memories it drew forward, at the reminder of her life before. But Iris was dead, had been murdered in Killian's office in a fit of rage. Iris wouldn't have been able to watch her daughter die for the greater good. But Thorne? There was no doubt in her mind that she could sacrifice Elora to save what humans remained.

The End.

Acknowledgments

My last acknowledgments page left a lot to be desired and I am sure this one will as well. As author after author have said, writing this is hard. I am always worried I will forget someone and then they will hate me forever. That may be an exaggeration, but forgetting some who was crucial and involved in this entire endeavor is terrifying. So, I will simply take the easy way out and thank my family, friends, beta readers, ARC readers, my partner's Discord friends, and those who read the first book. Thank you for coming back for the second one. I hope to see you against for the final book in the trilogy!

Book 3 is coming mid-2025. Follow me on social media for updates and sneak peeks at future projects.

About The Author

Misty Thomas (she/her) is a parent, partner, educator, cat mom, and coffee addict. When she isn't teaching composition or writing, she spends her time with her family, playing video games, and reading an unholy number of books in an effort to escape reality. Her debut book, Tower of Blood, is the first in the Blood and Silk Trilogy.

Other Works

Blood and Silk Trilogy

Tower of Blood (Book 1)

She is running from her memories, and he is tasked with dragging her back.

Elora is a patient with a violent past and a life of repressed memories. She knows vampires exist, that they run the city, and control every aspect of their lives. But they tell her it is all psychosis, that her scars are self-inflicted to fit her delusions.

Damien is second-in-command to the most powerful vampire leader and tasked with a mission that every other vampire has failed to complete – find Elora.

But when he finds her, everything he knows is thrown into question. And when she is dragged back to the place her mind protects her from, she will learn exactly why she was being hunted.

First installment in the Blood and Silk Trilogy.

For 18+ readers. This is a fantasy novel that has depictions of trauma and abuse. Please read the content warnings in the beginning pages of the book before reading.

www.ingramcontent.com/pod-product-compliance
Lightning Source LLC
Chambersburg PA
CBHW071735110726
47908CB00006B/1591